DOCTOR LUCIFER

DOCTOR LUCIFER
A Medical Thriller

Anthony Lee

This is a work of fiction. Names, characters, places, and incidents either are the product of the author's imagination or are used fictitiously. Any resemblance to actual persons, living or dead, events, or locales is entirely coincidental.

Copyright 2024 © by Anthony Lee

All rights reserved. No part of this book may be reproduced or used in any manner without written permission of the copyright owner, except for the use of quotations in a book review.

Cover design by Aleksandar Milosavljevic

First paperback edition published in 2024

ISBN 9798322212836

DOCTOR LUCIFER

MONDAY

CHAPTER 1

I don't know which is worse: disease of the human body or disease of humanity.

I may be a doctor, but I'm not like the rest of them. Docs typically treat without judgment, no matter who the patients are or how they live. Not me. I question the value of my work now and then. Does it really improve society, or is it wasted on the worst among us?

Let me give you some examples. Last week, a patient came to me with severe hyperglycemia. Turns out he ignored his diabetes meds and overindulged on junk food, so I had to bail out his ass. Months before that, I started treating a man for pancreatitis when the police showed up. Guess what? The patient was suspected of raping his ex-girlfriend. Gee, I had no fucking idea what kind of guy he was. Then there's the COVID-19 pandemic, with so many needless deaths, anti-maskers, and anti-vaxxers. Don't even get me started on this.

Sometimes, that's what my job comes down to: wiping away physical sickness within the morally sick. Prolonging people's lives just so they could go back to being a nuisance, a troublemaker, a menace to society. Not all of the time, but often enough to piss me off.

I'm not supposed to be saying any of this, or even thinking it. If Hippocrates, the great Father of Medicine, knew about me, he'd call on the gods to strike me down. After all, I already took his sacred oath. The one that says "do no harm," preaching a duty to heal all without playing God. So I can't be judge, jury, and executioner, deciding who lives or dies. I am a doctor who can stand only on one side, the side of life. I became an angel of health to defeat the demons of disease. Even with the human race so critically ill, with selfishness and stupidity running amok, spreading like cancer, I have a job to do. No ifs, ands, or buts. No questions asked.

So here I am, standing on a high pedestal, basking in the light of praise from the mortals surrounding me. But my base is shaky. My foundation isn't solid like the true angels have. I must always watch my footing. Any misstep or misdeed as a healer and I am finished. The gods will punish me, strip off my wings. I'll fall from the heights of heaven, plummet towards the depths of hell, vanish into oblivion. But I won't let that happen. I've spent my life climbing to the stars, and after all this, I am not going to toss it all aside. There is no turning back. The only path left is towards the light, while the fires of sin burn not too far beneath my feet.

I must defend my honor, at all costs.

* * *

As a habit, I don't drive in silence. Commuting is such a waste of time that hauling my ass to work while doing nothing else is pretty much the equivalent of trimming my precious lifespan. That's why I have my radio on. The dashboard of my Tesla can provide different types of audio to keep me company, whether it be the news, music from radio stations, or favorite tunes in my Spotify playlist. It's all at my fingertips. Right now, I'm flipping through various Southern California FM stations and seeing what songs randomly come up. I soon come across a catchy one: the all-girl eighties rock hit "Manic Monday" by The Bangles. I bob my head slightly to the rhythm and almost mutter the lyrics, too. Yeah, it's so appropriate for today. Something upbeat to start a new week, while longing for the weekend that just passed.

Of course, that's just for normal people, the five-day-a-week nine-to-five folks. I'm not one of them. I'm a hospitalist, a doctor doing nothing but inpatient care. My work goes from no later than 7 AM to no earlier than 5 PM, twelve days straight. Then six full days off, and repeat the cycle unless I opt for extra vacation time. I'm also paired off with a nocturnist, who watches over my patients whenever I'm off duty to get my nightly rest.

It's now day ten and I'm almost dead. Plowing through today, tomorrow, and Wednesday is going to be a fucking pain in the ass.

I'm done with music for now, so I tune in to KNX for the local news. The current segment is wrapping up, something about computer malware and how it's important for everyone to not open strange and unfamiliar emails. Gone are the days when the morning anchor dished out the latest stats about daily COVID-19 cases and deaths. Thank you, Pfizer, Moderna, Johnson & Johnson, and Novavax for those vaccines, plus the Food and Drug Administration for clearing them. These elixirs are giving us auras of protection, the magic we desperately need. It's also made my job a hell of a lot easier. The last COVID-19 patient under my care was a little more than a month ago.

What a way to start the year. Now I'm back to solving other bodily afflictions, like in the pre-pandemic era. Sure, it's the familiar endless cycle of "new day, same old shit" and it's still grueling work, but at least I can breathe. No pun intended.

Another ten minutes and I'm in north Anaheim. Up ahead is Ivory Memorial Hospital, a big shiny white tower that beckons the sick to enter. As one of its healers, I help project the pride of this place. I am Dr. Mark Lin, board-certified internist. Any adults needing nonsurgical care, they may come to me. Anyone else can find other white coats in this place. Don't forget the nurses, pharmacists, technicians, and other ancillary staff, too. Healthcare is a team effort, as this medical center likes to put it.

After parking my Tesla, I head up to the hospital's eleventh floor where the Department of Internal Medicine resides. My cubicle is buried in a back corner, well hidden from the entrance to this office space. There, my first few tasks are always the same: log into my work computer and contact Dr. Jay McKinnon, the nocturnist whom the chief often likes to assign to me. Just as I would hand off my patients to Jay at the end of the day, he would return them to me with updates. I would usually send him a text to find out where he is in the hospital and wait a few minutes for a response.

Not this time. Today, he just happens to come into the room and sit in his cubicle, only three spots down from mine.

"Morning, Jay. Hope you had a good night's sleep."

"You mean a good day's sleep."

"No, I really mean a good night's sleep. Did any of my patients keep you up?"

"Thankfully, no. Doesn't mean I relaxed all night, though."

"How busy were you?"

"I'd say one nurse call every twenty minutes."

"In other words, the usual?"

"Yeah."

I nod. Even though this hospital is lucky enough to hire nocturnists, it only managed to attract a small handful. The result: each nocturnist covers the patient load of three or four daytime hospitalists, nowhere close to a chill one-to-one ratio.

"I know how hard it can get," I say.

"Don't worry about it," Jay responds while logging into his desktop terminal. "It's totally doable."

"You enjoy the night shift?"

"Do you even need to ask?"

"Just making sure."

"Of course I love it, you idiot. Wouldn't you like handling stuff without extra hassles?"

"Good for you. Don't quit this place."

"Oh, I won't. I'm satisfied. Unlike you, who sometimes complains about being overwhelmed."

"Me, complain?"

"Remember when you gave me your patient list a few days ago? You were pretty damn tense, and you didn't hide it."

I nod and put my hands up in surrender.

"OK, fine, I had an unbelievably awful day," I say. "Anyway, can we do the handoff thing now?"

Jay smiles and adjusts his glasses, then pulls out his hospital-issued tablet from his white coat pocket. On its screen, he taps open an app containing his notes about the patients I signed out to him yesterday. I take out my own tablet from my coat, access the same app, and wait for Jay's overnight notes to be transferred wirelessly to mine.

"I'm only teasing you, Mark. You know how much I appreciate your work. I don't remember the last time I ever got swamped on a night shift because your patients were so unstable."

"Good to know. Even if I'm just lucky."

"It's not luck. It's good patient care. Seriously, you got dedication. You don't go home until they're nicely tucked in."

"Well, thanks for the kind compliment. Hurry up so you can get your daytime beauty sleep."

Jay laughs a little, then looks down at his tablet and slowly scrolls down with one finger. I listen while reviewing the same notes.

"All right, first patient. Christopher Flint, congestive heart failure. I got called by the nurse a little after midnight. Said he was constipated."

"Wait. What?"

"According to her, the patient had that problem earlier in the day, and even wondered if he should have asked for a laxative then. Maybe he didn't think it was a big deal at the time. Anyway, it sounds like he decided at the last minute, so late at night, to get that little request over with."

"So you gave him something."

"Yeah, a dose of Dulcolax."

"But vital signs were OK otherwise?"

"Yep. Nothing out of whack with that, or anything else."

"Cool. Next patient?"

"Uh, let's see. There was one new admission that I took at around seven last night, so he's on your list now. But let me get to your existing ones first."

"OK."

"Darnell Jackson is fine. I even took a peek at his glucose levels when things weren't busy. He's not back to DKA, that's for sure."

I nod with satisfaction. Jackson is a type 1 diabetic. He needs insulin every day because his own pancreas cannot make it. Due to chaotic life stressors, he missed an insulin shot at home, so that his blood sugars skyrocketed to the point of diabetic ketoacidosis and paramedics had to rush him to this hospital. The ICU took care of his DKA with an intensive insulin regimen, before transferring him to me on the medicine ward. My job now is to finish controlling his blood sugars and determine the insulin doses that he could continue at home after he is discharged.

"Doris Schafer with pneumonia didn't prompt any calls," Jay goes on. "And all the rest... Tony Palacio, Mrs. Green, Mr. Choi... no, nothing happened with any of them. So that leaves the new patient."

On my tablet, I spot the new name in the list: Donald Chester, a 68-year-old man with a history of liver cirrhosis secondary to long-term alcohol use. I listen to Jay while glancing at his notes.

"Donald Chester came in because of hematemesis. Vomited a lot of blood. Never happened before. He's also had some indigestion and loss of appetite over the last three days. Obviously, all of this scared him and his wife, especially the bloody vomit. So she drove him to the emergency department here. Doc ordered a CT abdomen, and the radiologist spotted not one but two things: esophageal varices and a suspected gastric tumor."

Wow. This is the kind of case that could excite a roomful of docs in grand rounds meetings: a clinical presentation with two possible causes. Possibility number one: blood leaving the esophagus, stomach, and intestines flows into the portal vein in the liver, but if the liver is known to be cirrhotic, blood has a tough time passing through. It backs up. Veins in the esophagus stretch wider, what we docs call esophageal varices. If those vessels break, the patient bleeds down into the stomach and could maybe puke it back up. Possibility number two: A stomach tumor results in pooled gastric blood just by growing and poking through little blood vessels nearby. So which is the source of the bleeding here: the esophageal varices, the stomach tumor, or both? Holy crap, this patient might be an alcoholic, yet his case is both mentally stimulating and emotionally intriguing. I can do this one.

"Was he unstable at any point?" I ask.

"Miraculously, he wasn't. When I spoke to him and did a physical exam, he was a little worried but otherwise awake and asymptomatic.

Blood pressure and other vital signs were within normal limits."

"Maybe his own blood clotting did the trick, whatever the bleeding source is. Obviously, we need a GI consult."

"Already called for one. Joanne Li is the on-call gastroenterologist. She'll evaluate Mr. Chester today."

I nod, making a note to follow up on that. I also need to fit in a surgery consult for the stomach tumor. That would have to come second, because variceal bleeding seems to be the more immediate risk right now. All of this will likely occur in the afternoon.

"Anything else?" I ask, even though I know the answer already.

"You're all set, buddy, and so am I. Well, almost. I still have to wait for two other docs to do handoffs with."

At that moment, Jay pulls out a smartphone from his coat pocket and glances at it. Then he smiles.

"What do you know? They just texted me."

"I'll let you get to it."

"I'm almost there. I'll definitely get some good beauty sleep."

"Good for you, man. You deserve it."

"Whoa, hold on. I'm getting another text."

Almost simultaneously, I feel a vibration. I have two smartphones, one work and one personal. The work phone in my left pants pocket is the one buzzing.

"That's weird," I say, pulling it out to check.

"You're getting it, too?"

"Getting what?"

"A text message from the top, hospital administration. Oh gee, looks like everyone is receiving this."

I say nothing as I slowly read my screen.

ATTENTION!

To all staff at Ivory Memorial Hospital:

Our email system has been flooded with numerous spam

messages, causing a systemwide slowdown of email communications. It has come to our attention that a form of malware, spreading rapidly via email, is likely responsible, not just in this hospital but also with many incidents elsewhere.

As an urgent cautionary measure, the Division of Information Technology has shut down email servers and disabled all related applications. Technicians are currently working diligently to resolve this matter as soon as possible. Until further notice, please refrain from accessing ANY email (work OR personal), and encourage patients and other staff to communicate with you by alternate means, such as phone and text.

We apologize for this inconvenience. Thank you for your cooperation. Remember, healthcare is a team effort.

Jeffrey Winters, MD
Chief Executive Officer
Ivory Memorial Hospital

"What the hell is going on?" I ask breathlessly.

"Beats me," Jay says with a frown.

"Has the CEO ever sent a message like this?"

"I've been here almost nine years. All I ever heard from him were those emails celebrating hospital milestones and annual holidays."

"Then something is definitely happening."

"It's probably a big news story now."

"Wait a minute. I heard something about malware this morning on KNX. I should look into this."

In my cubicle, I open Google Chrome on my desktop computer. I head straight to one of my go-to news sources, *The Associated Press*. I verbally read the top headline, loud enough for Jay to hear.

"Lucifer's Worm cripples computer systems worldwide."

"Whoa. What does the article say?"

I skim the text while reciting the key points.

"It starts with someone getting a weird email message, with the subject line, 'Here's something interesting I found.' The user opens it, only to find a short message in the body: 'Hahaha! You have just unleashed Lucifer's Worm! Now face the wrath of the demon itself!' The opening of the email triggers the malware to replicate and send itself to every email address found on the computer and any connected servers. Address books and mailing lists are major factors in the spread."

"Oh my god, really?"

"And when this happens, all other network activity slows down. In some cases, even grind to a halt."

Jay says nothing. But I hear a long exhale come out of him.

"It gets worse," I continue. "The article talks about some serious consequences of Lucifer's Worm. At a Bank of America branch in Houston, all of its computers have crashed. And there's madness in a Cleveland courthouse because everyone's machine has gone haywire, disrupting case processing there. There's even the possibility that online retailers like Amazon are going to temporarily shut down their websites, starting today."

"It's like we're going through another pandemic."

"More like a cyber pandemic. But the idea is the same: cripple one thing so many people depend on, the world goes into chaos."

"COVID-19 cut off interpersonal contact everywhere. Now Lucifer's Worm decimates email."

"Exactly."

"I sure hope I can still sleep today."

"What in the world is going to happen next?"

"I don't want to know."

Me neither. I take a deep breath. Time to change the topic.

"So, Jay, how are things with that woman you're dating?"

"No luck. She's not returning my calls. But it was hard for us to coordinate schedules, the end of her work day with the usual time I wake up in the afternoon."

"Sorry to hear that."

"At this point, I'm better off looking for ladies of the night."

"You don't mean—"

"No, not that kind, idiot. Someone whose circadian rhythm matches mine. Don't forget smart and beautiful, too."

I stifle a laugh. Jay has a funny way of calling me an idiot.

"How about another nocturnist here?" I ask.

"None catch my eye."

"Are you even looking?"

"Of course I am. At one point, I even thought about getting to know Joanne Li. But she's married with two kids, you know."

"Just remember you're not alone. I'm a bachelor, too."

"Thanks for the encouragement."

"Sure. Don't sweat it. I think you'll be fine, as long as you—"

All of a sudden, a loud high-pitched squeal pierces my eardrums from above. I freeze and hold my breath, waiting for the voice over the PA system.

"Code Blue, room 832. Code Blue, room 832."

I glance at the patient list in my tablet. Shit, it's Christopher Flint, now on the brink of death!

I jump out of my seat and run for the door, nearly crashing into two docs coming into the room, no doubt Jay's last two handoffs. Out in the hallway, an elevator opens up. No one inside. I dash in and press eight. The doors close. Then I clench my fists, suddenly remembering how goddamn slow these elevators are, even for a three-floor descent. I should've rushed down the stairs.

Yeah, I'm a real idiot.

Once the doors open, I dash down the hall in big, careful steps. Past the nurse's station. Then a right turn. I slow to a quick crawl as I carefully maneuver through the doorway of 832 and a crowd of staff inside. I reach the patient.

Flint's mouth is open, filled like a bowl of putrid stew.

CHAPTER 2

In any resuscitation effort, step one is to not panic. Step two is to take charge, make sure all the right things are done. Like the clearing of Flint's vomit, already underway thanks to a lady in purple scrubs wielding a suction cannula.

There are also random irregular waves racing across the heart monitor at 160 beats per minute. I palpate the patient's wrist with two fingers. Holy shit, I don't feel a pulse.

"Defibrillator?" I shout.

"Someone's getting it," a man says.

I nod and look at Flint. A big man in black scrubs stands over the patient, hands on top of the sternum, ramming his weight down repeatedly. Each compression shakes Flint's massive body. The patient is still unconscious. Behind the man in black, a woman in pink prepares an endotracheal tube. She moves behind the head of the bed, already pulled from the wall before I had arrived. The chest compressions stop, and she tilts Flint's head back to open his mouth. Metal tongue blade in her left hand, she lifts the jaw up. ET tube in her right, she slides it down the trachea without a hitch. Way to go. Then she attaches an Ambu bag to the tube and squeezes it, ventilating Flint's lungs.

My recent ACLS retraining comes flooding back. Emergency life support is all about the first four letters of the alphabet.

A for Airway. Make sure it is open and clear. Check.

B for Breathing. Manually get air flowing in and out. Check.

C for Circulation. Chest compressions to keep blood moving. So far so good, a checkmark for now.

D for Defibrillator, the newest letter. Use that device once it arrives. Still pending, and it better get here quick.

The chaos continues before me. Ambu bag breaths alternating with chest compressions. The monitor still showing ventricular fibrillation, the bottom chambers of Flint's heart contracting chaotically. Not enough cardiac muscle coordination to propel blood forward. Now I can feel my own heart fluttering fast, plus my own quick and shallow breaths. It isn't the nurses and their frantic activity. I have great trust in them. No, it's the patient. How much time does he have left? If only humans could have lifespan clocks.

"Defibrillator!" someone shouts from the doorway.

"Hurry up," I yell.

A man in gray places a kit besides Flint's left foot, opens it, and pulls out the defibrillator and metal paddles. I pull down the top left part of Flint's gown to expose his chest. While the gray man hooks the paddles to the unit, I hear another sound piercing the noise in the room.

The same alarm that brought me down here, followed by the PA system.

"Code Blue, room 915. Code Blue, room 915."

Shit, shit, shit! That's another patient in my list: Doris Schafer. What the hell am I supposed to do now? No way I can leave just yet. I'd be abandoning Flint, letting him die by default. All I can do is hope that the second Code Team from the ED gets things rolling. Damnit, I'll have to pick up the pieces later.

In the midst of this, the gray man holds the paddles down on Flint. I gesture everyone to move back. The gray man gives the shock. Flint's body jolts, 360 joules stunning his heart. The team resumes CPR. More Ambu bag breaths and chest compressions, back and forth, back and forth...

But nothing. Flint is still in V-fib.

Next step: another 360 joules. Same drill. Everyone steps back, gray man shocks, back to work. Then I throw in another measure.

"Give him epinephrine," I say.

"I'm on it," a woman in blue says, filling a syringe with one milligram of the stuff. Please let it jumpstart his heart.

CPR continues over the next few minutes. I stare at the heart monitor, waiting for signs of returned spontaneous circulation. I glance at the response team doing the breathing and circulating for Flint. No need to say another word yet. This is a well-oiled machine, an orderly symphony with the conductor getting a brief moment of rest.

But we're not done. The V-fib has not gone anywhere.

"Shock him again," I say. "Three hundred sixty joules."

The lifesaving becomes routine, to the point of it being a blur. The only break to that monotony is my verbal order for another medication, amiodarone. Anything to restore Flint's heart, even to the point of throwing the kitchen sink.

My mind also races through a differential diagnosis. Of all the possible causes for V-fib, which is the most likely here?

I know Flint has longstanding congestive heart failure. He came here because of CHF exacerbation, with breathing difficulty getting worse. All because his heart, already weakened from a heart attack several years ago, couldn't pump well enough, causing blood to back up and forcing its fluid portion to seep out of the capillaries surrounding his lungs, making those pulmonary tissues difficult to stretch.

All of a sudden, it hits me. I had given him a new medication yesterday. Was that the reason he's gone into V-fib?

Oh god, it better not be.

I can't think about that right now. The heart monitor has stopped showing waves. It's displaying a flat line only.

No heart contraction.

"Asystole!" I scream.

The man in black slows down a bit. Exhaustion kicking in, obviously. I step in and take over, doing the heavy two-handed chest compressions myself. I stop to gasp for air while the woman in pink squeezes air to Flint. Then another round of compressions. Another set of breaths.

Compressions... breaths... compressions... breaths...

"Rapid Response, room 903," the PA system announces after a

crackle of static. "Rapid Response, room 903."

Damnit! That's Darnell Jackson. Rapid Response calls without the wailing alarm may be a step down from the life-and-death Code Blues, but they're still not a matter of "wait until I have a chance to get there."

I force my chest compressions on Flint even harder, still seeing the flat line on the monitor. Soon, I realize that I'm the only one moving. I stop to take two deep breaths, then I do one more series of compressions.

It finally sinks in. It's over.

Flint is dead.

"OK, that's it," I say while panting heavily. "Nothing more we can do. Thank you, everyone, for your hard work."

Then I rush out of the room, without a word of explanation.

* * *

The good news about Doris Schafer in room 915: the second Code Team got to her as expected. She's intubated and bag-ventilated. Not dead right now.

The bad news: the cold stare from the nearest nurse, Cheryl, a lady in purple scrubs. Several other healthcare workers surrounding the bed also give me looks.

"I'm really, really sorry," I say nervously. "I got stuck with the Code Blue that got called before this one. Another patient of mine."

"Really?" Cheryl responds.

"I'm not kidding. What happened here?"

"Looks like anaphylaxis. We gave the patient epi, which helped. But intubation was still a challenge."

"How much of a challenge?"

"It took three tries."

Great. Just great. A near-fatal allergic reaction that really made the patient's throat swell. Definitely enough to ruin my already terrible morning.

"Is she stable?" I ask, trying not to sound stupid.

"Seems to be, so far," Cheryl says. "She's going to the ICU."

"OK, I'll take care of the official transfer orders later. I must get to the Rapid Response. Also my patient."

"What, are you serious?"

"Yes."

"God, I am so sorry."

I'm already out of the room. I run down the hall, triggering a shout from the nurse's station to slow down. I reach room 903 in no time.

Inside, the thin black man shakes vigorously in bed, face grimacing, eyes closed. Darnell Jackson's right hand clenches that of his wife Nina, while another man, the patient's brother Jerome, leans in close. A young nurse named Tiffany quickly turns to me, with a somewhat frantic expression.

"Dr. Lin, he started shaking a few minutes ago. Now it's much worse."

"You gave him insulin?"

"Yes."

"What's going on?" Nina asks in a shaky voice.

I have only one possible answer. Knowing Jackson's medical history and hospital course thus far, plus this recent insulin injection, I am looking at the other extreme of the blood glucose level spectrum.

"Give him IV dextrose," I tell the nurse. "D fifty."

Tiffany nods and runs out. I step closer to the patient.

"Darnell, can you hear me?"

His eyes open very slightly. Through the tremors, I could register a nod. Good, he's still responsive.

"You might be going hypoglycemic," I say in my best calm but firm voice. "The nurse is going to give you some sugar water through your IV. Just hang in there. It's going to be OK. Trust me."

"Doc," Nina says, "how is it possible for him to go from hyperglycemic to hypoglycemic? I thought you were careful with his insulin."

"I'll review what's been given to him. Hopefully, I can figure out what happened. I honestly did not expect this."

"You sure you know what you're doing?"

"I'm pretty sure. Believe me, your husband is not the first diabetic patient I've ever taken care of."

"Doctor, should I also give him this?" Jerome asks, holding up a small box of Minute Maid apple juice.

"No. The IV dextrose should be a good start. We don't want his blood sugars to get too out of control."

At that moment, Tiffany comes in with a new fluid bag, which she hangs on the IV pole. In no time, the solution of 50% dextrose in water courses down the tube, through the IV port in Darnell's left arm, and into his veins. The next step is simple: wait.

"You're gonna be OK, baby," Nina says to her husband. "Just sit back and let them take care of you."

"Don't forget to pray," Jerome says calmly. "We'll be right here with you. We're not going anywhere."

I slow down my breathing. I have narrowly averted a Code Blue, this time saving a life instead of letting it slip a third time.

But what the hell is going on here? Jackson's insulin regimen out of the ICU was at least a good start: a long-acting insulin once each morning, plus a short-acting one before each meal. It brought his glucose down to as low as 190 milligrams per deciliter, still above target but at least far from DKA. So two days ago, I upped the dose of the premeal short-acting insulin. It definitely helped. His glucose inched further towards normal.

Still, did I screw this up? Have I overdone it?

After about ten more minutes, Jackson is resting calmly. His shakes are practically gone. He is breathing and looking at me with eyes wide open.

"Are you OK?" I ask.

"Yeah," he says softly.

"I'm so sorry this happened."

"Don't let me die, please."

"I won't. I promise."

The patient nods. Then I turn to Tiffany.

"Check his blood sugar again."

The nurse proceeds to grab a fingerstick kit nearby.

"Looks like things are under control again," I say to the patient and his family. "Again, I am terribly sorry. I will absolutely look into what led to this, so that I can prevent it from happening again. Do any of you have any questions?"

All three Jacksons shake their heads, expressions neutral. Thank goodness. I am ready to get out of here.

"For now, we'll continue with the current treatment plan. No changes to his insulin, while still monitoring his blood sugars. Hopefully, we'll get those levels stable so he could finally go home safely."

The patient and his brother nod simultaneously.

"Thank you, Doc," Nina says.

* * *

Doris Schafer has already been wheeled out of her room. Looks like there's no more emergency with her, so there's no super urgent task from my end. Therefore, I head into one of the staff restrooms at the end of the hall. It's a narrow room with a single toilet and sink, much too small for a second person to fit inside comfortably. It's also not a place to get some fresh air. But you know what? It's fine by me. I want a quiet place I could have to myself, even for just a few minutes.

I take a piss, wash my hands, and wet my face. In the mirror, I see a real sourpuss, wearing a tense but neutral facial expression. I might as well have a police mugshot. It wouldn't look any different at all. Whatever. I've had enough tough shit thrown at me within just one hour. Does it really matter if I might scare some people away? At least I don't seem to be scowling too much.

My black hair is slightly out of place, not neatly combed back like it was this morning. I dab those hanging strands with water, then bury them between its neighbors. That's better. I also make sure my clothes are tidy: green necktie straight and center, light-blue dress shirt tucked into tan khakis, white doctor's coat covering most of everything. The navy blue stethoscope slung around my neck completes the look. I'm all dressed for success now. Of course, if only my work for today would actually allow some success. I deserve to salvage the rest of the day, without any more nightmares to ruin it all.

Currently, I have nine patients to attend to.

#1: Christopher Flint, dead

#2: Doris Schafer, anaphylaxis, ICU-bound

#3: Darnell Jackson, hypoglycemic Rapid Response averted

#4: Donald Chester, new patient

#5 through 9: Other patients with various conditions, all stable, with two likely going home today.

During my rounds, who goes first, second, third, etcetera? Shit, this is complicated. I take a deep breath, then form a plan. I would assign priority by acuity. Complete tasks for the most serious cases first, then work my way to the lowest-risk patients. That means the two potential discharges would have to wait a little while. I hope they won't bite my head off once I get to them.

One more minute, and I'm heading out.

Any escape from the insanity of clinical medicine is akin to breathing in new life. Even a moment to relieve biological needs is heaven. I could refuel, recharge, and reenergize quickly, then return to the battlefield. There is no end to the war against disease. Only victories in individual fights. Any soul I save, any sickness I banish, adds to my glow as a physician. I could soar with bigger wings, taking me to greater heights. I could build up my honor and proudly show it to the world.

At the same time, I must tread carefully. Something tells me that the rest of the morning will not be so kind.

CHAPTER 3

First things first: pronounce Christopher Flint's death.

I stand over his lifeless body, attuned to the silence through the stethoscope over his chest. No heartbeat echoes, no breath flows. I move the stethoscope's diaphragm around to different spots over the thorax. Same findings as expected. I also check for any pupillary light reflexes and motor responses to pain. After a thorough few minutes of postmortem examination, I check my watch. Time of death: 8:24 AM.

Behind the nurse's station is a room full of desktop computers. I go in and sit at a terminal in the back corner, out of sight from pretty much anyone passing by outside. I log into Icarus, the Integrated Clinical Record System, and open Flint's chart. As quickly yet carefully as I can, I type a note describing the Code Blue, the interventions attempted to revive him, the time of death, and the cause of death. I also complete the death certificate, where I have to list, in reverse order, the sequence of key clinical events leading up to the patient's death: ventricular fibrillation minutes before death, due to congestive heart failure for five years, due to acute myocardial infarction for about the same period of time. That sounds about right. I submit everything and let out a big exhale. Hospital staff will now handle the morgue transfer, and all the rest.

Now, the really hard part: notifying next of kin.

I'm not talking about just any surviving family member. Lisa Flint, the patient's widow, is the epitome of overpowering, overbearing, and overcontrolling. In every phone conversation and face-to-face meeting, she would nitpick all sorts of details and write them down in a small notebook. It could be doses of inpatient medications, how often the nurse is cleaning his bedpan, that sort of thing. One time, she had the nerve to question whether CHF is reversible. The problem wasn't the question itself. CHF can be reversible in certain cases, depending on the cause. That's the simple and clear answer I provided. No, the real issue was how she refused to accept the fact that her husband's CHF may not be reversible because it was caused by a myocardial infarction, a heart attack, destroying some of his heart muscle. It's as if she saw online articles about the reversibility of CHF with specific causes, but extrapolated that wishful thinking to her husband who was not an applicable case.

All of this occurs no matter if she's alone with me or at her husband's bedside. She's the one in charge. But I don't like her stubbornness. Hell, even the patient hates it, based on his frequent eyerolls whenever his wife speaks.

And now I have to call her. Goddamn it.

I pick up the phone next to the computer, call her work number, and breathe nervously with the ringtones.

"Hello. Lisa Flint speaking."

"Hi, this is Dr. Mark Lin at Ivory Memorial Hospital. I'm calling about your husband, Christopher."

"Of course. Who else would you be talking about?"

"Well, I'm afraid have some really bad news."

I leave it right there. This is the kind of thing that has to be fed piece by piece. No point in torturing someone by making them swallow it whole. At that moment, I hear what sounds like a chair squeaking. I can tell Lisa is priming herself for a powerful blow to the gut.

"What is it?" she asks a bit anxiously.

"This morning, Christopher went into cardiac arrest. I rushed to him, along with the hospital's code team. We did everything we possibly could: defibrillating him, injecting some meds, the works."

I pause. She says nothing.

"I'm sorry, Lisa. Christopher has died."

Another moment of silence. Then, a sudden wail that rattles my eardrums, making me jump in my seat. I close my eyes and cover my face with one hand. It's like I've stabbed her in the heart, then ripped it out through her ribcage. But this isn't my fault. No way. Deep down, I know I did all I could.

"Dr. Lin, I'm coming as soon as I can. Maybe in an hour or so, since I have a long drive from Irvine."

"I'll be here. And again, I'm—"

She hangs up, just like that. Damnit, my morning is fucking ruined. Normally, I would be halfway through morning rounds on all of my patients. Not this time. I haven't even yet checked the first of nine off my list.

Once again, how the hell did Flint just die like that? I look through Flint's chart documents from the past two days, reviewing thoroughly what I did. I remember how totally fine he looked. He was his usual jolly and upbeat self, even as he already had a solid medication regimen: the diuretic called furosemide to make him pee more, the ACE inhibitor lisinopril to lower his blood pressure, and the beta-blocker metoprolol to slow his heart down a little. Yet, fluid still surrounded his lungs. So for the first time yesterday, I added digoxin to make his heart muscle contract more powerfully. I was pretty damn careful with that, too. I prescribed 125 micrograms of digoxin, a relatively small dose, knowing Flint's history of renal insufficiency.

But wait. Something's wrong here.

My eyes stay glued to the screen, at the nurse's medication administration record. At the row for digoxin, given to him this morning at six. Oh my god, could it be? Does this line actually say...

No!

Flint got 250 micrograms of digoxin. Impossible!

This can't be happening. Right away, I open the physician orders tab of the chart, then select the entry for digoxin. And I look really, really hard.

My eyes aren't deceiving me. It's the same dose. 250 goddamn micrograms.

No way in hell did I order that! I clearly recall what I did, every step of it. And don't ask me if I was impaired, because I wasn't. To this day, and to the day I die, I never let a single tiny bit of alcohol or drugs enter my body. It's all shit to me. I keep my mind and body pure. Can't do my job otherwise.

Then I notice something else. The order for 250 micrograms was submitted yesterday afternoon. Definitely not right, because I ordered 125 micrograms in the *morning,* hours before the timestamp of this one. Right away, I change a record display setting on the screen, to show physician orders that are discontinued or expired in addition to the active ones. I scan the list, then slowly shake my head.

My 125 microgram order isn't there at all. Not around the time I submitted it, or anywhere in the order record.

Now it looks like I ordered 250 micrograms in the afternoon, from the start. If this case goes to a medical malpractice court, I am so fucked. I lean forward and cover my face in both hands. I'm not crying, but I don't want to show myself to the world right now. I can't let anyone see me like this.

Goddamn it, goddamn it, goddamn it!

"Excuse me, Dr. Lin?"

I look up. Nurse Tiffany is at the doorway.

"Are you OK?" she asks slowly.

"Oh yeah. I'm just having a rough morning. Don't mind me."

"Sorry to hear. Some days can be like that."

"What's up?"

"I got Mr. Jackson's blood sugar level."

"Which is?"

"Two hundred twelve."

I nod. It's still elevated, but at least it's nowhere near 400 milligrams per deciliter at ICU admission. Even though there was no chance to check his glucose when I suspected hypoglycemia, it didn't matter. The dextrose did the trick.

"Did Mr. Jackson skip any meals?" I ask.

"I don't think so. Yesterday, the nurse from the previous shift noted that he did eat dinner."

"All of it?"

"Yeah. And you know his wife takes real good care of him. She's definitely making sure his meals and diabetic meds aren't off."

So Jackson's hypoglycemia wasn't because food intake was lower than normal, so that insulin brought his glucose down way too low.

Uh oh, wait a second. What about the insulin itself?

"Tiffany, how much time passed between you giving him his insulin and you noticing him shaking?"

"You're talking about Humalog, right?"

"Yeah, the short-acting insulin."

"Hmmm... maybe like twenty minutes. I was going to give him his meal a little after that."

I quickly open Jackson's chart in Icarus. I go straight to the last physician order for Humalog. Then I freeze, seeing something out of place.

Actually, two things.

One, the order for Jackson's Humalog is for 200 units per milliliter, not the 100 units I had originally ordered.

Two, it was placed yesterday early afternoon, a little after one o'clock. Not two mornings ago, which I goddamn remember well enough.

Shit, it's the same kind of anomalies as with Flint's digoxin.

I clench a fist under the table. How in the world could both Flint and Jackson have medication errors? I almost stomp the floor thinking about it, but I stop myself. Through a narrow slit between my lips, I take some deep breaths.

"Dr. Lin, do you want me to give him Lantus?" Tiffany asks, referring to Jackson's long-acting insulin.

"Yeah, go ahead. And keep checking his finger sticks periodically. Let me know if his glucose goes low again. Or if he gets symptomatic."

"I will. Are you OK, by the way?"

"Oh, I'm doing fine."

"Just thought I'd ask. You looked a little uptight a moment ago."

"Don't worry. I'll live."

"It's OK to admit you're stressed out."

"I'm not. I really am OK."

"Just don't forget that you're human."

I nod just to be polite. Tiffany smiles and leaves, and I turn back to the computer screen. Then I close my eyes. I don't want to think about this anymore. But I can't get away. I have to push forth, get all my crap done before the morning is over.

All of a sudden, I remember another patient. What about Doris Schafer? She almost died, too. Are any of her meds screwed up?

I open her chart. First, I read the note left by the physician handling the Code Blue. The nurse sounded the alarm because Schafer had a swollen face and couldn't breathe. With suspected anaphylaxis, the patient got epinephrine. Because she wasn't fully conscious and breathing freely, she got intubated and hooked up to an Ambu bag. The record doesn't say it, but I recall nurse Cheryl telling me there was difficulty with the intubation.

The patient was admitted because of pneumonia. Pretty straightforward case, with coughing, difficulty breathing, and an abnormal chest X-ray. I had started her on an antibiotic called azithromycin, something that could defeat several species of bacteria, even without knowing which one was the culprit. I also made sure not to give her ciprofloxacin, because she was allergic to that antibiotic.

Now I'm shaking intensely. I open the chart tabs for both physician orders and medication administration. Nervously, I switch back and forth between them.

I confirm my worst fear.

Schafer didn't receive her next dose of azithromycin this morning. She got ciprofloxacin instead. And here is an order for ciprofloxacin submitted late afternoon yesterday, which is definitely not right. Just like my order for azithromycin that is no longer there.

Then, without going anywhere, I spot something at the top of the screen. Where the chart mentions allergies, it just says "None." Not ciprofloxacin, as I remember seeing before. At least I think that's what it said previously. I hold my breath and feel another gut punch.

Without logging off my terminal yet, I briefly step out of the room. I prepare to ask the charge nurse for Cheryl, but turns out I don't need to. She is coming down the hall, having just exited a patient's room.

"Cheryl, can I talk to you? In here?"

She nods and approaches me. I get back in my seat at the computer as I gesture for her to come over.

"About Doris Schafer's anaphylactic reaction. Was it you who noticed it?"

"Yeah," Cheryl says, with a slightly stern face. "After I gave her the Cipro."

"How soon after giving it to her did you see her face swell up?"

"Really quick. Like maybe two minutes."

"Here's the thing. Yesterday, when she got admitted, I ordered Zithromax, because she's allergic to Cipro."

"Seriously?"

I nod slowly.

"You didn't see anything strange with the Cipro order?" I ask.

"No, not at all."

I stop to think. Because nurses work in shifts, a different nurse was assigned to Schafer late yesterday before Cheryl took over this morning. Based on the timing of the supposed order for Cipro, the previous nurse probably had no idea that the first antibiotic given was actually Zithromax. So Cheryl wouldn't know either.

"Well, something is very wrong here," I say. "I did not order Cipro, even if it says so in the chart."

"Really? You sure you're not impaired or anything?"

I glare at Cheryl.

"I am pretty certain that I was not then and that I am not now," I answer deliberately. "And do you understand that I was stuck with the Code Blue before Schafer's, because that was also another patient of mine?"

"Yes, yes, I get it."

"Good, because I would've gotten to Mrs. Schafer if I could. Speaking of which, I need to call the patient's husband to let him know the bad news. I'll let him know that you and the team tried. Is there anything you want to make sure I tell him?"

"No. I think you know the story."

"OK. Thanks, Cheryl. You can go."

Once the nurse leaves, I pick up the phone and dial the phone number listed in the patient's chart. Given that Schafer is 71 years old, I assume Ronald Schafer, her husband, is also retired and living at home.

Sure enough, he is.

"Hi, Mr. Schafer. This is Dr. Mark Lin at Ivory Memorial."

"Yes?"

"Well, I'm sorry to be bothering you, but I have some bad news."

"Oh god. Is Doris dead?"

"No, but she's in critical condition."

I wait for Ronald's next comment. All I can hear is his breathing that has a slight wheezing quality.

"What happened?" he asks.

"This morning, she had an anaphylactic reaction. A severe, potentially life-threatening allergy. She's in the ICU now. As for how that happened, I'm looking further into it. But I regret to inform you that some kind of medical error might have occurred. She may have gotten the wrong antibiotic."

"What? Are you serious?"

I pause, giving him a moment to let it sink in further.

"Did you order the wrong medication?" Ronald asks tensely.

"No," I answer quickly. "I know which antibiotic I ordered, and I remembered to make sure it wasn't the one she's allergic to. Yet, something happened that led her to get the incorrect one. Like I said, I'm looking into this."

"It's still your fault, you know."

"I understand your frustration."

"No, you don't, you prick. I trusted you to look after her."

Here we go. Time to brace myself for some fiery abuse. He sighs heavily before continuing.

"At first, I thought you seemed all right. But now I think I shouldn't have. You goddamn docs are all the same. Not knowing shit, then messing things up. And you still act like you know better than us!"

"I get what you're saying, sir."

"Do you really?"

"I'm trying to look at this from both sides. I know that you are unhappy. At the same time, I am also trying to figure out where the problem lies. Healthcare is a team effort, after all. There's also nurses, the pharmacy..."

"Are you trying to deflect blame here? You're the one in charge."

"Again, I'm going to find out—"

"Fuck you, Dr. Lin! If I hear that my wife is dead because of your sorry excuse for care, your ass is going down!"

I stiffen, as if taking a hard kick in the crotch.

"I am sorry this has happened," I say, trying to sound sympathetic. "I get it. At the same time, please calm down. Let's work together to find a way through this. There's no need to be uncivil. OK?"

Ronald breathes loudly, like a fire-breathing dragon ready to bellow out a roar and shoot its flames.

"Whatever," he says. "At least you're not taking care of her in the ICU, right?"

"That's correct. A critical care doc is doing that."

"Then again, is that doc any better than you? Or any other goddamn physician who doesn't know crap?"

"I can't say."

Ronald says nothing. Fine by me, because I've had enough of this shit. Doing the best I can to save a life and then still getting a beatdown because things turn out wrong, not to the family's liking.

"Do you have any other questions?" I ask gently.

"No, I have no goddamn questions. I'll go visit my wife later today. And I don't want to talk to you anymore. All right?"

"Understood. Have a good day, sir."

I wait a few seconds. Then he hangs up. So do I.

In a daze, I do one more thing for Schafer in Icarus. I type a brief note in her chart, documenting my acknowledgement of the code doc's note and explaining that my attention with another simultaneous Code Blue prevented my immediate presence for this one. I also make sure to do a similar kind of note for Darnell Jackson's Rapid Response. It's the least I can do to save my own ass.

* * *

Six more patients to round on, but at least the pace is picking up. I start with two patients whom I expected would get well enough by this morning to be discharged home. Sure enough, they have, and I complete their discharge paperwork, finally easing the tension of their long wait. Three other patients are making progress with their conditions. I only have to adjust a medication for one of them. At least one may be able to go home tomorrow.

That leaves Donald Chester, the new patient I see for the first time. He is asymptomatic at least. The only thing he's feeling is anxiety. What is it that made him vomit blood over the past couple of days?

Dr. Joanne Li, the consulting gastroenterologist, would find the answer. Her note in Icarus documents her initial evaluation of the patient and confirms that he will be wheeled downstairs to the GI procedure suite. That will happen later today, meaning it'll likely be sometime this afternoon. He will undergo upper endoscopy, with a scope going down his esophagus into the stomach. For now, all I can do is wait for Joanne's findings. At least I am reassured. She is great with bedside manners and knows her specialty inside and out.

It's now a few minutes before eleven. I check my work phone. No message about Lisa Flint arriving yet, but I'll be ready.

I am back in my office cubicle in the meantime, away from the frontlines below. It's amazing that I finished my hectic morning rounds with still some time to spare. Now my remaining work for the day is follow-up stuff, things like making sure what I ordered is carried out and taking further steps based on any new developments. Obviously, the talk with Lisa and Chester's endoscopy are the biggest tasks left.

Killing time, I open Google Chrome on my cubicle desktop to check the news. I go to the website of *The Wall Street Journal*. As expected, Lucifer's Worm is dominating the headlines. I skim past the stuff I know already, about a spam email message and mail servers getting flooded. The part about businesses temporarily shutting down isn't surprising either. But halfway down the article, I stop and lean closer to the screen.

Some businesses are now seeing other things going wrong.

Hundreds of customers of an online clothing retailer were shocked to find that their submitted product orders suddenly displayed items they never paid for. A major news website had the phrase "Fucking Fake News" plastered numerous times all throughout its pages. But it isn't just businesses. Law enforcement agencies got hit, too. There is the website of the Minneapolis Police Department that got defaced, made to look like blood and feces smearing it. Same thing occurred with police department websites in Los Angeles, New York, and Chicago. Hell, even U.S. government websites got defiled with the same shit, like the Department of Justice, the Department of Homeland Security, Immigration and Customs Enforcement, and the U.S. Marshals Service.

What the hell is going on here?

This is so unreal. Nothing like this has ever happened before. Then again, COVID-19 also came out of the blue. I thought of the phrase I used this morning with Jay McKinnon: "Cyber pandemic." You know what? That's exactly what this is: a mysterious force that causes widespread chaos and destruction, leaving us scrambling in fear, desperately looking for answers, and bitterly pointing fingers at just about anybody.

How bad is this going to get? And for how long?

But wait. What about me, and my situation? Three patients crashing, with one already dead. All with medication orders I know I didn't place. All with errors I know I wouldn't make. All suffering tragically because of them. The more I think about it, the more I believe it deep down.

I did not fuck up any of this.

Never once in my career had I ever screwed up so badly that I harmed my patients. I know this to still be true. In fact, if there was any criticism I received during my residency training, it's that I was too careful, not that I wasn't careful enough. So really, the fault lies in something else, something well beyond my control: a dark force from the void.

Lucifer's Worm.

With this realization, I stand up triumphantly. I vow to fight off any attack on my career and reputation. I will protect myself against any vicious effort to bring me down and destroy my very being. I'll even throw Lucifer's Worm into the arena, let everyone know that it is this beast from hell that's doing the killing, not me. Of course, that means I have to put together a strong case. I must find a connection between Lucifer's Worm and three medication errors, then convince the skeptics.

I must defend my honor, at all costs.

Instantly, I snap back to reality. My phone just buzzed briefly. A new text has come in, from one of the nurse's stations on the eighth floor. The message makes me forget about pretty much everything else:

Lisa Flint is here, ready to talk to you.

CHAPTER 4

I approach the nurse's station, slowly and deliberately, knowing the grief I am about to face. Lisa Flint, a thin middle-aged woman with shoulder-length red hair, stands facing the charge nurse behind the counter. Then the nurse points in my direction, and Lisa's head turns. Her mouth is curled slightly downward, not surprisingly. But when I get within a few feet of her, her expression doesn't change. Her face is stone.

"Lisa, I'm really sorry about your husband," I say calmly.

"Whatever," she says quietly.

I wait before she continues.

"I wish I could've gotten here much earlier. Work obligations and freeway traffic made it tough."

"Understood."

"Now I can't even say goodbye to Christopher, face to face. Do you know how heartbreaking that is?"

I nod slowly. The patient had already been taken to the morgue and is now awaiting next steps from the newly-widowed Lisa. This hospital does allow families to visit loved ones in the same room they die in, but only for a limited time. Lisa had arrived a little too late. She missed her one window of opportunity.

"You'll be able to claim his body," I say, even though it is obvious. "This is a difficult time, no doubt. For all of us."

"I can't believe he's gone. Just like that. I mean, I saw nothing wrong with him the other day. Now what am I supposed to do?"

Again, I nod. It's the easiest way to acknowledge her pain, without pushing her too close to the edge.

"Do you need to sit down?" I ask. "There's a small conference room where we can talk quietly."

"Fine. Lead the way."

I escort Lisa to a room at the end of the hall. It contains a rectangular table with chairs along one side of the room, plus comfy seats and a couch in the rest of the space. We sit in soft chairs facing each other directly, with only about five feet of space in between. But Lisa still stares at the floor.

"Do you need some water to drink?" I ask politely.

"No, thank you," Lisa says quietly.

I wait a few seconds. Lisa takes out a pack of tissue from her purse. She pulls out one sheet and dabs the tears that are beginning to stream down her cheeks.

"He looked fine before," she says, sniffling. "I don't understand how this could've happened, him dying so suddenly."

"Would it help if I review the events leading up to today?"

She nods while opening her purse to take out a small notebook and pen. I remember her habit quite well: notetaking that is so careful that it's like she's jotting down every word I say. She isn't the first family member of a patient to do this, though, and I don't mind notetaking overall. Just not from this person, who would follow up with questions here and there as if trying to trap me into looking stupid or incompetent.

"Do you understand your husband's medical history?" I ask.

"He had congestive heart failure," Lisa says, flipping through her notebook. "And a prior heart attack. You also call that a myocardium, uh... what's that term?"

"Myocardial infarction?"

"Yes. That's what made his heart weak, right?"

"Correct. The heart attack was the precursor. Since that event, his heart had a difficult time pumping blood. That's CHF."

"Could it ever be reversed?"

There goes that question again.

"Not in his case," I say, shaking my head no. "Heart muscle that dies is replaced with scar tissue, not new muscle tissue. That's why his

CHF was permanent."

"So all we could do was just keep giving him meds?" Lisa asks calmly. "Every time he got worse?"

"Essentially, yes. Do you understand the purpose of each medication?"

"I think so. Furosemide to help him pee, to keep him from having too much fluid within him. Lisinopril to control his blood pressure. And metoprolol... oh, that's the beta-blocker. To slow his heart a little."

"You are well-informed. That's good."

"What I don't get is why he kept coming in and out of the hospital."

"There are several possible reasons CHF exacerbation can occur. One is noncompliance to fluid restrictions. If the heart is weak, then too much liquid in the blood could strain it. Christopher did consume food and drink beyond the recommended limit. That fluid accumulation was what made him keep coming back."

"I do understand that. After the last time he was here, I can honestly say I recorded everything he ate and drank."

"What about his medications?"

"Same thing. Believe me, I kept track of his doses."

I nod. Lisa's statement seems genuine.

"So after all of this, why did he have CHF exacerbation again this time?" she asks with curiosity.

"After having CHF for so long, it looks like his heart had gotten even weaker, gradually decreasing in function."

"Couldn't you just give him more high-dose diuretics, clear out all that fluid, and let him go?"

"If he took his meds and restricted his fluids, under your careful watch, and his heart still had trouble pumping blood, it likely means a new problem had entered the picture: weakening of the heart muscle itself."

Lisa pauses to let it all sink in. I take a moment to remember how, almost every day since Christopher Flint was admitted, she would visit and ask me so many questions, sometimes repeating what she asked the day before. Yesterday was the one day when she couldn't stop by or call me, because she had a one-day business trip to take.

I had not filled her in on the one fateful decision I made.

"What about trying different medications?" she asks. "Like replacing furosemide with another diuretic. Maybe another one would work better?"

"I doubt changing meds within the same class would make a difference here. Not if his existing ones weren't causing problems."

"So what's next?"

"With cardiac function declining, he needed a boost to that."

"How?"

"A medication to help his heart contract more strongly."

Lisa slowly looks up at me. Now that familiar ice-cold expression is back. My own heart begins to race.

"Is that what you did?" she asks, now starting to tense.

"Yes."

"And you didn't tell me?"

"I remember that you said you had to be away for business. And I really felt he needed this medication."

"Why didn't you consult with me first?"

I sigh quietly. In case it isn't obvious, this is the reason she, of all patient advocates, really gets on my nerves.

"I can assure you that I carefully weighed the benefits and risks. With his weakening heart, I felt that doing everything we did before without adding anything new would not be enough for him. The medication I prescribed, called digoxin, would improve heart contraction, addressing that issue."

"Wait a minute. Digoxin?"

"Yes."

"Do you even know how dangerous it is?"

"I'm aware of the potential side effects."

"But you gave it to him anyway."

"Again, I felt its benefit would outweigh the risk."

"You still should've told me."

"Yes, I understand you like to be kept in the loop, but—"

"Then why didn't you call?"

"It couldn't wait."

"What? Was he dying at that moment?"

"No, it's not like that."

"But he died after you gave him one dose of it. Right?"

I nod. Slowly, while maintaining eye contact.

"He went into cardiac arrest this morning," I say. "But despite all of our efforts, we unfortunately couldn't save him."

"You... you goddamn bastard!"

"Lisa, please—"

Without warning, she stamps one foot on the floor. The point of her high heel makes a loud crack that shatters the silence. Then she points a finger at me, shaking.

"You really should've told me," she scowls. "Because if you had, I would've said no to that, and you and I would not be having this conversation!"

"As a physician, it's my job to determine what's best for the patient."

"Oh, you think you're so smart, huh? Well, let me tell you. I've been reading up on treatments for congestive heart failure, including digoxin. And not just stuff from WebMD and the Mayo Clinic."

I nod slightly. Then she continues.

"I've also looked at journal articles saying that the risk for mortality goes up with digoxin. Plus first-hand accounts from people on Facebook who had taken it, and anyone who knows someone who suffered from it. So don't you even dare call me stupid."

I raise my hands in surrender.

"I'm not suggesting that at all. It's good that you are taking an active role in your husband's care."

"OK, so why are you questioning me?"

"I just want you to understand that reading up on medical topics is also best when done comprehensively. Not just anecdotes."

Now, Lisa's mouth curls into a tight ball. And she stands up, takes two steps forward, and looks down on me.

"You know what?" she says intensely. "I've had enough of you.

Because of your incompetence, my husband is dead, and I'm going to be struggling like hell trying to keep our house and everything."

"Lisa—"

"Shut up, you pig."

With that, she whips one hand across the left side of my face. A pain explodes as my head jerks the other way. Lisa's heels clank quickly as she scurries to the door. She stops and turns to me.

"Don't even think about trying to stop me," she says. "I swear to you. I'm going to make you pay for this."

Then she walks out.

* * *

At last, it's lunch time, one of my favorite times of the day because I can really get away from it all. Well, not always, since disease never sleeps. A Code Blue or Rapid Response could strike even between twelve and one. Whatever. I'm ready to recharge and savor every minute of it.

In the hospital cafeteria, I purchase a ham and cheese sandwich on a baguette, an apple, and a bottle of Tropicana orange juice. I pass through the general public seating area and into a room designated as a staff dining room. There, I find a large empty square table in the back corner. I sit there and close my eyes, then breathe.

In...

Out...

In...

Out...

Again...

And again...

Then I'm no longer aware of it. My head dips forward in a moment of relaxation. I start to forget about the soreness in my face I had a short while ago, whatever the hell that was from. I begin dreaming about a beach.

And just like that, I hear a snap, right in front of my nose.

"What the hell?" I say breathlessly while opening my eyes.

Dr. Thomas Chandler, a thin black guy with a big grin, is standing on the other side of the table, leaning toward me.

"Are you awake now?" he asks with a smile.

"Yeah, thanks to you."

Thomas sits down. Then a blonde lady approaches us and sits next to Thomas. It's another colleague, Dr. Jane Larsen. Although I can be content with sitting alone, as I had originally expected, having two friends is indeed better. Can't argue with that. I take the first bite of my ham sandwich, while Jane adds ranch dressing to a chicken salad and Thomas puts ketchup and mustard onto a hamburger beef patty.

"Did you get enough sleep last night?" Thomas asks.

"I got six-and-a-half hours."

"You slept like a baby?"

"Sort of. But ideally, I'd get eight or nine hours."

"You probably won't get Alzheimer's disease then," Jane says, with her usual warm and friendly smile.

"It's amazing how, many years ago, we had no idea what caused Alzheimer's," Thomas says. "Turns out it might be sleep deprivation."

"I'm not surprised," I say.

"How come?" Thomas asks.

"I remember reading about one of those animal studies, where they found less clearance of beta-amyloid in the brains of sleep-deprived mice. Knowing that beta-amyloid is the protein that accumulates in the brains of Alzheimer's disease patients, and seeing how plenty of Americans don't get enough sleep, I already guessed the connection right there."

"And here we are," Jane says. "A small human study shows it, too."

I nod. The best evidence is always the direct kind.

"There ought to be a new public service announcement," Thomas says. "Get your sleep, save your brain."

"That's a good slogan," Jane says, laughing.

"But it's pretty hard for people with high-stress jobs, like firefighters."

"Or cops."

"Don't forget doctors like us."

"Hey, speaking of which, who's the surgeon on call?" I ask.

"Why?" Jane asks.

"I have a patient who might need a surgery consult later."

"It's Dr. Samuel Pierson," Thomas says.

Oh, hell no. Anyone but that asshole with a scalpel.

"If I officially need to get a surgery consult, I am not looking forward to talking to him," I say.

"Why not?" Jane asks.

"You ever dealt with him before?"

"I have."

"How did he treat you?"

"He is rather intense. He has this way of putting you down for any request you have. It's like he only wants to deal with the important stuff."

"Don't you have a problem with that?"

"I do, but that's just the way he is. All you can do is put on some thick skin whenever he's around."

"Easier said than done."

"Sounds like you really dislike him."

I stare back at Jane.

"Wouldn't anyone feel the same?" I say. "Besides, he's treated me worse than he treated you."

"How so?" Jane asks.

"Much louder and more abrasive. I'll spare you the details."

"If you have to call him about your case, just focus on the patient's best interest. Nothing more important than that, right?"

I nod, then close my eyes and sigh. For almost a full minute, I don't even bother eating my sandwich.

"Mark, are you OK?" Thomas asks.

"Sort of."

"You're still not thinking about Dr. Pierson, are you?"

"No. Something else."

"What?"

"You remember what happened this morning over the PA system?"

Thomas and Jane pause to think.

"There was one Code Blue," Thomas says. "Oh wait, there were two."

"Plus a Rapid Response call," Jane says, then turns to me. "Mark, were any of them your patients?"

"Yeah. Guess how many."

Both of them freeze. Then, simultaneously, they slowly let their jaws drop.

"Have you ever had three of your own patients crashing one after the other?" I ask, starting to tense up. "This is beyond ridiculous."

"I'm sorry, man," Thomas says sympathetically.

"What happened with each of them?" Jane asks.

"Here's the short version," I answer. "The first one is dead. The second one is critical. The third one survived."

"I see," Jane says, poking through her salad with a plastic fork. "How did you manage each case?"

"First one was V-fib. I made sure things were done per ACLS protocol. He wasn't coming back, but I kept trying. That's when the second Code Blue got called. Now imagine yourself in the same situation. A patient before you is still crashing, and now another one, on a different floor, is also about to die, supposedly. Do you just stop what you're doing with patient number one and rush to patient number two? Or do you hope that the Code Team from the emergency department can hold the fort until you get there?"

Thomas and Jane nod in thought, then take bites of their respective meals. I give them a few moments to savor their food, and to think about my dilemma further.

"I take it you remained with the first patient?" Jane asks.

"Yep," I say. "Until he died. Then I had my chance with the second patient, who had anaphylaxis. When I got there, the Code Team already finished. They intubated her and took her to the ICU. So it's now in the hands of one of the critical care docs downstairs."

"So that leaves the third patient, the Rapid Response," Thomas says.

"Right. And that was simply a matter of a diabetic patient who was shaking, so I gave him dextrose for suspected hypoglycemia. He's OK for now."

I take one bite of my sandwich. Then another.

"Once again, I'm sorry you had to go through that," Thomas says. "I thought I had it bad. When I was in residency, I had four Code Blues in a single day. But there was time in between, like maybe an hour or two."

"Sounds like really bad luck," Jane says, then puts more salad into her mouth and munches on it.

"Tell me about it. What are the chances of that happening?"

"Really small."

"Like how small, would you say?"

"One in a million, maybe."

"Still better than my luck," I comment.

There is a pause as Thomas and Jane continue their lunch. I swallow another glob of bread, ham, cheese, and lettuce, followed by a few gulps of good old citrus. Then I turn to Thomas.

"There's one thing that makes my situation not like yours at all," I say with a hint of seriousness.

"What's that?" Thomas asks.

"A possible underlying reason for all three events."

"I'm listening."

"Think about what the CEO texted us. About the spam email getting in everyone's inboxes."

"You think that has something to do with it?"

"Anything is possible," Jane says. "I saw the news on my phone about an hour ago. It's all part of some malware called Lucifer's Worm."

"Whoa, I haven't checked the news all morning," Thomas says.

"It gets worse," I say. "There are strange things going on beyond just email servers getting slowed down and affecting all kinds of work. Like websites getting defaced. It's pretty bad out there."

"How is that possible?" Thomas asks, intrigued.

"I don't know yet. But here's why I bring this up."

Quickly, I bite into the last quarter of my sandwich. I use the time to compose my thoughts.

"I looked at the Icarus charts for those three patients this morning,"

I explain. "In each case, I saw something very wrong with their latest medication order."

"Can you be more specific?" Jane asks.

"The patient with V-fib has CHF. I had ordered digoxin. But when I checked back, there's an order for it with the dose doubled."

"Oh my god."

"I'm afraid that's what might've killed him."

"Are you sure you clearly remember ordering it?" Thomas asks.

"Totally sure. I was not sleep-deprived, if that's what you're asking. Seriously, have you ever had a situation where you ordered a medication, confirmed that the medication got ordered and administered to the patient, but then the next day you see an entirely different medication order instead?"

"And it was your name on it?"

"Yes."

"Man, what is going on?"

"I don't know. But let me explain what else happened. For the second patient, I ordered a specific antibiotic for her pneumonia. But now I see an order for a different medication, which she is allergic to. Nurse gave her that one this morning, triggering the second Code Blue."

I am speaking so intensely that I stiffen when I'm done. Thomas and Jane also tense up. They slowly lean closer.

"So the third patient had a medication error, too?" Jane asks.

"Yeah," I say. "Rapid Response patient had his insulin dose doubled."

"How are the patients' families handling this?"

"I'm not going there."

"Oh, that's fine. My god, you had such an awful morning."

I finish the last of my sandwich and orange juice. In the midst of conversation, I had not noticed that Thomas and Jane had already finished their lunches.

"So what are you going to do?" Jane asks.

"Maybe I should get in touch with the IT department here. I need to explain that it may be no coincidence that these medication errors have something to do with Lucifer's Worm. There's no way this is some random fluke."

"Not with medication orders you never really signed."

"Right."

"Do you think it could happen again?" Thomas asks.

I look at my friend.

"What are you talking about?" I ask.

"Could a fourth patient suffer from a strange medication order?" Thomas says, somewhat quietly. "Or a fifth?"

"I hope not. But I'm not taking any chances."

"Do you think you could prevent a repeat of this morning?"

I shrug slowly.

"I don't know. I think all I can do is just be wary of anything."

"Whatever happens, I hope you get through it," Jane says. "And when you go home, get some rest."

"I will. Thanks."

With that, the rest of lunch involves random chitchat between Jane and Thomas. Meanwhile, I'm lost in my own thoughts. If Lucifer's Worm is causing medication errors, why is it happening only to me? Come to think of it, am I really the only unlucky doc here? Suppose it's actually going on hospital-wide. Other physicians and their patients might suffer, too. Another reason to get hold of the IT department and give them a heads up.

Eventually, Jane leaves the table with her cafeteria tray. Thomas waves and also walks off. I could do the same right now, but I need another moment to myself.

It's now a few minutes until one o'clock. Not a single overhead alarm has summoned me to my patients. Not even a single text message on my phone. But as I stand, I know my luck will run out soon. It is time to be vigilant. More like hypervigilant. Whatever it takes to make sure no more lives slip through my fingers.

Not one more.

CHAPTER 5

As expected, Donald Chester had undergone upper endoscopy in the GI suite and is now back in his room. I review the procedure note by Dr. Joanne Li, detailing the steps she took as well as her findings.

The upper GI bleed likely came from esophageal varices, those veins dilated with blood struggling to flow through the liver. At least one of them might have ruptured. Joanne documented that she endoscopically placed bands around three veins that appeared most troublesome. Problem solved.

But what about the other issue, the stomach tumor? Joanne spotted it through the scope, but saw no mucosal erosion where the tumor was. So that was not the source of bleeding. However, she did take a biopsy sample of that mass, so that someone in the pathology lab would cut it into slices, examine each one under a microscope, and determine if the tumor is benign or malignant based on the tissue characteristics observed. The end of Joanne's note includes the phrase, "recommend surgery consult, and possibly oncology consult depending on biopsy results." No surprise there. I already thought about all of that even before Chester got wheeled down for endoscopy.

On my tablet, I confirm who the on-call surgeon is. Yep, it's Dr. Samuel Pierson. Why does it have to be him, of all people? I pull out my hospital-issued smartphone and send a quick text to Pierson, mentioning my need for a consult along with the patient's name and medical record number. Then I wait. Hopefully, it won't be long at all. It's amazing that 21st century technology allows me to communicate this quickly in a hospital setting. Because my work phone uses a special secure messaging system, not anything connected to the wide-open 5G network, all texts to and from other staff stay right here, without going anywhere past the confines of this place.

I also think about how Chester is on the fence between two specialties. Usually, patients are either on the medicine service under the care of internists, or on the surgery service with surgeons seeing them through. It's not often that a patient is on the medicine service but needs a surgery consult. If anything, the reverse is more common, with patients having some problem corrected with surgery and the surgeon consulting with an internist for various side issues that require medications. I sure hope Pierson doesn't get pissed off about being a consulting surgeon rather than a primary one.

At last, Pierson responds, in the form of a return call. Here goes nothing.

"Hello, Dr. Lin speaking."

"All right, I got your message," the deep serious voice of Pierson says. "Make it quick. I got a lot to do as it is."

"Sure thing. The patient, Donald Chester, is a sixty-eight-year-old man with a history of alcoholic cirrhosis. Admitted for hematemesis. He just underwent upper endoscopy and had esophageal varices banded. But he also has a stomach tumor, found incidentally on CT before admission. It's a bit large, like two centimeters. The GI doc's biopsy is pending, but I figure a surgeon would need to get involved regardless."

Now there is a pause. I wonder what Pierson is thinking. My guess is that he's brainstorming questions to throw at me. Would they be for getting more details about the case or finding excuses to bail out? The last time I asked Pierson for a consult, he attempted the latter, and I had to yell just to keep him in line.

"Let me ask you this," Pierson finally says. "Is the patient bleeding now?"

"No."

"Not even from the tumor itself?"

"Dr. Li in GI confirmed the bleeding was not from the tumor."

"OK, so what's the problem?"

"He still has a tumor."

"So?"

"Do you really need me to explain?"

"Well, shouldn't you?"

I shake my head in disgust. What the hell is wrong with blowhard, arrogant doctors? People expect compassion from medical professionals. More like demand it, if you ask me. Yet, there are white coats like Pierson who are still full of shit, give other people shit, and make them feel like shit. Oh, and make others bow down to these so-called gods of healing.

"You know something?" I say. "I thought you were so smart that the obvious wouldn't need to be laid out for you."

"Are you insulting me?" Pierson growls.

"No, I'm trying to understand what you're thinking. Why would you be reluctant to see a patient with a known tumor?"

"I need to know if he's high-risk."

"Based on what?"

"Is the tumor benign or malignant?"

"Biopsy is pending, OK? But wait a minute. Does it really matter? If the tumor were malignant cancer, now is clearly the time to take it out. He doesn't have lymph node or distant metastases as far as I could tell, so he has a better chance for survival. And even if the tumor were benign, it could still cause problems when it gets bigger and bigger. So you tell me. What the hell is the hold-up?"

"I'm a busy guy here."

"So am I. Everyone in every specialty is busy. But that's no excuse for saying no to this consult, right?"

I hear nothing. I tighten my mouth, wondering if he just hung up on me. Then he responds, a little calmer this time.

"Listen to me. We have a lot of surgical cases on our plate. Think of how hard it was for everyone during COVID-19. It's like that here."

"Is every patient crashing one by one?"

"No. The surgeries may be elective, but I'm still talking about a long list."

"OK, I get it. You're really, really overwhelmed."

"That's right."

"So why do you sound like you don't want to see the patient?"

"I'm just trying to prioritize, all right?"

I take a few deep breaths, but not silently. I am practically huffing and puffing into the phone's mic.

"My one question is really simple," I say slowly. "Will you see Mr. Chester?"

"The answer is yes. But... not immediately. If, based on the information you gave me, he is not someone who needs emergency surgery, then I'll get to him when I can. It may be later today. Or even tomorrow, if things get really busy on my end. Just know that I'll get to him. Eventually. *All right?!*"

I flinch as he yells that last sentence. It's a good thing I'm talking to him on the phone, not face to face. I'd punch him really hard in the nose.

"OK, thank you," I say, trying to be calm.

"Next time, don't you ever harass me like this again."

"Hold on. Was I harassing you?"

"Get your goddamn head out of the sand and stop being in denial! I don't appreciate your tone with me."

"What?"

"Right there. That's your goddamn tone."

"Look, I'm just doing what's best for my patient."

"By questioning my authority?"

I clench a fist until my knuckles turn white.

"What are you talking about?" I ask.

"I decide when to see the patient."

"While I'm the primary doc handling this case. I'm the one who determines what consults are needed."

"And I can tell you if they're warranted, and if I have the time."

"All right. I get it."

"Do you? Because you can't stop arguing."

"Look, Dr. Pierson, I'm done here. I'm not gonna take this crap from you anymore, OK? I don't need to explain how my focus is helping my patients get better, just like you're doing with yours. And I really don't need to get into how refusing to do our jobs is an invitation to malpractice. You want your ass sued because you refused to take care of a patient? I certainly don't. And you know what else? Being a hero does not mean saving the day whenever you want. It's when someone needs help, at any time. I guarantee you that the next time a patient of mine needs surgery and he or she dies because you didn't do a damn thing, it'll be your sorry carcass getting hung out to dry."

"You want to watch your mouth next time?"

"With you? No."

"You take that back."

"Forget it, I'm through with you."

"Hey, don't you dare talk to me like that!"

I hang up without a thought.

* * *

The rest of the afternoon goes by without a hitch. By the time it's almost four, my nerves have calmed somewhat. I can at least walk into a patient's room and not look like I'm ready to start a fight.

Remembering what happened to Darnell Jackson today, I enter room 903. The patient is awake and accompanied this time only by his brother Jerome. I greet them both with a slight smile.

"I wanted to stop by and make sure you're still doing OK," I say.

"I'm good," Jackson says.

"No further problems this afternoon?"

"Not at all."

"Is Tiffany the nurse treating you OK?"

"Oh, she's an angel. Bless her."

"Doctor, did you find out what went wrong this morning?" Jerome asks.

I nod slowly. Then I take a deep breath. I can tell the two men are bracing themselves for the worst.

"It appears that a mistake was indeed made. Darnell's short-acting insulin was given at a higher dose than what I had ordered. Right now, I can't tell exactly how that happened. I just know that it did. I'm so sorry."

Jackson frowns, while the brother shakes his head.

"So you're still looking into it?" Jerome asks.

"Yes," I answer without hesitation. "Just give me some time. I hope to have some clarity on the matter soon."

"At least I'm relieved this morning is behind us. But surely you won't let this ever happen again, right?"

"Of course."

"You promise?"

"Absolutely."

Jerome nods slowly, with a somewhat relaxed smile. For now, he and his brother look reassured. I have made my amends. Hopefully, I have their trust too.

I finish following up on patients' lab results, imaging studies, and whatever else, then I head back upstairs to my cubicle. Knowing what I know now, I am not taking any chances. At my terminal, I go through each patient's chart in Icarus. Every single progress note, physician order, nursing medication record, etcetera, from the past week goes through my radar. Inside and out. No stone unturned. I make sure nothing appears screwy. It takes me a whole hour to comb through all of these recent records. Other than the medication orders for Christopher Flint, Doris Schafer, and Darnell Jackson that I already saw, there is nothing out of the ordinary. Whatever harmed these three patients hasn't struck anyone else.

Not yet, probably.

I'm not letting this go. Not when the spam emails from Lucifer's Worm flooded this hospital, plus most other places around the world. Not when something computerized went haywire and killed one patient, just as chaos reigns elsewhere.

There has to be a connection. I can feel it.

On the hospital's intranet website, I navigate my way to the homepage for the Ivory Memorial Hospital Division of Information Technology. The site has a simple setup, with a welcome message and links related to things like in-hospital device security and tech support for clinical applications. But one thing is definitely unusual: the bolded all-caps line warning us not to access Ivory's email system because server troubleshooting is ongoing. I'm not here to simply read stuff, of course. I need someone to talk to, pronto.

Hence, I click on the "Contact Us" link. On the next page, there are phone numbers and email addresses for various senior IT staff members. I just need one. The most logical one to go to is the name listed at the top: Rajesh Krishnan, the division's director. I pick up my desk phone and dial Rajesh's number. Maybe I should just leave a voicemail. It's a little after 4:50 PM, so he might be gone for the day.

But after four rings, I hear a slightly accented male voice.

"Information Technology, Rajesh speaking."

"Hi, this is Dr. Mark Lin, one of the internists here. Can I ask you a rather strange question?"

"Is it about our email system?"

"Sort of."

I hear Rajesh laugh a little. It's one of those pleasant-sounding chuckles. A good sign, in my opinion.

"Let me tell you," Rajesh says. "You are definitely not the first person to call and ask for a status update. I can at least say that we're making good progress. There's still plenty more spam email to clear, plus server repairs and whatnot. But I'm going off on a tangent. You say you have a question to ask."

"Yeah. Before I get to that, have you paid attention to what the news is talking about? About this thing called Lucifer's Worm?"

"Absolutely. This hospital is one of many unfortunate victims of this malware. Right now, experts like myself are still awaiting more info about what it does. But it's starting to look like it does more than just flood and crash email servers."

"That's what I wanted to ask you about. What would you do if there is something else going on in our network, other than email flooding?"

"Like what?"

I take a long deep breath.

"Medication errors."

"Can you be more specific?"

"A dose increase or a drug substitution."

"And you spotted them in the system?"

"Yeah, but only after they harmed or killed my patients."

"Really? Oh my goodness."

I say nothing in response. Better to wait until this fully sinks in for Rajesh. Moments later, he speaks again.

"You are the first physician to report something like this to us. Because this is so new, I can't really say yet what's going on."

"Can you at least look into it?"

"I will try my best. Are you sure there was no human error on your part with those medications?"

"I'm one hundred percent sure."

"Can you tell me more about those medication errors?"

"Let me give you the patient info first."

"OK."

I give Rajesh the names and medical record numbers of the three patients who were cursed today. Then, while consulting records in Icarus for reference, I provide the relevant details. For each case, I walk Rajesh through the sequence of clinical events and my discovery of the chart errors. From his periodic utterances of "Uh huh" and "OK," I can tell he's getting it. In the end, I hear what sounds like a pen scratching a notepad. I smile, knowing he's jotting the info down.

"You never placed those three new orders you mentioned?" he asks.

"Not at all. In fact, I already left work around five yesterday. Those orders in my name were placed while I was gone."

"I see."

"That's one reason I know they're not mine."

"Are you in any kind of trouble because of this?"

"Not yet, but I'm still anticipating it."

I hear a soft exhale from Rajesh.

"Obviously, none of this is a coincidence," he says. "Three medication errors, all happening during the spread of Lucifer's Worm."

"So if this can happen three times, it could happen again, right?"

"Anything is possible. Believe me, we in IT are on full alert."

"So am I. A short while ago, I finished combing through my patients' charts for more fatal errors. There's nothing new this time, but I'm just afraid that another patient down the line could suffer or die because of something wrong in the system."

There is a pause.

"OK, I think I have enough to go on," Rajesh says. "Is there anything else you need to tell me?"

"No."

"All right then. I, along with my staff, will look into the technical irregularities you mentioned."

"Thank you, thank you," I say with a huge exhale.

"My pleasure, Dr. Lin. And once again, please accept my humblest apologies for what happened to your patients."

"I appreciate it. But wait, I have another question. How long will it take to figure it all out?"

Once again, I hear silence.

"It'll depend on how much we uncover," Rajesh answers. "Also, we'd be doing this alongside work on the email server side."

"Right. But could I least speak with you again tomorrow?"

"Absolutely. Just wait for me to call you. If you don't hear from me by, let's say, three o'clock tomorrow, give me a call back."

"Got it. Talk to you then."

I hang up, then sigh with relief. Just two more days to go, if I can survive them.

CHAPTER 6

"Good lord, what an awful day you had," Jay McKinnon says to me.

I have just told him about the triple alarms this morning, and the fates of those three unfortunate patients. But I hold back the stuff about Lucifer's Worm and medication errors. As much as I would hedge my bets on a connection, I still need solid confirmation, or at least something to rule in the possibility even further. Plus, I don't want to confuse Jay any more than I should.

Besides, I really want to get the hell on home.

Thank goodness the handoff procedure goes by quickly. I only have a small handful of patients in my care, and the main details about them are pretty straightforward. I do emphasize that Donald Chester still has not been seen by Dr. Pierson yet, but I hope it will be tomorrow. It better be.

"How did Samuel treat you?" Jay asks.

"Not good, and I don't want to get into it."

"I don't blame you. I've had bad moments with him myself."

"During the graveyard shift, while he's on call?"

"Yeah. Like one time when I got called on a patient who suddenly had really bad abdominal pain. Developed appendicitis while hospitalized. So I called Pierson and, well, he gave me crap about it."

"Why?"

"Because he was busy. You know, his usual excuse."

"But the patient did undergo emergent appendectomy, right?"

"Oh yeah. The patient came out fine."

"Dr. Pierson operated?"

"Yeah, he did. But it didn't have to be preceded by some pointless hassle."

I stand up and stretch my arms upward.

"Any questions?" I ask Jay.

"Nope. You're good to go. Just be sure to rest well. And do something relaxing to clear your head."

"Such as?"

"Anything besides watching the news. Lucifer's Worm is really spreading fast, in case you haven't heard. Some people are thinking an apocalypse is coming."

"Like it's worse than COVID-19?"

"Yeah. I mean, what would you do if you own a business and it comes to a grinding halt out of no fault of your own?"

"Sure, I get the sentiment."

"It may not be a physical illness, but it definitely impacts mental health."

Yeah, just like mine. I nod at the realization.

"Well, Lucifer's Worm is hell on earth," I say.

"Metaphorically speaking."

"Literally, too."

"Whatever. Get outta here, you idiot."

I laugh as I turn and head out.

* * *

I climb up the stairs to the roof of the parking garage, situated between Ivory Memorial Hospital and Ivory Memorial Clinic. I get into my Tesla, shut the door, and lean back. Damn, it feels good to be done. Nothing can bother me now. No Code Blues, no Rapid Responses, no nurse calls. No patients to take care of.

It is time to take care of myself.

I turn on the engine and the dashboard music player. My Spotify playlist has over a thousand songs, but I don't want to do shuffle play this time. Instead, I scroll down the list to one song I need right now: "Bad Day" by Daniel Powter. The soft piano notes play through my car speakers, with the singer's heartfelt voice enhancing the beautiful melody. I make my way down the garage inclines and out the exit. I now head east in the streets of north Anaheim, with the orange hue of the sunset shining in my rearview mirror.

I drive casually in the right lane, letting everyone speed past as they wish. I am at the speed limit, but whatever. I want to play it safe, keep moving without worrying about playing defensive driver. All I want is my personal space. Just me, my Tesla, and my music. And this song is perfect. Already, my spirits are being lifted from the depths.

Once the song ends, I play it a second time. This is good. I don't want the feeling to stop. Hell, if I ever get stuck on the 5 Freeway for an hour, I'd savor the downtime for this kind of therapy.

There's no need to worry about that, though. My commute is all city streets, typically no more than half an hour. I now head northeast on Santa Ana Canyon Road, taking me up into Anaheim Hills. I let out a sigh of contentment. As intense as my job can get sometimes, the pay is real nice. Six figures for my crazy-ass work schedule. I could still live high above the rest of society, without coming face to face with the assholes of humanity and the madness that permeates them.

Minutes later, I turn off the music player. One song on repeat plus three more random tunes have done the trick. My mind is clear.

Up ahead is my two-story home at the end of a cul-de-sac. I pull into the garage, then enter the house. But instead of going upstairs to my bedroom, I head straight to the backyard through the patio doors. The sun is almost fully below the horizon, and the slight breeze is nice and cool. I bask in the faint orange glow that will quickly fade to black in a matter of minutes. I take in the fresh air, before noticing that it isn't entirely so.

There is a faint waft of smoke. Not thick like with a building on fire, but light with a flavorful aroma. Someone was grilling meat not too long ago. The smell comes from my left. Over the fence separating me from my neighbor, I hear the sound of something metallic scraping against concrete.

"Ken?" I call out.

"Yeah, Mark?" a voice answers back.

I walk over to the middle of the fence where I have two cinderblocks vertically stacked. I stand on the top one and look over into my neighbor's backyard. It's a simple setup, with a lush green lawn alongside a spacious patio. There are chairs arranged around two circular tables, which have used disposable plates, forks, and cups. One of the tables also has a remnant square section of a big cake. Nearby is a water cooler, along with a barbecue grill that is off but still has thin smoke rising from it.

Kenneth Randall, a thin old man approaching seventy years of age, begins cleaning up the tables.

"What's the occasion?" I ask with a smile.

"My good friend Bill celebrated his birthday," Ken says. "Known him since I moved here years ago. He and I go way back."

"Tell him happy birthday."

"I will. Hey, do you want a burger? I still have plenty of leftover beef patties."

Now that he mentions it, I feel my stomach grumbling.

"Sure," I say. "If you don't mind bringing a plate all the way here."

"No problem at all, friend. You want any condiments? I got ketchup, mustard, and mayonnaise."

"Yeah, why not? Put them all in there."

"Lettuce, tomato, and pickle?"

"That's fine."

"And since these are somewhat small beef patties, how about I give you two? Unless you think one is enough."

I pause to think. Then I smile.

"Ah, what the hell. Give me two."

Ken laughs as he quickly gets one big paper plate and puts together the two hamburgers. He carries the plate over to the fence and I reach down to grab it from him. I take my first bite without hesitation.

"This is great," I say after swallowing the delicious burger. "I may not be in my twenties any longer, but my metabolism is nowhere close to shot."

"Wish I was still as young as you," Ken says with a chuckle. "At my age, I'm lucky if I can avoid fracturing a hip."

"You're doing OK healthwise?"

"Oh yeah. Every day, Edith and I take a walk down the street and around the neighborhood. Gotta keep those bones strong, you know."

I nod and savor another piece of burger. Ken and his wife Edith are both retired after decades of service in healthcare. He had been a pediatrician. She had been an inpatient pediatric nurse. They met while he was in residency at Presbyterian Hospital in New York, years before it merged with New York Hospital to become New York-Presbyterian. Then they moved to Orange County about a decade ago and continued their tradition of working at the same medical center, planning quality time around each other's schedules. In fact, their colleagues threw small parties for them every year to celebrate each of their wedding anniversaries.

"How about you?" Ken asks. "How are you doing healthwise?"

"Decent."

"You get plenty of exercise?"

"As a hospital physician walking all over the place, definitely. As long as I'm not scrambling to dying patients, like today."

"Tough day, I take it?"

"Very. Guess how many patients crashed on me?"

Ken looks up at the sky to pick a guess.

"Six?"

I stifle a laugh while shaking my head.

"Higher or lower, Mark?"

"Lower, thank goodness."

Ken strolls toward the water cooler as he speaks.

"Five?"

"Lower."

"Four?"

"Getting warmer."

"Three?"

I nod. He looks me with wide eyes, then reaches down to pull out a fresh can of Diet Coke from the cooler.

"Now, were they crashing at different times?" he asks.

"No. They were practically simultaneous."

Ken opens the can and takes a sip, then approaches me at the fence.

"That's too bad," he says. "Are those patients OK?"

"Just one of three. First one died while I tried to resuscitate him. Second one is in the ICU. I couldn't get to her because the second Code Blue got called while I was still busy with the first one."

"Jesus."

"Yeah, no kidding."

"So you had a chance with number three."

"Right. And his issue was minor, relatively speaking."

Ken drinks from his can. I finish my first burger and start on the second. I am glad Ken isn't probing any further into my issues, probably out of respect. I really don't want to get into my theory about Lucifer's Worm somehow being responsible, not when this is supposed to be my night off.

But I still decide to beat around the bush.

"Have you ever been accused of making a medical mistake, even if you believe you didn't?" I ask carefully.

"Oh, sure."

"Not regularly though, right?"

"Of course not. But each time it happens, I take a good look at myself, in case there is truly an error I committed. I can never forget the first time it happened. Did I ever tell you about it?"

"I don't think so."

"You don't mind if I tell you now?"

"Not at all. Go for it."

Ken pauses to compose himself and drink more Coke.

"This was back in the day at Presbyterian. Second year of pediatric residency. I had a patient who came in with fever and stridor, struggling to breathe. A real precious boy, about three years of age. Right away, I was forming my differential diagnosis. I knew it had to be something going on in his throat. But... I got careless. I did a throat exam on the boy, and at that moment, I really regretted it."

"Let me guess," I say. "Epiglottitis?"

"Exactly. That's what I suspected. It's practically a textbook case. And yet, for whatever reason, even as a second-year resident, I forgot about that one warning a med school professor had emphasized: do not perform a throat exam for suspected epiglottitis, or else it swells up and blocks the trachea."

"What happened next?"

"Obviously, we attempted intubation. It was much harder than I thought. But I was successful in the nick of time."

I nod sympathetically while chewing my second burger. Inserting an endotracheal tube is a challenge even in an adult. But a toddler with a swollen epiglottis, right where the ET tube needs to go through? I cannot imagine. Neither can I picture a cricothyrotomy, cutting through the skin and ligament right beneath the Adam's apple, in order to create a temporary airway just to buy the patient a little more time.

"It's a miracle he survived," Ken says quietly, looking off to the side.

"That's good, at least."

"Still, that night was so traumatic. I questioned whether I even deserved to continue, after working so hard to get this far. But as time went along, I just kept telling myself to not give up. Just learn from it."

"And yet, here you are. Retired after a long career in pediatrics."

"Yep. A little over thirty years."

"How did the boy's family handle it?"

"They were scared, as you can imagine. But they held onto hope and were grateful he survived. Even when I told them I was sorry for making a mistake that led to this, they were forgiving. I was relieved."

"Lucky you."

We both pause to consume our treats.

"Why do you say that?" Ken asks.

"I didn't tell you what happened with the families of my three patients."

"Oh?"

"For the two with unfortunate fates, their spouses got really mad. I don't mean just raising their voice. I'm talking about abuse here: being told 'fuck you' by one and getting slapped hard in the face by the other."

"Really?"

"Does it sound like I'm making this up?"

"Oh, I believe you. My goodness, I'm sorry."

I chomp on my burger, then stare at the last piece of it still in my hand. Oh, what the hell. I finish it quickly.

"It's frustrating to get yelled at, even after doing my best," I say. "I assume you'll give me the same advice: get up, learn, and move on?"

"You read my mind," Ken says with a smile, which I guess is his friendly effort to cheer me up.

"But here's the thing. People today are, I hate to say it, a real bunch of jerks. Am I insane, or are you seeing it too?"

Ken nods slowly.

"I know what you mean, Mark. Things appear to be a lot worse now. There seems to be a loss of values, of basic principles like empathy. Whatever our parents taught us growing up, it seems to have gone out the window."

"So I'm not crazy after all. I mean, think about the COVID-19 pandemic and the January 6th insurrection. Two shocking events showing us the absolute worst human impulses, right out in the open. How the hell could people be so damn selfish?"

"I don't know. But let's not forget the flipside. Both also brought out the best of us. Right?"

"What do you mean?"

"Just look at how much the Capitol riot woke up so many people, including those who never follow politics. And think of the healthcare workers on the front lines of the coronavirus. You were among them, right?"

"Yeah."

"So you're a hero to these people."

"I was just doing my job."

"But it's an important one."

I barely smile at the compliment.

"Is it me, or do a lot of people think way too highly of doctors, like we're on some kind of pedestal for the world?" I ask.

"What do you mean?"

"They glamourize the profession, romanticize it. They must think it's so cool we make so much money helping people."

"Anything wrong with that?"

"The problem is that's all they pretty much see. They don't know much about the other stuff: medical school debt, continuing medical education requirements, staying up to date with journals, the nuances of billing and coding, the endless paperwork. Oh, and don't forget the workload."

"It's all boring to everyone else."

"Yeah, but to ignore it is to not see its reality. This is why I never watch any of those medical drama shows on TV."

"Like *Grey's Anatomy?*"

"Exactly. How the hell could such a medically inaccurate show like that last, what, more than ten seasons?"

"I think it's nineteen now."

"Whatever. It's terrible."

"Have you ever watched it?"

"Yeah, one episode, featuring sex in the hospital. Come on now. Nobody I know in healthcare does that."

"What about the show *House?*"

"Also a load of crap. What kind of doctors focus only on one patient at a time from start to finish?"

"At least the cases are accurate."

"But are they common? No. They're rare diseases."

Ken laughs at my remark. None of it is funny to me, however.

"I take it you don't want to talk about the show *ER?*" he asks.

"Nope."

"What about the comedy called *Scrubs?*"

"Doesn't matter. TV medical shows suck."

"How about *Dr. Oz?*"

"Is everything on that show evidence-based?"

Ken doesn't answer. I can't tell if he agrees with me or not.

"OK, enough about me," I say. "What's your favorite TV medical show?"

"A really old one: *Marcus Welby, M.D.*"

"That's like in the sixties, right?"

"No, mainly the seventies. It ran from 1969 to 1976. I was a young adult when it first aired. Mind you, I didn't watch every episode at the time, nor after it ended. But the couple of times I did tune in, I was inspired by Dr. Welby, the main character, because he exemplified what a doctor should be: always kind and caring."

"Is that when you wanted to become a doctor?"

"Pretty much. My parents supported my decision, too, even if they weren't healthcare workers."

I nod as Ken smiles at his trip down memory lane. My own look back takes me elsewhere, to a moment in my medical school days when a professor mentioned Marcus Welby, explaining how that fictional doctor painted, in the minds of the public, an idealized picture of medical professionals. He brought it up as a way of explaining why people expect a lot from doctors. I consider it a blessing and a curse: a blessing for doctors back then, when people were decent human beings, and a curse for doctors today, when people are practically self-centered psychos. I don't feel like talking about it. So I say nothing in response to Ken's comment, and that ends tonight's discussion about medicine and TV.

He changes the subject.

"You must be starving. You scarfed both of those hamburgers down."

"Thanks a lot for this. Saves me the trouble of making dinner."

"No problem. Now, I must ask you one more thing."

"What's that?"

"Dessert. You want a slice of cake, too?"

I think of passing on that. But Ken is already heading to the patio table. He cuts a slice of the leftover cake, plops it on another plate, and comes back with it along with a plastic fork.

"Here you go," Ken says. "I insist."

I smile as I take the plate and fork.

"Thanks."

"Guess I'll leave you to enjoy your cake. What else will you do tonight?"

"Maybe watch some TV. I won't be tuning in to anything related to medicine, that's for sure."

"Whatever it'll be, have fun."

I smile, step down from the cinderblock, and head back inside.

CHAPTER 7

I begin to understand why people overindulge in sweet desserts: it feels good. I don't just mean the delicious taste. I'm also talking about its emotional benefit, the relaxing peace that comes with a dose of extra sugar. On a day like today, I definitely need it. I finish the cake that Ken gave me, then lean back on the living room couch. A slight drowsiness soon overtakes me. Food coma setting in. My body is prioritizing blood flow to its GI tract. Lots of pieces to pick up from the burgers and cake.

I pull out my work and personal phones from my pants pockets, then place them on the coffee table. They're now sitting next to the latest issues of *The New England Journal of Medicine* and *The Journal of the American Medical Association,* which I haven't gotten around to skimming, and an unopened box of Blu-ray discs for the television show *Breaking Bad,* which I haven't gotten around to watching since Jane gave it to me as a gift last Christmas. Of those two options, what am I in the mood for tonight? Reading scientific text or watching high-quality TV? Picking up updates on cancer medicine, or watching a high school chemistry teacher with lung cancer cook meth to fund his treatment? I start leaning towards the latter, thinking of the intriguing premise. Maybe I should start watching it now. Then again, do I really need something that depressing?

Nah. Maybe another time.

I spot the TV remote control next to me on the couch. I pick it up and turn on the television. For a while, I just surf the channels. Then I come across an image of outer space. It doesn't look like a documentary, so I guess it's some kind of sci-fi movie. Then I realize I'd seen this before. It's that Stanley Kubrick classic, *2001: A Space Odyssey*. This is the part where astronaut Bowman is trying to get back into the spacecraft, after using a space pod to rescue astronaut Poole from drifting off toward the void. Supercomputer HAL-9000 had tried to kill Poole by severing his oxygen hose during extravehicular activity. This scene is chilling, especially with the dialogue.

"Open the pod bay doors, HAL."

"I'm sorry, Dave. I'm afraid I can't do that."

I could stay on this if I want, but I need something fresh. I surf through more channels, with no fricking idea about what to stick with. Even with the gorgeous picture quality of the 54-inch flat screen bolted to the wall, I'm already getting bored. Come on, there has to be some quality entertainment here. Anything.

Then, I freeze.

I lean forward and stare at the bottom of the screen. The words fully register and hit me in the gut:

> *BREAKING NEWS*
> *LUCIFER'S WORM ENABLES WIDESPREAD HACKING*

At the moment, a pundit on MSNBC is giving viewers a recap of what experts already know about Lucifer's Worm, namely the spam emails and stalled servers. Then comes the punchline. There is malicious code within the email itself that not only duplicates and sends the email to other addresses found, but also leaves backdoors in the same system. New vulnerabilities placed in a secure computer mean that hackers can break in at will and do whatever the hell they want. Now there are many examples of strange events occurring today that could very well be explained by hacking.

For instance, the CEO of an electronic parts manufacturer in Ohio noticed his bank account significantly depleted. Nine million dollars gone without a trace. Earlier in the day, four people with no connection to each other or to this CEO were shocked to find an extra million dollars in each of their checking accounts. Investigations on both ends uncovered unauthorized bank transfers from the CEO to nine random people, each bypassing credentials while leaving no obvious records. The remaining five million dollars, probably divided up equally among five other people, have yet to be accounted for.

Meanwhile, Arizona has a major political mess. Two members of the U.S. Congress from that state, one Democrat and one Republican, each found their official websites defaced with vile hate-filled messages, graphic photos of sliced-up human corpses, devil's horns painted over faces in various photos, and digital blood splattered in random places. At first, they pointed fingers at each other. But today's development about Lucifer's Worm silenced the bitterness, with what some political commentators jokingly call rare bipartisanship.

There's so much other shit with these hackers that the anchor is now dishing out the rest of it in a laundry list. Social media accounts of various Catholic churches got hijacked to post sick drawings and photos of naked priests. The headquarters of a major fast food chain received ransomware to extort hundreds of millions of dollars. Several people were fired from their corporate jobs after private emails with friends bragging about flattering or sleeping with their bosses to get promotions were stolen and forwarded to everyone at their companies. Trading on Wall Street halted for most of the day because many stock prices and ticker symbols were randomly scrambled. And if the fiasco with law enforcement agency websites from earlier today isn't bad enough, multiple internal affairs records about cops committing police brutality have been stolen and dumped onto WikiLeaks.

I glare at the screen. Things are coming together now. This open season for computer hackers explains it all.

I pay undivided attention as the news segment continues with a guest appearance. The anchor is now interviewing a veteran cybersecurity expert, a man with graying hair and a stiff expression. The question for him is what we should make of the chaos surrounding Lucifer's Worm. His initial response goes straight to the point: be prepared for anything. Then he fires off a line of potential catastrophic scenarios, like destroying companies' operations and hijacking automated transit systems. Even unauthorized military strikes through national security breaches aren't out of the question. The man's tone carries an urgency that is contagious. I am feeling it, too. When asked if he has any idea who could be behind the development and release of Lucifer's Worm, he keeps his response open-ended. Anything is possible, he says. It could be millennial hackers or foreign cyberterrorists, like from Russia or China. The only thing that seems clear is intention. Whoever these perpetrators are, they don't care for petty cybercrimes, like stealing confidential information. No, they are relentlessly unleashing destruction and chaos, raising hell so to speak.

Just when shit couldn't get any more insane, the interview is interrupted with another piece of breaking news. A large section of Philadelphia has lost power, due to hackers striking the city's power grid. Right away, this is integrated into the conversation in progress. Now the interviewee is emphasizing, with greater tension, that everyone must act, from cybersecurity experts fighting back to regular folks getting ready for any unimaginable disaster. That's when he utters the phrase I had used earlier today: "Cyber pandemic." I close my eyes and let out a long, heavy sigh.

Goddamn, the world is going to hell. Again.

I tune out most of the chatter from the TV. My digestion of burgers and cake still proceeds, though the food coma is waning. I probably won't fall asleep on the couch now. Besides, whenever crisis strikes, I can never rest. Like right now. My brain goes into overdrive, processing all that has occurred. Pieces that seem too different from each other suddenly feel like a match made in heaven.

Three medical crises. Three mysterious medication orders. Widespread spam email, plus its secondary impacts. The missing link of backdoors and hackers. It makes perfect sense now.

A computer hacker tried to kill my patients. Lucifer's Worm made it possible. How else could someone replace my medication orders with new ones? As far as I can tell, there really is no other way.

I'll say it again. Deep down, I know that I made no mistakes. None.

Not with those three patients. Not with any patient, for that matter. I am a doctor with a squeaky clean record. No accidental patient deaths, and certainly no intentional ones either. Since day one of residency, nobody had ever accused me of carelessness. If anyone wants to challenge that, I dare them.

After a few moments of rest, I sit back up and flip through the channels again. Ultimately, there is no escaping Lucifer's Worm. I see local news coverage of it on KCAL 9. I don't bother watching or listening to it. But something else catches my attention: a buzzing sound, obviously a smartphone vibrating. The work phone remains still, its screen still black. No, it's the other phone getting a call.

I hold it up and check the caller ID.

Unknown
1 (666) 666-6666

What the hell is this? Curious, I answer it.
"Hello?"
I hear nothing at first. But then, a deep rumbling sound fills my ear, mixed with an increasing loud guttural roar.
"Who is this?" I ask in a shaky voice.
"*Your worst fucking nightmare,*" a very low voice growls.
"What?"
"*You heard me. I am your executioner, the bringer of your doom.*"
I say nothing. All I do is wait.
"*Do you know why you're going down?*"
"You tell me, asshole."
"*You are a sinner. You take away life.*"
"Who are you?"
"*Call me... Doctor Lucifer.*"
"Why are you doing this?"
"*You deserve to be punished.*"
"What for?"
"*For being the fraud you are.*"

There is no point in arguing. But I don't hang up. I need answers. I don't know if staying on the line is the best way to go about it, but what options do I have? One thing is clear. Doctor Lucifer is not giving up. Neither am I.

"*A Code Blue for the patient was announced this morning. I was unable to reach her due to a simultaneous Code Blue with another patient on my service.*"

"Wait a minute. Is that—"

"*The patient was intubated and is now transferred to the ICU. Please see this morning's note by the Code Team physician for further details.*"

"That's my chart note!"

"*For Doris Schafer, right?*"

I grip the phone real tight.

"It's you, isn't it? You're the one trying to kill my patients!"

"*Now you know what I can do.*"

"You didn't kill Mr. Jackson, though."

"*But what about... Code Blue called this morning. Arrived at bedside with Code Team. Patient found unconscious with vomitus in mouth. Oral cavity cleared by suction. Intubation successful. CPR initiated. Cardiac rhythm was V-fib. No return to spontaneous circulation after epinephrine; amiodarone; and three defibrillator shocks, each at 360 Joules. Patient became asystolic. CPR proceeded before being discontinued. Time of death: 8:24 AM. Cause of death: V-fib secondary to CHF.*"

I slowly shake my head. That's my last Icarus note on Christopher Flint.

"I'm gonna get you for that."

"*How are you going to find me? Huh?*"

"I will, you psychopath!"

"*I don't think so. You know nothing about me, but I know all about you. And your patients.*"

"Don't you dare lay a finger on them."

"*That's exactly what I will do. Can you guess who's next?*"

"What are you going to do?"

"*That's for you to find out. You are forever bound to me. The blood I shed is on your hands. The death I bring is yours to keep.*"

"That's where you're wrong. I will find a way to clear my name. I will hunt you down and make you pay."

"*You think you can stop me?*"

"Hell yeah."

"*You dare try to defeat me?*"

"I fucking will!"

"*It is settled. We will play a game of wits. Doctor L versus Doctor L. You stop me from bringing death. I stop you from saving life. First one to fall suffers eternal damnation. Last one standing holds the power.*"

I nod triumphantly. It's on. It's time for war, a battle over who lives and dies. A game of medical whack-a-mole where only one outcome is acceptable: me beating the shit out of this demon motherfucker. I know this sounds stupid, but the precariousness of the situation is not lost on me. Everything is on the line: my patients, my job, my career, my reputation. Ultimately, my honor is the wager and the prize, something to win back or lose for good. Only one Doctor L is going to triumph, and that will be me.

There is nothing more for me to say. It doesn't matter, actually. I glance at the phone's screen and see no active call. Doctor Lucifer has already hung up. I check the call log and look at Doctor Lucifer's number again, a one plus ten sixes. A phone number in North America, filled with the devil's digits. How fitting. No way I'll ever forget that.

Taking a deep breath, I pick up the disposable plate and fork and toss them into the trash. I take my two cell phones upstairs to my bedroom. I change out of my clothes and get ready for bed. Then I hear the personal phone vibrate once on my nightstand. A new text has arrived. What is it now?

The message comes from the same number as Doctor Lucifer and consists of just one short sentence:

Tomorrow, your ass is going down.

TUESDAY

CHAPTER 8

I didn't sleep at all last night.

More precisely, I barely got enough deep sleep, the kind that would truly clear my mind and let me wake up refreshed.

A constant dull ache grips my head as I get up to shower. Savoring my breakfast of Raisin Bran in milk, a glass of orange juice, a cup of strawberry yogurt, and a banana does help me a little. But in the end, I have to fight through this.

It all comes down to one thing: anxiety. Knowing what I now know, running away is not an option. The only thing to do is outsmart Doctor Lucifer. I must be hyperalert, because I have to do it right. Any slip in my work, neglect of the most minute out-of-place details, would mean death and destruction. Death for a patient, destruction for me. If there is any moment where an ounce of prevention is worth a pound of cure, this is it, though I know I must put in way more than just a measly ounce. I would seriously do this, once I get to the hospital in about fifteen minutes. For now, the current game of survival is getting there in one piece, by resisting drowsiness, ignoring pissed-off drivers passing by, and keeping the precious Tesla in my lane.

Through texting upon arrival, I confirm that Jay is on the eleventh floor, in the Department of Internal Medicine. That is reassuring. It means he isn't occupied with a patient crashing, especially one of mine. During the handoff, Jay reports that the night had been remarkably quiet. Nothing eventful with my patients, and no new admissions that would be added to my list. I know either of these things could change in the daytime, of course. But morning rounds go by just like that, easy breezy. Even when I make sure each patient's Icarus chart has no irregularities of any sort, including sections with little to no direct bearing on my work, there is nothing to freak out over or scream about.

Thank goodness.

The last patient I see is Donald Chester. He seems to be doing fine, with stable blood pressure measurements and no major drops in his hemoglobin level or hematocrit. It looks like he had no further GI bleeding. The banding of his esophageal varices did the trick. But the stomach tumor still remains unaddressed. Too bad Dr. Samuel Pierson still hasn't stopped by to evaluate the patient.

"Good morning, Mr. Chester," I say, putting on my best show of kindness. "How are you feeling today?"

Chester, a medium-sized black man with a gray beard, smiles at me. "I'm doing fine, Doc."

"Any problems since yesterday?"

"Nope."

"Any vomiting?"

"Not at all."

"What about diarrhea?"

"Didn't move my bowels yesterday."

I nod. If he had evacuated any stools, I could find out from him and the nurse's input/output assessment if his feces looked red or black, signs of GI bleeding. But based on everything else, I'm not worried about that.

"Let me examine you real quick," I say.

I put on my stethoscope and confirm that his heart and lungs sound normal. Then I place the stethoscope diaphragm on the surface of his belly. Normal bowel sounds. Good. I place one hand on his abdomen and feel around in several places with a slight press. Nothing out of the ordinary like pain or stiffness.

"Obviously, the only thing left is that stomach tumor," I say. "I already contacted the on-call surgeon yesterday about evaluating you."

"No surgeon came to see me," Chester says.

"I know, and I'm sorry that he still hasn't shown up. Let me make another call to him if I have to. If you need surgery to take out that tumor, and I'm going to assume it's likely, the decision ought to be made today."

"You mean I might be in the hospital longer?"

"Maybe."

"Couldn't I just go home now and then get my surgery later?"

I slowly shake my head.

"It's hard to predict how much bigger the tumor will get," I say. "And if it's cancerous, there's the risk of it spreading beyond the tumor site, to lymph nodes and then the rest of the body. Better to take care of it while you're still here. You know what I mean?"

"Yeah. Makes sense."

"Great. I'll make sure things move along. Take care, sir."

The patient smiles and waves goodbye. I leave the room and feel my work phone vibrate. I walk down the hall as I read the new text that has just come in:

Mark, please see me in my office as soon as possible.

Good Lord, it's Dr. Roger Garrison, Chief of Internal Medicine. What in the world could this be about? I stop to send a quick reply:

Dr. Garrison, I should be there in about an hour.

It would be enough time for me to log into Icarus and type progress notes for each of my patients, plus submit any new orders where applicable. I pray that Doctor Lucifer won't do anything with these new record entries. But knowing him, I'm ready for whatever he's going to dish out.

I turn towards one of the computer workrooms, then I freeze. Dr. Samuel Pierson is heading out that room. He's a tall man in a white coat surrounding light-green scrubs. His face has three distinct features: a bald head, rectangular-rimmed glasses, and a straight, expressionless mouth. He stops once he sees me. Then he approaches.

"Hey," Pierson says, in a plain tone without a hint of friendliness.

"I'm going to see your patient now."

"Mr. Chester, right?"

"Yeah. It got so late yesterday after these other urgent operations."

"Understood."

At that moment, Pierson points a finger at me. Lightly, but still pointing at me nonetheless.

"Do me a favor. Next time you ask for a surgery consult, don't be such a dick. You try being a surgeon one day, getting calls and texts left and right from just about everyone in this building."

"Just wanted to make sure my patient is taken care of," I say, ignoring his direct insult. "If I sounded pushy, I'm sorry."

"You weren't pushy. You were goddamn threatening."

"Threatening?"

"Well, it wasn't nice at all. Don't you remember raising your voice?"

"Yeah. I lost it, OK?"

"See what happens when you admit being wrong?"

"To be fair, you did the same thing."

"No, I didn't."

"Whatever. Let's move on."

"Fine. Now just relax. I'm going to see Mr. Chester and evaluate him. Don't you dare rush me."

I nod slowly and leave it at that. I got what I wanted. There's no point in pushing the matter any further.

* * *

Besides the giant room with cubicles and the adjoining lounge and conference room, the Department of Internal Medicine also has a hallway leading to its leadership offices, including those for the Chief of Internal Medicine, two Assistant Chiefs, and administrative assistants. I stroll down to the chief's office at the end of the hall. The door is open and I get ready to knock, but I don't need to.

Dr. Roger Garrison, a thin bearded man with glasses, is at his desk on the phone. He holds up one finger as he continues his telephone conversation. No surprise there, considering how busy he often is. In addition to his duty of overseeing matters for hospital internists like myself, Garrison is also dedicated to clinical research. He recently co-authored a medical journal article describing a study about whether hospital-acquired infections differ between community hospitals and academic medical centers. It's amazing how he, a board-certified infectious disease specialist who is barely forty years of age, could juggle patient care, research, and administrative work all at once.

"Come on in," Garrison says moments later, hanging up the phone.

I carefully step into the office and sit down in the chair opposite him. Garrison looks down on his desk for about a full second, slightly frowning. I begin to shake inside. Something is definitely up.

"Mark, let me begin by saying thank you for your hard work as usual. The pandemic has no doubt taken a toll on us all for two years. Even as we've reached the light at the end of the tunnel, the stress and exhaustion may still linger. And of course, we must always be on the lookout for new COVID variant strains. The virus may very well remain with us, like seasonal influenza."

I nod calmly. But I still wait for the punchline.

"How are you doing now?" he asks.

"I'm hanging in there," I say with a casual demeanor.

"Are you taking care of yourself outside of work?"

"Of course."

"Able to get enough sleep each night?"

"So far, yes."

"Any unusual levels of stress?"

I don't answer right away. Then I figure out where this is going.

"Yesterday was awful. I had not one, or two, but three patients crashing on me. First one coded. Then, while I was still handling the first code, the second coded and the third had a Rapid Response call. Ultimately, I could only work on two out of three. An available Code Team handled the second patient to the end. I ran to the Rapid Response and got that patient under control."

Garrison nods slowly. What is he thinking? Is he being understanding, or is he ready to pounce on something I said? He takes a deep breath.

"I'm sorry that has happened. It's rather incredible to say the least. I've never experienced, or even heard of, any instance of three patients declining so quickly and simultaneously, let alone two. I imagine if I were in your shoes, I'd do the same thing: attend to whatever I can, prioritizing the most critical cases."

"I tried my best."

"I'm sure you did. Nevertheless, we have a serious issue at hand. Actually, more than one. It's so dire that even the CEO is involved in this."

Holy shit. Even Dr. Jeffrey Winters? I exhale quietly.

"What is it?"

"Just as you arrived, I was on the phone with the head of the Patient Services Division. She informed me that the families of two of your patients have filed complaints against you. In fact, one of them already got in touch with a malpractice attorney. A lawsuit may be headed our way."

I swallow nervously.

"Which patients?"

"One of them is Doris Schafer," Garrison says, consulting a small notepad. "What happened with her?"

"Mrs. Schafer was the second Code Blue, the one I couldn't get to in time. She had an anaphylactic reaction to an antibiotic. I don't know how that could have happened."

"Were you careful with her medications?"

"That's the thing. I was checking her allergies list before ordering the antibiotic. But somehow, Schafer got the wrong one."

Garrison nods slowly. So far, my initial plan is working: give him only the essentials. Leave out the landmines for now, like the supposed alterations in her Icarus chart.

"After you ordered the antibiotic, did you check to see that the patient received it properly?"

"Yes, when I followed up in the afternoon."

"There were no problems then?"

"No."

"But this morning was different."

"Correct. Something must've happened in between."

"Any idea what that might be?"

"I have a theory, but you'll think it's crazy."

Another pause. I've just thrown a wrench into the works. Knowing him, Garrison is mentally rearranging the pieces.

"Is it going to take a while to explain?" he asks.

"Maybe."

"Like how long?"

"Probably a couple of minutes. In fact, I have a feeling it also involves the other patient, if it is who I think it is."

"Then hold that thought."

Garrison opens a desk drawer, pulls out two pages of a printout, and slowly hands them to me.

"I need you to look at this. It's related to the other patient. This is the reason why the CEO is now involved."

I take the pages and begin reading. It's a typed letter, dated today and addressed specifically to the hospital CEO.

Dear Dr. Winters,

I am writing to tell you that one of the doctors on your staff has done something horrible. Specifically, I am talking about internist Mark Lin, MD. Because of his unacceptable incompetence, Christopher Flint, my husband, who had been under his care, is dead.

Christopher has had congestive heart failure for many years, following a myocardial infarction that left much of his heart's left ventricle scarred and dysfunctional. His condition was not always easy to manage, especially in the beginning when he had not gotten used to dietary and fluid restrictions and he kept getting hospitalized for CHF exacerbation. Medications were also an issue, because he didn't always take them as prescribed.

As his wife, I had a really long talk with him. About a year ago, I had to explain the following:

1. If he has too much fluid in his body, his heart can't pump well, the reason he must limit what he eats and drinks from now on.
2. His three medications, which he must never skip, help even further.
3. The steps above can mean the difference between being able to walk to the bathroom and being able to walk at all.
4. Our financial situation is already precarious. At the time, he was still unemployed and trying to find work, and I was at wit's end trying to hold up our house with just my income.

When I told all of this to Christopher, he finally took everything more seriously. Since then, he had only two CHF exacerbations in a single year, a huge improvement. Then he never had to come back to the hospital for many months, until just a few days ago. I thought it would be a routine hospitalization where he would get high-dose IV diuretics and whatever before being discharged back home again.

But I was wrong. It turned out that Dr. Lin prescribed digoxin, without ever telling me in advance.

Before my husband's recent hospitalization, I've done more extensive research into the management of CHF, including the use of digoxin. I learned how dangerous it can really be. I've enclosed two documents:

1. A copy of an article that explains how, based on meta-

analysis of multiple published studies, the risk of death goes up when a CHF patient receives digoxin
2. A newsletter from an organization on cardiac care

I'm also a member of a Facebook group for people with CHF, and I've seen horror stories of death or near death because of that drug.

If I knew Dr. Lin would be adding digoxin to Christopher's regimen, I would've flat-out said no, knowing how much of a risk this is.

When I met with Dr. Lin yesterday, he was abusive, rude, and condescending. He showed no sympathy for me as I grieved my painful loss. Most importantly, he kept arguing with me when I tried to tell him that digoxin is dangerous. He even said that I should listen to him because he, as a physician, is the one with the knowledge and expertise, not me.

Therefore, I am holding Dr. Lin and Ivory Memorial Hospital responsible for Christopher's death. You will be hearing from my lawyer very soon, because I do intend to take the matter to trial if Dr. Lin refuses to provide a fair settlement. I will also report this to the Medical Board of California, see to it that Dr. Lin faces appropriate disciplinary action.

I await your prompt response.

Regards,
Lisa Flint

"She can't be serious," I say, dumbfounded.
"Did you act rudely toward her?"
"No."

"You sure?"

"Yes, she's lying about all of that!"

Garrison holds up one finger in front of his lips. I immediately take a deep breath and calm down.

"Let me ask you this," Garrison says, "what did happen during your meeting with her yesterday?"

"I remember that she was relaxed. We went over my care of her husband in detail. I answered her questions. She asked why he got CHF exacerbation even while on those meds, and I explained that his heart was weakening further. Basically, she was fine until I brought up digoxin."

"Do you think you were condescending at any time?"

"Not at all."

"Honest?"

"One hundred percent."

Garrison momentarily consults his notepad.

"One thing can determine if she really has a case or not: whether you followed standard of care for CHF."

"Is there any reason I didn't?" I ask.

"At first glance, it would seem no. From Mr. Flint's chart in Icarus, you had started digoxin because his CHF wasn't corrected, despite everything else. You had even ordered an echocardiogram, which showed that the patient's ejection fraction is now thirty-two percent, down from thirty-nine percent the year before."

"That's correct, yes."

"But your note stated that you would order digoxin at a dose of one hundred twenty-five micrograms. I don't see an order for that. Instead, you ordered two hundred fifty micrograms. The nurse's record shows that the patient received that dose."

I only nod. Better let him do all the talking.

"Don't you think two hundred fifty micrograms is rather high for him?"

"I didn't order that."

"What are you saying?"

"I had originally ordered digoxin at a dose of one hundred twenty-five micrograms, sometime in the morning yesterday. I did not submit an order for two hundred fifty micrograms of digoxin."

"Well, I don't see any other orders. How do you explain this?"

There is only one way to save my ass now. I have to present the theory, put forth what I know and believe into one seamless presentation. It would no doubt sound crazy to Garrison. But what can I do?

"Did you follow the news yesterday?" I ask.

"I did," Garrison says, with no expression whatsoever.

"You know about this malware going around called Lucifer's Worm?"

"Yes."

"What about the newest development, about how the worm makes computer systems vulnerable to hacking?"

"I've heard about that, too."

"Then consider this. Doris Schafer and Christopher Flint crashed simultaneously in the same morning. In each case, it's because of a medication order, one that does not match what I had originally submitted. How likely is it that, for each of those patients, a computer hacker erased my original order from the morning and put in a new one the same day in the late afternoon or evening, which then got processed and led to the patient getting the altered medication the next morning, triggering a catastrophe?"

Garrison remains silent. I maintain a firm stare, hoping this would send the message that I am fucking serious. I also see no signs that he is aware of my deliberate omission of Darnell Jackson falling victim to a supposed hacker's sabotage of Icarus. If the other two cases already put him on edge, I better keep my lips sealed.

A moment later, he sighs.

"Mark, how likely is it that this scenario you propose is really what happened? It sounds farfetched."

"I see no other way."

"Can you honestly say you were aware of all the steps you took?'

"Yes."

"Well, even if your theory of computer hacking is plausible, although highly unusual, I still need solid proof."

"For Christopher Flint, I had documented in a progress note my plan to prescribe digoxin with a starting dose of one hundred twenty-five micrograms. Why would I then order the dose doubled and do so later in the day, not right away in the morning?"

"It might look like you weren't paying attention. That would be considered negligence, wouldn't it?"

"So what should I do?"

"Do you have direct evidence of the computer hacking you allege?"

"It depends."

"How?"

"I called the IT department yesterday afternoon. The head of IT said he would look into it, after I gave him the names and medical record numbers of the patients involved. I'll need to follow up with him later today."

I can tell this is too much for the chief. He looks down and sighs again. I also place the copy of the Flint widow's letter back on his desk.

"Here's what I'll do," he says. "I'll speak with Dr. Winters to figure out what to do with the complaints, especially the one from Mrs. Flint. Meanwhile, please continue to be careful when taking care of your patients."

"What about the computer hacker theory? If I get some info from IT, should I pass it along to you?"

"If you feel it's definitive."

"Can we use that if Mrs. Flint's lawsuit goes forward?"

"Hard to say."

It is my turn to look down. I shake my head. How the hell could this much shit hit the fan, not just yesterday but also today? Goddamn it.

"She is angry, no doubt about it," Garrison says. "She went to Patient Services, but in addition to completing the standard complaint form, she insisted on having this letter forwarded directly to Dr. Winters. That, along with the complaint about the other patient, was why the head of Patient Services called me. She was concerned that both issues involve one doctor specifically."

"I understand."

"At the same time, Lisa Flint also appears not to be fully rational. For one thing, it isn't entirely up to the patient's family to decide what treatments are best. The doctor is trusted with such decisions, especially if the situation is urgent. Also, the article she enclosed with her letter may be from a peer-reviewed journal, something robust, but the other enclosed newsletter is by an obscure organization trying to appear legitimate."

"So her case isn't really all that strong?"

"Possibly. But who knows?"

Damnit. This nightmare is far from over. I guess I could offer an amount of money that sounds good for a settlement. Better than a courtroom evisceration of me and my career.

"The spouses of both patients are demanding answers," Garrison says. "Mr. Schafer may not be considering a lawsuit like Mrs. Flint is, but it would be best to treat his grievance just as seriously."

"Should I start preparing some kind of defense, for both cases?"

"Perhaps you should."

"I'm asking in case IT does get back to me."

"Right now, it's still too early to know where things will go. Meanwhile, you sound quite confident about this computer hacker theory of yours."

"I am."

"Well, don't get carried away. I don't want you to get into any more trouble because you lose your focus."

"OK."

"At this point, just get back to work. Your patients need you."

"Anything else you need from me?"

Garrison shakes his head. Then he shoos me toward the door, as if batting away a pesky fly.

CHAPTER 9

Minutes after leaving Garrison's office, I receive a text from Dr. Ellen Roberts, one of the emergency physicians downstairs. A new patient is going to be admitted, and I will be the treating physician.

I'm not surprised. In this hospital, the procedure for inpatient admissions is simple: hospitalists with the lightest workloads would handle the newest cases. I've discharged plenty of patients home since yesterday. I am also not complaining. I definitely prefer this over the traditional system of being on call every now and then and assuming work for every new patient, even if it's a shitload of admissions.

I take the elevator down to the emergency department and head for ED room 3 where my new patient is. From the Icarus chart on my tablet, the patient is Clara Summers, a 58-year-old woman with diverticulosis, a condition of multiple abnormal pouches in her large intestine. This morning, she was fine sitting on the living room couch, but when she stood up quickly, lightheadedness set in, and she wobbled to the side before falling to the floor. Because she is divorced and currently living alone, there was no one else at home to help her. Her saving grace was the fact that her cell phone was sitting on the coffee table within reach. She called 911, used much of her remaining strength to crawl to and unlock her apartment door, and remained still. Paramedics arrived and brought her here.

In the ED, Ellen started the patient on IV fluids because of slightly low blood pressure. The ED doc also ordered tests that included a blood chemistry panel, a complete blood count, and a CT scan of the head. The only real abnormality detected was still serious enough to warrant hospitalization: a hemoglobin level of 9.4 grams per deciliter, a big drop from her usual level of 12 to 13. Through conversation, Ellen learned that, starting about two days ago, the patient first noticed streaks of blood in her toilet paper whenever she wiped herself after defecating. While they weren't gigantic bloodstains, they weren't trace amounts either. With other bleeding sources being fairly unlikely, Ellen concluded that Summers had bled excessively from her diverticuli, directly into her bowel movements. Even if the patient had never stood up to look in her toilet before flushing, Ellen had enough clinical suspicion for diverticular bleeding as the cause of the patient's lightheadedness.

The emergency doc's role of stabilizing the patient is done. It is now my job to transition the patient upstairs and go from there.

I enter ED room 3 and notice a thin black woman with slightly graying hair lying in a gurney. Her expression is neutral, neither smiling nor grimacing. But I can tell she is scared. I quietly knock on the open door to announce my arrival.

"Hi, Ms. Summers," I say gently. "I'm Dr. Lin. I'll be taking care of you while you're here in the hospital."

"Hello, doctor," the patient says. "You can call me Clara. No need to be formal, even if I'm really old."

"Nah, you're not old. Age is just a number, right?"

The patient laughs a little.

"Am I going to be OK?" she asks.

"You will be, and I'll make sure of it. Tell me what happened."

Clara inhales deeply and exhales slowly, then begins providing her history of present illness.

"I was in the living room watching TV, just sitting quietly on the sofa, because it's my day off today. Then I needed to get a drink of water. I stood up, and then everything got blurry, and I was going to faint. I tried leaning back, but I ended up tilting to the side. Then I kept going that way, stumbled a few steps, and then bam, I'm on the floor."

"Did you lose consciousness at any time?"

"No."

"You were still aware of things?"

"That's right. Though when I was on the floor, I was feeling like I was going to black out soon."

"And did you?"

"No."

"What about chest pain, or the feeling that your heart is beating fast?"

"No to both."

"Any strange sensations, like smells or flashing lights?"

"Nope."

"Any recent use of alcohol or drugs?"

"I don't do any of those things."

I nod. Even though Ellen documented her own patient history, I still have to do it, too, in case anything new could make the picture clearer. Here, I don't have to worry about things like a cardiac event, seizure, or substance use being the culprit for the lightheadedness and fall. I proceed to ask a couple more symptom-related questions to cover the bases, things like headache, vomiting, difficulty breathing, and abdominal pain. Then I pick up the stethoscope lying across the back of my neck and ask her to sit up for me. Clara has no trouble gripping the side rails of the gurney and pulling herself to an upright position. Her lungs and heart sound normal. Then I instruct her to lie down, after which I hear normal bowel sounds through the stethoscope, and feel no stiffness or tender areas in her abdomen as I gently press different sections of it. I complete my physical exam with confirmation of no abnormal discoloration in her feet and hands, signs of impaired peripheral circulation. Hence, this part of my evaluation hasn't revealed any new diagnostic clues.

I'm satisfied for the time being.

"I understand from Dr. Roberts that you had seen blood in your toilet paper after using the bathroom," I say.

"Yes, that's correct."

"How much blood would you say you noticed?"

"How should I describe it?"

I stop to think, and quickly come up with something.

"Try picturing coins of different sizes. Would you say, over the past week or so, the blood in the paper looked small like a dime, or bigger than that?"

Clara pauses to think of her answer.

"It's mostly been like the size of a quarter," she says. "One time, it was bigger than a half-dollar."

"Did any of that alarm you?"

"Honestly, no. I was still feeling fine. Plus, I thought it might've been hard stool scraping me on the way out."

I nod politely. Then I refer back to my tablet, skimming the list of past progress notes in her Icarus record.

"I see that you've had major bleeding episodes before because of your diverticulosis. Is that right, Clara?"

"Yes. But the last time was three years ago. Never went back to the hospital since then, so I thought that was forever behind me. Maybe that's why I didn't really get scared about this latest bleeding."

"Understandable. Well, based on what I see, it looks like you indeed had some new diverticular bleeding. It would certainly lead to lower blood volume, causing you to feel lightheaded this morning. Does that make sense?"

Clara nods with a slight smile.

"Therefore, you'll be here in the hospital for a little while. I may order some blood to be infused into you. That will make sure you don't become anemic. Hopefully, with time, the bleeding will stop so that your blood pressure and red blood cell count become stable."

"Sounds good."

"Any questions?"

"No, doctor. Thank you."

"Meanwhile, I have an important question. If you go into cardiac arrest, with your heart suddenly stopping for whatever reason, do you want us to try resuscitating you, with measures like defibrillators?"

"Yes, please."

"And if you go into respiratory arrest, where you stop breathing, do you want us to put a tube down your windpipe and connect you to a ventilator?"

"Yes. I may be old but I'm not ready to leave this world yet."

I smile as the patient laughs.

"It sounds like you want everything done, Clara."

"That's right."

"I'll note that in the chart. Also, is there any family member you want me to inform, just in case?"

"The only family I have now is my son. Right now, he's in his junior year of college."

"Where at?"

"UCLA."

"What is he studying?"

"Mechanical engineering."

"Wow. Good for him."

"Thank you. I know he's busy there, so I'm thinking you don't need to contact him. Unless I am close to dying, in which case you better let him know. He is listed as an emergency contact."

I nod. Clara seems like a strong woman, someone who insists on tackling a crisis herself, yet not afraid to call for help if need be.

"All right then," I say. "I will get you upstairs. You just sit tight and let us take care of you."

"Bless your heart, Dr. Lin," Clara says, with another big smile.

Just down the hall is a computer workroom, containing ten terminals spread across five long tables. I sit at the one closest to the door and log into Icarus.

First things first: the admission H&P. This is my detailed documentation of the history and physical exam from my encounter with Clara, plus other stuff like lab test results that I copy and paste from other parts of the chart. It takes only a few minutes because of my eighty-word-per-minute typing speed. Then I wrap it all up with two things. Number one, my assessment: fainting secondary to suspected diverticular bleeding. Number two, my plan: admit the patient to the medicine ward, IV normal saline, check blood pressure every six hours, draw blood every six hours for serial monitoring of hemoglobin and hematocrit, and a blood type and screen. The idea is to observe Clara to see if she continues bleeding, in which case I will order units of blood to be transfused into her. How much blood she will receive? Only time will tell.

With the H&P finished, I complete a physician's order form, which consists of different sections for orders related to nursing, lab tests, imaging studies, medications, and the like. It is user-friendly, too, with check boxes marked with the click of a mouse and other boxes to manually type in. I make sure that every item in my plan is accounted for here, before I e-sign and submit the form.

A few moments later, a woman with wavy blonde hair, glasses, and light-blue scrubs walks in and approaches me. It's Dr. Ellen Roberts.

"Hey, what's up?" I ask.

"You're taking good care of Clara Summers, I assume?"

"You know me. Always on top of things."

"Of course. You were Doctor of the Month for three months last year, during the pandemic."

"Gee, after the madness of the Delta variant surge, I totally forgot about that."

Ellen laughs at my sarcasm.

"You're a diligent physician, Mark, so I shouldn't worry. But the reason I'm here is to let you know about the blood bank downstairs."

"What about it?"

"They're out of O negative blood."

I stop and look at her.

"You're kidding."

"Afraid not. I just got word from them. Apparently, the last bag of O negative blood just went out. I'm guessing I was the one who ordered it. We had an accident victim who needed blood so badly."

"We're not a Level One trauma center."

"Far from it. Ivory Memorial is Level Four. We can still handle the basic traumas, of course, like this patient who got hit by a speeding car at an intersection just a couple of blocks from here."

"Was he a driver or pedestrian?"

"Driver. But it was a high-intensity impact."

I let out an audible exhale.

"I take it you're telling me about the blood bank because of Clara Summers?"

"Exactly. You think you'll transfuse her?"

"Depends on her serial H-and-H levels. If there's no more O negative, I sure hope there's still some other blood left."

"All I can say is good luck."

I nod as Ellen gives me a reassuring smile.

"Hey, did you hear about the double Code Blue yesterday?" she asks.

"Oh, don't get me started."

"Why not?"

"Both codes were for my patients. Same for the Rapid Response right after."

"Oh my god, really? Sorry I asked."

"No worries. You didn't know."

"Are you OK, though?"

I shrug.

"For now, I'm all right. Still, it's freaky to have a triple threat, as if it's a supernatural force at work, not mere coincidence."

"Like some kind of invisible hand?" Ellen asks, giggling a bit.

"More like demonic possession. Forget a medical doctor. You need an exorcist, like Father Karras."

"Who?"

"The priest in the movie *The Exorcist*. It's the best horror movie ever made, in my opinion."

"Ugh, I can't stand horror. That scene with the girl and what she does to herself with the crucifix... oh god. That was sick."

"What kind of movies do you like?"

"Mostly other kinds. I do love science-fiction. I don't have a favorite, though. There's just so many good ones to see."

"OK, what's the first one that comes to mind?"

"Uh... the *Terminator* movies, mainly the first two. The action is great, while it makes you think about whether it's dangerous to have computer technology that's way too advanced with artificial intelligence. Or automation."

"Hello, Skynet."

"You're telling me. Never mind robots for war. I'm still wary of self-driving cars. Wouldn't want to ride in one, or be on the same road as them."

"I have yet to encounter a single driverless car."

"In ten years, that might change."

"As always, I'll be going with the flow, so I don't care."

"Good for you."

I nod my head. Then Ellen checks her phone, presumably to read a text message. She puts it away.

"I'll be back," she says, doing her best Schwarzenegger impression.

"Hasta la vista, baby."

"Hey, don't call me that. You're lucky my husband isn't here."

"Why, are you married to Arnold?"

Ellen stares at me.

"All right, I'll shut up," I say.

Then she laughs out loud before leaving the room. Pretty soon, I do, too, after logging out of Icarus.

I head to the hospital cafeteria, and on the way, my work phone rings. I don't recognize the number, but I guess the caller has to be within this building.

"Hello?"

"Dr. Lin, this is Rajesh Krishnan in IT. I wanted to follow up with you about our conversation yesterday, regarding the medication errors with three patients."

"Yes?"

"Our team has looked into the matter. Based on what we've found, we really need to talk to you."

"How long will it take?"

"Maybe fifteen minutes to half an hour."

"That long?"

"There's plenty to discuss. Also, it would be better if we could go over all of this in person."

"Why not on the phone?"

"Trust me. It's much easier that way."

I pause. A mix of excitement and anxiety sets in. There could be stuff from IT that could clear my name. At least, I hope so.

"What time would be most convenient?" I ask.

"Any time this afternoon. Earliest is one o'clock. Our department is in the basement. Just use your badge to open the double doors by the elevators."

"I'll see if I can be there a little after one, assuming nothing urgent comes up."

"OK. See you then."

I hang up, then step into the cafeteria. I am starving like hell.

CHAPTER 10

The Division of Information Technology is located in a part of the hospital's lower level that I've never set foot in. I'm familiar with the hallway running past the elevator lobby, with the radiology department located at one end and the clinical laboratory, blood bank, pathology lab, and morgue at the other. What's new to me is a pair of double doors near the elevators, with a sign that reads "Authorized Personnel Only." Opening them requires flashing a staff badge against a card reader, which I do here for the very first time.

The world I step into is much quieter. There are no clinical personnel scrambling to and fro. This is where the miscellaneous departments of the hospital do their thing, including hospital linen and laundry, janitorial services, and telecommunications. Logically, information technology is next door to telecommunications, though I have to navigate a maze-like labyrinth just to get to it. Man, I feel like a lab rat.

The door to IT is open, but no one is inside. There is an empty desk with a computer, probably for an assistant who must've taken a late lunch. I also notice doorways leading to three other rooms. Rather than wait, I knock on the open door.

Almost immediately, an Indian man, who is mildly chubby and has early signs of graying hair, emerges from one of the other rooms.

"Are you Dr. Mark Lin?" he asks with his familiar slight accent.

I nod, and even hold up my ID for good measure.

"You're Rajesh Krishnan?"

"Yep, that's me," he says, smiling. "Come on in."

I walk in and follow Rajesh into a much larger room. A giant rectangular table occupies the middle of the space. Along one wall is a table with multiple desktop computers, each displaying what I guess are real-time statuses for the many application systems used in this hospital. On the other end is a door to a server room. There are also four offices, one of which belongs to Rajesh.

"Have a seat," he says.

I pick a random spot at the table, before two men emerge from one of the offices. One is a thin man with glasses and a goatee, wearing khakis and a blue button-down shirt. The other is a portly man with curly hair and glasses, wearing a red, long-sleeve shirt. For a moment, I swear I'm seeing Gilligan and the Skipper with reversed bodies. The colorful pair place laptops onto the table, along with stacks of printouts.

"Dr. Lin, this is Patrick Flanigan," Rajesh says, gesturing to the man in blue, then pointing to the man in red. "And that is Walter Laramie. Both of them are IT technicians who mainly work with the cybersecurity section of this department. But they do have some understanding of clinical applications too."

"Hello," I say, raising a hand in a flitting wave. "I take it you both looked into the issue I reported?"

"Yes, we did," Patrick says. "And let me tell you. In all the years I've worked here, I have never seen anything like what we're about to discuss."

"Well, don't leave me hanging," I joke.

"I think it would help if we first explain a bit about what we do here," Walter says. "Not all of it, of course. Just the parts that pertain to the problems you reported. Rajesh, is that OK with you?"

Rajesh nods politely. I can also see him smiling, as if content with trusting his staff to run the show.

"Our department keeps track of activity on the hospital's network," Walter continues. "All tests and medications ordered, all notes entered, that sort of thing. We keep a running log of it all, so that if something goes wrong, we can look back and see if anything is out of the ordinary."

"When I do all of that clinical stuff with Icarus, what kind of information is tracked and stored?" I ask.

"What do you mean?"

"Like, does it log the contents of orders and such?"

Walter shakes his head. I guess I shouldn't be surprised.

"It's mainly basic stuff," he says. "Like who entered it into the system, what day and time. And the IP address, too."

"What's an IP address?"

"It's like an ID number for a computer. It usually doesn't stay the same all the time, though. But if there's something unusual with it, we can at least try looking into it, just in case it yields something."

"How do you know if someone unauthorized is in the system?"

Walter turns to Patrick and offers the chance to answer that. Patrick nods, then leans forward to speak.

"We have what is called an intrusion detection system. It contains rules to help distinguish normal activity, like your routine clinical tasks, with abnormal activity, like a hacker doing some damage. When unusual stuff occurs, it triggers alarm notifications. Does that make sense?"

"Perfectly," I say, nodding.

"OK, good. Because here's what happened."

I hold my breath as Patrick consults some of the printouts in front of him. The pages are nearly an inch thick. Is there really that much material to go over?

"Two days ago, Sunday afternoon, Walter and I noticed some flags," Patrick says. "At 4:12 PM, an unauthorized user, some hacker, accessed the network. No user ID, no IP address, so each of the hacker's actions going forward was easy for us to see in the activity log. That includes the hacker viewing a bunch of pages in multiple patient charts. Yes, just viewing pages within charts also shows up in the log. Then, at 5:37 PM, the hacker deleted the record of a physician's medication order, related to one specific patient, that had already been submitted. Minutes after that, the user created a new medication order related to the same patient, which the pharmacy appeared to have processed. Obviously, we found your name attached to all of this."

"Which patient are you talking about?" I ask.

"Based on decryption of patient info, Christopher Flint."

"But the log doesn't show the contents of the orders?"

"No."

"Because I need proof of what was in the order that got deleted. That patient's widow is threatening to sue me."

Patrick frowns. Then I notice Walter and Rajesh doing the same. Oh boy, am I really screwed for sure?

"I'm sorry you're going through that," Patrick says. "But sadly, our system doesn't work at the level of detail you're hoping for. You see, it's already a monumental task just to store hospital-wide activity data without all the minutiae like text within patient encounter notes and physician orders."

I sigh heavily.

"What did you do when you noticed those flags?" I ask.

"Honestly, we had no idea what was going on," Walter chimes in. "Also, we didn't know what HIPAA says about a situation like this. We actually spent time trying to find out anything to guide us."

Anyone who works in healthcare has to understand and honor the Health Insurance Portability and Accountability Act, HIPAA, the federal law making sure that confidential medical information and patient privacy are treated as sacred at all times by healthcare workers. Any violators would face serious penalties, like prison.

"Then Lucifer's Worm became priority number one, after spreading so quickly," Patrick says. "Walter and I got busy with that, before Rajesh told us about your phone call to him. In the end, we decided that, whatever HIPAA says about this, patient safety is at stake with what we do. If any hospital site inspectors have an issue, that'll be our statement."

"At this point, let me share my side of the story," I say before leaning forward. Then I give them the key details of Christopher Flint's case: his medication dose error and subsequent death.

The room goes silent. All three IT specialists nod slowly.

"I'm really sorry," Rajesh says gently. "Please understand that we are taking this matter very seriously."

"Thank you," I say. "Meanwhile, when I submitted an order form for Flint, it didn't just contain an order for a new medication. It also contained orders for a physical therapy consult and another set of routine lab tests. I haven't noticed anything wrong with those. Have you, by any chance?"

"No," Patrick says.

"How is it the hacker could just screw up the medication order, but not the other stuff I requested?"

"Simple. You may be completing one order form, filling out different sections for different types of items, but once you submit the form, the items are treated as separate streams of data, not one big block. The part of the form for medications is one block. The part of the form for physical therapy is another. And so on. That's how the hacker could just target that medication order. Somehow, he intercepted that one thing specifically, removed it, and slipped in something similar but deadly."

"And there's no way to track him down?"

"Not with his information masked."

"So what about Lucifer's Worm? It goes around as a spam email message, while leaving backdoors along the way so that hackers could break in through those points. Is that something you've resolved?"

"Not quite. The worm spreads so quickly that even as we're rapidly patching up security breaches and clearing out that email from the servers, there may still be some remnants of each. The automated fix we've applied is doing what it can. Believe me, we are still on this. It's not over yet."

"Any idea of an estimated timeframe?"

"I'm afraid not."

I close my eyes and shake my head.

"OK," I say. "Enough about Flint. What about the other two patients I reported to Rajesh?"

"Darnell Jackson is pretty much the same story as Christopher Flint," Walter says. "And Doris Schafer, too, though there is much more to her case than just a medication order substitution."

"How so?"

"According to our logs, some other things got changed right after."

I stop to pull out my tablet from my white coat pocket. From my patient list, I open Schafer's chart in Icarus.

"Can you give me details?" I ask, somewhat anxiously.

"Let's see," Walter says, leafing through printouts. "First off, the hacker made an edit to the overview section."

"Meaning?"

"The top bar displaying the patient's name, medical record number, date of birth, etcetera."

I scan that part of Schafer's chart, immediately spotting the irregularity that I'd already seen yesterday.

"It says she has no allergies," I say. "Which is definitely not correct, because I remember it saying she's allergic to ciprofloxacin. That's why, on Sunday morning, I had ordered azithromycin. Then, after she had anaphylaxis, I found out that order disappeared, and a new order for ciprofloxacin was put in place."

"This is beyond insane," Patrick says quietly.

"Look at this," Walter says. "Records also indicate the hacker edited some pages in the patient's chart."

I stop. I remember having gone through Schafer's chart yesterday, but I covered only pages from the past week.

"You know which ones specifically?" I ask.

Walter pauses to review his information.

"They seem to be patient encounter notes. The hacker altered about twenty of those pages in total."

I scan the list of note entries in Schafer's chart. I don't have time to open each one, but I suddenly have a new hunch. Many of the notes document the patient's office visits with her primary care provider. Often, they reiterate details of the patient's medical history. I open one of the notes at random and skim the contents.

Then, I nod slowly.

"One note by the PCP says the patient has no allergies," I say. "It just says 'allergies, colon, none.'"

"Can you explain what you're thinking?" Rajesh asks.

"If the hacker deleted the allergy in the chart heading, I'm guessing he must've done the same with any other place where allergies are mentioned, like whenever a clinic physician sees the patient and includes in the visit note the pertinent past info about the patient already documented previously. You know, things like past medical history, allergies, and history of substance use."

"Is that what you're seeing?"

I open more of the PCP's office visit notes at random. Sure enough, each one says "Allergies: None," not "Allergies: ciprofloxacin." I nod my head slowly.

"Wow," Patrick says. "This hacker is dead serious."

"Wait a second," Walter interrupts, looking at the same printouts as Patrick, along with his own laptop screen. "These pages were altered practically all at once."

"What do you mean?" I ask.

"Each record of a page edit by this nameless hacker has the exact same time stamp: 6:02 PM. The only difference is the seconds. The first three pages were edited at 6:02 and five seconds. Next two were at 6:02 and six seconds. Then three at 6:02 and seven seconds. And so on, all the way to 6:02 and twelve seconds."

"How is that possible? You can't manually delete an allergy from multiple pages so quickly."

There is a pause. Every one of us is trying to figure it out. I have no idea, so I leave it to the other three.

It is Patrick who breaks the silence.

"Maybe the hacker used an automated method. You know how, in a text-editing program or something like Microsoft Word, there's a Find and Replace function to automatically replace all instances of certain text with another? Maybe the hacker has a way to do something similar here."

"So he was trying to make it look like the patient has no allergies at all," I respond. "And it looks like I gave her an antibiotic that she's allergic to. If her husband insists that she does have a known allergy, and can easily back it up based on past medical records he or his wife may have already..."

I frown, and momentarily close my eyes.

"This won't look good at all," I say.

While the three IT men look at me, I resist the urge to blurt out the one burning question in my mind. Who the fuck is Doctor Lucifer? The moment I find out who this asshole is, I will kick his ass straight to hell.

I look back on the tablet, seeing the words "Allergies" and "None" staring back. All of a sudden, it hits me like lightning. I quickly sit straight up. Everyone else stares at me.

"There's something else," I say breathlessly.

"What?" Patrick asks.

"Schafer's chart specifies the word 'None' for allergies. That's not normally what it should say."

"What should it say?"

Instead of answering, I open a different patient's chart on my tablet. I glance at the chart's overview section. I nod, then show the tablet screen to Patrick.

"This other patient of mine doesn't have allergies, either," I say. "But where it says 'Allergies,' it says 'No Known Allergies.' That's what it's normally supposed to say for any patient who has no allergies. Not the word 'None.'"

Everyone else stays quiet for a moment.

"Sounds like the hacker isn't too versed in medicine," Walter says slowly, with a hint of surprise.

"Or he isn't fully familiar with normal protocols in Icarus," Patrick adds. "An interesting find, Dr. Lin."

"Whoever the hacker is, he's out to get me," I say, somewhat softly.

"Any idea who?" Rajesh asks.

"No."

"Once again, I am sorry about what you're going through now. If anything, I am glad you contacted me to have us look into this."

"I know, and thanks again for your help. I appreciate it."

"Absolutely. And from this, it's become very clear how vulnerable we are to cyberthreats. Going forward, we will certainly look into ways to improve our network security, so that no more patients end up suffering like this."

"Meanwhile, I'm still a sitting duck. If the hacker is planning another attack, I sure hope there's a way to act before he does."

Rajesh nods. He does it with an air of confidence.

"This is what I think we should do," he says. "Patrick, Walter, I'm going to have you keep an extra eye on the activity log in real time. If anything gets flagged, look into it and find out which patient it involves, then contact the treating physician, whether it's Dr. Lin or someone else. Give them a warning as soon as you can."

Patrick and Walter nod, like two soldiers ready for war.

"In addition, give Dr. Lin one of your business cards," Rajesh continues. "He should be allowed to get in touch with you just as you may wish to contact him."

The two technicians quickly step into their offices, retrieve a business card from their desks, and return to give them to me. Rajesh gives me one of his as well, from a thin stack he keeps in his pocket.

"This is a great idea," I say. "I'll stand by for any calls from the three of you."

"Similarly, if you have questions for us, give us a call," Rajesh says. "We'll be around."

"In case I don't pick up, just leave a voicemail," Walter says.

"Or you can just text," Patrick says. "It's up to you."

I nod. Rajesh, Patrick, and Walter look at me with slight smiles. It feels good to go into battle with a team of allies. I won't have to do this alone. But just as I am ready to leave, one of my smartphones rings. Not the work phone in my left pants pocket. The personal phone in my right. I pull it out and see an incoming call.

From the devil's number: 1 (666) 666-6666. Here we go again.

"*The blood is on your hands!*" Doctor Lucifer growls.

I just hang up. Then I get a new text message. I open it. It's from the same number, containing the exact same words.

"He's back," I say breathlessly.

CHAPTER 11

"Who's back?" Patrick asks.

"The hacker," I say. "I didn't mention that I've also been getting threatening phone calls, which I suspect are coming from him."

"He's on the move now," Walter says intensely, staring at his laptop. "Look at this."

Rajesh and Patrick rush to look at the same screen. Slowly, I come around the conference table and peek as well. The screen is fully occupied by a window containing some kind of list, with rows upon rows of new entries appearing every few seconds. I spot a few that are shaded light red.

"What's going on?" I ask.

"Hang on, let me filter out the normal activity," Walter says, clicking a mouse button a few times.

Just like that, the many unshaded rows disappear, leaving behind only the red highlighted ones. We can now see every trace of the hacker's latest actions.

"Dr. Lin, if you look at the bottom here, the earliest entry says the hacker entered the network at 11:45 AM today," Patrick says.

"That's more than an hour ago," I respond.

"Yeah. Nothing we could do, though."

"What else does the list say?"

"A few minutes later, he started viewing just one patient's chart."

"Must be his target."

"Probably."

"Which patient is it?"

"I'll have to do a little decryption to find out. It's not like the name and medical record number are right there in front of us. HIPAA, you know."

I nod. Then Walter chimes in.

"At 11:58 AM, a lab test order got deleted. And now, starting just several seconds ago, a series of lab test results have been edited. Hmmm, wait a second. I see the letters BLD in these entries."

"Meaning?"

"I think it's related to blood."

I remember what Doctor Lucifer said moments ago: *the blood is on your hands.* With haste, I open the Icarus chart for Clara Summers in my tablet and jump to the orders section. I look for what I had submitted.

"No," I growl, clenching a fist.

"What?" Walter asks.

"I had ordered a blood type and screen, but it's now gone. This is for a patient with a bleeding problem. I placed an order for the blood bank to determine her blood type, because she might need a blood transfusion while she's here. That was sometime between eleven thirty this morning and twelve noon. If the hacker removed that order..."

"Then the blood bank may not have gotten it?" Patrick asks.

"Right," I say, more frantic now. "That would mean delays in getting blood ready for her. Speaking of which..."

I open the chart's lab results section, then select the tab labeled "Type and Screen." I hold my breath.

What I see nearly stops my heart.

"The patient has had blood transfusions in the past," I say. "Each time, she would've had an initial blood type and screen, followed by a crossmatch for confirmation before the actual transfusion. A person's blood type does not change, so you would expect the same result for every type and screen and for every type and cross."

"That's not what you're seeing?" Patrick asks.

"No. Instead of the same blood type for all eight of her tests, I'm seeing each one with a different blood type, none identical to each other."

"Let's count how many edits we have."

I wait as Patrick performs some kind of mental count. Walter points a finger at the screen and slowly moves his hand down, probably doing the same thing.

"I see a total of twenty-three rows corresponding to blood test result edits," Patrick says. "Also, there are little identifiers indicating which test result got edited. I see eight different ones, meaning each of those eight blood type results got changed at least once."

"Dang it," I say loudly. "The hacker is trying to hide the patient's blood type. He doesn't want me to even guess it."

"The only thing left is here at the top," Walter says. "One instance of an uploaded image getting deleted."

There is a section in Icarus that I know involves the uploading of scanned images: the one called Outside Records. If a patient receives care at any other hospital and provides records from there, they could be scanned and stored into Icarus for reference.

I open that part of Clara's chart, wondering if this is what the hacker struck. It leads to a short list of scanned external records. One of them is labeled "UC Irvine Emergency Transfusion." It is marked with a yellow triangle containing a red exclamation point. I try to open that record.

I get an error message: "Image Not Found."

"The patient received a blood transfusion elsewhere once," I explain. "The record of that had been scanned into her chart. That whole document is now gone, which is too bad because I assume the blood type is mentioned in there."

"Dr. Lin, wouldn't this be an issue only if the patient is actually bleeding?" Rajesh asks with concern.

"Yes. At the same time, I must be prepared. You never want to be stuck in a crisis situation with no way out."

"I'm no physician, but I would hope that if she's still stable, we could buy some time to get to the bottom of this."

"I get what you're saying. And I hope we can beat the hacker in whatever sick game he's playing with me."

I suddenly remember the deleted order for the blood type and screen. I pull out my work phone and call the blood bank from my contacts list. Then I wait. Somebody better answer me, or there will be hell to pay.

"Blood bank, Bill speaking," a voice answers.

"This is Dr. Mark Lin, internal medicine. I ordered a type and screen for a patient about a little more than an hour ago. Patient's name is Clara Summers."

I read off the patient's MRN from my tablet. Then I hear some faint keyboard presses. Several seconds later, Bill speaks.

"I don't see an order. Doctor, are you sure you sent it?"

"Positive."

"Why not just resubmit it?"

"There may be a glitch in the system. I can't explain, but believe me when I say that even the IT department has confirmed something is wrong. Is there any way I could just do a verbal order over the phone? I'll sign it in the chart later."

"Is it urgent?"

"Not right now. But her case is worrisome enough that I don't think this should wait any longer."

There is a pause, which goes on a little too long.

"Tell me again the details of the order," Bill says.

I rattle off my name and state that I ordered a type and screen sometime between eleven thirty and noon.

"OK, Dr. Lin, I'll make sure a tech draws some blood from her."

"Thank you," I say, before abruptly hanging up and turning to the three IT men. "And thank you, everyone, for your help. I'm going to leave now in case my patient dies on me. Can any of you text me with updates about this patient from your end? Her name is Clara Summers. I'm pretty sure she's the hacker's current target."

"Will do," Walter says.

Then I dash out of the room.

* * *

I reach the seventh floor in no time. There may not be any Code

Blue or Rapid Response alarms, but I'm not taking any chances. I want to be as close as possible to room 719, where Clara had been taken to. I step into the computer workroom behind the 7 East nurse's station. Besides the terminals, there are two round tables with chairs, good for doing non-computer work. I sit at one of them, pull out my tablet, and flip through Clara's chart.

What exactly does Doctor Lucifer have in store? What kind of trap is he setting up? Based on the chart hacks, probably confusion. And chaos. But only if I really don't know Clara's blood type in a life-and-death crisis.

If only I can figure it out.

I peruse the list of chart notes and open some of them at random. Is there any mention of her blood type that Doctor Lucifer missed? Or at least some kind of clue to her blood type? I need a lead, a jolt to get me going.

Sure enough, after a few minutes of aimlessly looking around, I find something, in a rather unexpected place.

A note by Clara's primary care physician about an annual check-up visit lists several things about her past medical history, including a hemolytic blood transfusion reaction several decades ago. No details are provided, but "hemolytic" means that the red blood cells transfused into her just burst, because of a blood type mismatch.

Every person has an ABO blood type: type A if red blood cells have surface antigen A, type B for RBCs with surface antigen B, type AB if both, or type O if neither. Every person also has an Rh blood type: Rh positive if RBCs have Rh factor on the surface or Rh negative if not. That means eight possible blood types. Whichever antigen is absent, the person has antibodies to it. Any packed red blood cells transfused into a patient must not have surface antigens that could react with the patient's antibodies.

The fact that Clara had even one transfusion mismatch in her lifetime means she is not AB positive. Someone with A, B, and Rh antigens on their red blood cells would have no antibodies to them, and could safely receive any type of human RBCs. So that leaves seven possible blood types. Which one is hers?

I think about it further, brainstorming ways I could possibly deduce the blood type without making a dangerous one-in-seven guess. But then I stop.

I hear a commotion outside.

"I got a patient bleeding," a woman shouts from far away.

"What's going on?" another woman responds, presumably the station nurse just right outside.

"She's pouring out blood between her legs."

"Which patient?"

"Clara Summers, room 719. Should I call a Rapid Response?"

I shoot up from my chair and hasten out of the room. The station nurse is standing, looking down the hall at an Asian woman in pink scrubs frantically working a smartphone. I make my way to her without a hitch. She looks up. I recognize her as a nurse named Anita. She's really frightened right now.

"Oh, Dr. Lin," she says, struggling to putting away her phone. "I was just about to call you."

"I was behind the nurse's station. I heard you screaming."

"Ms. Summers is bleeding really fast."

I head straight into the patient's room. On the bed, Clara is grimacing, with tears streaming down both cheeks. Her hips are sitting on an absorbable underpad, which has a red stain emerging from the side of her thigh. I grab a pair of rubber gloves from a nearby box, put them on, and lift her hospital gown. I carefully move one of her legs slightly to the side. A thick, dark red pool soaks the pad.

And it's growing.

"Anita, get her normal saline, quick," I say. "Clara, how are you feeling?"

"I'm scared."

"Are you having pain?"

"No. Just bleeding down there."

"Can you feel where it's coming from?"

"It's my rectum."

"What about vaginal bleeding?"

"Definitely not that."

I nod and turn my head. Anita already has a fresh IV bag mounted on a nearby pole and is now attaching its tube to the port in Clara's arm. Then I take my own action for the patient. I hold her hand in one of mine.

"It's gonna be OK," I say, trying to be soothing. "We're going to give you fluids, and likely some blood, too."

"Am I going to die?" Clara asks, almost sobbing.

"No, you won't."

"Will the bleeding stop?"

"I'm hoping it will. If push comes to shove, we'll have a surgeon go in and remove the bleeding part of the colon. But we're going to try to avoid that."

I keep holding Clara's hand. Soon, she closes her eyes, and her grip of my hand tightens, almost crushing my fingers. This is now a game of chance. Many cases of diverticular bleeding thankfully resolve on their own. If I actually believe in a higher power, I would be praying for this outcome. But in reality, actions speak the loudest.

"I'm going to call the blood bank," I say calmly. "Just take some deep breaths and let us handle things. You'll be fine."

"You sure?"

"Absolutely. One hundred percent."

"Thank you."

"By any chance, you know your blood type?"

"No, I don't remember it."

"Has anyone ever told you what it is?"

"I think so."

"How long ago?"

"Oh, a very long time. I can't seem to recall it. Let me see..."

Clara pauses to think. I am taking a deep breath, while mentally crossing my fingers. Come on, please give me something.

"I only know that I'm negative," she says.

"What do you mean?"

"Blood type negative. I can't say for sure if it's A negative, B negative, or whatever. It's something negative."

"But you're certain about the negative part?"

"Yes. I think so."

I nod. Clara seems confident enough. I turn to the nurse.

"Anita, keep those fluids going. Stand by for blood transfusion. I'll be outside if you need me. OK?"

"Got it."

"Can you also change the bed pad? It'll be easier to see if the bleeding finally slows down."

"Will do. Thanks for stopping by."

I head out and use my work phone to call the blood bank, making sure I'm out of earshot from room 719. I feel the phone vibrate momentarily. Likely a new text. But then Bill answers the call.

"This is Dr. Mark Lin again. I gave you a verbal order for a type and screen several minutes ago for patient Clara Summers."

"Oh yeah. I do have a tech coming up right now."

"Well, we have a problem. The patient is bleeding profusely, so it can't wait. Can you please tell me if you have any O negative blood in stock?"

"Let me check."

I remember Ellen Roberts telling me about that blood type being depleted, but I want to be sure. Who knows if the blood bank actually got a new batch of O negative in the last hour, even if it's, let's say, only two bags?

"Nope, we're still out," Bill says.

"OK, how about this? Can you check to see if the blood bank has records of past blood typing tests this patient had?"

"What for?"

"Figuring out her blood type, if we can't do a type and screen."

"Uh, are you sure..."

"Just do it, please."

"OK, hold on."

I rush to the nurse's station. I place my tablet on the counter, using my right hand to sift through Clara's medical record while holding the phone to my ear with the other. Then I feel the phone vibrate again. This time, I look at the screen. There is indeed a new text message. While the call is still active, I check the text.

Walter Laramie messaged me three minutes ago.

> *Dr. Lin, the hacker has altered multiple records in the blood bank. All for patient Clara Summers. No blood bank record for her was left alone.*

Goddamn it! Doctor Lucifer is one fucking speed demon. I wish I hadn't missed this text. I also beat myself up for not even thinking of checking with the blood bank in the first place, before Clara's blood type records there were altered.

"Hello, Dr. Lin?" Bill says.

"Yes?"

"This will sound crazy, but the patient's past blood typing results are totally different from each other. It keeps changing from one to another. Looks like something is very wrong with our system."

"Yikes," I say, pretending to sound shocked. "I'll tell you what. Let me hang up and get back to you. I'm going to find out what her blood type is, then call you with an urgent transfusion order. Can you stand by for me?"

"I'll be right here."

I hang up and go back to Clara's chart. I feverishly review the notes on the tablet, my breathing becoming rapid and noisy.

There has to be some other clue to her blood type. I've gotten as far as eliminating type AB positive, the universal recipient, along with A positive, B positive, and O positive, assuming Clara's memory is reliable. I still need to go from four possible blood types to just one. Come on, man, think!

Anything will help me at this point. I start casting a wide net. I don't care which doctor wrote each patient encounter note or what clinical condition was involved. I'm even reviewing a series of records about

Clara visiting a psychiatrist. So what if they talked about her being severely shaken after a serious car accident and being diagnosed with acute stress disorder? A meandering fishing expedition is still better than staying put and just letting her crash.

At that moment, I freeze.

One of the psych notes is about a psychotherapy session, where a mental health therapist helped the patient cope with her own trauma through optimistic thinking. The therapist briefly noted some affirmations the patient would proclaim each day, like how she was blessed to be alive, proud to be a wife up until her divorce, and happy about her son's high school graduation. The note even mentions the patient's gratefulness for having a blood type that is compatible with more than one blood type, not just her own.

I ball a fist with excitement. I can scratch off O negative. The only RBCs that can be safely donated to O negative patients are O negative RBCs. I also sigh in relief. Clara isn't doomed because the blood bank has no more donor O negative.

But I still have three possibilities left: A negative, B negative, and AB negative. There is no donor blood type other than O negative that is compatible with all three, and guessing is not a safe bet, even with these odds. I have to keep looking.

I spend another few minutes combing the chart. Still nothing, even after skimming orders, lab results, referrals, and scanned outside medical records. I quickly walk to room 719 and peek through the door. Anita is carrying a used bed pad to the biohazard container in one corner of the room.

"How many pads have you used so far?" I ask.

"She's on her third one," Anita says.

"Is she still bleeding?"

"Yeah. It's not slowing down."

"Did you check her blood pressure again?"

"Yes. It's still holding up, around one fifteen over seventy-five."

At that moment, Anita approaches me and whispers.

"What's going on with the blood transfusion?"

"Problems with the blood bank. I'm still working on it."

"The patient is getting agitated."

"Do what you can to keep her calm."

"I'm trying."

"Just don't say anything about blood bank issues, OK? For her sake, keep quiet about that."

"What exactly is the problem?"

"I have no time to explain. Just keep her distracted."

Anita nods and heads to the patient.

Back on my tablet, I notice the miscellaneous sections of Clara's Icarus chart. One of them is labeled "Education," for documenting patient educational sessions like diabetes management classes and storing copies of Ivory Memorial pamphlets created for patients. So far, Clara had received health materials related to breast cancer, hypertension, arthritis, and diverticulosis.

Then I spot one curious item, about blood transfusions, probably because of her diverticulosis. I open that document.

The window that appears lists two items in a side bar. One is a clean electronic copy of Ivory Memorial's full miniature booklet about blood transfusions. The other is a scanned image. I do know that some nurses giving educational materials to patients like to scribble a few extra notes in the pamphlet before giving it to the patient, and scanning the additional stuff into Icarus is a way to document that in the system. So immediately, I open the scanned image. It contains two back-to-back pages from the booklet.

Specifically talking about blood types.

Immediately, I spot the additional stuff in black pen. In a blank space to one side, a sentence had been handwritten: "Iron-rich foods you like: beef, shrimp, chicken, beans, spinach, broccoli, watermelon, strawberries." The nurse probably gave Clara some advice about which foods could help prevent iron deficiency anemia, given the patient's history of multiple blood transfusions.

The main feature of the two pages is an 8-by-8 grid indicating, with checkmarks, which of eight donor blood types is compatible with which of eight recipient blood types. Looking at the recipient blood types, four of them have small dots marked beside them in black ink: A negative, B negative, A positive, and B positive. Along the donor blood types, I see similar black dots next to five of them, each compatible with at least one of the four dotted recipients. It's as if the nurse had shown Clara examples of what blood types are safe to receive for transfusion depending on the recipient's blood type, marking each example with a black pen. I keep my eyes on those dots, wondering what the nurse and the patient were discussing at the time. I can only guess what they were saying.

But then, I see it.

The dot next to recipient B negative looks like it was made by swirling the pen tip around and around in the same spot. Every other dot for marked recipient blood types is slightly smaller, merely a quick touch of the paper with the pen tip.

Same thing with donors B negative and O negative. Slightly more pronounced dots next to those, unlike the other marked donor blood types.

I'm guessing that after the nurse explained the general examples of compatible blood transfusion, she ended it by marking more clearly which blood type was actually Clara's and which donor blood types were safe for her.

I call the blood bank.

"This is Dr. Mark Lin, calling about Clara Summers."

"Yes?" Bill says.

"Her blood type is B negative. Can you send up two units of that?"

"Are you sure that's her blood type?"

"If I weren't certain, I wouldn't be calling."

"And this is still urgent?"

"Yes, please do this stat."

"Sure thing."

I hang up and run back into room 719. Anita is changing Clara's bed pad again. I'm guessing it's number four.

"Two units of blood are coming," I announce.

"Hallelujah!" Clara says, smiling and almost laughing. "Oh my goodness, what took you all so long?"

I hold the patient's hand like before. I wonder if Anita blurted out the blood bank problem to Clara, or if the patient assumed it herself.

"I'm so sorry for the delay. There might be problems downstairs. But it does look like you're going to be OK."

"I won't die then?"

"Nope."

"Thank you, Jesus. Bless your heart, Dr. Lin."

I nod and smile.

"Thank you. Now, just relax, Clara. Think about all the good things you have in your life. Being alive. Your son. Just count all of your blessings. Can you do that?"

"Oh yes, I will."

With that, I say nothing more. Clara closes her eyes and smiles. I can tell she's in her own little world, a personal heaven away from the horrors of reality.

Soon, a man in white scrubs enters the room, carrying two bags of blood. Anita mounts them next to the IV saline and connects one bag to Clara's IV port. I watch the tube turn red all the way through. Then I look at the patient.

It's now the moment of truth.

For the next few minutes, I stand over the patient, gauging her facial expressions and body movements. So far, nothing changes. She remains still. In this context, that's good. I even ask her if she's experiencing any symptoms, like fever, chills, or pain. She answers no for each one.

An hour later, when I check back in, Clara is still asymptomatic. Knowing that hemolytic transfusion reactions can occur even as late as two weeks post-transfusion, I'm not ready to declare it being out of the question. But that's OK. If something does happen down the line with that, she'll be in good hands, whether mine or someone else's.

For once, I feel like a guardian angel. The light has prevailed over the dark.

Still, I cannot tell if this is winning the war or a victory in just one battle. Yes, Doctor Lucifer has failed this time. But he'll be back. I just know it. Whoever the fuck he is, he's still out there and ready to strike again.

I am not out of the woods yet.

CHAPTER 12

Once I leave room 719, I call IT. Given that the last person who communicated with me was Walter Laramie, I decide to speak with him.

"Hello, this is Walter."

"I just want to thank you and Patrick for your hard work, keeping an eye out on Clara Summers's records."

"Hey, glad I could help. How is the patient?"

"She's done getting her blood transfusion. The hacker thought he could conceal her blood type, making me risk not transfusing her or giving her the wrong kind of blood. Turns out he overlooked one thing in the chart."

"What was it?"

"A patient pamphlet about blood transfusions. The nurse had subtly marked her blood type on one page, before scanning it into her chart."

"So... you managed to get the blood type?"

"Exactly."

"Well, that's a relief. I'll be sure to let Patrick know the good news. Boy, am I glad we're doing this."

"It does look like your department and I can work together. Next time you see some unusual activity and it involves a patient, you call the attending doc, although I'm pretty sure it'll be me again."

"Don't worry. I've been on this ever since Rajesh told us."

"Good. All right, you take care. We'll be in touch if need be."

"Thanks, Dr. Lin."

After hanging up, I go back to my tablet to do some follow-up work, mainly checking lab results, an imaging study, latest vital signs on patients, etcetera. I also note that Clara Summers's next hemoglobin and hematocrit test would be done in about two hours.

Just then, I get a call from the ICU. A patient is going to be transferred out to the medicine ward, and I would be the doctor assuming care.

The patient is Laverne McDonald, a 76-year-old woman with an artificial hip and a cardiac pacemaker. She was admitted straight to the ICU a week ago because of severe bacterial pneumonia. The pathogen was one of those microorganisms with some antibiotic resistance, impervious to first-line antibacterial drugs. It took a little extra time to find a suitable regimen, but it worked. Her condition improved enough that she could breathe on her own without mechanical ventilation. All I have to do now is make sure her pneumonia is fully cleared, or at least close to it, then send her home.

I visit her in room 811, confirm she is still somewhat short of breath but otherwise breathing OK, and notice fine crackling sounds when I listen to her lungs. If things go well, she could be discharged within two days.

But knowing that Doctor Lucifer sent another patient to the ICU with a deadly antibiotic, I am still treading water.

I receive a new text message from Dr. Jeffrey Winters, the CEO. He says that, thanks to the hard work of the IT department, the hospital email system is now back online. He does warn us that some copies of the spam email are still going around, so that if it lands in our inboxes, we should delete it immediately without opening it in order to prevent further spread. Interestingly, he refers to the spam email this time as Lucifer's Worm. The whole world is probably calling it that now.

With no high-priority tasks, I head to the computer workroom behind the 8 West nurse's station to check my work email. My inner peace returns, even if only temporarily. Nothing like silence to soothe the soul. No texts or calls from nurses. And for that matter, no warnings from my IT allies, Patrick and Walter.

Soon, Jane Larsen enters the room.

"Hey, Mark."

"Hello. I trust your day is better than mine?"

"Is it bad like yesterday?"

"No, but I could still use a breather."

Jane flashes a warm smile. Gotta love her positive spirit, the bright sunshine for my black cloud. In all the years I've known her, she has never been angry or hostile toward anyone, at least in my presence.

"Well, enjoy every minute of it," she says, logging into a terminal. "That's what I've always told myself ever since med school."

"I never asked you this. Where did you get your MD?"

"Baylor. Also did my residency there."

"You went to college there, too?"

"No. But I do root for Baylor University's sports teams."

"Are they any good?"

"Have you even been following college basketball? Baylor won the championship on the men's side, a few years ago."

"Really?"

"Oh yeah."

"And the women's basketball team at Baylor?"

"Champions two years before that."

I laugh and shake my head in embarrassment.

"I'm sorry, Jane. I don't follow sports."

"Not even college athletics?"

"Nope. Going to college is supposed to be about getting an education, not sports fanaticism."

"Hey, nothing wrong with hitting the books. I take it you're one of those studious academics."

"Of course."

"Do you dislike the idea of college sports?"

I pause to think.

"I wouldn't call it a dislike. I would say it's overhyped. I get that it can provide a needed break from academic rigor, and it brings in big bucks for the school. But when the biggest news out of a college or university is about the performance of its sports teams, not something else like major contributions from researchers, it makes you wonder where people's priorities really lie."

"That makes sense."

"Honestly, I don't even know the teams at my own alma mater."

"Where did you go for college?"

"UC Irvine. Also for med school and residency."

"Whoa, you did all of that in one place?"

"Yeah. Can you imagine being tied to the same academic institution for eleven years straight?"

"That's amazing. Now, if you're really dedicated, why not just practice medicine there until you retire?"

I stop and look at Jane. She laughs in response.

"I really needed a change in scenery," I finally say. "I just got tired of the whole academic medicine thing."

"I don't blame you. Some of the attending docs I had were too much."

"Hey, have you checked out the news today? I'm wondering if there's anything new with Lucifer's Worm."

"Depends on what you mean by 'new.'"

"Just major developments, like whether things are getting way worse or way better overall."

"Well, the situation isn't too different from yesterday. Too many businesses and organizations are scrambling to function with their computer systems down. I do feel bad for them. Still, I did hear many are having an easier time clearing out that pesky email message and getting back on track."

"Like in this hospital. You got the CEO's text?"

Jane nods in response. Then, to change the topic, she says, "Hey, before I forget, let me ask you something. Peter and I will be going out to dinner tonight, and he wants to meet some of the people I work with. You want to come?"

I've never met Peter, but Jane speaks fondly of him. He's her fiancé. They're getting married sometime this year.

"How many are coming?" I ask.

"So far, Thomas is the only other person."

"You know what? I'll go. Where are we eating?"

"Luigi's on Harbor Boulevard. An Italian restaurant close to Disneyland. That sound good to you?"

"Sure. I haven't had Italian in a while."

"Me neither. It'll be nice to have some of that again."

As I continue deleting emails, my work phone vibrates. Incoming call. I put up one finger, signaling Jane to hold, as I answer.

"Hello?"

"Dr. Lin, this is Bella. I'm taking care of Mr. Donald Chester."

"OK."

"He's refusing surgery."

I pause. This is definitely a first.

"What do you mean?"

"The orderly came here to wheel the patient to the OR, but then the patient panicked and said no."

"You tried talking to the patient?"

"I did, but no luck. He wants to talk to you now."

I shake my head and sigh.

"All right, stay there. I'm coming over."

* * *

This isn't really a life-and-death situation, but I still move quickly as if it is. I rush down one flight of stairs and make my way to room 705. Near the doorway is a gurney next to a man in blue scrubs. I move past him to reach the patient, Donald Chester, who is frowning. And almost crying.

"Mr. Chester, are you OK?"

"No."

"What's wrong?"

Chester shakes his head vigorously.

"I can't do it, Doc. Please don't let Dr. Pierson operate on me."

"How come?"

"He's a mean fellow. You know how he spoke to me this morning? He talked like a drill sergeant, just being rough and barking questions here and there. Then he just said surgery is today, and walked out."

"Just like that?"

"Yeah."

I frown. I know how much of an asshole Pierson really is.

"I'm so sorry he treated you like that."

"It ain't your fault, Doc. You're all right. It's just that Dr. Pierson has no bedside manners. None."

"Your surgery is important. You know that, right?"

"Yes, I do. I know I need it. The problem is the surgeon himself."

I nod and quietly take a deep breath. This is one of those times where I have no choice but to think on my feet. Medical school never taught me how to handle curveball dilemmas like this one.

"What would make you feel better?" I ask.

"I want another surgeon."

"A different one to operate on you?"

"Yes."

"Is that what you want?"

"Absolutely. Either get me someone else, or I'm not going."

I sigh, then nod again.

"OK, let me see what I can do. But keep in mind that this is a very unusual situation. I'm not really sure how this will end up."

"You will try though, right?"

"I'll do that now."

I leave the room. The nurse named Bella, an older Filipino woman, approaches me, and I tell her I'll arrange for another surgeon. The next step is going to be painful, but I have to do it. I take out my work phone and call Dr. Pierson.

Amazingly, he actually answers.

"It's Dr. Mark Lin, calling about Donald Chester."

"Yeah?"

"You're really not going to believe this, but... the patient doesn't want you to operate on him."

"Are you serious?"

"He insists."

"Why?"

"To put it kindly, it's your demeanor towards him. He was very put off by it. Basically, you scared him off."

There is silence on the line. I can't tell how Pierson is reacting, but I expect nothing but the worst.

"That's a load of crap," Pierson barks.

"I swear I'm not making this up. He really isn't happy about the way you talked to him this morning. In fact, let me get straight to the point. He wants someone else to do his gastrectomy."

"*What the hell?*"

I have to pull my phone away. Goddamn, he is fucking loud.

"That's what he told me," I say calmly. "I don't think trying to convince him to just stick with you is going to work."

"Have you even tried?"

"Yes. And he's firm about it, all right? How else can I put it?"

"So what do you want me to do?"

"Can you ask another surgeon to take over his case? It shouldn't be too complicated, I assume. I think it's the only way to keep this patient calm."

"Well, what if I were to say no?"

I stop to think of an answer.

"Then I'll contact the on-call surgeon."

"You better not!"

"Oh, I will."

Then I hang up. Honestly, it feels good to cut off that jerk.

I access my tablet to find out which surgeon is on call today. It's Dr. Gary Thorberg. Good, that is reassuring. I met the guy before and he seems very nice. Probably has good operative table manners as much as bedside manners. I dial Thorberg's number.

"Hi, this is Dr. Mark Lin, internal medicine. Listen, I'm sorry to bother you, but I have a very unusual situation on my hands."

"What's up?" Thorberg asks pleasantly.

"Well, I have a patient who originally came in for bleeding from esophageal varices. That problem is solved, but he also has a stomach tumor. He's supposed to go to surgery right now, but he refused at the last minute because he felt that Dr. Samuel Pierson, the surgeon who did the consult, was rude and condescending to him."

"Oh gee. That's unfortunate."

"And before you ask, yes, I did talk to Dr. Pierson. He's refusing to let another surgeon do the operation. I was wondering if there's a way you can do his surgery instead. I realize the patient might end up getting surgery later because you need to review his case first. But the patient is so upset over what happened that he's adamant about having someone else operate. I doubt he'll change his mind."

I stop to take a deep breath. The phone remains silent for another moment. Please, come on, this is important.

"I'll tell you what," Thorberg says. "Give me the patient name and MRN and I'll see what I can do."

"Seriously?"

"Yeah. But you also have to understand my dilemma. Will I get into serious trouble for doing this?"

"Don't worry, Gary. I'll take full responsibility. If anyone says anything, just have them run it by me."

"You'll do that?"

"Absolutely. You have my word."

"OK. Name and MRN?"

I give him the details about Donald Chester.

"All right, Mark. I'll get to it when I can. OK?"

"Sure. Thank you so much."

Thorberg hangs up. I let out a sigh of relief. But then I toughen myself up again. The next step will be brutal. I call Pierson right back.

"Dr. Lin here. I just spoke with Gary Thorberg. He'll see the patient."

"What? How dare you!"

"I'm sorry, but I had no choice."

"Oh, come on. You really think that's the only option?"

"What would you do?"

"I'd tell the patient he would have to trust me."

"You really think that would work?"

"If he doesn't put his faith in me, that's too bad for him."

Did Pierson just say that? Man, I wish I could record this call. But I'm not physically or legally able to do it, goddamn it.

"Do you know what you're saying?" I ask slowly. "You're suggesting that the patient is supposed to bow down to you if he wants to be treated, and if he refuses and has poor outcomes later, that's his fault."

"I didn't say that."

"But it sounds like it."

"Putting words in my mouth, are you? Well, I should report you to your chief. What's his name? Roger Garrison?"

"Are you even paying attention to the patient's feelings here?"

"Of course I am."

"No, you're not."

"How do you know?"

"Do I even have to explain?"

"Explain what?"

"That you're a self-centered pig who cares more about your reputation as a surgeon than what your patients are going through."

Pierson doesn't answer. But I hear a little heavy breathing, like a raging bull ready to maul someone's ass.

"I'm sure you know that patients are the number one focus," I say. "If they're not comfortable with something, you listen to them and figure out a way to honor their wishes if possible. Is that not something you agree with?"

"All right, fine."

"So why so upset? Just let someone else take over."

"I don't take anyone meddling in my affairs lightly. You had no right to just call another surgeon."

"It's the only way, OK?"

"Then let me tell you something. The next time I see you, I don't want to hear a fucking word out of your mouth. Mark my words. If you dare cross me again, I will make you regret it. You hear me?"

"Hold on, are you threatening me?"

"What does it sound like I'm doing?"

I pause to take a deep breath. And clench my fist.

"Can we just stop this?" I ask slowly.

"Whatever. Now get out of here."

Without hesitation, I hang up.

Not once do I have any regrets. If this asshole wants to play games, fine. I'll beat him and emerge victorious. If this gets me into trouble, then so be it.

CHAPTER 13

To my relief, the rest of the day is uneventful. No Code Blues, no Rapid Responses, no nurse calls. Not even one notification from IT, which is perfect. I call Jay McKinnon, who tells me that he is in the ED, doing patient handoffs with other hospitalists. I head down there, aching to meet my friends for dinner.

In the ED workroom, Thomas Chandler is the one currently signing off his patient list, wirelessly exchanging data between his tablet and Jay's. I wait a few minutes before he is all finished.

"Mark, are you hungry?" Thomas asks, smiling.

"Hell yeah. I'm starving. Now let me do my signout before I collapse here and Jay has to send me upstairs."

Thomas laughs. I begin the usual patient handoff, giving Jay the key bits about each patient and the main issues to watch out for. At first, I wonder if I should just leave it there. But then I think no. Without holding back, I explain the situation about a computer hacker killing my patients, Lucifer's Worm, and how he tried to screw me over today by concealing a patient's blood type. I also mention the IT department officially confirming it all for me, so that there's no question about what's going on.

"That is horrible," Jay says breathlessly.

"Man, I'm amazed you've survived it all," Thomas says.

"I'm trying," I say. "I bring this up because I don't know if the hacker will strike overnight after I leave. So if you can, Jay, pay extra attention to my patients. But don't ignore other patients, in case the hacker decides to take a break from hassling me and go after some other doc."

"Should I actually comb random charts?" Jay asks. "You know, in case I may spot errors in advance?"

"No need," I say. "Just be extra vigilant. And once you resolve a situation, look in the patient's chart in case there is something out of the ordinary. You really don't want to miss that, you know."

Jay nods.

"Aye, captain," he says. "Anything else?"

"Nope. You're good to go. Have a good night."

I sigh with relief, then walk with Thomas side by side through the ED hallway. We head out the front entrance and toward the street. That's where we would turn and stroll to the parking garage next door. I can feel the excitement of dinner building up.

But suddenly, I stop.

So does he.

We spot a crowd of protestors on the sidewalk, in line with the hospital's main doors. Many are holding picket signs, with messages like "Down With Doctors," "Doctors Are the Disease," and even an explicit one: "Fuck Ivory Memorial Hospital." Some also have various objects to make noises, like plastic buckets as makeshift drums. One person seems to be the leader, standing aside with a bullhorn in one hand as everyone else is facing that individual and doing their chants. Goddamn, who the hell are these fools?

"Did something happen here today?" I ask.

"Not that I know of," Thomas answers. "None of my patients had anything tragic happen. What about you?"

"Not really."

"What about anyone else?"

"Other docs in the hospital? Beats me."

"In any event, no need to stick around."

Then I notice the protest leader has already turned to me. I stop. The long red hair comes into focus. Then the face.

Lisa Flint!

"You know her?" Thomas asks.

I turn to my friend.

"The widow of a patient who died," I answer, not daring to make eye contact with Lisa. "The first Code Blue I talked about yesterday, one of the hacker's targets, killed with a digoxin overdose."

"Really?"

"She's not letting this go."

"Come on. Let's get out of here."

Sadly, the only escape is backward. Lisa begins approaching us, then moves faster. The crowd does the same. I move toward the ED's sliding doors, picking up the pace. Thomas follows me with equal stride.

"Dr. Lin, don't you go anywhere!" Lisa screams.

The moment we cross the threshold of the entrance and enter the waiting area, I yell to the triage desk.

"Get security! Angry mob coming!"

The triage nurse, panic in her expression, verbally relays the message behind her. I quickly swipe my ID on a reader to open the double-doors leading into the ED proper. Thomas runs in first. Suddenly, a commotion breaks out from behind, but I don't look. I just focus on the hallway ahead, the portal to safety.

But something yanks me back.

"You killed my husband!" Lisa screeches close to my ear, clenching the back of my collar in a tight fist.

"Calm down," I manage to croak.

"Give me a settlement, or I'll see you in court."

"Can we talk about this?"

She pulls my collar again. Now she's cutting off my trachea, her vise-like grip not giving me mercy. All I can do is try to shake free. I heave to my left, then right, but I'm still stuck. Next thing I know, Lisa's tremendous pull sends me stumbling back. My left foot suddenly crushes one of hers. As she lets out a high-pitched squeal, her grip releases. But now I sail downward, until my ass pounds the hard floor, followed by my torso.

I turn my head to the side. Lisa, with a contorted face of rage, still maintains her balance. Then, one of the seated visitors, a thin middle-aged man, gets up and marches to her. He gets in her face.

"Hey, lady, get the fuck out of here!"

"Says who?" Lisa barks, turning to him.

"Says everyone here waiting for help."

"It's none of your business."

"It is now!"

Suddenly, the man drives both hands into Lisa's shoulders, shoving her back a step. Then she swings a fist towards his face, which he blocks. She tries again with her other hand, to no luck. Now the two lock arms like the horns of dueling rams. I take the opportunity to get up and scramble deeper into the ED.

That's when two beefy male security guards run past me. One grabs Lisa's arms and holds them behind her, then leads her out. The other does the same with the short-tempered man. Soon, a third security guard slowly walks past me to observe that order is restored. Then he turns to me.

"Are you OK?" he asks.

"Yeah," I say, still panting. "Thank you for coming."

"What happened here?"

I tell him everything rather quickly, while still covering the salient points. In the middle of it, Thomas joins me. He has nothing to add to the story.

"Should we call the police, have assault charges pressed against her?" the guard asks me gravely.

I glance through the open doors of the ED entrance. Lisa looks my way, hate filling her eyes, before she is pulled out of view. I wait before answering.

"No."

"Are you sure?" Thomas asks.

"Strange as this may sound, she might regret her mistake."

"After what just happened, you just want to give her the benefit of the doubt?"

I nod slowly.

"The important thing is that it's over. Somehow, I think this will force her to cool down, make her think twice about doing something so stupid."

The truth is, I don't want to be staying here for an hour talking to the police. Besides, I am so fucking hungry right now.

* * *

On the way to the parking garage, I say nothing to Thomas. As a friend, he is showing much concern for me. I have no objections to that. But each time he asks me something, I only answer nonverbally.

"Are you hurt?"

Slight head shake.

"You want to talk about it?"

Another head shake.

"Will you be OK?"

A nod, though I'm not sure I mean it.

We get into our individual cars and drive out of the garage. Because Thomas's assigned parking space is on a different level from mine, neither of us can follow the other. But that's OK. I know where to go. Plus, I do need a little extra time to myself, to clear my mind before dinner. The last thing I need is to meet Thomas, Jane, and her fiancée Peter in a sour mood. I consider pulling up my Spotify music playlist on the dashboard, but decide that even that wouldn't make much of a difference now.

All I want is peace and tranquility.

Nothing is more shitty for doctors than pissed-off patients, at least in my opinion. I know this sounds harsh. I'm even aware of the common advice for doctors facing angry patients, like listening to their concerns, because chances are that it's something like fear driving their emotions. But take a look around. How many people would rather solve their problems through force, rather than peace? I don't know the number, but if you ask me, I don't think it's small. Not even close.

My nerves gradually calm down. On Harbor Boulevard, I pull into the parking lot for Luigi's Italian Bistro. It's a fairly nondescript place on the outside, but through the windows, it looks like a decent fine-dining establishment. I park in a spot close to the entrance, a few spaces down from where I see Thomas's white Kia already parked. I get out and enter the restaurant, my stomach now growling.

Looking around, I find the table in the back where Thomas, Jane, and a man in glasses and light-blue button-down shirt are already seated. I take the last open seat, next to Thomas and across from Jane.

"You made it," Jane says, smiling. "Allow me to introduce you to my wonderful beau, Peter Carpenter."

I shake hands with Peter.

"Nice to finally meet you," I say with an exaggerated smile. "Jane says a lot of good things about you."

"Good to know," Peter says with a laugh.

"Did everyone order already?"

"We're thinking of getting one really large pizza so we can all share," Jane says. "What do you think?"

"Sounds good," I reply. "What toppings?"

"Pepperoni, sausage, mushroom, bell peppers, onions, garlic. Oh, and olives and pineapple, too."

"Fine by me."

As if on cue, a waitress comes by to take our order. Jane rattles off what she just described, and the waitress nods with a smile before taking the menus and leaving. Jane then leans forward toward me and speaks.

"Mark, before you got here, Thomas told us what happened in the ED, how you got attacked. Are you OK?"

"Yeah, thanks for your concern," I say, still somewhat solemn. "I'll live."

"What exactly was her problem?"

"Remember yesterday when I told you one of my Code Blue patients died? That was the widow."

"You're kidding."

"No. Dead serious."

"Mark, you want to tell her about the computer hacker?" Thomas asks.

"Wait, what's going on?" Jane asks, confused.

I fill her in on everything I had told Thomas and Jay earlier. I do it carefully to make sure she understands all of it.

"I should add that the hacker also has my personal phone number," I say. "He's been threatening me over the phone, too."

"Oh, man," Thomas says breathlessly.

"You might as well broadcast it hospital-wide," Jane says. "If you really think the hacker could strike anywhere."

"Right now, it's just me he's after," I say. "Still, what's happening to me is just like what's going on in the rest of the world, after Lucifer's Worm got unleashed."

"Wow," Peter chimes in. "I've heard so many news stories about hackers doing bad stuff. I never heard of one hitting a medical center."

I sigh quietly.

"He might be the only one," I say.

"Are you going to be all right?" Peter asks.

"I hope so. But seriously, how in the world could someone create this kind of malware that could do so much damage?"

"I don't know, but in the world of cyberspace, anything is possible."

"Did I tell you that Peter is a computer expert?" Jane asks me.

"No, you never mentioned it."

"Huh. I thought I did. Anyway, he works as an IT guy. Right?"

Peter nods and kisses Jane on the cheek.

"So Peter," I say. "I've heard of computer viruses that trigger when you open a strange file attachment in an email message. But something unleashed just by opening the email itself? That's unheard of, isn't it?"

"Not really."

"What do you mean?"

"It's been done before. It occurred with the computer worm called BubbleBoy, back in 1999. It went around just by opening the malicious email, not any file attachment. But there's a catch. It only happened with an old version of the Microsoft Outlook email program, specifically the one used in Windows 98, when Internet Explorer was version five. It had a vulnerability that BubbleBoy exploited."

"Wow, I didn't know that. So Lucifer's Worm is much more advanced, but otherwise does the same thing?"

"Pretty much. What's scary is that I cannot fathom how the hacker, or hackers, coded this. We're talking about something that could replicate in a lot of different email clients, not a specific one."

"Why was it called BubbleBoy?"

"You ever watch *Seinfeld?*"

I shake my head.

"There's an episode where Jerry and Elaine are on their way to meet a guy in a bubble, but George and his girlfriend get there first and end up playing a game of Trivial Pursuit with the bubble boy," Peter explains. "The hacker must've been a fan of the show."

"Was the bubble boy immunocompromised?"

"What does that mean?"

"He means a weak immune system," Jane says. "I don't remember the episode mentioning that specifically."

"But it was still funny when the bubble popped," Peter says.

Jane laughs a little, then playfully slaps her man.

"Anyway, hackers have all kinds of inspiration for naming their creations," Peter says. "Another notable example: the Melissa virus, named after a stripper in Florida."

"That's pretty weird," I say. "What about Lucifer's Worm? Do you think its creator is a Satanist?"

Peter nods and smiles. "You know, that's a good question."

"Peter, what is the difference between a computer virus and a computer worm?" Thomas asks, like an eager student.

"A virus is a malicious program that attaches itself to an ordinary program. Running that ordinary program activates the virus. In contrast, a worm can propagate without any user action triggering it."

"Are there other types of malware?"

"There's also the Trojan horse. That's a malicious program disguised to look like a harmless regular application."

"I just realized something," I say, almost smiling. "If Lucifer's Worm were actually a computer virus spreading worldwide, the hacker might call it COVID-19. Or maybe COVID-24, just to be timely."

Peter laughs.

"That's an interesting thought," he says. "It's funny how computer and medical science have a few similarities, like viruses."

"Worms, too," Thomas says. "As in ringworm and tapeworm."

"And you do hear about quarantines in both fields."

"There's quarantining in computers?" I ask, confused.

"If an antivirus program detects malware, it isolates it," Peter explains. "Quarantines it, so to speak."

"Didn't even know that. Now, is there a computer equivalent of bacteria?"

Peter looks up in thought, then shakes his head no.

"What about antibiotics?" I ask.

"Not quite," Peter says.

"Or fungi?"

"No. But as I mentioned, computers use antivirus software, just like there are antiviral medications."

"You know something? Infectious diseases aren't the only medical specialty with similar jargon as computer science. What about neurology? Both the human brain and the computer have memory, right?"

Peter starts giggling.

"Mark, you're funny."

"Nah, it's such a stupid joke," I say.

"But it's witty."

"It's as lame as saying computer mice are like laboratory mice, because both will die if you abuse them."

This time, the whole table laughs.

"Now that's even funnier," Jane says, still trying to compose herself.

I smile as the laughter dies down. Then the conversation proceeds to the little things in life, like the weather, TV shows, and football. I don't really say anything. I just listen. I don't know if it's hunger, frustration, or even depression that's keeping me quiet. I have no desire to speak right now.

Minutes later, the pizza arrives, on a dish that's nearly as large as the wheel of a little kid's bicycle. The aroma is undeniably a delight.

"Bon appetit, everyone," Jane says.

"Wow, this looks really good," Thomas says.

Each of us takes a one-eighth slice. I pick up my knife and fork to savor my first bite while keeping my hands clean. Man, I haven't had pizza in many months. I've forgotten how delicious it is.

"I want to do a quick poll for Mark and Thomas," Jane says. "This is something Peter and I talked about recently."

"What is it?" Thomas asks.

"As you know, we're going to get married later this year, down in San Diego where my parents live. Which name do you think sounds better for me: Jane Larsen, Jane Carpenter, or Jane Larsen-Carpenter?"

Thomas pauses to munch on his pizza.

"I'm thinking Larsen or Carpenter," he says after swallowing. "The combined hyphenated name is too long."

"Mark, what do you think?" Jane asks.

"There's a problem with the second option. If people call you Dr. Carpenter, would they think of you as a lifesaving woodcutter?"

Jane bursts out laughing. So do Peter and Thomas, nearly at the same time. Goddamn, I had no idea it would be that funny. I begin giggling a little, despite myself.

"So you think I should keep my maiden name?" Jane asks, still smiling.

"It's up to you," I answer.

"Which is what I said the other day," Peter says.

Jane nods and brings a slice of pizza to her mouth to chomp on it. Then she raises her glass for a toast, to life and friendship. We clink our glasses and sip. Then my three friends continue talking while I eat in silence.

A few minutes into the meal, my personal phone vibrates. I read the incoming text message:

> *I will get you tomorrow, you white-coat piece of shit! Don't you ever fuck around with me!*

Yep. The devil's phone number is shown as the sender. Once again, what is going on here? At this point, all I want to do is survive. I just need to get through one more day of work. Just one. That's all I ask. If I can do that and Doctor Lucifer doesn't manage to destroy me, I'll be home free.

At least for a little while.

"Buddy," Thomas says, patting me on the back, "you all right?"

I nod, although very slowly.

"Hey, listen, if you're still upset about what happened in the ED, I understand. It's not easy to forget that."

"I just want the nightmare to end," I say firmly. "I never asked for any of it to happen. I'm not just talking about what happened an hour ago. I'm also talking about all of today, and all of yesterday, too."

"None of it is your fault at all," Jane says. "I know you. I've seen you work. You are no doubt a dedicated physician."

"Maybe you need a break," Peter says. "When was the last time you took a serious vacation?"

I look at him, my face still serious.

"Sometime before the pandemic," I answer.

"He's right," Thomas says. "Maybe ask for extra time off. Not just six days. Make it a few weeks. Just get away from everything."

I nod slowly.

"Sure. And whether I'm far away or staying home, I could also watch some more movies. They always help me."

"Maybe try some feel-good movies this time," Jane says. "Nothing wrong with drama, which I know you're kind of a big fan of, but if you're feeling down, you don't want to reinforce it, right?"

"Sometimes I like comedies. You know what one of my favorites is? *Groundhog Day,* which I've seen multiple times. Because it's a metaphor for life itself: the same thing happening over and over again."

"How about I make a film recommendation?"

"OK. What?"

"*The Hangover.*"

"Haven't seen that one."

"Oh man, that movie is hilarious," Thomas says.

"I think you'll like it, Mark," Jane says. "Knowing that you don't drink alcohol, this one will remind you to never start."

"Isn't one of the actors also a doctor?" Peter asks.

"Yeah, Ken Jeong," Jane says.

"That's right. Imagine going from wearing a white coat to being butt-naked in this movie."

Jane and Thomas laugh their loudest yet. I even look around to see if other patrons are turning their heads toward us with annoyed expressions. Thankfully, none of them do.

"All right," I say, smiling a bit. "If I'm the only one at this table who hasn't seen the movie, I'll put it on my list."

"Not far down your list," Jane teases. "The top of it. It shall be your very next one to watch. Because I say so."

"Yes, mother."

She giggles at my sarcastic remark. And on that note, I finish the rest of my dinner, in total silence.

CHAPTER 14

Something is wrong with me. No doubt about it.

I wasn't fully engaged in conversation with my friends tonight. I know it for a fact. I also know that it isn't easy to put on a fake smile and act like everything is OK. I don't do that sort of thing. If I'm genuinely happy and I can honestly say it, sure, I'll join the fun. But if I'm not satisfied with where things are, I'm not going to sugarcoat it.

Why am I like this? Hard to say. Maybe I have too many problems right now to care about how everyone else is doing. Then again, I've been like this my whole life. I've always been antisocial. Not the kind of antisocial with rebellion against authority. The kind where I want to be alone. Unsociable is more like it.

Another possible explanation: I crave attention and approval and I never got enough of either. I can't count all the times I did the right things in life to show I was a worthy individual, only to get picked on in school because young people valued slackers. In my world, there is no such thing as praise for good deeds.

Goddamn it. Everything is fucking backwards.

I think about things like this as I drive home from Luigi's. The sun is still just above the horizon, such that the evening sunlight illuminates my way home. As usual, things gradually get quieter as I leave the busy main road and navigate through the quaint avenues of Anaheim Hills, terminating in the cul-de-sac that shelters me from the rest of society. It is all too quiet once I park in my half-empty garage and shut its automatic door. I walk through the house and then into the backyard for a few minutes, basking in the stars of the night sky, as if the only ones who could honor my presence are the angels above. I think about saying hi to my neighbor, but I assume he and his wife are already inside for the night.

Maybe I'll give him a call, see if he's in the mood to talk.

I head back into the house and shut the patio door. Although I've eaten already, I need to figure out my dinner plan for tomorrow. I open the refrigerator and look inside. Besides breakfast stuff like milk, eggs, yogurt, and orange juice, I have various vegetables like carrots, broccoli, celery, bell peppers, and green beans. I also have packages of raw meat in the freezer. Maybe I could do some homemade stir-fry pork, swimming in oyster sauce plus chili. It's one of many recipes my father taught me. All my life, he's worked as a chef in a Chinese restaurant in the heart of Orange County. He still does now.

I pull out my phone and dial Kenneth Randall's number. I crash onto the living room couch as I hear the ringtones.

"Hello?"

"Ken, it's Mark."

"Oh, hi. What are you doing up so late?"

"Late? It's only eight o'clock."

"I know. I'm just teasing ya."

"Well, I hope I'm not disturbing you or your wife."

"No worries. We're just catching up on the news. I see that Lucifer's Worm is still going around. Maybe at a slower rate, but still, it's not over yet."

I smile and say nothing. It's a rather chilling reminder about how tomorrow could possibly suck ass.

"Let me ask you this, Ken. What was the absolute worst experience with a patient, or a patient's family member, you've ever had in your career? Was it the epiglottis case you talked about?"

There is a pause. He's thinking, I can tell.

"Depends on what you mean by 'worst experience.'"

"OK, I'll cut to the chase. Have you ever gotten sued for malpractice?"

"No, not once. Are you getting sued?"

"I might be."

"You mean it's not official yet?"

"No, but there's still a serious threat of one."

"Is there a chance that it won't move forward?"

"I don't know. I'm just assuming the worst."

During the silence, I ball up like a fetus. But I refuse to cry.

"Mark, it sounds like you're anticipating so much so soon."

"I know, but the person involved is furious with me. And before I forget, yes, this is about the patient of mine who died yesterday."

"If it was just yesterday, you still have time on your hands. After all, the plaintiff would have to obtain medical records and then demonstrate that what you did or did not do was the reason for whatever serious negative outcome the suit is about. Anything can happen from now until then, right?"

"I suppose. But let me tell you. I've never had a patient's loved one who is so angry towards me."

"Maybe she's in pain."

"Even if that's true, it's still a problem when the anger stemming from that pain grows so much that the pain itself is forgotten. Because that's when the only focus is trying to destroy the other person. That's what I'm up against, you see."

The phone is silent again. I'm guessing I've made my point about how fucked up my situation with the Flint widow really is.

"I'm sorry if I'm ruining your evening," I say apologetically.

"No, no, don't worry about it. This is a difficult time for you."

"I guess all I can do is keep making it clear that I did the best I could, and whatever went wrong was not because I was negligent."

"If that is true, then you shouldn't worry so much."

"I'll try."

"Just take the night off and don't think about a thing."

"That's what I'm trying to do now. Anyway, thanks for lending an ear. I'll leave you and Edith to be."

"OK. Goodnight, Mark."

I lie down for a while, letting the tension pass. Then I open the

Breaking Bad disc box on the coffee table, take out the first disc from the set, and pop it into the Blu-ray player beneath the wall-mounted TV. I get ready to hit the play button when the phone rings. Aw, man. Is that Ken again?

No, it's Thomas Chandler.

"Hey, man," I say after picking up.

"Mark, just wanted to check on you again."

"Well, I'm doing OK so far."

"Seriously, if the ED incident was too much, there's no shame in talking about it."

"I believe I already said everything I needed to."

"I'm not forcing you to. I'm just saying."

I pause to see if Thomas would tell me anything else. Then I break the silence.

"The only thing that matters to me is getting through tomorrow."

"Then you're off for six days, right?"

"Exactly."

"It's just one more day. Why worry?"

"You know why."

I wait for his response.

"The hacker," he says.

"Right. It may be one more day, but it's at least ten hours of work. Anything can still happen at any time, you know."

"Are you scared?"

"How can I not be? But there's one good thing. I narrowly saved a patient's life today, and it's a patient whose records the hacker altered."

"There you go, man. Just do it again if you have to."

"I only hope a new threat, assuming there will be one, isn't impossible to beat. I want to emerge victorious, not crash and burn."

"Just stay positive and you'll be fine. What are you doing right now?"

"About to watch *Breaking Bad*. Finally getting around to watching it."

"The box set that Jane got you for Christmas?"

"Yep."

"I haven't watched the show myself, but I hear it's a really good one. All right, man. Enjoy yourself."

"Take care."

I hang up, then use a remote control to start the show. I find myself getting into the story, while also asking a question: How fucked up does the American healthcare system have to be for a chemistry teacher to use his knowledge to cook and sell drugs, just to fund his lung cancer treatment? The idea isn't that farfetched. I've heard of people committing crimes on purpose because some prison inmates get better healthcare than free citizens. What a sad state of affairs.

And that's when I'm finally distracted, by yet another phone call. I pause the Blu-ray player, the TV showing a still of the main character holding a gun outside an RV.

I answer the phone without looking at it.

"*So, the motherfucking doctor is still alive!*"

Doctor Lucifer. I should've known.

"What do you want?"

"*I'm going to take you down, pummel you until you beg for mercy.*"

"Literally?"

"*You know what I mean.*"

"But why?"

No response.

"Why are you harassing me?"

"*You fucking doctors deserve it. For all the shit you do for tons of money. For all the selfish pride that consumes your ego.*"

"What do you mean?"

"*Do I have to explain?*"

"OK, so you hate asshole doctors. Is that right?"

"*Yeah. So?*"

"Then why me?"

"*You're one of them.*"

I shake my head, then quickly change the subject.

"You tried killing four of my patients. That makes you the asshole, doesn't it?"

"*But who's taking the fall?*"

"You're the evil one."

"*No one knows a thing about me.*"

Is this bastard bluffing? I ignore it and answer back.

"Here's the thing. You only killed one out of four patients. You only have a twenty-five percent success rate."

"*I'm not done. Tomorrow, you will see my true power. I will fucking get you, and I will get you good.*"

"Try me, you bastard."

Doctor Lucifer lets out a grumbling laugh.

"*It is you who is the bastard, Dr. Mark Lin. You evil, hateful, murderous, sorry excuse for a healer.*"

"I am no killer."

"*You will be. Because I will make you.*"

"No, you fucking won't!"

I end the call. Doctor Lucifer is getting no mercy from me. Why should he? Goddamn prick.

After putting the phone down, I watch the last few minutes of the *Breaking Bad* pilot episode. As expected, I find myself wanting to watch more of the show. But not tonight. I am tired, not to mention scared shitless. I turn off the TV and Blu-ray player before heading upstairs to my bedroom. I shower and change into sweats before hopping into bed.

I wait for deep sleep to kick in. But all sorts of mental questions race here and there, keeping me up.

Who is Doctor Lucifer?

Why is he tormenting me?

Why me specifically, not anyone else?

What have I done to deserve this?

Is Doctor Lucifer actually a doctor, or working with one?

How in the world am I finally going to slay this beast and defeat him once and for all?

Pretty soon, my mind becomes a haze, and the world fades away. The last thing I remember is heartache. And tears in my eyes.

WEDNESDAY

CHAPTER 15

As usual, I step into the hospital via the ED and text Jay McKinnon to see where he is. He doesn't respond right away.

That's OK, though. I figure he's busy with a patient. Usually, he would return my text within five minutes or so if he doesn't answer right away. So I head up to my cubicle on the eleventh floor, then pocket my fully charged tablet. I also log into my desktop computer to open up my usual applications.

Then I wait another minute. Still no signs of Jay texting or calling back. Gee, where the hell is he?

Rather than waste time sitting, I make use of it by checking my work email. There is one message that catches my eye. The subject line reads, "CEO Statement on Workplace Violence." Right away, I know what it's about: Lisa Flint attacking me yesterday. Sure enough, I guessed correctly. Without mentioning any names, Dr. Jeffrey Winters references the incident and goes on with a generic PR-friendly commentary about how such violence, regardless of who and where, shall not be tolerated. At least the man at the top isn't sweeping this under the rug and burying the truth. I'd be really pissed if he did.

Next, I peruse the latest patient updates on my tablet. It would at least provide sort of a head start when Jay finally returns for the handoff formalities. So far, peeking in each chart, particularly the top of the patient notes list, yields nothing remarkable. It seems like Jay had a quiet night when it comes to my patients.

But then I open the record for Laverne McDonald. Whoa, whoa, whoa. Here's something I never expected.

Jay has posted a note about her, timestamped only a minute ago.

> *At 6:47 AM, I received a call from the nurse about the patient complaining of heart palpitations. Upon my arrival, patient was minimally responsive. EKG on telemetry showed pattern consistent with ventricular tachycardia, with rate of 130 beats per minute. Systolic blood pressure hovered around 95. Code Blue was immediately called.*
>
> *After arrival of Code Blue team, patient was given oxygen via face mask and IV normal saline. Suspect pacemaker-mediated tachycardia based on EKG showing minimal pacer spikes. Adenosine given as IV push, but tachycardia persisted. On-call cardiologist was consulted, who used a magnet over the pacemaker. Heart rate then reduced to around 100 BPM.*
>
> *Patient now transferred to the Step Down Unit, in coordination with Cardiology, for pacemaker interrogation.*

Holy shit! All of this occurred before I had set foot in the hospital. Even the Code Blue alarm. Goddamn, this is shameful. Imagine not being there for a patient, at the worst possible time. I would hate to see her in person right now.

As if on cue, my work phone rings. No surprise about the caller.

"Hello, Jay?"

"Mark, sorry I didn't respond."

"I just found out what happened. I saw your note on Laverne McDonald, the one you just submitted into Icarus."

"I'll tell you more about it. Are you at your cubicle?"

"Yeah."

"I'm coming up."

Jay ends the call, and I wait. It only takes about two minutes before he walks in with a stunned expression.

"Are you all right?" I ask.

"I'll be fine. I'm just a bit shaken."

"I don't blame ya."

"Honestly, I have never encountered pacemaker-induced tachycardia. But at least I remembered bits about it. You know, from past readings on the topic, while flipping through the journals I subscribe to."

"Well, thanks for taking care of it. I feel bad that I wasn't the one there for her. It's like I've disappointed her."

"Don't feel that way. Technically, your shift hadn't started when this happened. It's no different if this happened at, let's say, midnight."

"Was the patient in any kind of pain?"

"Hard to say. When I shook her and asked if she was OK, she barely moaned. She must've been terrified, if she was even awake."

I nod, recalling the words "minimally responsive" in Jay's note.

"At least she hasn't expired," I say.

"Plus, we're talking pacemaker-mediated tachycardia. The prognosis for it is generally good. Expect to see her back on the wards later this week."

"Though I'll be off service."

"You're off after today?"

"Yep. My six days begin then."

"The patient will still be in good hands."

I sigh. But at least I feel somewhat better.

"I suppose you're right, Jay. Anyway, you want to get me up to speed on my patients? I have a computer hacker to outsmart."

Jay nods as we prepare our patient handoff routine. About ten hours to go before reaching the end of the tunnel.

* * *

Other than McDonald's unexpected departure from my list, morning rounds proceed without a hitch. Donald Chester underwent surgery last night, with Dr. Gary Thorberg performing the operation and now assuming the role of consulting surgeon, replacing Dr. Samuel Pierson. As Donald's initial reason for hospitalization was nonsurgical in nature, I am still his main doctor. Other patients are doing fine, too, including Darnell Jackson whose blood glucose is so much more improved that he might go home tomorrow. Tony Palacio, the last patient I visit for the morning, is feeling somewhat better, with the IV antibiotics I had started for him for bacterial gastroenteritis.

I step into the 9 East workroom and log into a terminal. I have plenty of notes to write and orders to submit, but it would all be a piece of cake. An inner peace fills me. Everything could be all right, after all.

Then I get a call. From Walter Laramie.

"Dr. Lin, Patrick and I are seeing new signs of the hacker's movements."

"What's going on now?"

"He's viewing a chart in Icarus, belonging to Tony Palacio. He's one of your patients, right?"

"Yes."

"And let's see... oh, now he's going through another record. The patient is... Donald Chester."

"What should I do? Review those charts for irregularities?"

"No, we have a better idea. Where are you at?"

"Nine East, in the computer room behind the nurse's station."

"We'll be there in a couple of minutes."

Before I can respond, Walter hangs up. But I feel good. He and Patrick are on this. If we are going to work together in person, maybe I could beat Doctor Lucifer again, at whatever game he has in store for today.

I get pretty close to finishing all initial tasks on my patients. Then the two IT technicians come in. This time, I see a much better approximation of Gilligan and the Skipper. The thin Patrick Flanigan is wearing a red, long-sleeve button-down shirt, while the puffy Walter dons a similar blue shirt, with short sleeves. They sit at the circular table along one wall and place their laptops down.

"Are you busy, Dr. Lin?" Patrick asks.

"No. I'm almost done with my stuff."

"While we were in the elevator, our real-time log started showing the hacker looking in a third patient's chart: Darnell Jackson."

"Looks like my whole patient list could be vulnerable. But you don't see the hacker doing anything else?"

"Other than reconnaissance, no."

I nod. At least we're not in the hacker's attack stages. Yet. But what the hell is he going to do? Looks like all I can do is wait and see, then act quickly at just the right moment.

"I got a question," I say. "How is it that this hospital can still be vulnerable to cyberattacks?"

"What do you mean?" Patrick asks.

"It's been two days since the hacker first targeted my patients. Aren't you guys in IT close to putting a stop to this?"

"So far, we managed to get rid of nearly all copies of that Lucifer spam email. It's barely replicating in our network. But we haven't addressed all the backdoors those emails kept placing. That's a separate issue with a separate fix. The random coding of the backdoors makes it super complicated, so it's not like there's an easy one-size-fits-all deal. Believe me, Rajesh and others downstairs are working on it."

"They're still not done?"

"I would say there are hundreds of backdoors remaining in our system. Maybe a few thousand. Who knows?"

"So the hacker can still break in."

"Right."

Great. Just fucking great.

"Is there really no simple way to stop all hacker activity?" I ask. "Like, I don't know, put up an airtight foolproof firewall?"

"It doesn't exactly work that way," Walter says. "It's true that much computer activity in this network is the vital clinical work occurring within this building. But some of it does involve connection to the internet at large, such as sending emails to people outside the hospital. We can't just seal every one of us in and keep everyone else out."

"What about blocking users who aren't authorized?"

"It's tricky," Patrick says. "The easiest way to put it is this: the hacker has multiple ways to evade us. We're playing digital whack-a-mole."

"He's really clever, isn't he?" I say with a sigh.

"I hate to say it, but yes," Walter answers.

"So what's going on with the log right now? Any new hacker activity, with my patients or anyone else's?"

Both Patrick and Walter check their individual laptop screens. A few seconds pass before they turn to me.

"Just more chart combing," Patrick answers. "No edits or deletions yet. You see anything, Wally?"

"No. And don't call me Wally. Patty."

"Wally and Patty?" I ask, smiling. "You guys like teasing each other?"

"Sometimes, when things get tough," Walter says, almost laughing. "Though Patrick's the one who usually starts it."

"I do not," Patrick says playfully. "OK, I do. But you know I'm just kidding around, buddy."

"Oh sure," Walter says, smiling. "Use me as a punching bag. I can handle it. Unlike you, wimp."

Instead of a verbal comeback, Patrick just laughs.

"Is the hacker looking at the same three patients?" I ask.

"So far, yes," Patrick says.

"Hmmm. Maybe the next target will be one of those three. I still cannot imagine what he's going to do."

Moments later, my personal phone rings. It's the familiar demonic phone number again. Doctor Lucifer. I answer anyway.

"*I will stab you in the fucking heart!*"

Then I receive a text, with the exact same words. I put the phone back in my pants pocket.

"Something is going to happen," I say.

"How do you know?" Walter asks.

"Just a gut feeling. Given what I've gone through so far, I'd rather be safe than sorry. You know what I mean?"

"For sure. I totally get it."

Next thing I know, I'm staring at the door. Someone has come into the room. But it isn't just anyone.

Dr. Samuel Pierson, dressed in light-green scrubs underneath a long white coat, marches in and takes a seat at the computer terminal closest to the door. He gives me about seven feet of space. Patrick and Walter are maybe a shorter distance from Pierson than that. I ignore the surgeon and turn to the IT guys.

"At this point," I say. "I'm really relying on you two to help me out. Anything unusual you see, let me know. Call me or text me. Whether I'm available to respond right away, don't worry about it. Just let me know and I'll take it from there."

"Sounds good," Patrick says. "Also, we might end up being too busy with other stuff in our department. We can't guarantee that we'll keep a constant eye out for you. You understand, don't you?"

"Absolutely."

"In addition, don't hesitate to call us," Walter says. "If you see something strange, let us know, in case we can look further and then pass along more stuff we see."

"Great. Basically, if anything bad happens, at least we can prove it's not entirely my fault."

"*Oh, come on! It's always your fault!*"

It's the booming voice of Pierson that shatters the peace. I glare at the surgeon. So do Patrick and Walter.

"What's your problem?" I ask.

"My problem?" Pierson barks, turning to me. "My problem is you, the one who screws up everything."

"What did I do?"

"You took away my case and gave it to Gary."

I sigh heavily.

"Look, it wasn't my idea to begin with," I say. "The patient wanted another surgeon because he was terrified of you. Is that really hard to understand?"

"I could've done just as good an operation."

"But the patient didn't want you to. Just let it go, OK?"

"Why should I?"

"It's just one patient refusal. You'll always have many more surgical cases coming your way. No need to get upset."

The next thing Pierson does surprises me. He stands up and then slowly walks to me. He is now towering above me, looking down. I slowly get up to meet his gaze. We are only inches apart, close enough for his hot breath to hit my face.

"You should not have dissed me the way you did," Pierson says softly, pointing a finger at my chest.

"I was listening to my patient and his wishes," I say, even more softly. "Shouldn't you do that, too?"

"I don't need you lecturing me."

"I'm just trying to help."

"By interfering with my case?"

"Your case?"

"Yeah, I was supposed to be the one doing his surgery."

"Don't forget. I'm the main doc. You're the consult."

Pierson's mouth tightens, hard as stone. In the lower part of my vision, I barely see two clenching fists.

"What are you doing?" I ask nervously.

"What do you think I'm doing?"

"You're threatening me. Come on, Dr. Pierson, this is stupid. Just calm down, will you? Let's talk this over."

"Not until you apologize."

I slowly shake my head. Big mistake.

Pierson quickly grabs my shirt with both hands. He shakes me violently. I attempt to pry his hands off, but can't.

"*Do I have to fucking make you?*" he growls.

"Let me go!"

But he doesn't. Instead, he shoves me backwards. I trip over my chair and stumble into the wall behind me. I lean into the wall to stop short of dropping to the floor. As I straighten up, he takes two steps closer. Then my adrenaline skyrockets, time slows down, and nothing matters except this deadly mano a mano, face to face with the embodiment of every asshole doctor who has ever given me shit. I don't know if it is rage, fear, or a mixture of both. I just know something has forced my next move.

A solid upward kick to Pierson's nuts.

Then he pins me to the wall. Behind him, Patrick and Walter rush in my direction. For a moment, they disappear from view, behind Pierson's body. Then a pair of hands grips his left forearm. Another pair grabs the right. While Patrick and Walter try pulling Pierson off, I use the force of my own hands to loosen his fingers locked around part of my shirt. It is enough. The forces of blue and red pull the green monster off me. Patrick slips and falls down. So does Walter, who momentarily holds his balance and sends Pierson flying toward the other side of the room into two consecutive wheeled chairs. The surgeon faceplants into the floor. Walter gets up, breathing heavily through his mouth.

He and I help Patrick back onto his feet. Pierson slowly gets up, grimacing. Then the surgeon stops, realizing he is now cornered. Not just by his three adversaries, but also by the five or so heads peering in from the doorway.

"You should be ashamed of yourself," I say loudly. "And don't you dare try to hide from this. We all saw it."

This time, there is no pushback from Pierson. Not even a hint of an apology. All he does is leave the room, standing tall and looking ahead without any sign of remorse. The witnesses step aside nervously as the surgeon disappears from sight.

"Are you all right, guys?" I ask.

"Yeah," Patrick says, panting.

"My god, I've never seen anything like this," Walter says.

"You ain't seen nothing yet," I say bitterly.

"Are some doctors really that bad?"

"They can be."

Then I walk out.

* * *

Time for another retreat to my safe space.

I enter the staff restroom at the end of the hall, another one of those tiny enclosures rivaling an airplane lavatory. I take a piss, wash my hands, and just stand there. No way I'm going back out. I have to wait until the heat dies down, along with my racing heart, body tension, and inner turmoil. I even close my eyes as if I'm meditating. It barely helps, but whatever.

If anyone is still bowing down to Dr. Samuel Pierson, worshipping him on a pedestal without seeing the piece of shit he really is, I dare them to explain the chaos in the 9 East workroom. If they still stand by his side, fuck 'em. They're full of crap, too. I've had enough of people like him, selfish pricks who never put others first. And if they happen to don a white coat and flash a medical degree, shame on them for bringing down the profession. I didn't sign up for this bullshit.

All of a sudden, it dawns on me.

It's one of those moments where certain things seem to fit, where the stars appear to line up just perfectly. I now have a theory, though a very flimsy one. It's only a remote possibility and I have absolutely no proof of it. But the more I think about it, the more I wonder if it might be true.

Could Doctor Lucifer actually be Dr. Samuel Pierson?

Sure, he's not likely a computer expert, let alone a hacker. But does that necessarily mean he's working alone? Far from it. He could be working with a computer hacker. Pierson may be manning the phone with the vicious threats while his ally is doing the cyber grunt work. I don't know. I really don't. But I can't help but wonder.

I step out of the restroom and head toward the elevator. Then I get an incoming text, on my work phone. It's from Dr. Roger Garrison. My heart stops upon reading it.

Mark, come to my office. NOW!

CHAPTER 16

One thing I've always taken pride in is never getting into trouble. All my life, I stayed as far away from it as humanly possible. No one could ever accuse me of being a truant or a criminal. I have no records of either. I can also attest to never setting foot in a school principal's office, police station, courthouse, jail, or prison for breaking a serious rule or two. Growing up, I was the kind of person who made parents and teachers proud. Personal responsibility was my middle name.

Yet, here I am: arms crossed, face neutral, staring straight ahead. Yeah, I'm in some really deep shit.

From behind his desk, Dr. Roger Garrison eyes me coldly. His lips curl downward and remain that way.

"Do you have any idea what you've just done?" he asks, an octave higher than his usual conversational tone.

I wait without moving my head in any direction. I just blink. No point in making this worse. I decide to just let Garrison take the lead.

"Well?" he says.

"I didn't start the fight."

"Doesn't matter. You still hit him back."

Technically, I kicked Pierson back, not hit him back. But whatever. This is no time to debate semantics.

"He made the first move, then tried to make a second," I say, finally putting my arms down. "I had no choice but to defend myself. It's not like I could just ask him to stop. He was beyond that point."

"What the Chief of Surgery told me is that, according to Dr. Pierson, you were the one who attacked him first."

"That's a lie."

"Is it?"

"Yes. That's not what happened."

"Then what did?"

"Like I said, he came at me first. If you don't believe me, ask all the witnesses. Some nurses saw it, after hearing some noise outside the room. And don't forget the two men I was in the room with."

Garrison sighs and tilts back in his chair. I can tell this isn't what he was expecting. It's now his turn to cross his arms.

"All right, Mark. What's your version of the story?"

Carefully, I walk him through every moment in the 9 East workroom. When I get to the part with Pierson entering the picture, I make sure to slow down. The details have to really sink in for the chief. I treat him the way a prosecutor sways a cold impartial jury with an airtight closing argument. I give him a word-for-word recall of the verbal banter, then the blow-by-blow account of Pierson's attacks followed by my retaliation. I especially mention Patrick and Walter who pulled the surgeon off me, to make it clear it wasn't all me. I tell this part of the story with my eyes closed, trying to conjure up vivid mental images that could help me describe it. At last, I reach the end of the tale, with Pierson walking out the door and through the crowd of shocked onlookers.

It is time for the chief's verdict.

"I swear I'm not making this up," I say calmly, after a long silence.

Somewhat to my relief, Garrison nods. Then he leans forward on his desk and folds his hands.

"I suppose you have been under tremendous pressure lately, Mark. That amount of stress could certainly make any typically sane person lose their cool."

"Sounds about right."

"And you were, to a certain extent, acting in self-defense."

"I was."

"I imagine another thing may be a factor: the incident in the ED yesterday, with Lisa Flint attacking you."

"You know about that?"

"One of the ED managers sent me an email about it. He recognized you and mentioned your name."

I nod slowly.

"Has it bothered you since it happened?" Garrison asks.

"Of course. Then I just slept it off."

"Is this something you want our Department of Medical-Legal Affairs to address?"

"Meaning like a lawsuit?"

"That and whatever other options are on the table."

"As awful as this was, maybe Mrs. Flint was having a very rough time with her husband's loss."

"You don't wish to take any action?"

"For now, no."

"And you're sure about this?"

"Yes, because I'm already dealing with so much as it is. I don't need anything else besides the lawsuit Mrs. Flint wants to file."

"How did you come into contact with her in the ED in the first place?"

"It was the other way around."

"How so?"

"It started as a protest outside the emergency department. She was probably trying to gain enough attention to pressure this hospital into firing me or offering some other kind of compensation for her husband's death. I was leaving for the day through the ED entrance. When she saw me, she chased me into the ED, and I had to run back inside for safety. That's when she attacked me, demanding that I give her a generous settlement or else. Looking back, it seems she is in a real rush for justice, given that it's only been a little more than a day since her husband died."

Garrison slowly takes in a deep breath. He's obviously digesting this. I'm not sure if the ED manager knew about the protest before the attack. No matter. The chief is finally hearing it from me.

"It looks like this will really hurt her case," he finally says.

"I agree."

"She didn't follow through with her complaint to Patient Services, letting them investigate the matter. She just went straight to harassing you. If a malpractice lawyer asks if she made any effort to discuss the matter or compromise, it will be pretty much impossible for her to proceed with taking us to court."

"Because she hasn't satisfied any pre-lawsuit requirements."

"Right. So there's no need to worry about her."

I look down at the floor. At this point, I don't care anymore. Whatever he wants me to do about whatever, I'll do it. Just let me get through my day so I can get the hell out of here. That's all I ask.

"Meanwhile, there's another thing that can put this matter to rest. I finally spoke with Rajesh Krishnan, the head of IT."

"Wait. He called you?"

"No, I called him this morning. I wanted to follow up on what you talked about yesterday. We had quite a long discussion, about everything a mysterious computer hacker has been doing to your patients. What you had suspected yesterday."

I sit up in my chair. Holy shit, he's actually listening to me now?

"I'm sure it's hard to believe," I say.

"He told me about what IT found, what you had gone through, and how you all pieced everything together. He also explained how you are now working together with two of his associates, in order to stay one step ahead of the hacker."

"Do you know what happened yesterday?"

"What are you referring to?"

"I had a patient whose blood type, well, got concealed in her record. It was the hacker's doing, and IT was noticing it in real time."

Garrison nods in recognition.

"Yes, Rajesh did go into that. I have to say. It's quite stunning what transpired. I'm also amazed that you still managed to figure it out. Good job with that."

Yay. The first compliment from the chief all day. I nod with a tiny smile, then put my poker face back on.

"Now I understand what happened two days ago, with three patients affected at once," the chief says.

"I would prefer not to talk about it again."

"No need to, but I want to mention this. Given the evidence that we have about a computer hacker sabotaging the system and killing Christopher Flint, we can now build a defense should his widow proceed further with her litigious actions."

"Finally."

"I know I wasn't keen on the idea before, but after all the things Rajesh shared with me, I can see you're onto something."

"So if we do work on a defense against whatever Mrs. Flint throws at us, what would that involve?"

"Rajesh will begin preparing a report that details the actions of this hacker, based on the information they have as well as what you provided to them."

"Would I be helping out with that?"

"No, don't worry about it. I do not want any of it to interfere with your patient care duties. OK?"

I nod. That's a relief.

"At the same time, the hacker could still strike any moment," I say. "Before the incident with Dr. Pierson, the two IT technicians were informing me that the hacker was combing charts of my patients again."

"Couldn't they somehow block the hacker directly?"

"Not without affecting certain work-related functions."

"Are you ready to respond if something happens?"

"I think so. That's not to say I'm not afraid. Because I am."

"I understand."

I let out a heavy sigh. Garrison straightens up in his chair. I see no hint of displeasure. If anything, I sense worry.

"I imagine that if I were in your shoes, Mark, I'd be very afraid, too. This is an unfortunate situation."

"You know what else is unfortunate? Not knowing who this hacker is or why he's doing it. There's an infinite number of possible answers to each of those questions, and I don't have anything to narrow them down."

"I get it, Mark. I really do. At the same time, try not to obsess over it so much. This is undoubtedly another source of your stress. Remember, you want to manage that, keep it to a minimum where possible. It starts with not letting one thing become too great a concern. Do you know what I'm saying?"

I nod without hesitation. Then I feel a vibration. In my pants pocket. My work phone. I check it.

It's a text from Walter Laramie.

> *The hacker has altered a medication order. ID of patient pending. Call if you need assistance.*

"What is it?" Garrison asks.

At first, I consider lying, just to avoid complicating things. But now that the chief is on my side, I give him an honest answer.

"It's one of the IT guys. The hacker has done something. I have to go."

"OK, Mark, get back to work. I'll speak with the Chief of Surgery to update him. Good luck."

I leave the office, reinvigorated. I have been validated, but I'm also on edge. Which patient is next on Doctor Lucifer's hit list? It is surely coming, and soon.

I approach the elevators as I try to text Walter back. But then the phone vibrates, and I answer right away.

"Dr. Lin," a woman's voice answers, somewhat frantically. "This is Becky, the nurse for Mr. Darnell Jackson, room 903. I need you here immediately. His heart rate is only fifty beats per minute."

"Hang in there. I'm coming down."

I end the call and hold my head high. It is time to go into battle, another holy struggle. The angel versus the demon. Life versus death. Dr. Lin versus Doctor Lucifer.

A fight for the soul of a helpless mortal.

CHAPTER 17

Darnell Jackson isn't dead, but he sure looks like it. Eyes closed, mouth open, head turned to one side, and not a tiny hint of movement anywhere. First things first: check his mental status. I gently shake him.

"Mr. Jackson, can you hear me?"

I barely hear a grumble. His eyes remain closed. At least he hasn't expired.

I check for a wrist pulse. There is one, but it's faint and infrequent. I don't need to count the beats and look at my watch to know the patient is bradycardic. Why in the world is his heart beating so damn slow?

The nurse named Becky, a brunette in pink scrubs and thick-framed glasses, looks at me with concern.

"What's his blood pressure?" I ask her.

"Ninety-seven over forty-six."

"Pulse ox?"

"Ninety percent so far."

"He got his meds as scheduled?"

"Yeah. He got his insulin this morning."

"Both types?"

"Yes. And he got propranolol a bit later."

Suddenly, I hold my breath. My heart now has its own abnormal rhythm, a fast one. Goddamn it! That's what Doctor Lucifer has done, right under my nose.

"Propranolol? I didn't order propranolol."

"Oh my god, you didn't?" Becky says, gasping. "I don't get it. Why is it in his medications list?"

"Something's very wrong. When did you give him propranolol?"

"About fifteen minutes ago, I think."

"How much?"

"Three milligrams, IV."

Shit, this isn't good. Given Jackson's comorbid illnesses, that heart medication would be too much for him, certainly enough to slow his heart.

"Call a Rapid Response," I say urgently.

The nurse runs out and yells the same message to the nurse's station. I pull out my tablet and frantically access an online medical resource called *UpToDate*, quickly reviewing the management of beta-blocker overdose to make sure I don't screw this up. The hospital PA system announces a Rapid Response for this very room. I put my tablet away and get to work.

I shake the patient once more, but this time, he makes no sound at all. I press a button on the bedrail to lower his head all the way to horizontal. Footsteps begin echoing faintly from the hallway, then quickly grow louder before exploding into the room all at once. I throw out rapid-fire directives.

"I need a milligram of atropine, plus an EKG. Becky, start him on normal saline, half a liter."

I place my hand just above the patient's open mouth. Minimal breath coming out. I order someone to use a face mask and Ambu bag. Meanwhile, another person is prepping a syringe, presumably with the atropine to get the heart going and counteract the propranolol. Across the room, Becky rushes back into the room with an IV bag, which she begins hanging on the IV pole. I remind her to check Jackson's blood pressure again sometime after starting the infusion.

Nearby, a woman in blue has already gotten an EKG machine ready. She attaches the electrodes to Jackson's chest before pressing the record button. As I wait, I feel Jackson's wrist pulse again, which is still slow and weak. Once the EKG spews out its sheet with Jackson's cardiac tracing, I glance at it. There are normal P-QRS-T complexes, but spaced pretty far apart, just like the patient's pulse. Classic textbook bradycardia.

The Ambu bag breaths are inflating Jackson's chest, making it rise and fall. Airway and breathing, check. Circulation, still a big question mark.

"Blood pressure ninety over fifty-two," Becky announces. "Pulse ox ninety-three percent."

"Check his blood sugar, too."

"OK."

Knowing that Jackson has type 1 diabetes, I have to watch out for hypoglycemia, because beta-blockers often enhance the effect of insulin. If that were the case, I would also tell Becky to push a bolus of IV glucose.

I feel for another pulse. No improvement. Knowing how much time has passed roughly, I ask someone to give another one milligram of atropine, and get epinephrine ready, too, just in case. Moments later, I watch a syringe deliver an IV push. Atropine dose number two, done.

Minutes go by. Becky tells me his blood sugar is 160 milligrams per deciliter. Higher than normal, but hey, at least he isn't hypoglycemic like around 40 or whatever. His heart rate remains a little over 50 beats a minute, still better than crashing down towards zero. The man is holding steady.

After a little more work, I'm beginning to think Jackson will make it. Maybe he won't be one of the worst case scenarios for beta-blocker overdose, but I better not get cocky. I try speaking to the patient and he still doesn't respond. He's still too out of it to stay here on the regular ward floor, while not sick enough to go back to the ICU.

There is only one place to send the patient to.

"Take him to the Step Down Unit," I say to the room. "I'll do the transfer orders."

The staff begin clearing the space, then move the patient's bed toward the doorway. I make mental notes of the key items for the transfer orders.

Assessment: bradycardia, secondary to inadvertent beta-blocker administration. I'm trying to avoid the word "error" and any other form of it.

Plan: telemetry monitoring, vital signs every four hours, blood glucose checks also every four hours.

Medications: same as before, with no propranolol of course.

The idea is to watch over Jackson, giving him enough time for his heart to get back to normal on its own. If anything goes wrong, the Step Down Unit team will handle it. He'll be out of my hands, for better or for worse.

Once I follow the bed out of the room, I stop in my tracks. The wife and brother have arrived. Nina and Jerome stand in the hallway, wide-eyed as their beloved Darnell is wheeled past.

"I can explain," I say quickly.

Both of them approach me. Their eyes and mouths narrow and tighten, switching from disbelief to borderline rage.

"Dr. Lin, what's going on?" Nina shrieks.

"Darnell's heart slowed down," I say carefully.

"But why?" Jerome asks incredulously. "He looked much better yesterday. What happened?"

"A really bad mistake occurred," I respond.

"Mistake?" Nina utters loudly.

Next thing I know, she is turning to her brother-in-law, who returns an equally baffled expression. Both look at me again.

"I am just as shocked as you are," I say, trying to sound soothing. "What I'm about to say is not going to be easy to hear."

"Just tell us," Nina says, crossing her arms.

I sigh before answering. Here goes nothing.

"There was a very unfortunate medical error. Darnell received a heart medication that slowed his heart down. It's not something I ordered at all, yet the nurse somehow thought I did. I still need to look into it to find out what exactly went wrong. I am really, really sorry that this has happened."

Nina closes her eyes tightly. I don't see tears coming down, but I know there is pain. Jerome puts one arm around her, and then buries her face into his shoulder. While comforting her, Jerome speaks up, with restrained tension.

"How the hell could there be another mistake? Come on. You're supposed to be the doctor. I thought you said it won't happen again."

"I do take responsibility for this," I say. "Again, I'm sorry."

"Whatever, man. Is he going back to the ICU?"

"No. He'll be in the Step Down Unit. That's the transitional unit right outside the ICU. We can take comfort knowing he's there instead of the ICU."

"He's not going to die, is he?" Nina asks, turning to me.

I shake my head.

"I think he'll be fine. He'll need to be monitored to see if the effects of that heart medication wear off. Should there still be problems, there are other treatment options they can do for a slowed heart."

Nina and Jerome say nothing. They step about ten feet away from me and look at each other, their backs turned toward me. I look away, yet my ears can barely pick up their words.

"I thought Darnell was in good hands," Nina says. "After what just happened, I'm not so sure."

"I know," Jerome says. "We'll keep watching over him, just like each and every day. I pray he'll make it."

"I hope you're right. I'm just... I'm just so upset over this."

"I am, too. But we can't give up."

"Of course we won't."

"I know you've been let down by doctors before. I, too, have my doubts. But what else can we do?"

"I just want Darnell home again. I miss seeing him happy and living life, without any needless suffering."

There is silence after that. Quickly, I pull out my tablet and pretend to sift through it. I can't get caught eavesdropping on a conversation supposedly out of earshot from me. My only role is to help the patient, and despite my best efforts, Doctor Lucifer has thrown two strikes on Darnell Jackson. I do take comfort in one thing, though. I would not likely be seeing this patient or his family for the rest of the day. That would spare me the humiliation of a third strike to throw me out.

I wait for Nina and Jerome's next move. They simply walk further down the hall, leaving me all by myself.

* * *

In the 9 West workroom, I complete my transfer orders for Darnell Jackson, then remove him from my patient list. In a way, this is a cleansing, a purge, so to speak. I have nothing against the patient at all, but I don't need any reminders of how I am being increasingly cursed. Plus, I really need to watch who's left on my service.

I look at the clock. 12:30 PM. But I'm not hungry anymore. I've lost my appetite with one setback after another.

I haven't checked my work phone since coming down from the eleventh floor. The only new thing is Walter's follow-up text confirming that Darnell Jackson is the patient associated with the altered medication order. Then I think about his previous message. If I had more time, I could've scanned my patients' charts until I come across some indication that Darnell Jackson would be getting propranolol, then I could call the nurse to tell her not to give that drug at the last minute. But what's done is done.

I would now have to get the details after the fact. I text Walter my delayed reply.

> *Something did happen. I need to talk to you and Patrick. Call me or see me in the 9 West workroom within the next few minutes.*

For a while, I do some follow-up work with my other patients. Then nurse Becky comes in, and I put it aside.

"Dr. Lin, do you have a minute?"

"Sure. What's up?"

Becky pulls a chair from a nearby round table and sits down, facing me while I am at my computer terminal. She pulls out a pack of Kleenex from her scrub pocket as tears begin filling her eyes.

"Tell me the truth," she says, dabbing her eyes with tissue. "Did I make a really big mistake?"

"No," I answer without a thought.

"But I gave him propranolol, and look what happened."

I look at her with sympathy. Becky is quite young, likely in her twenties, though she could easily be mistaken for a teenager. I'm also guessing that she graduated nursing school not too long ago.

"It's not your fault. You were doing your job as you've always done. It's pretty hard to notice something so unusual like this."

Becky nods slowly.

"Dr. Lin, I'm just afraid the family will sue us for malpractice. Who's going to take the blame?"

"It's not going to be you. It may be me, but I'll fight it if I have to. Especially if I figure out how this error occurred. And I think I know where to start."

"Where?"

"You know about Lucifer's Worm flooding email systems, while leaving openings for hackers to break into networks?"

"Yeah, it's eerie."

"Long story short, I talked to the IT department here. I have proof that a hacker has gone into this system and screwed things up to harm my patients."

"Really?"

I don't answer yet, because I spot Patrick Flanigan and Walter Laramie entering the room with their laptops.

"Perfect timing," I say. "Becky, this is Patrick and Walter. They are two IT technicians who've been helping monitor the hacker's movements."

The nurse nods with a smile, her eyes still red. The two men wave and say hello. I continue to speak.

"Guys, the patient Darnell Jackson mistakenly received a medication slowing his heart down. He'd gone from the ICU to this floor, but now had to be transferred to the Step Down Unit because of this grave error. I need you to help us figure out what exactly the hacker did this time around."

Fixated on their laptop screens, Patrick and Walter pull up the latest network log information. I wait for them to find the best place to begin.

"After scanning different records earlier this morning, the hacker accessed a patient's chart," Patrick says. "Not for one of your patients, Dr. Lin, but a patient for another physician. Then, at 10:04 AM, a medication order from that chart underwent some kind of editing."

"Walter did send me a text about an altered med order," I say. "But sadly, I didn't have time to look into it."

"Not too long after I texted you, we saw something else," Walter says. "Deletion of the altered order for that other patient, followed by the creation of a new medication order for one of your patients, who we now know is Mr. Jackson."

I hold up a finger, signaling for everyone to pause. I need time to ponder on this. But several seconds later, nothing is obvious.

"How far apart were those two actions?" I ask.

"They're practically simultaneous," Walter says.

"We were trying hard to figure this one out," Patrick says, scrolling through the log some more. "Eventually, we got it."

"Yes?" I say.

"The hacker changed a medication order for a patient not in your list, then moved it into Jackson's chart. If that moving process involving cutting something in one place and pasting it somewhere else, that could explain the two log entries being simultaneous. Does that make sense?"

"Now it does. The hacker altered an order for the heart medication propranolol, changing the patient's name to Darnell Jackson and the physician's name to mine. Then he moved it to Jackson's chart, to make it look like I ordered it."

For the first time, Becky speaks up.

"Then how come I got the order to give it?"

Patrick nods before giving his answer.

"There's something else. The hacker also went into the inpatient pharmacy system. We have record of an alteration made to one specific document there."

"Normally, medication orders have a two-step process," Walter explains. "Step one is the physician submitting the order. That creates a record for the chart. In response to step one, step two is a second copy of that order going into the pharmacy's system. We believe that's what the hacker went for."

"In order to make the same changes," I say, nodding.

"Right," Patrick says. "And theoretically, if there are any kinds of flags or safeguards to prevent medication errors, the hacker could've made other changes to bypass them."

"Anything else after that?"

Patrick and Walter shake their heads.

"That would result in you seeing instructions to give propranolol," I say to Becky. "Is that what happened?"

"Yes. And to be quite honest, I was surprised to see that. But then I looked in the chart and saw that you ordered propranolol, so I thought you did order it. Obviously, it's now clear you had not."

"That's why the fault does not lie with you. Or even me for that matter. It's whoever this computer hacker is."

"I can't believe someone could be so cruel, hurting a patient this way."

"And he's already struck other patients' records, all involving me."

"That's awful."

Patrick and Walter turn away from their laptops to face Becky.

"It's unbelievable what hackers are capable of," Patrick says. "I don't know how much you follow the news, but do you remember when a hacker broke into a computer at a water treatment plant in Florida and actually attempted to add high levels of a dangerous chemical to the drinking water supply?"

"Oh, I think I heard about that," Becky says.

"The hacker had remote access to that computer," Walter says. "He was able to move the mouse cursor and change the chemical settings. Thankfully, the supervisor noticed the moving cursor and put an end to it."

The conversation among the nurse and the IT specialists continues, but I get distracted. My personal phone buzzes, followed by my work phone. I answer the personal phone first, knowing exactly who's calling.

"*See? You're not so clever after all. You really are a bad fucking doctor!"*

I quickly end the call without a word. As I get ready to answer the work phone, I stand up quickly.

"I have to go," I say. "Patrick, Walter, thank you for your help again. And Becky, I hope you feel better. Don't cry, OK?"

"I won't," she says, with a bigger smile this time. "In fact, I feel much better now thanks to all of you."

As I rush out of the room, I answer the work phone. The caller is a nurse named Brian, who is taking care of Tony Palacio in room 926. The news from him is even more strange than what I'd already gone through today.

The patient has disappeared.

CHAPTER 18

In 9 East, I spot Brian, a lone thirty-something male nurse in light-blue scrubs. He emerges from room 926 and looks down the hallway. Then he tilts his head up slightly. He waves once he spots me, and I speed toward him.

"What happened?" I ask.

"I don't know," Brian answers, somewhat nervously. "I last saw him about ten minutes ago, when I checked his vital signs. Then, when I came back in to give him his medications, he was gone."

"He wasn't in the bathroom?"

"No."

"Did he simply take a walk around this floor?"

"Nope. I even checked the wardrobe. His clothes and belongings aren't there, either. I think he's split for good."

I close my eyes and sigh. This is just great.

"Has anyone else seen him?" I ask.

"That's the thing. I asked every other nurse here, giving them a description. Nobody saw him leave."

"Not even the head nurse?"

"Nope. I already asked her."

"All right. Time to call security."

Brian follows me to the nurse's station. Because he was the one who brought up the issue, I let him take the lead. The head nurse, a middle-aged lady in glasses named Jackie, looks up as we approach.

"Tony Palacio in 926 is gone," Brian says. "Can you call security, in case he hasn't really left this building?"

Jackie nods, picks up the station phone, and presses a speed dial button.

"Can you describe him?" she asks.

"About five foot six, short brown hair that's starting to go gray," Brian says. "Oh, and a small goatee."

"Body size?"

"Fairly thin."

"OK, wait."

Jackie holds up one finger as she kindly greets security and passes along the physical description of Tony Palacio. There is a pause, maybe like a minute long. Then she nods slightly, thanks security, and hangs up.

"Security checked its cameras, and they don't see him," Jackie says. "They will keep their eyes open, just in case."

"Maybe we should call the patient directly," I suggest.

"Exactly my thought. Let me open his record and find his phone number. You want to call him?"

I nod as Jackie turns to her computer. I smile a little, as if I could actually bring some cheer to this bummer of a situation.

"Have you ever had anything like this happen?" I ask Brian.

"Nope. Before today, the weirdest patient I ever dealt with was a man who totally faked his illness."

"Why was that bad?"

"He wanted the free hospital food, bed, and TV."

"He was mooching off the healthcare system?"

"Pretty much. I can't imagine what his home situation was like to drive him into doing something like that."

"Did he get caught eventually?"

"Yeah. And needless to say, the doctor who ordered his CT scan was really not happy about it."

"I can imagine. I'd be pissed, too."

Moments later, Jackie turns to us.

"OK, here's his phone number," she says, handing me a sticky note. "Record says it's a mobile number."

"Let's see if he still answers it," I say, pulling out my work phone.

I dial Palacio's number and wait. I half expect that I would be taken to voicemail, in which case I would leave a message warning him about leaving the hospital without notice. I'd have to force myself to sound polite, while still being firm.

To my surprise, he answers.

"Hello?"

"Mr. Palacio, this is Dr. Mark Lin at Ivory Memorial. Where are you?"

"Where do you think I am, huh?"

Palacio's voice booms. He is playing the role of tough guy. If he could possibly get hostile, I have to play my cards right.

"Are you in the hospital or not?" I ask.

"Hell no. I already got the fuck out of there."

"Can you explain why?"

"Do I have to?"

"I want to understand what you're concerned about."

I hear nothing. Maybe he's debating whether to just hang up on me. Or making some obscene gesture toward his phone.

"All right, Doc. You want to know why I left? I'll tell you. The hospital is a madhouse. A big fucking madhouse."

"What do you mean?"

"I was taking a walk in the hallway when I heard some noise. A few nurses crowded around a doorway, so I came by to look. Turns out you and some other doctor were fighting! What the fuck, man?"

I bury my face in one hand. Suddenly, I'm the one in deep shit.

"I am very sorry you witnessed it," I say calmly. "I found myself having no choice but to defend myself."

"Not from where I was standing."

"I get that it's a highly unusual situation, a one-of-a-kind deal."

"Hell yeah, it is. This is a hospital, not a fucking prison."

"Look, I'm not going to delve into greater detail about what happened this morning. But at least hear me out on this. It is unsafe for you to leave the hospital without being formally discharged."

"So? At least I'm a hell of a lot safer."

"You haven't finished your antibiotics."

"Oh, was I supposed to stay until the end of it? That's a whole fucking eternity right there!"

"My plan was to discharge you once your GI symptoms improved enough. It probably would be another day or so. Then I could prescribe antibiotics in pill form for you to finish at home."

"Well, I ain't gonna wait."

I stop to compose my next statement. A tension flows through me from head to toe. I begin gripping the phone, and clenching a fist in my other hand.

"Mr. Palacio, you must understand. If something were to happen to you from here on out, I cannot be responsible for the consequences, given that you chose to leave against medical advice."

"I don't goddamn care, all right? I'm sick and tired of doctors like you, who can't even control their fucking temper."

"Do you least comprehend what I'm saying?"

"Yeah."

"About how you're assuming the risks of what you are doing?"

"Yes, I got it, all right? It's all on me. Happy now?"

I nod, as if I were speaking to him in person. At this point, I know I cannot change his mind. At least I've made it clear that if my former patient gets sicker, or dies, no one could blame me for it. He chose to make a break for the exit. I was doing my job, following acceptable standard of care. A malpractice jury ought to see that clearly.

"If you happen to change your mind," I say gently. "You are more than welcome to come back. OK?"

"Whatever. I'm through with this."

"Remember, we're always here to take care of you."

Once again, there is silence. Then I look at the phone. Palacio must've hung up after his remark. I put the phone back into my pocket.

"He's really not coming back," I say, shaking my head. "I'll officially document that he has left AMA."

"Thanks for trying," Jackie responds. "I'll go ahead and add this to the Unusual Events database. Hope it will provide useful feedback on how to prevent this."

"Not a bad idea."

Then I turn to Brian.

"Thanks for your help. No need to feel bad about this, OK?"

"No worries," Brian says. "If anything, I'll probably look back on this and laugh."

I smile at him, then stroll to the elevator lobby, with a headache that starts to pound my skull. I realize I am turning into Tony Palacio. I, too, want to get the fuck out of here.

* * *

Nothing tragic happens for the rest of the afternoon. Thank goodness.

I get the break I so desperately need, not just for rest but also for food. The insanity of the day forced me to skip lunch. I have to settle for Nutri-Grain bars and apple juice in the doctor's lounge near my cubicle. After a much needed snack and nap, I do remaining follow-up tasks for my patients, the ones not performing some risky vanishing act. I also call Patrick Flanigan, explaining that my six days off begin tomorrow and suggesting that he and his team still keep an eye out for the medical hacker, in case some other doc becomes a new target. No one should suffer the same torture I did.

The last thing I do is the most important.

I write interim summaries within my patients' charts. Each one provides a quick overview of the patient's hospitalization thus far, the major issues already addressed, and what still needs to be done. I leave no stone unturned. I dot every *i* and cross every *t*. The daytime hospitalist taking over would have what he needs just from reading my summaries, without having to comb through huge chunks of every chart. Of course, the transition isn't just about the notes. I also call that hospitalist to discuss these cases verbally over the phone, so that he really would not be flying blind tomorrow. It takes a while but it moves smoothly. With that, he is all ready to go.

And so am I.

I hand off my patient list to Jay McKinnon in the ED, then head out through its rear door. I walk across the space between the hospital and the parking garage, taking my time and letting the exhaustion gradually fade away. I savor the freedom, the chance to finally get away from it all. As I slowly ascend the parking garage stairs, all the way to the top to get some serious exercise, I think about how I might relax: listen to music on the beach, go out to the movies, maybe do some sightseeing in Santa Barbara or San Diego. I haven't been to those cities in so many years.

On the top level, I spot my Tesla, sitting in its usual spot. No other vehicles occupy the adjacent spaces. There is something about parking on the roof that appeals to me. Maybe it's the sky directly above. Rain or shine, I like having my car out in the open. Also, not too many people park on the roof, so I appreciate the sense of peace whenever I am about to leave work for the day. Just like now. With the Tesla's key fob in my pocket, I hear the driver's side door automatically unlock as I get closer.

A powerful force yanks me back.

It pulls me to my left, then my right, until my face crashes into the glass. I reach back and to the side, but cannot grab my unseen attacker. I only suffer another cycle of torture: left, right, boom. And a third, after which I am thrown to my left and hit the ground shoulder first. I roll onto my back, wincing.

From my vantage point, a tall muscular man slowly approaches. Dressed in blue jeans, plain black shirt, and a dark green jacket. Thick brown beard barely concealing a stiff mouth. The furrowed eyes pretty much say it all.

He is going to fuck me up good.

"What are you doing?" I ask, as if that could actually do anything.

"Teaching you a lesson," the man says, his voice rough and deep. "For being a real shitty doctor."

"But why?"

"You know why."

"I don't know what you're talk—"

He cuts me off with a sharp kick to my right side. Directly in the ribs. I scream and grab the site of impact. Goddamn, he's wearing steel-toed hiking boots.

"Quit playing dumb!" the man growls. "You know exactly what the fuck I'm talking about!"

"I don't!"

"My family is in pain because of you."

"Who?"

Then he reaches down to grab my legs. I begin scurrying backward, but too late. He grips my ankles, and with a mighty upward heave, my world flips upside down. I scream for help, so loud my lungs could burst. I'm dangling from this giant's arms, facing away from him, my fingers just inches above rough cement.

In this awkward position, I can barely think. Even as I start to recall the last few days, I still have no idea who this man is talking about. But before I could speak, the big man makes his next move. He heaves himself back and forth. Like a pendulum, I am flung to my right, then to my left. My head bangs the car door, along with most of my body. I brace for another ramming, and sure enough, the second hit is worse. My vision blurs. My ears ring slightly. I feel liquid pouring out of my nose, while I'm panting through a wide-open mouth.

I have to fight back.

I flail my arms in all directions, desperate to grab onto something. Then, as I am hurled again for round three, my right hand hits the jackpot, locking onto his crotch. With all the strength I can muster, I squeeze as hard as I'm able. The man roars like a vicious beast. My ankles are suddenly free, and I drop front first.

But there is no respite. He yanks me up and drags me backward. Too exhausted to fight, I do not resist. Then he lifts me and drops me onto the hood of my Tesla, grabs my shirt in one tight fist, pins me down, and pummels me with punches from his other hand. I raise my arms, forming a tight shield to cover my face. Each blow strikes my forearms, sending pain rippling through my flesh and bones. I hold this defensive position, knowing that I'd rather sacrifice my arms than lose my head and neck. But he goes on and on and on. I count about twenty or so rock-hard poundings.

Unexpectedly, there are no more blows. But I hear a rustling, before something else penetrates my field of vision.

A gun!

I reach up and grip his hand, then force it to my left. The gun barrel now points at the windshield. I keep pushing hard as he pushes back. Each second, my arms quickly burn. My will to survive this life-and-death arm wrestle rapidly drains my strength. I'm down to my last burst of energy.

Suddenly, the attacker's other hand releases my shirt, but it goes for my neck. He's choking my windpipe, cutting off all of my air and any cries for help. My vision goes blurry again. My arms burn with fatigue, stiffen like rock, no longer a conscious part of me. But then I realize I can still move something else.

My right foot.

I shoot it upward. Even without looking, I nail the bullseye of his crotch. The man grunts. Then I send another upward kick, even more powerful than the first. This time, he roars. The vise on my neck loosens. I lift my upper body, giving me extra momentum to push the gun past the driver side mirror.

Right before a mysterious high-pitched voice shouts.

"Don't shoot him!"

Too late. The gun fires its deafening shot, an inadvertent pull of the trigger in the chaos. Now in a near-sitting position, I wrench the man's arm upward and to my right, pointing the barrel at his head. Without a thought, I press down on his trigger finger. Another shot, along with a simultaneous explosion from one of his eye sockets. Blood and fluid pour from it. His lifeless body drops with a loud thud.

I lie back on the hood of the car.

The sky, still a clear light blue, fills my vision. But none of it gives me any peace. I pant with my mouth wide open, hearing and feeling the two-way rushes of air. Blood quickly refills my head. Slowly, I slide off the car, grunting through the horrendous pain the moment my feet contact the ground. Looking down, the man is on his back. One eye stares upward, opposite a small overflowing red pool. I turn away to my left and stumble forward. I almost drop to my knees.

The gun is on the ground, several feet away. But further down, I spot something else: another corpse, right in front of the open stairwell door. Still fighting full-body soreness, I make my way forward. One step, two steps, then about ten more, just enough for me to see the face of the second gunshot victim.

Lisa Flint, a bullet hole right in the forehead.

I hold my breath. Seconds later, my stomach heaves. I turn to one side and let out a gushing stream of acidic mush. Then my vision shifts and fades again. My whole body softens, and I go down. I hit the ground face first.

I barely feel it, because I'm already out of it.

How long have I remained here? All I know is that I hear nothing for a while. What breaks the silence is a series of footsteps. Rapid ones. First distant, then louder and louder. A pair of black shoes and navy-blue pant legs appear in my visual field. I turn my head to see a black man in a security uniform, squatting next to me.

"Sir, are you OK?" he asks.

I barely shake my head. He grabs a two-way radio from his belt and speaks loudly and urgently into it.

"This is Cole. I'm on the roof of the parking garage. We have an apparent victim of assault, plus two dead individuals, presumably due to gunshots. Send paramedics immediately. And call the police."

Seconds later, I hear a response on the radio, but I can't make any of it out. Why the hell should I care anyway?

"Are you in pain?" Cole asks.

"Yes," I croak. "A lot."

"Problems breathing?"

"No."

Cole looks around to take in the rest of the scene. Meanwhile, a new sound wails in the distance: an ambulance, from the ED just next door. It muffles as it enters the garage at ground level.

I close my eyes, like a man waiting at the pearly gates.

CHAPTER 19

The ambulance ride is ridiculously short. Per paramedic protocol, I am taken to the nearest hospital. It is obvious which one.

Never mind the searing body aches, aggravated by each turn of the ambulance as it corkscrews its way down the garage. The notion of returning to the hospital I just left is insult to injury, pouring bitter salt into gaping wounds. I could be an escaped convict being taken back to prison and it would be pretty much the same humiliation. Well, not exactly. Prisoners try to flee. How often do doctors leave work for the day, get the shit beaten out of them, and wind up back in the same place they just came out of? I say the chances are one in a billion, and I am that sad statistic.

What will the reaction be from ED staff once I get wheeled in as a patient? It's time to find out.

The ambulance comes to a full stop, then the rear doors open. Slowly, my gurney is pulled out, its wheels making contact with the asphalt of the ED's ambulance bay. I am on the move now. Right there, I make my plan. I will say nothing and make no eye contact. In fact, I take it a step further. I close my eyes and keep them shut. But while it looks like I'm sleeping, I still keep my ears open.

I hear the double doors of the ED entrance slide apart. The ambience changes from outdoor city traffic to a cacophony of footsteps and faint beeps from medical devices. The next thing I know, I am stopped, while a conversation ensues between the male paramedic and one of the female triage nurses. There is a gasp from the latter, followed by the same voice muttering my name. I still keep my eyelids sealed.

Moments later, I am pushed forward, then turned once to the right. Seconds later, a stop, followed by a backwards rotating motion and a slow crawl to a stop, before the clank of the gurney's foot brake.

I open my eyes. I cooperate with the two paramedics as they help me transfer to an adjacent ED patient gurney. My body hurts, but I make it.

"The doctor will be with you soon, OK?" one paramedic says.

I nod, very slowly. Then the paramedic duo leaves, en route to the next person desperate for a second chance at life.

Taking a deep breath, I shift in my gurney into a more comfortable position. With my upper body already somewhat upright, I look around. I am surrounded by about three feet of space on all sides. The usual ED features are nearby, including a supply cart, medical gas outlets on the wall, and a stainless steel sink. The curtain conceals all activity outside this little bubble. I smile and laugh quietly. It is so peaceful that, for a moment, I don't mind just staying here all night just to sleep and recover, like this is my own little hotel room. But obviously, that's not going to happen.

If anything, I am getting nervous. Am I going to be admitted upstairs, or can I be discharged from the ED?

Pretty soon, a young female medical assistant emerges through the curtain to take my vital signs. I follow all instructions without saying a word. She also gives me a hospital gown and suggests that I put it on. Good idea, I tell her. After she leaves, I remove my tie, shirt, and pants. Holy shit, I have a purplish bruise over the right side of my chest, where the big man kicked me. I put on the gown to conceal my front. I feel more free and comfortable now. If I end up going into cardiac or respiratory arrest, staff should have easy access.

I continue to sit still. Even if this is the emergency department, it feels no different from a stuffy medical clinic. I look at my watch. Almost 7 PM. Being a hospitalist who mainly works upstairs, I have no idea how long my wait will be. Certainly, this is one of many reasons why people hate their doctors and take out their rage on white coats like me. Oh well. At least I'm already in the ED proper, not the waiting room. Still, I know the reality: too many sick people, too few doctors. It doesn't matter what the specialty is. Emergency docs are overwhelmed. So are internists. Hell, even the field of psychiatry is having a doctor shortage.

And some people have the nerve to say that America has the greatest healthcare system in the world. I beg to differ.

Then there's the late Lisa Flint and whoever that big man is. What's their connection? I'm guessing a familial one. He did say his family was in pain because of me. He was likely talking about Christopher Flint's death. That may have driven him to confront me as I was leaving work, while Lisa stood by to watch. They must've planned to get their revenge on me in the worst possible way.

But their scheme failed. Too bad for them. I'm not mourning because they deserve no sympathy.

At last, I spot a pair of feet stopping at the curtain. It parts slightly, and in comes Dr. Ellen Roberts. She covers her mouth and lets out a gasp.

"Oh my god. Mark, I can't believe it."

She comes over and hugs me gently. It hurts a bit, but that's OK. This is the most appreciation I've gotten all day.

"I'll be OK," I say, somewhat hoarse. "Just do what you have to do. And be honest with me. No sugarcoating."

Ellen smiles as she grabs a paper towel from a dispenser near the sink. She dabs the tears in her eyes.

"The triage note said you were assaulted on the parking garage roof. I am just so heartbroken right now."

"Thanks for your sympathy."

"Do you want to talk about it?"

"I have to anyway. After all, the more details you get, the better documented the patient history is, right?"

"As long as it's not traumatizing for you."

"Don't worry. I'd rather let it out than keep it in."

"Glad to hear that."

Simultaneously, the curtain moves a little. Ellen turns to see the security guard named Cole peeking through the gap.

"Excuse me, Dr. Roberts. Sorry to bother you. There's a police officer here. He wants to speak with the patient."

"Can it wait?" Ellen asks.

Cole hesitates to answer. Then I speak up.

"Let him in. I'm going to describe the assault in detail. It's something all three of you will need to know."

"Good point," Ellen says with a nod.

She pulls the curtain open a little more. Cole walks in, followed by a muscular Latino man in a black police uniform. The cop gives me a friendly smile.

"Hello, Dr. Lin," he greets. "I'm Officer Ramos. I'm with the Anaheim Police Department."

"Nice to meet you, sir," I say, shaking his hand.

"I'm sorry to hear what happened. I overheard that you're ready to share details about the attack. Is that right?"

"Yes."

"Are you sure you're up to it?'

"Absolutely."

"OK, good. Now, just relax and take a deep breath. Whenever you're ready, tell us what happened. No need to rush."

Officer Ramos already has a notepad and pen ready. So does Cole. Then Ellen smiles as she retrieves a clipboard and pen. It is time to tell my story, a single tale for three different professional reports.

"I finished my work here a little after five fifteen. I exited this building through the ED's back door. I walked to the parking garage."

"Did you see anyone following you?" Ramos asks.

"No. But I wasn't paying attention."

"I see. Go on."

"So I walked up the stairs to the garage roof where I had parked. The attack began when I got close to my car door."

I proceed to describe the assault, narrating the events as I replay them in my head. Parts of it are a blur, but I remember plenty of it. Each blow, kick, punch, and face slam, I relive it. Same for the struggle with the gun, Lisa Flint calling out to the attacker, the two shots, and my collapse after seeing Lisa dead. I stop at the part where Cole arrived on the scene. The three notetakers scribble the final details down.

Officer Ramos speaks next.

"Dr. Lin, are you familiar with the assailant?"

"No."

"What about the woman?"

"I do know her."

"How so?"

"She's the widow of a patient of mine, who died recently."

Ramos nods. I take it as a signal to expand my narrative.

"Her name is Lisa Flint. Two days ago, her husband Christopher Flint, who had been hospitalized under my care, died suddenly. Lisa didn't take it well. When we met in person later that day to discuss things, she yelled at me, even slapped me in the face. But it gets worse. She wrote a long complaint letter to the CEO of this hospital. Then yesterday, she held a protest right outside this hospital, before chasing after me into the ED and physically attacking me herself, demanding that I provide a settlement for the case or else she'll file a malpractice lawsuit against me."

"You didn't call the police?" Ramos asks.

"No. As crazy as this sounds, I thought it would be a one-time thing, just from a really bad day. In hindsight, maybe I should have."

Ramos turns to Ellen and Cole.

"Do either of you know Lisa Flint?"

"I do," Ellen says. "On more than one occasion. Whenever a member of the Flint family came to the ED here, she would often accompany him. And let me tell you. She was very irritating each time. I'm sorry to be so judgmental, but she would nitpick us doctors about everything we're trying to do for the patient."

"When you say 'patient,' are you referring to Christopher Flint?"

"Not just him. Other times, it was his brother Zachary."

I quickly lean forward to interrupt.

"Ellen, is Zachary a big muscular man with a brownish beard?"

"Yeah," she answers, nodding.

"Did he ever show a bad temper?"

"Quite often. Why?"

I stop to put it all together.

"Take a guess," I say with a straight face.

Ellen looks off to the side. Her face registers confusion, but then, her mouth and eyes widen in surprise. She also puts two and two together.

"Looks like Zachary Flint was the one who attacked me," I say.

Then I turn to Ramos. But the cop doesn't answer or change his expression. He probably isn't allowed to divulge details from an active investigation. I let it go.

"I have encountered him once before," Cole says. "The ED called me to stop Zachary from verbally abusing a nurse. He almost attacked her physically, but I came by in time to put a stop to it."

"I remember that," Ellen says, shaking her head. "In my opinion, Zachary is worse than Lisa."

"Here's what I don't get," I say. "She told him to not shoot me."

There is silence. I am trying hard to figure this out. Maybe Ellen is, too. As for Cole and Ramos, I assume they're waiting for us.

"Perhaps a guilty conscience," Ellen says.

"Seriously?" I respond. "She stood near the stairwell while Zachary, if that was him, was beating the crap out of me."

"Maybe that's what she wanted at first. Maybe she only expected a beating to teach you a lesson, but instead, the attacker went too far by pulling out his gun."

"I still find it hard to believe. Imagine Lisa actually knowing right from wrong. She was never reasonable from the start."

"You never know. Redemption can occur even with the worst people. Just take a look around. There are stories out there."

I shake my head and close my eyes. I want this fucking nightmare to end. No more talk about this crazy family, please.

"Dr. Lin, let me say again that I'm so sorry about what happened," Ramos says. "I do thank you for giving us a detailed account. It's unfortunate that a matter of grievance with a healthcare service had escalated to this."

"I appreciate it," I say, somewhat relieved. "And in case it isn't obvious, everything I did was in self-defense. I was so terrified that I'd do anything to survive. I hadn't even expected the gun to go off the first time."

"At this point, I think it's best for you to focus on your recovery. Dr. Roberts, I hope I haven't taken up too much time."

"Not at all," Ellen says. "If anything, Mark was smart enough to tell his story once, for all of us."

Ramos nods and smiles. Then he pulls out a few business cards from his pocket and hands one each to me, Ellen, and Cole.

"If there's anything about this case that you need to add, feel free to contact me," Ramos says. "Thank you, everyone. And Dr. Lin, I hope you get well."

I nod my thanks as Ramos and Cole step out of the space. Ellen makes sure the curtain is fully closed. Then she and I go back to our doctor-patient relationship.

"Where are you hurt, Mark?"

"Lots of places."

"Which are the worst ones?"

"Mainly my forearms. Plus the bridge of my nose and the right side of my chest. Yeah, I'd say those three."

"How would you describe the pain?

"A dull soreness."

"On a scale of one to ten, how bad is it?"

"Maybe a seven or eight."

Ellen shines a penlight into my each of my eyes, obviously to check my pupillary reflexes. Then she holds up one finger and tells me to follow it. She traces an imaginary capital H, and my eyes gaze at her moving finger the whole time. She also instructs me to open and close my jaw, smile, and frown. Plus, I stick out my tongue while she shines her light at the back of my throat. Then I turn my head left and right. Even in my sorry state, none of this is foreign. This is the part of the physical exam for checking the cranial nerves. She then proceeds to listen to my heart and lungs, examine my belly, and inspect and palpate tender impact sites. Ellen is a pretty thorough emergency doc, I must say.

Next, she uses some gauze and distilled water to wipe parts of my face, especially the areas beneath my nose. Much of the white cotton turns a thick dark red. The last thing Ellen does is apply a small adhesive bandage to my right cheek.

"Here's what's going to happen," Ellen says. "You'll undergo a skeletal survey plus a CT scan of your head, thorax, abdomen, and pelvis. I don't need to explain all the things I'm ruling out, right?"

I nod. There are plenty of serious things that could possibly turn up: intracranial bleeding, rib fracture puncturing my lung and causing pneumothorax, a ruptured spleen. Even a broken nose isn't out of the question. But what are the chances that a radiologist will see none of those abnormalities, paving the way for an all-clear discharge out of here? Given my history of present illness, I'd say a small chance.

I still cling to that hope no matter what.

"Please let me be OK," I say.

"I hope you'll be fine," Ellen says, starting to head out. "Try not to think about it too much. Just get some rest while you wait."

"Yay. Back to my little slumber."

"See you in a bit."

Then she pulls the curtain, and I close my eyes.

* * *

Tonight is all about firsts: first time getting beaten up this badly, first time fighting off a gunman, first time killing someone by accident, first time killing someone intentionally, first time being an ED patient, first time being a patient in the same hospital I work in. Now it is my first time getting a serious dose of ionizing X-rays. Starting off, a series of plain radiographs, covering every single bone from head to toe. Then the CT scan, where I lie on my back while sliding through a fancy cylinder and following the audio and visual cues to hold my breath or breathe normally. None of it is painful, of course. If anything, there is a soothing placebo effect just from going through all of this.

But later, I shudder.

It takes only one serious complication from my beating to warrant hospitalization. Just one thing to go horribly wrong for me to be thrust back into this place haunted by Doctor Lucifer. If he knows I'm a patient here and the doctor assigned to me isn't vigilant, I am totally screwed. If that's the case, I might as well say goodbye. My life was never great to begin with, and it still isn't. If Doctor Lucifer is going to take it away from me, then so be it. The only thing I ask is that it be painless and quick. No prolonged suffering. Just a one-way trip out of this godforsaken world.

Or better yet, I could just sign out AMA, against medical advice. Just get the fuck out of here and accept whatever happens. At least I would escape the clutches of the devilish doc. I'd be free like Tony Palacio, that patient who already had the guts to do it. Strangely enough, I'm really envying the guy now.

I don't know what to do. All I want is the radiologist to finish reading my damn images, tell me if I'll be going upstairs or heading home.

After another fifteen minutes, someone does finally come. But it's not Ellen peeking through the curtain gap.

"Mark?" Jay McKinnon says with an astonished look. "Oh my god, man, what happened to you?"

"You didn't hear any big news down here?"

"No, I was upstairs. I was just walking by when I saw you. Sorry if you wanted to be alone."

"No, don't worry about it. Long story short, someone attacked me on the parking garage roof, just as I was ready to leave. It wasn't some random assault. It was done by an angry family member of a deceased patient."

"Oh, gee. I'm sorry."

"Remember what I told you about the hacker in this hospital, and one of my patients died as a result?"

"Yeah."

"That's what it was about."

"Are you kidding me?"

I shake my head slowly.

"This hacker is bad news, Jay. If it turns out I'm going to be admitted, I sure hope it'll be you watching me overnight."

"You trust me on that?"

"With my life."

Jay smiles.

"Anything for you, buddy. Listen, I have to take care of a new admission. I'm praying that you'll go home instead."

"Sure. And even if I do, be wary of strange things tonight, in case the hacker decides to target someone else."

"I know. I got it."

With that, Jay moves on, and I resume my wait.

I check my watch. It's now 8:40 PM. If I have to hazard a guess, Ellen will come back within the next half hour. She better, or else I'm walking out of here. I'm more comfortable with the idea because I'm feeling better. I'm breathing fine. My body soreness is now like a five out of ten on the pain scale. I can even move my arms and legs without wincing. At this point, I'd bet a hundred dollars that I will not be admitted. Even if hospitalization is indicated, I'll just sign out AMA.

Either way, I'll be gone in a flash.

I wait another ten minutes. At last, Ellen returns.

"Please tell me I won't be going upstairs," I say.

"You won't," she says.

"Seriously?"

Ellen nods and smiles. Cha-ching.

"Except for a nondisplaced fracture in your nasal bone, all of your X-rays are negative. CT is clean, too. No intracranial or intrathoracic hemorrhage. No pneumothorax. Not even a hematoma."

"How do my ribs look?"

"Totally fine."

"No fracture? Because I got kicked there, you know."

"The radiologist report says 'no rib fracture.' If it makes you feel better, I even looked at the films myself. My assessment is the same."

I look up, raising a fist in triumph.

"You have some really strong bones, Mark."

"I've been drinking milk all my life. My parents made me."

"Good for you."

"Plus, those old milk commercials really got me into the habit."

"The funny 'Got Milk' ads?"

"Not just those. The ones from the 1980s, too. You know that slogan 'Milk: It Does a Body Good'?"

"Oh yeah. I saw those back in the day."

"I remember a teacher in school showing us some of those old milk commercials. I wanted to be big and strong, too. Now it looks like milk saved my life."

Ellen laughs and pats me gently on the shoulder.

"Anyway, you can go home," she says. "The only treatment I would recommend is some over-the-counter analgesics, if you happen to need them. Tylenol, Bayer, Advil, whatever you prefer."

"Any activity restrictions?"

"No, but make sure you can tolerate whatever you do."

"Anything else?"

"Maybe you should request some time off."

I think about it for a moment.

"This isn't a doctor's recommendation as much as a friend's suggestion," Ellen says sympathetically. "I'm worried about you, because you've just been through something so horrendous."

"Thanks for watching out for me. Believe it or not, today is actually my last day of the hospitalist twelve-day stretch."

"Hey, there you go. But seriously, do you really want to be back here after only, what, six days off?"

"Depends on how quickly I recover."

"How do you feel about such a short break?"

"I say no."

"You want more time off?"

"Yeah."

"So what's stopping you?"

I nod. Ellen is right, one hundred percent.

CHAPTER 20

At last, I am back on the parking garage roof.

Being here suddenly takes on a whole new meaning. Anyone else would think nothing of it, but I lived through the horror defiling this place just hours earlier. I am standing close to where Lisa Flint had fallen, as well as the spot where I threw up. All signs of them are now gone. Same for the attacker's body and the blood streaking the side of my Tesla. The cleanup crew did a fantastic job, banishing the curse that was unleashed here.

But nothing will ever wipe away the memories. They will haunt me for a very, very long time.

I approach the car door and hear it click open. But I don't enter yet. Seeing the driver side mirror, I recall how the emergency department has no mirrors, obviously to make sure that patients, especially the mentally ill ones, are not startled by their own reflections. So I move closer to this mirror and lean my face up against its shiny surface. Immediately, I pull away. Then I look again, forcing myself to stare at the hideous beast.

There is swelling over the bridge of my nose, near a partially black right eye. Similarly, half of my upper lip is thickened, to the point of concealing the lower one. An adhesive bandage stretches vertically over my right cheek. My hair is disheveled, with strands hanging down over my eyes.

In essence, I look like shit.

I get into the car. At last, I am truly in my own little world, away from the awfulness all around. I don't even press the ignition button yet.

I just savor the silence, the peace that starts to fill me. At first, it feels good. It calms me down. But ultimately, it only helps a little. Based on the chain of events over the past three days, my luck is godawfully bad. There is also the one menace underlying this whole mess.

Doctor Lucifer, whoever the fuck he is.

It's time to move. I power the engine and make my way down the garage. Once on the street, I decide to just go in random directions. I have no destination, no purpose. This is one of those times where driving isn't merely a means to a place of salvation, it's salvation in and of itself. The opportunity to go anywhere, see whatever passes by, is what I need tonight. To move is to be free.

But that's not all. I need my other form of therapy: music. Silence alone isn't going to do justice.

On the dash, I turn on the radio and access my Spotify playlist. I still have it on shuffle mode. I use one finger to cycle through random songs. At the same time, I turn right onto Harbor Boulevard, heading south. It takes a few more seconds before I settle on the right kind of tune for my mood: the rock song "Boulevard of Broken Dreams" by Green Day. Hearing this is like having someone who understands. The song may be a far cry from something celebratory, but I need it. Its theme centers on being alone, going somewhere without another soul, another companion, by one's side.

Something I know all too well.

I am an only child born to Chinese immigrants. Mom and Dad grew up in a poor village located miles from Beijing. Looking for a better opportunity, they came to the United States, with all the cash they could muster by selling all but their most essential possessions. If that wasn't tough enough, Mom was also three months pregnant. My parents survived only because of the generosity of another Chinese family in the city of Garden Grove, in Orange County. Having already gotten settled on American soil a decade earlier, they provided my parents with temporary shelter and resources to find work. Eventually, Dad got a job as a chef at a Chinese restaurant, while Mom earned her income in a dry cleaning shop. Six months later, shortly after my parents changed their legal names, I was born at the UC Irvine Medical Center.

I might not recall early life so clearly, but I definitely remember two things.

The first was daycare. Not daycare in the usual sense, because my parents couldn't afford it. No, it was more like prison, with good intentions. Before preschool, I had to spend my days in a playpen, in the back room of the dry cleaning shop where Mom worked. I was given some toys plus a TV showing cartoons. But rule number one was to be quiet. Rule number two was to never leave the playpen, because it was never safe outside.

The second memory was a visit to a pediatrician for a checkup. When we got home, Mom and Dad explained who doctors were. They were the greatest people in society. They were rich, well respected, and loved by all, because they took care of people, made them feel better, and helped them live longer. No other job lavished such grand rewards. Medicine was the holy grail of professions. It was the ticket to prosperity and happiness, even for someone who lived in misery and poverty before. The more my parents hammered this home, the more I desired it, craved it, to the point of fighting for it.

I wanted a fulfilling life beyond my wildest dreams. Yet, here I am, having achieved that life, which is nothing more than an endless nightmare.

I look back on the road. Still southbound on Harbor, this time alongside the eastern border of Disneyland. My sight of it is blurring a little, because tears are suddenly getting in the way. I wipe them away with one hand. I get ready to change the music, but I don't need to. As I turn right onto Katella Avenue, Spotify happens to know what I need: a sad piece by Imagine Dragons, called "Demons." It is about exactly that: personal demons. Pain, fear, anger, grief, you name it. They built up, even within my own soul.

As early as age eight.

In school, I was the envy of parents and teachers. I got A's in every subject, because I loved to learn. There were so many fascinating things with math, English, science, geography, history, literature, music, and art.

The admiration from adults was awesome. Yet, it came with a terrible price. Other kids stayed away from me. No one wanted to be my friend. They ignored me, or worse, bullied me into submission. I'd been insulted, pushed, shoved, and even dumped into filthy trash cans. But I never sank to their pathetic level, especially as fighting would dishonor both me and my family. I was better than that.

In fact, I had to be the best.

My parents said so. They told me that many young people were competing to get into medical school, not just me. The only way to win was to beat them every step of the way. That meant straight A's in every school year, stuffing my college applications with extracurricular activities, acing the SAT, whatever it took. They didn't wait to tell me this. I may have been just a kid, but Mom and Dad said to always look toward the future. A good education and career were the most important things in life. Everything else, like friends and dating, took a back seat, because they were distractions.

Was that really a good idea, resisting a social life? No, but with the kind of people surrounding me, I had to. Kids who flunked their classes were trouble. They were not a good influence. I knew it and, of course, so did Mom and Dad. Teens who got into drugs or other risky shit were out of their fucking minds. Those punks were worthless, with no future, likely on their way to being poor out in the real world. Not me. I was prepared. My parents got me ready for the long climb to the top. I would reach the heights of heaven, far from the hell on earth that could drag me down if I allowed it to.

On the dashboard, I scroll through the list to my go-to song for emotional tension. Nickelback's 2006 single "Savin' Me" could mean a lot of different things. For me, with just the powerful rock vocals and instrumentals, it is about inner turmoil, crying out for help, wanting a second chance. I was smart as hell, yet invisible to the rest of the world. Did anyone ever see what I accomplished or the positive traits I possessed?

Do I even have any worthy qualities?

Damn this curse! Being an intellectual has its price, a terrible one. I have a solid life foundation, but no one else to stand on it with me. In fact, one of the two people who did got yanked away from this world.

That occurred when I was twelve.

I was in the backseat of Dad's Toyota. We were on our way to Disneyland, the happiest place on Earth. Dad was driving while Mom took the front passenger seat and I sat behind Dad. Just as we crossed a street, with the theme park starting to become visible, a giant blast to my right suddenly rocked the entire car. Glass shards flew in all directions. I closed my eyes, shielded my face, felt my whole body jolt back and forth. I didn't dare to look. I only waited, until I heard the sound of Dad opening his door, running to open mine, and unbuckling my seat belt before pulling me out. Seconds later, I opened my eyes. Dad was by my side, panting heavily like I was.

But where was Mom?

She wasn't conscious when the paramedics freed her from the wrecked Toyota, sitting near the Chevy pickup that crashed into us. I couldn't bear to look at the ambulance taking her away. I only hugged Dad and poured tears into the side of his shirt. Later, we came to the hospital that admitted her. Not just any hospital. The UC Irvine Medical Center, the same place where she gave birth to me. It would be about an hour before we finally saw the doctor. That's when he told us: she was dead. Again, I buried my face into Dad's chest. I couldn't hear the conversation between Dad and the doctor, but I still managed to hear two words close together: "bleeding" and "brain."

I had to miss school for a week. It was my one and only chance to say my final goodbye to Mom. Watching the burial was no easier. The gaping hole in the ground for her casket was as wide as the gaping hole in my heart. How could I possibly fill it up again? Thankfully, Dad gave me some answers. The best way to honor Mom and keep her memory alive was to never forget her wisdom. I would continue to be a good person always doing the right thing. I would never stop working hard to achieve success. I would make the best out of the opportunity I still had for a stable, secure, and prosperous future.

I would also learn that the driver of the Chevy was drunk. That was another hard lesson for me: alcohol is poison. I vowed never to taste a drop of that shit. I am sure Mom would be proud of that, too.

Where am I now? Oh yeah, still driving west on Katella. The next street is Beach Boulevard. I decide to get into the left turn lane. While waiting for the green light, I scan the Spotify playlist. After some depressing music, it's time for something different. Is there anything more upbeat I could listen to? I soon find another rock tune that might fit, though it would still be semi-dismal.

Ah, what the hell. I select the track, press the play button, and slowly turn south onto Beach.

"How Far We've Come" by Matchbox Twenty is about two things: achievements and tragedies. Here is a buoyant and catchy song that covers both. An optimist would cheer on the message about pushing forth even in the face of adversity. A pessimist like me gravitates to the parts about the world being so shitty.

In high school, I didn't give a fuck about social status. The only status that mattered to me was academic: 4.0 GPA, 2150 on the SAT, volunteer work at the UC Irvine Medical Center, and the school's chess club to solidify my college applications. Sure, I knew which groups of classmates hung out together, which ones dated and then broke up, what their hobbies were, but all of that was just news from afar. I especially stayed away from the most troublesome people in my class: the cheerleader who got pregnant at sixteen, the car enthusiast who totaled his older brother's Ferrari, the drug addict who got expelled and then arrested, and the many who were just total assholes in general. I didn't need anyone like that to pull me down, off my path to future success. Like I told myself many times, I would be better than these people. If anything, finally becoming a doctor would give me the respect I deserved, and it would make up for the lack of appreciation throughout my early life.

Loneliness did get to me during senior year, especially the month before graduation. Any chatter about the prom only pissed me off. Every pretty girl I passed by was taken, or otherwise some other guy already asked her to be his prom date. There was still one chance, however.

In the middle of the fall semester, a girl in calculus class was struggling with the subject. I had never talked to her once, ever. Yet, here she was, a beautiful and kind girl loved by all, destined to be prom queen, who could not wrap her head around derivatives, integrals, and other fundamentals of calculus. I went up to her and offered to tutor her. The girl said yes. Hence, we would meet after school to review whatever stuff confused her. Later, she would also seek my help in between classes. I found this fulfilling, even if my relationship with her over much of the school year did not go beyond mentoring. I was helping someone in need. Even better was how she went from almost failing calculus to hovering between a B plus and an A minus. That's when I finally popped the other big question, asking if she'd like to go to the prom together. She said yes to that, too.

Sadly, it was not meant to be.

On prom day, she did not show up to class. Any morning class, not just calculus. Then, during lunch, the school principal circulated the tragic news: the girl had been shot to death the night before. The one who killed her was a guy in my class. Not just any guy. Her ex-boyfriend, whom she broke up with a couple of weeks before. While we were all grieving, he had the nerve to get in my face, give me the finger, and walk off without a word. Not too long after that, the police came on campus and arrested him.

That motherfucker may be rotting in prison, but that didn't stop my relentless searing heartache. What would've happened if I didn't ask that girl out to the prom? Would she still be alive? Those questions kept me up for weeks.

Eventually, Dad noticed my bitterness and I had to tell him the whole story. He hugged me tightly, just like he had five years earlier. His messages were also similar as before: do not be pulled down by grief, keep working hard for a better life, never forget the people you love. And most importantly, becoming a doctor will still bring you much fulfillment. In essence, move on and keep going.

With that, I barreled through the rest of my education.

First, my college years. Majored in biochemistry and molecular biology. Avoided the slackers, drunks, frat boys, all that dirty shit. Studied hard but barely talked to roommates. Graduated Magna Cum Laude.

Next up, medical school, same institution. Fought to keep up with the tremendous amount of material in years one and two: anatomy, physiology, histology, pathology, pharmacology, microbiology, etcetera. Year three: hospital and clinic rotations, covering the big medical and surgical specialties. Also the first year of being treated like shit. Residents and attending physicians being the biggest fucking assholes on the planet. Not all of them, but still plenty enough to sour this med student's reverence for the profession.

Was this what my tuition paid for: higher-ups on the totem pole quizzing us to boost their own egos, making us do menial tasks, telling us to just go read and look stuff up? Where the hell was the education and training of future doctors? It's called medical school for a reason, for fuck's sake! Might as well have an army instructor give someone a machine gun and tell that person to just figure out how to use it.

Whatever. If this shit was supposedly temporary, I might as well just put up with it and get it over with. That's what I did in year four, when I did more specific clinical rotations, like radiology, gastroenterology, cardiology, and infectious diseases. I chose internal medicine because adults were easier to handle than kids. Plus, I wasn't cut out for surgery, pun not intended. So on Match Day, I got the result I wanted: a three-year internal medicine residency. Yes, same place again. On graduation day, Dad rejoiced in me getting my MD. Supposedly, I was finally there. I would be catching the holy grail in no time.

I was dead wrong.

Residency was hell on earth. Eighty-plus hours a week of nonstop in-your-face, soul-draining work. Either you knew what to do or you didn't. There was no helping hand, no emotional support, no empathy, no mercy. Not even a decent lunch break, good night's sleep, or enough time to unwind. All of this from a profession that supposedly stood for good health. A profession that society puts so high on a pedestal, without a goddamn clue about the mistreatment behind closed doors. After three years of this, I got my additional credentials: California medical license and internal medicine board certification.

And after eleven years at the same institution, I was done. I settled for a smaller community hospital. I chose Ivory Memorial Hospital in Anaheim.

In the end, I have nothing left.

There is no holy grail. Everything my parents ever told me is bullshit. I have the title but no real prestige. I have the money, but I still have no hordes of people showering admiration, except maybe Dad's friends, but that's only because he always shows me off to everyone as the ideal person their kids should strive to become.

And forget the respect and love from patients. This is no longer the good old days of decades past. Many of them now question the experts, insist on being know-it-alls themselves, and accuse us docs of being greedy, self-serving frauds who only care about the extra dollars in our wallets. Even if I am trying to do my job with honesty and integrity, this is the goddamn thanks I get?

Am I really expected to save everyone's life, including these many flawed individuals? The more I think about this, the more I want to scream.

My philosophy on life, based on Mom's words, is simple: be good to yourself and others. Love and appreciate oneself, then do the same with people around. Nurture the mind, then cherish the world. Develop and grow new skills, then achieve something inspiring. Have a positive, meaningful impact on ourselves and the world, because we only have one life. Sounds good, right? Yeah, until you see the jerks and morons on this sorry planet...

People who put themselves first while mistreating others, then wonder why the fuck everyone hates them.

People who already think they're special, without having done shit to deserve that kind of reputation, while expecting everyone to bow down to them.

People who see nothing wrong with themselves, yet cause problems that they only blame on others.

People who would rather cover up their own flaws, instead of working to fix and improve them.

People who are quick to fault others, because they're too impatient to figure out their own problems.

People who think helping others means weakening oneself, as if the goal in life is to dominate the competition.

People who insist they're always right and never listen to others, even in the face of constructive feedback.

People who stubbornly resist learning anything new, to the point of falling behind because they miss out on stuff they could really use.

People who find reality too complicated to understand or too uncomfortable to stomach, and instead of working to fully comprehend and accept it, they deny it, oversimplify it, or even believe total nonsense just because it sounds so good it must be true, all before doing some really dumb shit based on a terribly inaccurate view of the world.

So now we have a giant cesspool of assholes in this world: bullies, abusers, slackers, cheaters, murderers, thieves, terrorists, bigots, racists, rapists, narcissists, violent domestic partners, awful parents, brutal cops, asshole doctors, drug dealers, brainwashed cult followers, psychopaths, sociopaths, greedy rich people, con artists, crooked politicians, heartless dictators, etcetera, etcetera, etcetera. You know what I say? Fuck these losers! Fuck these awful, degenerate, stupid, selfish, devilish disgraces to humanity! How much damage to society have they done altogether? How different would things be if they had never done any of their shit to begin with?

As a medical doctor, I treat diseases of the human body. I understand their etiology and pathophysiology, their causes and step-by-step processes, in order to make sense of the conditions' signs and symptoms, plus how to diagnose and treat them. But diseases of humanity, I can't do shit about that. I can spot flawed human thinking and behavior leading to frustration, anger, hate, and destruction, but that's it. As far as I know, there's no easy cure for disease of humanity. And don't get me started on the prognosis. It's pretty negative to say the least.

Call me bitter, angry, cynical, whatever. I get it. I'm aware of it. I also know that I have very high standards. I've learned the importance of morality and wisdom, and appreciated how my life shot up because of them. I'm not going to let the scum of humanity get in my way, stop me, or yank me down. I've worked hard to get here, goddamn it.

I turn my attention back to Beach Boulevard. The 405 Freeway overpass is up ahead. Meanwhile, I need one last good song to heal me, just one more for the night. After a little while, the next random tune is "Fight Til the Bitter End," by a rock band called Black Tide. Yeah, just what I like: a hard reminder to keep going and never stop fighting, even when times get tough and things look bleak.

I can see that I'm straddling a moral fence. I stand in limbo, between heaven and hell, each side pulling me in a spiritual tug-of-war but stuck in a stalemate that only I could break. The direction I take is a matter of choice. Which path do I want: the steady one up to the faint light or the quick one down to the powerful darkness? Obviously, the former. But do I have the strength, the will power, to escape the clutches of the abyss? I take a slow deep breath, then another. And another.

Then, I feel a bit lighter. A weight has come off my shoulders. I have just let something go.

I guess I should stop caring about who my patients are and whether saving human bodies also saves humanity. I'm not really some kind of god or guardian angel, right? I'm just a healer, a mortal human practicing a sacred craft. Nothing more than that. Am I pure in heart and spirit? Far from it. I still have a long way to go.

But at least my job seems a bit simpler. After years of looking up to the stars, maybe it's time to just come back down to earth. Don't expect to rescue humanity anymore. Just save lives, one at a time, whichever ones I can. I'll have to keep telling myself this over and over, each and every day, especially if I'm still close to slipping back into disillusionment. Even with the world quickly falling apart before my very eyes, and especially if it finally comes to a tragic end, I have a duty to the people around me.

Because the Hippocratic Oath said so.

CHAPTER 21

I take a deep breath and turn off the audio in my car. I'm done with music for tonight. It has definitely satisfied me and eased my tension. But now I am starving. After being forced to miss lunch and dinner and only managing a quick afternoon snack, I am desperate for calories and nutrients.

The clock on the dash reads 10:05 PM. Aw shit, I hope I can find a food joint soon. Any place still open?

At this point, I reach the end of Beach Boulevard, where it forms a T-intersection with the Pacific Coast Highway in Huntington Beach. I have two choices: turn right to head north towards Seal Beach, or turn left to go south towards Newport Beach. I choose the latter, just for the sake of staying closer to home. As I relish in the silence of the trip, I think about how PCH is a segment of California State Route 1, which runs along most of the coastline, spanning from Dana Point in Orange County all the way north to Leggett in Mendocino County. With major highways connecting the northern and southern parts of the state, I still can't believe California is so friggin' huge. SoCal is a whole world in and of itself.

I reach Balboa Boulevard and decide at the last minute to make a right. This is a recognizable street in Newport Beach, because it runs through the middle of the Balboa Peninsula, a great hangout area with a beach, pier, marina, and restaurants. This is obviously where I might be able to grab a late-night bite to eat. Amazingly, a street parking spot just opens up, and I snatch it. Next question is where to dine in, not to mention which establishments are still open at this hour. After minutes of wandering, I find a good spot, a place called Newport Balboa's Bar and Grill. I step inside.

The faint smell of cigarette smoke stings my nostrils a bit. The place is about half full, still enough to generate random chatter filling my ears. I grab an empty stool in the middle section of the bar. Menus are already placed periodically along the counter, and I pick one up to glance at the food options. Given my state of hunger, I'd take anything, maybe more than my usual intake. Eventually, I give my order to the bartender: a well-done 12-ounce ribeye steak with mashed potatoes and steamed vegetables, plus a glass of ice-cold water. Then I sit still and observe the scenery.

I'm amazed how so many people would still hang out at night in the middle of the week. Then again, I suppose it's better than Fridays and Saturdays. Overly large crowds are not my thing. Neither is alcohol. All of those bottles on the wall in front of me, containing bourbon, whiskey, vodka, whatever, I could care less about. Same for wine and champagne. It's all poisonous shit to me. In a way, my father was also an influence. In addition to hammering home all that stuff about becoming a doctor, he told me to always do what I preached. That meant being a doctor who doesn't drink, smoke, do drugs, eat unhealthy food, or refuse to get any exercise. To this day, I still maintain that discipline.

There are plenty of large overhead TVs along the walls of the interior. They are tuned to cable sports channels like ESPN and Fox Sports, showing live games, highlight footage, stats, news headlines, and commentator analysis. Sports are another thing I could care less about. I wasn't good at any of them in school, and many kids didn't want me to play with them anyway. Whatever. I still had my own little world to enjoy. Early on, it was *Sesame Street, Mister Rogers' Neighborhood,* Disney movies, TV cartoons, and books. After puberty, it became music and cinema of all genres, plus television dramas. Also throw in cerebral activities like crosswords, Sudoku, and puzzle video games. If optimal health was based on taking care of the mind, body, and soul, I've scored two out of three. The soul remains my void to fill.

Pretty soon, two men sit in stools immediately to my right. The one next to me is a thin man with short black hair and graying strands, wearing blue jeans and a red flannel shirt. The other man two stools down is a heavyset blonde with a ponytail, whose dark pants and vest plus a plain white T-shirt suggest he is some sort of biker dude. They each order a bottle of Budweiser and start chatting away. Their conversation covers lots of things: college football, the Dodgers and Lakers winning championships during the pandemic, government stimulus checks, local businesses that reopened, planned home improvements, the weather, and models of new cars coming out. As usual, I don't feel like socializing, but hey, listening to them keeps me from total boredom.

By this time, a big plate with my order arrives, along with a napkin, fork, and steak knife. I carefully slice a piece of steak and taste it. At last, the juicy flavor of meat. I mix it with a lump of potato and a bite of a broccoli head. Then I add some steak sauce to the big slab of meat before taking another bite. I take my time savoring dinner, all while letting my mind wander freely.

Doctor Lucifer cannot harm me now, but he's still on the loose. After one death, one ICU transfer, one Step Down Unit transfer, and one near-catastrophe with blood, not to mention the threat of a looming malpractice lawsuit, I can't rest knowing he can kill again. I've lived this nightmare already. No one else should have to. Now, the same nagging question comes back to haunt me.

Who is he?

It could be anyone in the whole world, and I have absolutely no leads. The past three days have been all about one thing: survival. Lucifer strikes, I stop the damage. Too bad Lucifer has covered his tracks so well. Meanwhile, who would have such a strong grudge against me? So far, just Dr. Samuel Pierson. No doubt he hates me and vice versa. What are the chances that it's Pierson, the epitome of asshole doctors, who is calling with threats and directing a hacker to target me? It's tempting to believe, but I must be rational. Start with facts first and then formulate conclusions, not the other way around like a lot of idiots do. But where do I even start?

I turn back to the conversation on my right. The two men are getting serious now. They're talking about the economy and Wall Street, mainly complaining about how the top 1% don't give a shit about the rest of the 99%. I don't say anything or make eye contact, but I imagine myself nodding in agreement.

There is silence again. I cut into my diminishing remnant of steak. Then I feel a nudge against my arm.

"Hey, are you all right?" the man to my right asks.

I look at him with a neutral expression. Then I remember my face being banged up. I have forgotten all about it.

"I'm hanging in there," I answer.

"You got into a fight or something?"

"As a matter of fact, yes."

"Today?"

"Yeah."

"What happened?"

"I, uh, got into a car accident. Road rage ensued."

The man whistles, believing this story I've cleverly made up at the last second. As he inquires further, I decide to keep it going.

"So the other driver beat you up?"

"Pretty much. I had no choice but to defend myself."

"Yikes."

"Soon, the cops showed up. Let's just say the other guy is not going to be a problem now. That's all that matters."

"Sounds like the police took care of him good."

"You can say that."

"I was about to ask if you got beaten up by some racist asshole. You know, with COVID-19, anti-Asian hate, and all that."

I pause to sip some water.

"Nothing about the other guy screamed racism," I say.

"Still, sorry you got hurt."

"No worries."

"It's just pathetic. I have a lot of Asian friends I hang out with, and three of them already had to call the police on some racists yelling at them in public. How stupid are these bigoted jerks? My buddies didn't actually bring the virus to America, even if they're of Chinese descent. They grew up here."

"Just like me."

"And even if the virus did ride along with some folks coming here, they had no idea they were carrying it. So you can't treat them like they brought it intentionally."

"To me, anyone who refers to the virus with a geographical name firmly attached deserves a real ass-whooping."

The man nods and laughs. Then he holds out his hand.

"Hey, the name's Rick. What's yours?"

"Mark," I answer, shaking his hand.

"And I'm Hank," the biker dude next to Rick says, raising his hand.

"Hello, Hank," I say.

"You from around here?" Rick asks.

"Born and raised in OC."

"I'm originally from Bakersfield. Moved here to be at the water. Hell of a lot better than being inland."

"You like it here?"

"I do. I now run a boat shop here. I'm glad it's picking up again. Man, for a year and a half with COVID, I had to close and live off the savings I had, plus whatever government checks I could get."

"Me too," Hank says. "Had to shut down my motorcycle repair business. Not permanently, though. That's back up and running now."

"Cool," I say.

"Still, did we really have to go through all of this?" Rick asks. "I mean, how the fuck could this virus just sweep across this country?"

"Carelessness," I say, holding up my glass of water. "If there's a new infectious disease going around, you make sure it doesn't reach us. You don't sit on it."

"You know one thing about the pandemic that pisses me off?" Hank says. "Rich-ass motherfuckers getting aid money they don't need at all."

"I hear ya," Rick says.

"Let me tell you what happened to my good friend. He's the one who owns a little restaurant in Seal Beach, called Bob's Cove."

"I think you mentioned him once."

"Yeah, well, he ain't as lucky as us. His business went under. He and his wife had to move in with her parents."

"Jesus."

"You'd think the COVID aid for small businesses would go to people like Bob. But no. A lot of it went to millionaire cocksuckers."

"Nobody gives a fuck about the regular people."

"You said it."

During their spirited chat, I had eaten half of my steak and chowed down most of the mashed potatoes and broccoli. I keep my eyes on the plate, taking another sip of water. Rick and Hank have had it rough. Sure, they made it through the past two years OK, but not without the bumps and rollercoaster drops. I understand their pain, sort of. I've shot up the socioeconomic ladder so high that I'm truly not the best person to know their struggles. My parents had pushed me to avoid a low income like theirs.

"All right, your turn," Rick says to me. "What do you do?"

Aw shit. This is not a question I want to answer.

"I'd rather not say."

"Why not?"

"Because it's stressful as hell."

"OK, how about you give us clues and we'll take a guess?"

"Fine."

Rick smiles and keeps his eye on me.

"First question," he says. "Did you get any COVID-19 stimulus checks from Uncle Sam?"

"No," I answer.

"Not really poor then. Does your job require a college degree?"

"Yes."

"Graduate degree?"

"Yes."

"OK, now I'm thinking high-paying professional."

I slice off another piece of steak and eat it. Rick goes on.

"Are you an engineer?"

"No."

"Businessman?"

"No."

"Lawyer?"

"Keep going."

"Doctor?"

"Oh, hell no."

"Wait a second. It sounds like you must be a doc."

"I never said I am."

"So what are you then?"

"Keep guessing."

"All right. You a professor?"

"No."

"Scientist?"

"No."

"Salesperson?"

"Not even close."

Rick drinks from his beer bottle as I sip some of my water. My secret is safe for now, it seems.

"You're not gonna tell me, are you?"

"No."

"Why not?"

I turn to Rick with a stiff eye, then answer.

"I'll tell you what. I'll mention what kind of setting I work in. How about that?"

"OK."

"I work in healthcare, in a hospital. As for my job, it pays well, but it has its downsides. It's hard as hell. There's a ton of work. You get hounded left and right with stuff. You're practically expected to be perfect. If you screw up, some people could lash out. Any big mistake, the game's over."

"Sounds like you're a high-ranking nurse."

"Believe what you want."

"If your job is so bad, why not just quit?"

"Hard to find a different line of work."

"Really? Lots of people switch jobs."

I sip some more water. There is one reason I never bothered to quit medicine and find something else. Medical school gave me no other options. All of the choices were variations of the exact same thing: patient care. If you dare to deviate from that, you're on your own. None of my med school instructors ever talked about things like working for a pharmaceutical or biotech company, going into hospital administration, or working for the government like in the U.S. National Institutes of Health.

Then there is my six-figure med school debt. Forget my six-figure salary. Much of that already goes into paying some of that damn loan off, and I'm still not finished. In my book, many doctors are not rich people.

"It's not that easy," I say.

"You could be right," Rick says. "So what about the people you work with? Are they nice to be around?"

"Some. But not all."

"Any real jerks?"

I nod as Rick keeps looking at me. Damnit, he still isn't going anywhere. That's when I think of a good story I could use, a mostly true one. I focus on the one person I definitely want to describe.

Dr. Samuel Pierson.

"There's this one surgeon who's a real asshole. Picture a tall thin man who is bald with glasses, and has a stiff mouth wherever he goes. Every time he speaks, he fucking raises his voice like he's screaming."

"Sounds like he deserves an ass-kicking," Hank says over Rick's shoulders. "That is one fucked-up doc."

"Believe it or not, I did kick his ass before."

"Yeah?"

"He came into the room I was working in, all bad boy and shit. Then he walked up to me to start a fight, because that's how he is. He grabbed me, then pushed me back. I kicked the fucker right back. And he went down, hard on the floor."

"Goddamn," Rick says, mouth gaping.

"Did you get in trouble?" Hank asks.

"Yeah," I say. "But it was worth it."

Rick and Hank whistle, then smile.

"You taught that sonofabitch a lesson," Rick says.

"I did, but if only I had another chance. If I really got my way, I'd tie him up in a chair, go apeshit with some punches to the face."

Rick and Hank start laughing.

"Throw some kicks in, too," Rick says.

"Or spit in his face," I say. "Better yet, let's throw in some screaming, torturing, beating, cutting off the hands, scary images, whatever. The worse, the better. I say every asshole doctor deserves the same treatment. Give them a taste of their own medicine, so to speak. Am I right, or am I right?"

At that moment, I cut through the piece of steak on my plate, slicing all the way through the meat with one hard press of the blade.

"Whoa, you are pissed," Rick says, laughing harder this time.

"Hey, I got a doctor story to tell," Hank says.

"Go for it."

"A few weeks ago, I went to the clinic for my annual checkup. Doc said I'm putting on a lot of weight, and my blood pressure and cholesterol are all out of control. So I asked him what should I do. He gave me the usual spiel: exercise, watch what I eat, that sort of thing. But he wasn't nice about it. There was no smile, no friendly manner. Nothing. Just hearing him speak makes me want to sucker-punch him."

"Why are doctors just a bunch of fucking assholes?'

"I don't know. They just are."

"I feel like I've had it with them. If you can't even treat someone with basic respect, how do you expect me to feel good about you?"

"I hear ya. Before leaving my apartment, I was watching the local news. You know what happened at Ivory Memorial today?"

"No."

"Some doctor got beaten up on the roof of the parking garage."

Oh shit, I don't want to be part of this conversation. I sip from my water glass, keeping my gaze forward the whole time.

"Hadn't heard about that," Rick says.

"The police said the attack appears to be done by a disgruntled family member, of a patient who died in that hospital," Hank says. "They didn't mention any names, but it still pisses me off."

"So one of the doctor's patients died, and the family got upset?"

"Pretty much."

"Sounds like a shitty doctor."

"Maybe. If he's that bad, I say fuck him. He deserved it."

That does it. I slam my left hand on the counter and turn my head swiftly in Hank's direction. I keep my mouth stiff and tight and lock my eyes on the big man. Hank freezes, with a mix of fear and confusion.

"You want to say that again?" I growl.

"Say what? The part about the doctor being so bad?"

"That and the part about him deserving a beating."

"What's wrong with that?"

"What's wrong is that you don't know the whole story."

"I'm just reacting to what I heard. And why should you be so offended?"

"Take a fucking guess."

Hank turns to Rick, who also says nothing. Then Rick's eyes widen with realization.

"Wait a minute," he says to me. "You're the doctor who got beaten up?"

"So I lied," I say coldly. "You know why? Because I'm fed up. I've had the worst godawful day of my life and I don't need any more shit thrown at me. I'm sick and tired of people who make a judgment without seeing everything, just like I'm sick and tired of all the stupid and selfish people who fuck things up for everyone else. I try really hard to help others and do my job, and this is how I get treated? Are people really that goddamn pathetic? Huh?"

By this time, Rick and Hank have stood up, hands slightly raised in surrender. Their faces register real fear. Then I see why: my right hand is still gripping the steak knife. I was pointing it at them the whole time I was letting my rage loose. I turn back to the bar. That's when I notice the bartender standing there, also nervous in my presence. I carefully put the knife down on my plate, then bury my face in my hands. I just want to be left alone now. I close my eyes for a while, waiting for Rick and Hank to finally go away and for other people to stop looking in my direction, assuming that my outburst did get their attention.

Damn, I really fucked up.

Minutes later, I pay my tab, then think about what Thomas Chandler and Ellen Roberts have said about taking time off. COVID-19 had kept everyone on their toes, turning healthcare workers like me into mindless drones. The whole time, I never bothered to deprogram and destress. A vacation is long overdue.

On the drive home, I listen to one more song on Spotify: a dark and bitter piece by Phil Collins called "I Don't Care Anymore." Because really, I don't care anymore.

THURSDAY

CHAPTER 22

I sleep for a very long time. But I still wake up with pain squeezing my head. I am also in bad need of a full-body cleansing, having been too tired to wash up after coming home last night. All I had done was remove my clothes, climb into bed, and close my eyes. I had forgotten to turn off the alarm in my phone's clock app, but I dozed through it.

It is now nine thirty in the morning. I get out of bed and take a long hot shower, letting every bit of dirt, sweat, and misery slip down the drain. I put on blue jeans and a green flannel shirt. Noticing the sunlight streaking through my bedroom window, I figure it's a good time to step outside. So I head downstairs and out the patio door. The sun is out, shining down on the grass in my yard with not a cloud in sight. I sit in one of the lounge chairs near the sliding door. Then I close my eyes. I start falling asleep again.

Is this really what I'm going to do all day, lounging around in the backyard? I hope not. That would be a serious waste of precious time off. One-sixth of it would be gone in a flash. But should I go out with a dejected, beat-up face? I'm not so sure, especially after I had scared away Rick and Hank last night. Who knows if anyone else might have a problem with it?

As I feel the breezy air cool my skin, I hear footsteps. They are coming from the fence to my left. Kenneth Randall's backyard.

"Hello, Ken," I call out.

"Hi, Mark."

Ken begins walking in my direction. I suddenly stiffen. Holy crap, he is going to see my face if he actually peeks over the fence. But then he stops short of the wooden planks. I sigh in relief.

"First day off?" he asks.

"Yeah. Are you just hanging around at home, too?"

"I was going to, but Edith and I made last-minute plans."

"For what?"

"Travel. We went on Expedia and searched around for vacation packages. Plenty of good ones for New York, Seattle, Boston, Chicago. But then we saw a great deal for a trip to Hawaii, and we decided to book it."

"Cool. When are you going?"

"Today."

I pause, then straighten up in my chair.

"You booked an impromptu flight to Hawaii?"

"Yep. We're going to leave in an hour. The flight isn't until mid-afternoon, but I figure we beat the traffic first."

"What part of Hawaii are you going to?"

"First, the main island Oahu. Then Maui for another few days."

"Oh, wow. Have fun."

"Thanks. So when was the time you took a vacation?"

I begin to laugh.

"Do you know you're the third person to bring that up lately?" I ask. "It's like everyone is giving me crap about it."

"Maybe that's a sign," Ken says, chuckling as well.

"It has been a long time since my last extended break."

"Well, there you go."

"I guess I've gotten so used to six days off every twelve days that I don't even remember what a real break is like anymore."

Ken laughs again.

"Maybe it's time you finally follow the advice," he says.

"Might as well. I still don't know where to go, though."

"Well, you got plenty of time to decide. There are lots of places you can visit. The world is an oyster for travelers, you know."

"Right."

"Say, what happened at Ivory Memorial yesterday?"

"What are you talking about?"

"The parking garage. The news last night said someone got attacked there. It was on all the channels."

Oh, here we go again. Time to cover it up, avoid drawing attention to myself. I must put it to rest.

"Well, I don't know a thing about it," I say nonchalantly. "I was pretty much gone for the day."

"They said the victim was a physician. The attacker was angry about a family member who died as a patient."

"Did they mention the victim's name?"

"No, there were no names at all. Not that it matters. I figure that person would appreciate the privacy."

Yep, I absolutely would. I still hope Ken doesn't look over the fence.

"It's too bad people would resort to violence," Ken says. "Sometimes I wonder if morals and values have really gone out the window."

"I think about that all the time," I say. "OK, maybe not all of the time, but enough that it bothers me."

"Even while on the job?"

"Sometimes. But more often when the day is done."

"Anything about being a doctor that stresses you?"

"People's lack of respect for it. That's the main thing."

There is a pause.

"What do you mean, Mark?"

"Patients used to trust doctors and let the experts decide what is best. Not anymore. Now they look up medical stuff on the internet, like they want to trap us in a gotcha moment and prove they know more than we do."

"Do you think you're being too harsh?"

"Not at all."

Ken doesn't say anything. I sigh under my breath.

"The thing is, it's not that simple," I continue. "People seem to think that it's just a matter of a symptom checklist, see if their own symptoms match how a disease is described. But do they understand all the workings of the human body, and the many caveats of diseases and conditions so that they can effectively sort out which possible diagnoses are more likely or less likely? Can they order the right tests and interpret the results correctly? Can they weigh the benefits and risks of every treatment option, not just fixate on one that sounds good from the start? If they really think they know more than us doctors, let's see if they can all of that without any medical training at all. No anatomy cadavers, studying, clinical rotations, residency. Nothing."

"They won't succeed."

"Yet, they act like they can."

"Mark, I can sense you're upset."

"Well, I am."

Because of the fence, I can't see Ken's expression. I'm going to assume he is frowning, shaking his head, or both.

"Let's put it this way," I go on. "If my car needs maintenance or repair, I could do it myself, if I have the knowledge and skills. But I don't, so I go to a mechanic. I trust that he can do what needs to be done, based on what he knows about how cars function. I could look up stuff if I want, then ask him if the problem is so-and-so. But I wouldn't try to prove him wrong or anything. I go to the mechanic for a reason. He's the expert, and I'm not. Even if I've had bad mechanics, I wouldn't put the next one in the hot seat."

"An interesting analogy."

"With some differences. Cars are artificial. The human body is not. Cars have complex inner workings, but nowhere as complicated as the human body. If a car stops working, it's not the end of the world. But when a human dies, that's it."

"I know it's difficult. It can be challenging for doctors to recognize a patient's autonomy, their right to make their own decisions if they're capable. Especially in today's time. Patients are really medical consumers. They want the best value for their money. Their own health is no exception."

"So what should I do?"

"I would say keep listening to them. You may be pleasantly surprised about how well some of them know things. And should they consider a path you know won't be helpful, you can gently offer your expertise. Right?"

"I'll try."

"You don't sound too sure."

I let out a sigh, a rather loud one.

"I put in the effort," I say. "I aim for the best outcomes. But not everyone appreciates it."

"How about the ones who do?"

"There are some, here and there."

"That's all that matters. Do you really need to please every single patient who comes into the hospital?"

"Would be nice, but yeah. It's not always possible."

"Just do your best."

I nod, even if Ken still doesn't see me.

* * *

In the kitchen, I change my mind about cooking something for lunch. I decide on a quick meal: a TV dinner. I pull one package from the fridge and heat the plastic tray of chicken breast, corn, and mashed potatoes in the microwave. The quality would be subpar compared to fine dining, but I'd take it for the convenience. Besides, I want to watch some TV while on the living room couch.

I use the remote to jump to CNN. Then I stop, staring at the chyron on the screen.

> *BREAKING NEWS*
> *TEEN HACKER ARRESTED IN CONNECTION WITH LUCIFER'S WORM; OTHER HACKERS STILL AT LARGE*

The live footage shows two FBI agents escorting a handcuffed teenage boy away from a high school. The young teen, wearing black jeans and a matching T-shirt with a white skull on the front, has his face tilted downward, his curly brown hair partly hanging over his eyes. I listen to the anchor reporting the latest details. The yet-to-be-identified kid in Cincinnati, Ohio, who is only fifteen years old, is the hacker who had struck bank accounts in a Robin Hood-type scheme, transferring money from the wealthy to random people with low balances. He had bragged about this to a fellow friend at school, who in turn reported it to the FBI with the help of his parents. Meanwhile, based on the vast scope of cyberattacks after the release of Lucifer's Worm, authorities are considering the likely possibility that this hacker is part of a network of hackers, not a lone wolf.

Obviously, several questions remain. Is this the hacker who unleashed Lucifer's Worm? How many hackers are involved? Where are they located? Why are they doing this?

One thing is definitely clear. Doctor Lucifer could not possibly be this fifteen-year-old. Changing medication orders and patient records is just too sophisticated to be pulled off by someone so young. The medical hacker has to have some knowledge of the field, or is at least working with someone who does.

About ten minutes later, I finish my lunch and lean back on the couch. The next segment features a live interview with a cybersecurity expert. Not just any. The same one who appeared on MSNBC earlier this week. This time, he talks more about the possibility of catching all of the other hackers and less about how they might strike next. Even with the optimism, I don't bother listening. In fact, I gradually doze off. The TV is still on but I filter it out. Pretty soon, I enter dreamland, that wonderful realm of blackness and nothingness where images and memories blend into random weirdness. My brain soon relaxes, as if resetting and clearing out its junk. I remain still for a while longer.

When I wake up, CNN is providing a recap of the breaking story about the teen hacker. There is nothing new, other than the fact that the kid and the FBI are now far away from the school. I switch to one of the regular broadcast channels and catch the local news. It is not long before there's an update on last night's hospital parking garage attack. Police have finally released the names of the two gunshot victims: Lisa Flint and her brother-in-law Zachary Flint. In a press conference, an Anaheim police officer explains that those two had intended to harm a specific doctor because a family member died in his care, but the doctor's acts of self-defense instead resulted in the deaths of the two Flint family members. The best part is that they're keeping the name of the assaulted doctor under wraps. Good. I don't know if it's police protocol or some action by Ivory Memorial's public relations department that had something to do with it. Regardless, I'm taking it.

I turn off the TV, with a great sense of relief.

That's when I spot my personal phone on the coffee table. It is blinking a light, indicating a new voicemail message. It was left a couple of minutes ago while I was asleep. I listen to the recording.

"*If you think you've gotten away, you are mistaken.*"

Doctor Lucifer. Goddamn it, he's back.

"*I will destroy you, unless you find me first. I will give you twenty-four hours to hunt me down. If you fail, I will kill someone and leave the blood on your hands. I dare you to catch me, motherfucker!*"

I shake all over as I close my voicemail box. What is Lucifer up to now? Is he really going to murder someone? Who will he kill? Goddamn, I don't know what to do. I have nothing to go by, no one to turn to. Helpless, I fall flat on the couch and ball into a fetal position.

Hoping to distract myself, I toss my TV dinner tray into the trash and take a piss in the bathroom. Then I get on my phone and quickly check news headlines from other sources. None of them tell me anything new, nor do they quell my fears. Next, I log into my personal email since I haven't checked that in days. I don't expect to see much. I have few regular email contacts anyway.

But there is one new message. Surprisingly, the sender's name and email address are completely blank.

SUBJECT: I dare you to catch me, motherfucker!

Slay the demon to win the game
Seek the water where the natives aim

Catch the dragon by trapping its tail
Round the lip of the British male
Kill the goblin to end the curse
Find the gold in the lady's purse
Strike the troll with blade or gun
Shoot the bear and the morning sun
Beat the ogre and end its malice
Pass the door of the moistened phallus
Stab the zombie and rip its jaw
End the journey at the lion's claw

CATCH ME IF YOU CAN!

Doctor Lucifer

What the hell is this? Some sort of ridiculous poem? If this is Doctor Lucifer's way of stringing me along, I'd say screw it, I'm done.

But then I remember the voicemail. Its last line is the same as the subject line of this email. And the voice said that if I don't catch Lucifer within twenty-four hours, he is going to kill someone. Is that true, though? Who knows if this would lead me away from Lucifer, not toward him? Damn this uncertainty. It's driving me mad. But I would also hate to be wrong after sitting on my ass. If someone does die and I could've stopped it, I won't be able to live with myself.

There is only one way to put that possibility to rest and that is to march forward. Taking a deep breath, I make my decision.

It is time to play Lucifer's game.

CHAPTER 23

For the next hour or so, I head south from home, first through a few winding roads and then on minor freeways before merging onto the 5 Freeway. It is smooth sailing until I pass the city of Irvine. About two miles of bumper-to-bumper traffic halt my progress. Whatever. It's not like I'm dying to get anywhere by a certain time. There's really only one purpose for this drive: clearing my head.

Later, I pass by San Juan Capistrano, which I had mentally noted as a landmark before my planned exit: Dana Point, where Highway 1 officially begins in SoCal. I sail down the off-ramp and merge onto the first leg of the 1, Pacific Coast Highway. At last, I am doing it: a road trip on Highway 1. Not all the way up to Northern California, but just from Orange County to Los Angeles County, still more than enough for me. After minutes of admiring the sights of SoCal, I turn on my dashboard stereo, with my Spotify playlist on shuffle mode as usual. This is what I truly relish in: just me, my music, and my Tesla, along a road that welcomes my presence.

In essence, solitude.

I drive through Laguna Beach as one of my favorite songs comes on. "Let the Music Play," an early eighties pop hit by Shannon, is one of the few tunes I actually love dancing to, at least in private because I hate dancing in public. There's just something upbeat about this one. I enjoy losing myself in its semi-fast tempo, loud and intense beats, and feel-good vocals, the perfect accompaniment to the gorgeous sights on my left: the nearly cloudless blue sky, the glistening Pacific Ocean, the early afternoon sun beaming down on waves that wash onto the long sandy beach. I also appreciate the song's title, because music is my therapy. Just play it for me.

The mood continues further up Highway 1. In Huntington Beach, the Bon Jovi song "Raise Your Hands" fills the interior of the Tesla. This one is loud, like front-row-seat concert loud, but I love it. If I need a boost, this dose of excitement is the cure. I could see myself standing tall, looking up to the sky, and triumphantly throwing my fists up, so high on top of the world that nothing could pull me down to the depths. I also begin laughing, as I realize that I'm crossing Beach Boulevard, the same intersection I reached last night in a totally opposite emotional state.

Eventually, I switch off the stereo. The healing for my soul is more than adequate. At least I hope so.

I carefully get off Highway 1 and make my way west into Long Beach. I follow Ocean Boulevard before turning left onto Shoreline Drive and heading to the touristy area, with attractions like the Pike Outlets shopping center, the Aquarium of the Pacific, and the Queen Mary. I park in a lot next to Shoreline Aquatic Park. A spiral notebook and a black ballpoint pen sit in the passenger seat, which I pick up as I get out of the car. With few visitors on this weekday afternoon, I find a good patch of empty grass in no time.

I sit down and open the notebook.

Before leaving the house, I had copied Doctor Lucifer's 12-line poem onto the first page. Now, with the warm sun and gentle cool breeze soothing me, it is time to decipher this damn thing. What is it all about? Why is he doing this? I read each line carefully from first to last, and do it again a few times.

The more I look at it, the more I see that this is indeed some kind of riddle, not some mere exercise in verse. The lines sound like a series of weird rhyming instructions. *Slay the demon to win the game. Seek the water where the natives aim.* Whatever the hell that means. I go through each word individually, which doesn't help much. Then I look at the whole thing at once, with all twelve lines in my central vision. I am staring at this like I'm gazing at one of those Magic Eye illustrations, where a 3D image could supposedly appear from a flat 2D picture if I move my eyes in just the right way.

After about five minutes, I stop.

There is a pattern here, involving alternation. The odd-numbered lines sound like variations of one thing, while the even-numbered lines sound like something else. With my pen, I quickly rewrite the first, third, fifth, seventh, ninth, and eleventh lines of the riddle on another blank page:

> *Slay the demon to win the game*
> *Catch the dragon by trapping its tail*
> *Kill the goblin to end the curse*
> *Strike the troll with blade or gun*
> *Beat the ogre and end its malice*
> *Stab the zombie and rip its jaw*

Yep. The third word in each line refers to a type of monster. But what does each line mean? None of it makes any damn sense. So, on the next blank page, I rewrite the other six lines of the riddle:

> *Seek the water where the natives aim*
> *Round the lip of the British male*
> *Find the gold in the lady's purse*
> *Shoot the bear and the morning sun*
> *Pass the door of the moistened phallus*
> *End the journey at the lion's claw*

Other than the first word being a verb, I find nothing in common with these six lines. With the two sets of lines on opposite pages of my notebook, I can see them both simultaneously. I attempt to look for patterns between the two sets. First line of left page, first line of right page, nothing. Line one left, line two right, nothing either. I try every combination of one line on the left and one on the right. Shit, this is a waste of time. Is this really just random fluff that has no meaning whatsoever?

Given my skill with crossword puzzles and word games, I try a different approach: word association. Look at each line and write synonyms of the key words. For the first line on the left, the key words are *slay, demon, win,* and *game.* Words related to these four: *slash, kill, defeat, destroy, devil, monster, beast, victory, achievement, champion, contest, fun, leisure.* Ugh, this is already giving me a headache. Then I look across the words I've written, in case there are striking connections.

Still nothing.

Just for the sake of avoiding stagnation, I do the synonym exercise for the first line on the right: *Seek the water where the natives aim.* I scribble a ton of words related to the act of looking for something, bodies of water, Native Americans, and pointing at an object. I divide them into groups of four. Then I focus on the words and let my brain loose, waiting for something. Anything.

My head starts hurting. I lie down on the grass and hold my notebook above my face, blocking the sun. I continue brainstorming, to the point of almost falling asleep. My eyelids begin to slowly close. I let out a loud yawn.

Then, abruptly, I sit back up.

Two words click together: *pond,* among the words related to *water,* and *arrow,* from the set of words similar to *aim.* I am suddenly thinking of Arrowhead Pond, the former name of the Honda Center, the arena where the Anaheim Ducks play their home games. It all makes sense now. *Seek the water where the natives aim,* if *natives* means Native Americans with bows and arrows.

If that line is pointing to a physical location, line two is probably doing the same. *Round the lip of the British male.* OK, what the hell is this about? Of course, I'm not giving up, not after nailing what I believe is the answer to line one. The first thing I wonder is if the last word really refers to a man or boy as spelled, M-A-L-E, or is intentionally misspelled and actually refers to postal mail, M-A-I-L.

After looking at the words, I write down a new one: *chap.* That is a British term for a man or boy. It can also describe dry lips, and line two does mention *lip.* Oh man, I am definitely onto something. Now, is there a place somewhere in Southern California called Chap or something similar?

Actually, there is.

I pull out my phone and open the Google Maps app. I scroll the map to the east of my current location in Long Beach, then zoom in on the east part of Anaheim. Yes, I knew it! In the neighboring city of Orange, there is an east-west street called Chapman Avenue. I scan it from left to right, then I stop and zoom in even more. The intersection of Chapman Avenue and Glassell Street is a roundabout, a circular intersection.

Shit, that has to be the meaning of *round,* the first word!

So that's two points on the map now: Honda Center and the Chapman Avenue roundabout. Is line three a third location? *Find the gold in the lady's purse,* it says. Somehow, the same strategy has to work here, too. But damnit, I need a break. So I lie down, cover my face with the open notebook, and close my eyes.

I sleep for about fifteen minutes before the phone in my pocket vibrates. I answer it without seeing who's calling.

"Hello?"

"Hey, Mark. It's Thomas."

Oh man, it's Thomas Chandler? What a surprise.

"What's up?" I ask.

"Just wanted to check up on you," Thomas says in his usual friendly tone. "Make sure you're OK, you know."

"Well, I appreciate it. But what's the occasion? Is this about dinner on Tuesday when I seemed so quiet?"

"That's part of it. The other thing has to do with last night. The assault at the parking garage."

"What do you know about it?"

"The Anaheim police had a news conference this morning. They revealed the identities of the attacker and the woman. And provided their pics."

Not surprised, since I already got a glimpse of them myself. But I do realize what happened. Thomas saw Lisa Flint's face on TV today, remembered her from the protest on Tuesday, and thought of me.

"Is it correct that you were the assault victim?" Thomas asks slowly.

"Yes," I say without thought.

"I'm really sorry."

"At least my name isn't out there. I'll keep denying it to the media, but not to you or any other good friends of mine."

"Hey, I would do the same thing."

"Right. Just let the public keep guessing."

"Did you get beaten up badly?"

"I did, but imaging in the ED cleared me for discharge."

"Are you feeling better though?"

"Yeah, sure."

"Where are you at now?"

"Long Beach."

"Seriously? You're hanging out all the way there?"

"Yeah. The Pike is pretty nice, I have to say."

"I took a girlfriend there once. Nice place for dinner and a movie, plus a romantic walk along the water."

I smile.

"Thomas, I gotta ask. Did anything strange or tragic occur in the hospital today?"

"Like what?"

"Code Blues or Rapid Responses that really should not have happened. Weird stuff like that."

"You're still worried about the hacker?"

"Why wouldn't I be?"

"Well, there was only one Code Blue that ended in death. It was a patient getting chemo for metastatic cancer."

"Nothing out of the ordinary, then."

"I'll still keep my eyes out, just in case. All right, man. Good to hear you're doing OK. I'll talk to you later."

I hang up. Since I am not really sleepy anymore, I go back to line three of the riddle: *Find the gold in the lady's purse.*

In the Google Maps app that is still open, I decide to just scroll around the map in random directions. I am zoomed in so that the window is showing individual streets of a specific city section or two. I take note of the places I see as I slowly move around.

The Santa Ana River in Orange County.

The city of Fullerton.

The city of Buena Park.

Knott's Berry Farm.

Little Saigon in Westminster.

The city of Fountain Valley.

The northern part of Huntington Beach.

Bolsa Chica State Beach.

I stop. Then I turn back to the notebook to reread the third line of the riddle. *Find the gold in the lady's purse.*

That's it! Bolsa Chica is the lady's purse. The gold is probably the beach sand. Line three, done.

Now I zoom the map out, so that the locations of Bolsa Chica State Beach, the Honda Center, and the Chapman Avenue roundabout are all in the same screen. I can imagine an elongated triangle, with the two spots in Anaheim and Orange marking its short side and lines from those two points going all the way to Bolsa Chica in the southwest to form the two very long sides. It's like a giant ice cream cone, with its tip at the edge of the Pacific Ocean. I laugh as I realize this is like geometry class all over again.

Next, line four: *Shoot the bear and the morning sun.*

I crack this in under a minute. Given that I am already looking at an imaginary cone, I naturally picture a line shooting out from the inside of the cone, as if the cone is acting as a cannon. The line of sight heads northeast. Assuming the *bear* is a polar bear near the North Pole and knowing that the *morning sun* rises in the east, line four denotes that particular direction on the compass.

This would mean the destination is coming up.

Line five sounds like a place en route to it. *Pass the door of the moistened phallus.* Time for word association again. I scribble stuff related to *pass, door, moist,* and *phallus,* then draw imaginary lines from one word to another. I'm suddenly reminded of a particular scene in a movie: Russell Crowe in *A Beautiful Mind* trying to crack a complex numeric code. In a way, I'm a lot like him: crazy, but brilliant as hell. Yet, I am stuck once again. My head pounds even harder this time. I am also cramped from being in a stationary position for so long. It's time to take a walk.

I carry my notebook and pen while strolling alongside the water. I decide to continue the word game just as a light mental exercise. I still take in the sights to ease the tension. Then I reach the end of the park, which is essentially the tip of a small peninsula. To my right is the majestic Queen Mary, a historic British ocean liner that was permanently docked here after its retirement. Up ahead is a marina, full of sailboats and motorboats of various sizes. I can't imagine living on a boat, being on water all the time. At least there are metal gates leading to each individual dock as a security measure.

With that, I go back to the riddle in my notebook. I had written plenty of words similar to *door,* but I hadn't thought of the word *gate.*

Three words now come together: *gate, water,* and *dick.*

Watergate. Tricky Dicky.

Answer to line five: the Richard Nixon Presidential Library and Museum, in the city of Yorba Linda. Looking in Google Maps, I stiffen with excitement. The northeast line indeed passes by that place.

Now, the final line: *End the journey at the lion's claw.*

It has to be the destination. My gut feeling also tells me that the only relevant key words are the last two. *Lion's claw.* What is that? I sit back down on the grass, open my notebook, and churn out synonyms and related terms for those two words. I draw imaginary lines between them, but nothing registers. Goddamn it, I am so fucking close!

I close my eyes and lie back on the grass, covering my face with the open notebook once again. My brain hovers between resting and thinking. I begin to picture a lion, then focus on its feet. They aren't claws, are they? Maybe they are. I always thought felines have paws, even the big cats. But what do I know? I'm not a zoologist.

I keep thinking how messed up this is. Doctor Lucifer hacking

Icarus. Instead of Icarus flying too close to the sun and having the wax on his wings melt, he is falling to his death a different way: a demon from the abyss rising up to kill him. I could very well be Icarus, an angel of health with his wings getting clipped. Forget the classic Greek tragedy. I have my own modern-day tragedy. It's funny how this reminds me of my early school days, when I learned about mythology. The major Greek and Roman gods, plus some half-gods. Also, some fantastic creatures, like the centaur, minotaur, satyr. I was even exposed to mythical elements from other cultures, like the Slavic character Baba Yaga, the djinni of Arabian myths, the griffin of medieval folklore...

I snap my fingers and bolt upright. The griffin is part lion, part eagle, with sharp talons for the front feet.

A lion with claws! As in, bird claws.

I go back to Google Maps in my phone, then perform a search for any place called "Griffin," G-R-I-F-F-I-N. There are some results, but none that could possibly be relevant. Then I try searching with spelling variations: G-R-I-F-F-O-N, G-R-Y-F-F-I-N, G-R-Y-P-H-O-N, G-R-I-P-H-O-N. Still nothing worth looking into. Then I get more creative with the letters, trying more funky spellings. After a few minutes, I am just about to give up. I decide to attempt a few more before I stop.

Jackpot!

G-R-Y-P-H-I-N yields a place called Gryphin Network Solutions. It is located in the eastern part of Yorba Linda. A line from Bolsa Chica State Beach drawn northeast past the Nixon library would practically nail this spot.

This has to be it!

Right away, I open my phone's web browser, search for Gryphin Network Solutions, and visit its official website. I learn that Gryphin offers products and services related to computer networking for business environments, things like internet routers, server equipment, firewall applications, and malware removal software. The company has been around for almost two decades, according to the website's "About Us" page. I also check out the page that introduces key members of the leadership team at Gryphin, including the CEO, CFO, and leaders of various company divisions. I scroll down the list, then quickly stop.

I look closely, and my breathing stops, too.

The Division Leader for Cybersecurity is Peter Carpenter, the fiancé of my friend, Jane Larsen.

What the hell is going on here? Is Doctor Lucifer really Peter, and did he think I couldn't crack his riddle? Or is Peter merely being framed by someone else who is Doctor Lucifer? I have no fucking idea.

I bury my face in my hands. My head is pounding. So is my heart. After all of this, the next step is going to be complicated. How in the world should I even approach this? I have to do something or else I'll run out of time.

Putting the phone away, I head back to my car.

CHAPTER 24

According to Google, my trip from Long Beach to Gryphin Network Solutions in Yorba Linda would take about 45 minutes if I head north on the 710 and east on the 91. I assume no more than an hour and fifteen minutes for actual driving time, given possible traffic delays. So far, I haven't encountered any. But this is only the start of the journey. Anything could happen at any time, on any freeway.

It is four twenty in the afternoon. If Peter's work day ends at five, I could possibly follow him, see what he's up to. Maybe find the perfect opportunity to confront him. Anything to get all the answers to my questions.

Is he Doctor Lucifer? If yes, then...

Why would he be doing this?

What does he have to gain?

Of all the physicians he could possibly choose to humiliate and torment, why me specifically?

Have I done something to deserve this punishment?

Does he really think I'm too stupid to figure out the riddle?

I reach the 91 interchange and then head east on that freeway. As I accelerate to match the traffic, my phone buzzes. It is an incoming call from Roger Garrison. I accept the call and turn on speaker mode, knowing that a call from the chief is always important and should never be ignored.

"Hello."

"Hi, Mark. This is Roger. Sorry if I'm bothering you at this hour."

"Not at all, sir."

"Are you busy?"

"I'm just driving somewhere. Don't worry. I'm hands-free."

There is a brief pause. Then Garrison speaks.

"I want to talk to you about the issue with Dr. Samuel Pierson. The Chief of Surgery and I reviewed the matter more closely, also taking into account the details provided by those who witnessed the altercation."

"OK."

"Based on the information gathered, we have agreed that Dr. Pierson was at fault, having initiated the fight. It's now clear that you were acting in self-defense. I'm sorry if I sounded like I was accusing you of wrongdoing."

"So you finally believe me."

"Even so, if you can avoid losing your temper no matter what, that would be most welcome."

"Yes, sir."

"Do you have any questions?"

"Just one. Will anything happen to Dr. Pierson?"

"As a matter of fact, he is suspended for a whole month, effective immediately."

Wow, is this really happening? After repeated dealings with that asshole, the gods are actually on my side for once.

"Am I suspended too?" I ask.

"Technically, no. You have not been issued any penalties. However, there's still another matter that I must go over."

"Yes?"

"I understand that you had been assaulted in the parking garage last night. I'm truly sorry that has happened. Are you feeling all right?"

I pause for a moment. I assume Garrison figured out I was the victim the same way Thomas Chandler did: the Anaheim police's press conference publicly mentioning Lisa and Zachary Flint.

"Better so far," I say.

"Are you still hurt physically?"

"Not really. But mentally, the trauma somewhat lingers."

"I can imagine. This, plus what I learned from IT about a computer hacker targeting your patients, would certainly be overwhelming for you. Would you agree?"

"Yes."

"Good, because I do think you need to rest. Therefore, I am ordering you to not return to work for the next four weeks."

"Will this affect my pay?"

"No."

"When do I return?"

"Just stand by for an update from me. The hospitalist schedule will need to be modified in light of this change."

"Understood."

"Otherwise, that should be it. Once again, I am sorry for the tremendous stress you are going through. I do believe your time off for the next month will be valuable. Take full advantage of it. I'll be in touch."

"Thank you."

"Goodbye, Mark."

I should be celebrating right now. But with a monster still on the loose, I'm not smiling until the job is done.

* * *

Gryphin Network Solutions occupies part of a wide three-story building, sharing it with other businesses having tech-sounding names. Parking spaces are marked all around. I pull into one that faces the street while allowing me to observe the doors of Gryphin in the rearview mirror. The view is perfect. Nothing is blocking it, not even a car parked in front of the entrance. I can easily hide any signs of a stakeout.

I check the time. 5:25 PM.

This is certainly the end of the work day for many. But I wonder if I've arrived too late, with Peter already having taken off before I came. I'm not giving up yet, though. There are maybe twenty other cars parked in this section of the lot alone. Surely, some of them belong to Gryphin employees.

Meanwhile, I still have no clear plan. Even if Peter were to come out and I tail him on the road, what would I do next? Spy on him during his evening activities? Confront him face to face and see what happens?

I sigh heavily. This is not a mission with an objective. This is a fishing expedition, a desperate effort to find anything, even one thing, that would shed light on this mystery about Doctor Lucifer and his cruel mind game. Why am I not giving up yet? Simple. Because I deciphered the goddamn riddle, and it led me somewhere. I have made it this far. I am not backing down.

I reopen my notebook, referring back to the scribbles of my thought process. I cannot imagine being wrong here. Are there any alternate answers for the six lines I cracked, other locations that could fit the cryptic clues? I doubt it, especially with the neatness of the geometry involving the cone and the diagonal line. Could I have just gone straight to the last line about the lion's claw? Maybe. I suppose I could research every single griffin-inspired company around the world until I find the one that could possibly be involved. But how much time would that take? An eternity, I imagine. Besides, the first five clues narrowed the geography to Southern California. No need to search the ends of the earth.

In the rearview mirror, nothing is happening.

I return to the notebook. What about the other six lines I put aside, the ones referencing monsters? Do they actually have anything useful? Ultimately, I don't bother. I am too tired to think anymore. Maybe those lines are indeed meaningless, only functioning as in-between clutter to confuse me.

I close the notebook and drop it on the passenger seat. About a minute later, someone is coming out of Gryphin in the rearview mirror.

Peter Carpenter. He is finally leaving.

Right away, I start the engine. I watch Peter in the mirror walk off to my right. I turn my head slightly that way, just enough to see him in my peripheral vision. He is getting into a white Toyota Prius that faces the building. I watch the car pull out and carefully proceed toward the street, stopping to let cars pass by. I reverse my Tesla and drive to my left, away from the Prius to avoid detection. The lot exit is just a short distance away. I stop there to let one car in the street pass by, then I slowly turn right. That car drives past Peter's Prius, which then turns right as well.

Now I am driving behind him, with lots of distance in between.

The Prius moves into the middle lane of the street. I keep going in my current one. The last thing I need is to tip him off to a pursuer. I have to do this carefully. Watching the speedometer, I keep my Tesla going at thirty miles an hour, five less than the posted speed limit. I could care less if anyone behind wants to pass, honk, or give me the finger. I just need to keep the Prius in sight.

Based on my sense of direction, I am going west. So far, there is only one instance of zigzagging, turning right on one street and then turning left onto another. I am now on a wide street with two lanes in each direction. The Prius is in the left lane while I still hold the right. Behind the Prius is a plain silver sedan. I change lanes to get behind it. I can still spot part of the Prius over the car in front.

Good. I can see Peter's car, but maybe not vice versa.

This goes on for about ten minutes. Then the Prius moves into the right lane and makes a right turn to head north. I am maybe a hundred feet behind, but at least he is unlikely to see me. When I turn onto the same street, I easily spot the Prius up ahead and to the left. I keep myself one lane over, instead of trying to go behind him.

As I proceed, an idea flashes before me. If Peter is going home, maybe I could call Doctor Lucifer's number stored in my call log, see if Peter, getting out of his car, answers his cell. That would confirm a connection.

Hell, maybe I should try it now.

I slowly inch closer to the Prius, just enough to barely make out the driver. With my right hand off the wheel, I use my phone to pull up the call log and then call Doctor Lucifer. I turn on speaker mode. While I hear a series of rings, I see no movement from Peter. He keeps both hands on the wheel without moving his head. After about the ninth ring, I hang up. Either Peter isn't Lucifer, or he is refusing to answer while driving.

I move into the same lane as the Prius. Good thing I do, because now that car is going into a left turn lane. So does the car in front of me.

I follow. It takes about two minutes before the green left arrow lights up and every car in line makes its turn. The Prius and the car in front proceed in the left lane going west. So do I.

After another uneventful couple of minutes, I notice a city limit sign. We are now entering Fullerton, Anaheim's neighbor to the north. The Prius still shows no indication of its driver spotting me. I am getting pretty damn good at this.

For a moment, I consider calling Lucifer again, but another idea strikes me. I pick up the phone and call Jane Larsen. Then I switch to speaker mode and put the phone in my lap. Jane answers immediately.

"Hello, Mark?"

"Jane, sorry to bother you if you're busy."

"Oh no, not at all. What's up?"

"Can I ask you a question?"

"What kind of question?"

"A really strange one, related to an even more bizarre situation. The question may sound intrusive, but it's kind of important to me."

I hear nothing for a few seconds.

"OK," she says slowly. "What is it?"

"It's about my situation with the computer hacker."

"Yes."

"Today, I got a threatening voicemail message, presumably from the hacker, saying if I don't catch him, someone is going to die."

"Really?"

"Then I got an email, likely from the same person, containing a weird riddle. To make a long story short, the lines of the riddle pointed to several places in Orange County. The last one is supposedly where he's ultimately pointing me to. It's some business called Gryphin Network Solutions."

I leave it at that. There is more silence, which I momentarily ignore as the Prius makes a left and I follow, still a good distance behind. This time, there is only space between my Tesla and the Prius. The gap must be wide enough to act as my shroud.

"That is unbelievable," Jane says. "Are you sure?"

"So far, yes."

"That's where Peter works."

At first, I consider playing dumb, pretending to be so surprised. But why would I? I've already disclosed so much to her. And she is my friend.

"I know," I say. "I saw him mentioned on Gryphin's website."

"So you're wondering if Peter is leading you on like this?"

"Pretty much."

There is silence. I hope I'm not losing her or pissing her off. So I present my question as carefully as I can.

"Based on how well you know him personally, is there anything to suggest that he would do something like this?"

"Absolutely not," Jane answers quickly without hesitation.

"One hundred percent?"

"Yes."

At that moment, the Prius turns left, and I follow. I enter an upscale residential neighborhood, a far cry from the busy main road I just left. I cut my speed to avoid catching up too quickly. The Prius makes another left.

"Mark, I've known Peter for eight years. He is the kindest, most wonderful man I have ever met. We have full faith and trust in each other. There are no secrets between me and him. We even understand each other's line of work fairly well. So I highly doubt that he is some kind of malicious computer hacker and hiding it from me."

"I'll take your word for it," I say politely.

"As much as I understand the stress you're going through, I don't have anything to offer that could help."

"It's fine."

"Hey, listen, I have to go. Peter is coming up to my house right now. I'll talk to you another time, OK?"

Immediately, I pull over to the curb without a word, watching the Prius quickly disappear. Peter isn't going home. He is meeting Jane, who turns out to live not too far from here. Without further delay, I turn my car around and head back out of the neighborhood. I peek at my phone.

The call had already ended. I let out a huge sigh of relief.

* * *

By the time I return to Anaheim Hills, my anxiety subsides. Jane had no idea I was so close by when I called, and Peter had no idea I was following him throughout his commute. I keep repeating these two statements to myself. I also look for a restaurant to clear my mind over dinner. I end up dining at a Thai place, ordering some pad thai with chicken. Once my meal arrives, the past hour becomes water under the bridge, my fears put to rest.

Meanwhile, I'm returning to the drawing board, back to square one.

Peter is not Doctor Lucifer. Yes, it's Jane's firm belief, not some concrete proof, but I am not going to argue and ruin her upcoming wedding.

Once again, who in the world is the medical hacker making my life a living hell? If he plotted to pit me against Peter, how did he know Peter in the first place? This is where I am totally stumped. Other than Jane, I don't know anyone who has a mutual connection with both me and Peter. My head pounds trying to come up with even one possibility. I let the delicious taste of noodles, chicken, and beansprouts soothe me, along with nice cold water to wash everything down. I also close my eyes for a minute. Then I get on my phone to read the latest news.

There are developments related to the arrested teen hacker.

First off, his name has been publicly announced: Adam Tyler. He is now cooperating with the FBI, confirming to authorities that he is not acting alone. He is part of a hacker clan, along with several others. He also says that one of the hackers is the mastermind behind the development and release of Lucifer's Worm. Otherwise, he has no idea who any of his cyber comrades are. Meanwhile, the FBI has possession of Tyler's laptop computer and other items, which could provide a treasure trove of clues for investigators.

I suppose I can sit and relax until the FBI catches all of the hackers. But I can't forget Doctor Lucifer's voicemail. Someone is going to die in less than twenty-four hours. That cannot wait.

My phone buzzes. I expect to see Lucifer as the caller, but

thankfully, it isn't him at all. Caller ID says Jane Larsen.

"Mark, about our conversation earlier. I'm really sorry I cut you off suddenly. I didn't mean to."

"You had plans. I get it."

"But don't think I was brushing aside the hacker thing."

"What is this about?"

For a moment, I hear a faint sigh. Something is going on.

"I had set up a nice candlelight dinner for Peter and myself," Jane says. "It was meant to be another special occasion in light of our upcoming wedding."

"I shouldn't have called then."

"No, don't say that. I admit that I didn't want any complications with this, which was why I abruptly ended the call. Again, I'm sorry. But then, during our meal, Peter asked me what was wrong. So I told him everything you had said."

"About the voicemail and the riddle?"

"Yeah."

"And?"

"Now he's worried, too."

"Why?"

"The same reason I am: your well-being. We're both concerned that this hacker has given you so much grief."

"Well, that's nice of you. But nothing is going to change unless this hacker is stopped. Right?"

"Which is why Peter asked me to call you back. He is offering to help you."

I freeze. My noodles dangle over the fork I'm holding in mid-air.

"How?" I ask.

"Let me turn on the speaker. He'll explain."

As I hear a bit of noise, probably Jane putting her phone down somewhere, I quickly eat the noodles and sip some water.

"Hello, Mark," Peter says.

"Hi there."

"Do you still have the email with the riddle?"

"Yes."

"Let me give you my email address so you can forward it to me."

"What will you do with it?"

"I'm going to look at the email's metadata, all the technical stuff buried under the stuff you see. Like IP addresses, if there are any."

"What will you do? Trace the email's origin?"

"Exactly."

I take another sip of water. My mood suddenly shoots upward.

"You don't have to do this," I say.

"No, but I want to."

"That's really kind of you. How long will the email trace take?"

"Depends on how complicated it is. I say give me a few hours."

"You think you can give me an answer by tomorrow?"

"Even better. Maybe by the end of tonight."

"But what about you and Jane? Your evening together?"

"We'll always have opportunities for that. But helping someone in desperate need, that's not something we're letting slip by."

I stop to take this in.

"I've always been taught to look out for the less fortunate," Peter says. "I'm also a fan of the Golden Rule."

"That's good," I comment.

"I also remember how funny you were and how much I enjoyed talking about the work you and I do. So it's sad to hear that you're in this situation. That's why I want to help you."

"Don't forget that you're also my friend," Jane says in a warm tone. "A close friend, too."

I smile. For a moment, the world seems a lot less bleak.

"So are you two giving up your evening just for me?" I ask.

"We'll still watch some TV together," Jane says.

"I can take care of the email tracing thing at the same time," Peter says. "You got a pen and paper?"

"I can type your email address in my phone."

"Sure thing. Here it is."

Peter spells out his email address, and I type it into a notepad app in my phone before saving it. I tell Peter to hold on. Then I open the phone's web browser, access my personal email, and forward Lucifer's email to Peter.

"There, I sent it," I say.

"Great," Peter says. "I'll get started on this soon."

"I can't tell you how much this means to me. Thank you for doing this. Next time we have dinner, it'll be my treat. How does that sound?"

"Can't really say no to that. Jane, do you agree?"

"Totally," she says. "Anyway, Mark, we'll let you go, but we'll be in touch. Just sit tight and get lots of rest, OK?"

For the first time today, I feel inner peace.

"I will," I answer.

* * *

I get home around eight o'clock. There are no missed calls, voicemails, or texts from Jane, and no email response from Peter. I figure he needs some more time. I head upstairs to brush my teeth, take a hot shower, and change into dark blue pajamas.

I also go downstairs to retrieve the *Breaking Bad* disc box and bring it up to my bedroom. I have a big TV and Blu-ray disc player there as well. Lying in bed, I watch the second episode of the series. It may still be the beginning of a long story, but shit is getting real. The teacher and former student now have to dispose a dead guy while holding another guy captive. There is a gross scene with an attempt to dissolve the corpse in a bathtub full of hydrofluoric acid. Because the tub is in an upstairs bathroom, the acid eats through the tub and the first-floor ceiling, and everything falls to the ground floor, guts and all. Once the credits roll, I turn off the TV and Blu-ray player with a remote, then switch off the lamp nearby. I start drifting to sleep. My tense body loosens. I focus on the silence of the room, which slowly fades from my consciousness.

A buzz interrupts it. It's my phone on the nightstand.

Jane has sent a text message.

Check your email. Peter finished it.

I access the web browser, which still shows my inbox because I had never closed the application or logged out of my email account. Right away, I see one new message, the first at the top in bold. Peter's reply.

Mark,

I am so sorry for the delay. Tracing the email message was harder than I expected. Had it contained only one IP address, it would've made things much, much easier.

In this case, the email header contained over two hundred IP addresses, as if the message got sent from one server and went through that many other servers before getting to you. Not sure if the hacker really did that or if he somehow created and slipped in many false IP addresses at once. The point is that he tried to mask the real IP address by surrounding it with 200+ misleading ones. I used an IP tracing application that could provide geolocation data based on an IP address and various databases, giving approximate latitude and longitude. However, that program only allows me to check the IP addresses one at a time, not all at once. That's why it took a super long time. But at least I got it done tonight as promised.

Anyway, I confirmed that only one IP may be real. It was buried in the middle of the list, not near either end of it.

I've attached a screenshot of the findings from that IP address, including the location of where the email was sent from. You decide if it's accurate or not. I hope this will help you.

Good luck.

Peter

I scroll to the part of the email displaying the attachment link, for a file called "IPAddressResults.jpg." I download it and then open it in an image app. The picture displays a screenshot of a desktop application window, with text details in the left half and a map marking a location in the right half. I zoom in on the map. I stare at the location marker, holding my gaze until I am convinced that I'm not crazy at all.

"Son of a bitch," I whisper.

FRIDAY

CHAPTER 25

The email had come from Ivory Memorial Hospital.

I spent all night thinking about it. The knowledge that Doctor Lucifer was right under my nose the whole time, sending me the riddle straight from my workplace, gave me no reason to sleep. I wonder if I somehow missed a vital clue that could've let me tackle the problem right then and there. Probably not. There just wasn't enough to go on.

Similarly, could I myself have narrowed the IP address to the hospital, or at least the general area, without Peter's help? I'm not sure. Even if I know what an IP address is and attempt to trace each one in Lucifer's email, I might not get the best results. Peter has the best resources, expertise, and knowledge. I don't. Then again, is the geolocation accurate? Nothing is one hundred percent certain, that's for sure. But what are the chances that the latitude and longitude pinpoint the exact location of Ivory Memorial Hospital, just by random chance? The marker didn't just narrow the location to Anaheim. It gave me the goddamn building, too. If that is correct, then only one question remains.

Among everyone working in the hospital, who is Doctor Lucifer?

I've already ruled out three of them: Patrick Flanigan, Walter Laramie, and Rajesh Krishnan. That leaves whoever else works in IT, and so far, I don't know anyone else. Whoever it is, he probably has some serious beef with the medical profession. Maybe he is bitter about not getting into medical school, then having his parents give him shit for failure and dishonoring the family. I really have no idea. My theories are weird enough to begin with. But given how fucked up this whole situation is, nothing seems out of the ordinary anymore.

In the end, I only get about four hours of real shuteye. Not four continuous hours of quality rest. Alternating periods of conscious brainstorming and deep dreaming, the latter totaling four hours. At this point, I no longer want refreshing sleep. I have a vital mission to complete.

Time is not on my side.

After showering and dressing in tan khakis and a green shirt, I drive to Ivory Memorial. I go through the main entrance like everyone else. Then I take the elevator down with a small group of folks. While they are headed to public areas like the radiology department, I use my employee badge to open the locked door leading to the private hallways and the IT department. I march forth to the entrance, which is open.

I peek in. The first room is empty at the moment. I decide to wait until somebody comes by. It happens about five minutes later. Rajesh Krishnan steps out from one of the back rooms.

"Dr. Lin?" he asks, frozen with surprise.

"Sorry to bother you, Rajesh, but there's something I need to talk to about. Something rather important."

"What is it?"

"Patrick and Walter kept me alert about the computer hacker targeting me. Kudos to them for their work. But we never talked about the possibility of an inside job, hackers operating from within this building."

Rajesh maintains a hard stare in my direction.

"That is nonsense. We are dedicated to operating a secure network. We take our work very seriously."

"Can you convince me?"

He sighs heavily, then slowly approaches me.

"Dr. Lin, what is the meaning of this?"

"I got an email from the hacker that basically taunted me into finding him. I had a friend do a trace of its origin, based on the IP address. Guess where it pointed to?"

"Here?"

"Yep."

"Are you sure? IP tracking isn't perfect, you know."

"If it's really just some other random troublemaker in Anaheim, how did my friend's tracing tool, which is supposedly more advanced than others, determine a latitude and longitude that just happened to mark this exact building?"

"I still think you're not being reasonable here."

It is my turn to do a quick time out. I look away, compose myself, and turn back to Rajesh.

"Look," I say. "I'm doing this because there's an urgency to it. The hacker also threatened me, saying someone is going to die. I don't know who, how, or when, but I want to be able to stop it."

"I'm sorry," Rajesh says. "I really don't know how I can help. If I do, I would gladly assist you."

"You're being honest with me?"

"Dr. Lin, do I have to explain myself here?"

At that moment, Patrick Flanigan comes out from the same back room. He glares at me, without the familiar friendly expression.

"What's going on?" he asks.

"Dr. Lin is wondering if any one of us in IT is the hacker," Rajesh says. "I'm trying to tell him that we're not."

Patrick moves to Rajesh's side.

"Dr. Lin, I know you've been under great pressure," Patrick says calmly. "But right now, we are super busy with things. Lots of things unrelated to Lucifer's Worm. And like Raj said, I don't know what we can do."

"I understand," I say, somewhat coldly.

"At this point, I think you should leave," Rajesh says to me firmly. "Please do not bother us, all right?"

I nod slowly, like a scolded child.

"I apologize for the inconvenience. Could you do me a favor and not tell Dr. Roger Garrison about this? He's got a lot on his plate, too."

"Fine," Rajesh says, arms crossed.

Then he points to the hallway.

* * *

I step into the elevator and press the button for the ground floor. Then I decide at the last minute to stop by the doctor's lounge instead, just for a quick snack, if anything. I hit the button for the eleventh floor after the doors open. Nobody comes in, and the elevator doesn't stop for anyone else.

I also think about saying hello to Jane and thank her personally for having Peter do the IP trace, even if it seems I am pretty much at a dead end now. But she isn't anywhere in the Department of Internal Medicine. In fact, none of the cubicles are occupied. I wonder if Dr. Garrison is in his office, but given my mandated time off, I'm not taking any chances by heading that way.

Quietly, I saunter to the lounge, pick out one strawberry-flavored Nutri-Grain bar, and devour it in two large bites. That hits the spot. I wash it down with water from the cooler, then discard the paper cup. Not wanting to be conspicuous, I sit at my cubicle. On a day like this, I absolutely value my space being in a back corner, with only one neighbor and the most amount of physical cover. I could stay focused on the computer, without making eye contact with anyone. If in the unlikely possibility that anyone sees me now and asks why I'm here, I could just say I'm tidying up a few things that I didn't have a chance to do a few days ago. Yeah, that's a convincingly good excuse.

To make that work, I log into my desktop computer and spend time going through my work email, reading new messages and clearing out old ones I no longer need to keep. I also log into Icarus to access my patient list. Although other doctors could add patients to it, like when an emergency doc gives me a new admission, it is still up to me to manually delete them when I'm done.

Yet, I don't. Not right away.

Part of me is curious, aching to know what happened to certain patients, the ones whom Doctor Lucifer struck. Another part says no, because I would be violating HIPAA. If it isn't required for me to do my job, I don't have a right to know. This is the federal government talking. Not respecting patient privacy could get my ass fined, fired, or imprisoned. No harmless slaps on the wrist.

Ah, fuck it. I open the first patient chart.

Donald Chester no longer has a hospital internist as the primary doc and a surgeon as a consult. Yesterday, he got transferred to the surgery service, with Dr. Gary Thorberg as the new primary. Makes sense, given that post-gastrectomy care is priority number one and the original issue of GI bleeding has practically been solved. So far, Chester is doing all right on postop day three. He's making good progress with healing of his abdominal incisions, breathing exercises to avoid lung collapse, and consumption of a clear liquid diet. I have a feeling that he'll be just fine in the end.

Clara Summers, the lady with diverticular bleeding, did not have any further bleeding episodes or other complications, including any signs of Doctor Lucifer striking again. Her hemoglobin and hematocrit quickly inched their way up toward her usual baseline levels. She was discharged from the hospital yesterday. Good for her.

This morning, Darnell Jackson got out of the Step Down Unit and is back on the medicine ward. His chart documents a lengthy discussion about how, for reasons they couldn't identify like I did, he erroneously received propranolol intended for another patient. That aside, his glucose level is coming down nicely. It's still elevated, but if his current insulin regimen is the right one, he could be out of here within a day or two.

Sadly, I cannot say the same about Doris Schafer.

Doctor Lucifer's second victim, with anaphylaxis because of malicious antibiotic switching, is still in the ICU on a ventilator, and in a coma. On Wednesday, the ICU doc noted that he suspected hypoxic encephalopathy, brain damage from lack of oxygen, due to the anaphylactic event on Monday and prolonged difficulty with intubation to provide oxygen support. Yesterday, the doc had a long talk with the husband, Ronald Schafer, about his wife's poor prognosis. Ronald wasn't ready to give up, though. When presented with the options of continuing care as usual versus stopping it altogether, he picked the former. Quite frankly, I don't blame him one bit. I'd probably do the same thing if this happened to a beloved family member of mine.

There is one more patient I feel like peeking in on: Laverne McDonald, the one who got out of the ICU for severe bacterial pneumonia, only to have a pacemaker malfunction two mornings ago. According to a note by a cardiologist, McDonald's pacemaker was interrogated, having its settings checked. He then described two grave errors: an excessively high base rate and an extremely high sensitivity threshold, both so out of the ordinary that he actually placed asterisks above this part of the note, on either side of the words "ATTENTION: UNUSUAL ADVERSE EVENT!" in all caps, as if screaming for me to pay attention.

Although this isn't my specialty, I know a few basics about cardiac pacemakers. If the heart doesn't beat often enough, like if it stops or skips a beat, the pacemaker would sense it, then send a jolt to the ventricles to stimulate a contraction, a heartbeat. The base rate is the minimum heart rate the pacemaker would try to maintain. Usually, it would be set around a normal level like 60 beats per minute. In fact, based on earlier records, that's what it's supposed to be for McDonald's pacemaker. But the cardiologist's interrogation tells a very different story.

A base rate of 130 beats per minute.

How is this even possible? This means that if McDonald's heart just happened to skip a beat, the pacemaker would suddenly force the heart to beat 130 times per minute, way too high for a frail old woman like her. That's exactly what it was on the telemetry when the nurse summoned Jay McKinnon. No way the patient could rest with that super high rate. So if she had been doing OK previously, that means only one thing.

Her base rate got changed, from 60 to 130.

The sensitivity threshold got raised, too. The result would be that the pacemaker would not detect even a normal spontaneous heartbeat. Therefore, the pacemaker, acting as if the patient's heart is not beating at all, would be guaranteed to trigger the dangerously high base rate of 130 BPM.

But how could all of this happen? Intrigued, I continue reading the newest contents of McDonald's chart. In the same note, the cardiologist stated that the patient would be observed for one day in the Step Down Unit to make sure no further cardiac issues came up. The next day, Thursday, the cardiologist noted that the patient would return to the wards upstairs. However, he also documented that the patient claimed to have had an unknown visitor, shortly before feeling palpitations the day before. The cardiologist attributed it to delirium, a state of confusion that might've been triggered by this sudden event and possibly this hospital environment being so foreign to her.

But then, this morning, the hospitalist caring for McDonald also noted it. For the second time, the patient was claiming that someone had been in her room the morning her pacemaker went haywire. Like the cardiologist, the hospitalist didn't know what was going on and also called it delirium.

I stiffen in my chair, because I have my own theory.

Doctor Lucifer is no doubt a very skilled hacker, having already breached the Icarus system several times. What is the likelihood that he also knows how to hack a cardiac pacemaker? At this point, anything is possible. Then there is the fact that he's an insider, someone employed by Ivory Memorial. Given that Laverne McDonald was a patient of mine just like his other targets, I'm willing to bet that he walked right up to her and did something to throw her pacemaker out of whack, before slipping out of the room unnoticed. The thought suddenly makes me shiver.

Someone in this hospital is a killer.

* * *

Laverne McDonald is in room 820. Getting in there will not be easy this time. I am not her current treating physician, nor am I even on duty. Then again, this isn't Area 51, with secret corridors and multiple high-level security clearance protocols. Casually, I walk past the head nurse who is fixated on a computer screen. Then I turn down another hall, not seeing any nurses looking in my direction. I slip into McDonald's room unnoticed, then knock very quietly on the open door.

The patient is in bed, awake and slightly smiling. Seated in a chair along the wall is a chubby bearded man with a similar friendly smile. I wave hello to both, then hold up one finger to my lips.

"Ms. McDonald, do you remember me?" I whisper.

The patient stares at me. Then she beams with delight.

"Yes, I do. Dr. Lin, right?"

"That's correct," I say. "Obviously, another doctor is taking care of you now. I'm actually off service, now that he's rotated into the schedule."

"It's still nice of you to visit."

"And who is this gentleman seated with you?"

"My son, Chuck."

I turn to shake hands with him.

"Nice to meet you, Dr. Lin," Chuck says.

"He was my first doctor here after getting out of the ICU," McDonald explains to her son. "Then I didn't see him anymore because I got taken downstairs."

"Because your pacemaker went crazy. Right, Mom?"

"Yep. Now I'm back up here and someone else is taking care of me. But he's pretty good, too, just like Dr. Lin is."

"I appreciate it," I say gently.

The patient smiles.

"I remember the pacemaker incident happening while I was commuting here," I say. "It seemed the night-shift doc took care of you just fine. He told me about it, and that gave me quite a scare. I'm sorry I missed you."

"No, don't be. It was just bad timing."

"Are you feeling OK now?"

"I'm doing pretty good."

"I ask because there's something I'm curious about."

McDonald takes a moment to press a bedrail button to raise her head. I move closer to both her and Chuck. I am standing almost between them.

"What is it?" she asks.

"I understand that you had a mysterious visitor," I say carefully. "Shortly before your pacemaker malfunctioned."

"I did."

"What happened?"

"I was just lying in bed, still asleep. I heard a noise, like footsteps. At first, I thought I was dreaming. Then I opened my eyes, and... and... oh my god."

Her expression does a one-eighty, with a smile that flips into a frown and eyes that widen into a blank stare. Chuck reaches up to hold his mother's hand in both of his. I say nothing. Instead, I just wait.

"A man was standing right by my bed," McDonald continues, voice lower. "Looking down at me."

"OK," I say softly with a nod.

"He gave me a smile. Not a friendly one at all, but a scary and creepy one. Almost like an evil clown smiling. And he held up something, like a cell phone or remote control. I don't know what it was. I just know that he took it out for a couple of seconds. And he kept making that horrid smile."

At this point, Chuck slowly stands up. He places one hand on his mother's shoulder, while still holding her hand with the other. I'm not sure if my visit is a good idea after all. But I have come to listen to her story, and listen I shall.

"Then, I felt my heart fluttering," McDonald says, breathing slightly heavy. "Boom, boom, boom, boom, boom, boom, boom. And the man just walked away, without trying to help me."

"What did he look like?"

"He wore glasses. He seemed somewhat big, too."

"What about hair?"

"Kind of dark."

"What did he wear?"

"Um..."

"Did he have a doctor's white coat?"

"No."

"Nurse's scrubs?"

"Not that either."

Maybe it wasn't a frontline healthcare worker. Or maybe it was, but not in their usual clothes. I keep looking at the patient. I need more detail, but I also have to be careful. The last thing I need is to trigger another catastrophic cardiac event.

"I only remember his shirt color," McDonald says. "It was blue."

Blue shirt... glasses... dark hair...

Who was it that looked like the Skipper from *Gilligan's Island,* two days ago on Wednesday?

Holy shit, it can't be.

Walter Laramie?!

I remain frozen, still looking at the patient. I nod while picturing what supposedly happened.

Walter had come in with some kind of device, used it to hack her pacemaker and jack up its base rate and sensitivity threshold. He waited until her palpitations started, then walked away. This was one cruel and sick act, not just to hurt this precious old lady but also to make me take the fall. Just like with every other patient of mine he harmed or killed through digital sabotage of Icarus records.

But wait. How could he do some hacking while I was physically in the same room with him? There had to be something else involved, something I hadn't considered. Maybe there is more than one evildoer in this hospital, not just Walter?

Whatever it is, I now have something to go on.

Walter Laramie holds all the answers. I just need to extract them, by force if I have to. I can't understand how the cardiologist and the current internist couldn't put two and two together. On the other hand, they weren't targets of computer hacking. I was, so I know exactly what to look for.

Now I'm glad I came to room 820.

The only thing left for me to do is to soothe the patient once more, then get the hell out of here.

"Ms. McDonald, I am so sorry to hear what happened," I say. "But you can rest knowing that your son is here."

"I know," she says. "You'll protect me, Chuck. Won't you?"

"You know I will, Mom," Chuck answers with a big smile. "It's going to be OK. I'll make sure of it."

I smile and pat McDonald's hand.

"Dr. Lin, thank you for stopping by," she says.

"Sure," I say. "But do me a favor. Don't think about that incident anymore. And don't mention to anyone that I came by. OK?"

The patient and her son nod. With that, I wave goodbye and walk out. Once I reach the elevator lobby, I drop my pleasant expression.

CHAPTER 26

Once again, I have crossed the forbidden red line of HIPAA.

I log into Icarus and search for Walter Laramie. There is one patient chart with that name, and I open it. Looking through random patient encounter documents, I come across a clinic note by the primary care doctor, which mentions, as part of the social history, the patient's occupation of IT technician in Ivory Memorial Hospital. Good, this is the Walter Laramie I know, not any other. So I head straight to the chart's contact information tab, commit his home address to memory, and search for it in Google Maps on my phone. Walter lives in west Anaheim, about a twenty-minute drive across town.

My work here is done. I leave the hospital.

In no time, I park across the street from Walter's house, a two-story wooden dwelling with faded yellow paint. The neighborhood seems decent, populated mainly with single-story homes of various colors and designs. At the moment, everything is quiet. No person roams the sidewalks, nor does a single car move anywhere in sight. Friday is, after all, a work day and a school day like any other.

I wonder what Walter is doing right now. Probably going about his daily work at Ivory Memorial. I will have to wait several hours until he comes home. Then I will confront his sorry ass, tell him that he's finished. He will pay for trying to kill my patients and making me take the fall. And who knows what else I will do?

On my phone, I check out the headlines for two newspapers: the *Los Angeles Times* and the *Orange County Register*. Nothing interesting so far. Not even any new developments with the FBI's investigation into the hacker clan. I smile a little, though. Knowing Doctor Lucifer and his movements, I am one step ahead of the feds. But I also shake a bit nervously. Unlike those professionals, I have no weapons on me, not to mention any kind of legal authority to make an arrest.

I turn back to Walter's house. It is now clear that waiting out here like a sitting duck is suicide. A neighborhood watch crew might have its eyes peeled. If I am to pounce on Walter, I need the element of surprise. I'll have to do it out of sight. There is only one place where I could do all of that: his backyard. I will need to heave myself over the wooden gate next to the garage, then get into a good hiding position.

Am I seriously going to do this? My morals say no. But my bitter heart says I have no choice. I have gone so far towards catching Doctor Lucifer that crossing one line after another is the last thing I should worry about.

While deep in thought, I hear a faint motor running. It's coming from Walter's house. Holy shit, the garage door is opening. It soon reveals a blue sedan that slowly backs out into the street.

Walter is in the driver's seat!

Quickly, I lean heavily to my right, almost lying on my side. For extra concealment, I open my glove compartment and pretend to search for something there. But I don't hear his car passing by. Instead, I heard it fade into the distance. He is heading off in the same direction I am currently facing. I hold my position for a full minute before closing the glove compartment and confirming that he is out of sight.

So Walter was home the whole morning. But now where is he going? I have no frigging idea. Perhaps he is coming to work late. Or he's not working today and he'll actually be back pretty soon. Either way, fuck it. I'm putting my plan into action.

I get out of my car and walk towards the fence next to Walter's garage. I turn my head to each side, spotting no other movement anywhere in the neighborhood. Without pause, I jump up, grab the top of the gate with both hands, pull myself up as hard as I could, and get one leg over. I carefully maneuver the other leg over before dropping onto some hard dirt.

Next step is to navigate a jungle. Thick, waist-high weeds cover every square inch of the backyard. I can barely see my feet as I inch my way forward, thorny stems poking and scratching my arms and legs. Goddamn, Walter never trimmed these plants. For a moment, I wonder if any animals are hiding beneath this sea of green. Then again, why would stray cats, raccoons, or whatever else want to hang around here?

The yard is no better around the corner of the house. The only break in the vegetation is a toolshed all the way on the other side. Even that is obscured by dense botanical overgrowth, making it look like a faraway house in a vast meadow. I turn to the rear of the house and spot a patio door. I head towards it, moving even more slowly than along the side of the house. At last, I am free. I'm now standing on a slab of concrete immediately in front of the glass patio door. I also notice it's partially open. Walter probably left it that way to let in some air.

Now what is my next move? Should I just stay here until he sees me? Maybe lure him out? Nah, that wouldn't give me an advantage. Plus, the wait might take forever, and I no longer any patience with him.

Then I spot the wooden stick on the patio door track inside the house. I pause to think. Given how many rules I've already broken, why stop now? If Walter had tormented me this much already, forget staying out here. I'm going all the way in. If there is going to be a showdown, it better be in his inner sanctum where he'd least expect me. Maybe I can find something to blackmail him with, too.

I turn back to the toolshed. I cross the weeds to the shed door, then open it. It is mostly empty, save for a few rotten cardboard boxes containing an assortment of items. Rummaging through them, I find a pair of grass shears, a tin water pitcher, a garden hose, and a few small plastic buckets, all of which I doubt were ever used regularly. Then I notice some even smaller things at the bottom of one of the boxes, like metal chimes, a miniature decorative windmill, a weathervane, and...

A wire coat hanger.

Just what I need. I pick it up, untwist it, and fully straighten it as best as I can. I exit the shed and return to the patio door. Holding the thin metal rod by the unhooked end, I slide my hand through the door gap.

Slowly, I maneuver the rod's hook until it slips under the wood stick. I lift the wood up, pull it to the side, and gently set it down along with the rod. Then, very carefully, I slide the patio door open. All too easy.

Once I step into the house and slide the door back to its previous position, my heart races like never before. I am entering uncharted moral territory, going against everything I believed was right. I've also put myself in maximum danger. What if someone else is home? What then? There will surely be a fiery encounter, with heated words and likely some violent blows. All I can do is defend myself and stand by my claim that Walter Laramie is a killer, in both cyberspace and physical space.

So far, the whole house is dead silent. I slowly walk through the dining area. Nearby are two doors, which I open to confirm that they lead to the garage and the basement. I move toward the front door of the house, then find myself treading carpet, which really helps dampen my footsteps. I also notice there are no wall decorations of any sort, not even a clock. Walter seems to be a slob, based on my glimpse of the kitchen, where I spot an open box of Apple Jacks cereal near a sink full of dirty dishes. In the living room, the décor is surprisingly simple. Just a sofa for two, a dark wooden coffee table, and a giant flat-screen TV mounted on the upper wall. Nothing more.

That's when I spot the stairs. All the interesting aspects of Walter's home life have to be up there. I head in that direction.

There are four doors along the upstairs hallway. The first leads to a nearly empty room, occupied only with a desk and cardboard boxes containing who knows what. The second is a small bathroom. The third is like the first, except the junk stored here fills the floor and, in certain spots, is stacked almost to shoulder height. Most of the stuff is electronic, like old desktop computers, a dismantled DVD player, a wheeled cart with a dusty flat-screen TV, and stereo speakers. Walter is probably a crazy tech geek, with a zeal for understanding the inner workings of things like that. This leaves door number four, which has to be the master bedroom, Walter's personal chamber.

It is so dark in there that, even in the middle of the day, I have to flip on a light switch. Then I see why. Black curtains hang everywhere, not just over the windows. They are also tacked onto all the walls, concealing every square inch. The only surfaces with some shade of white are the ceiling and the carpeted floor. Otherwise, this room is a computer nerd's haven. An unmade bed sits immediately close to the door. Along the back wall is a desk with a sleek-looking black desktop computer and a bulky silver landline telephone. A knee-high wooden shelf occupies the corner space, storing a bunch of video games for the PC. To the left of the desk is a bathroom and a walk-in closet.

In the latter, I quickly run my hands through stuff at random. I search the shoe boxes on the floor, the jackets and shirts on hangers, the sweaters piled on the top shelf. Then I stop. Behind the last pile of clothes on the upper shelf, I feel something that's made of smooth paper. I pull it out.

It is the box package for a video game called *Diablo,* its cover depicting a vicious red demon against a black background. Why is this deep inside the closet, wedged behind some sweaters, not out there on the games shelf? Something tells me it isn't because the box is overly large in comparison or because the game is way older than those other ones. Instinctively, I open the box and pull out its contents: a jewel case containing the CD-ROM game disc, an instruction booklet for the game, and...

A little red spiral-bound notebook?

This definitely doesn't belong. I turn to the first page of the notebook, containing large handwritten text:

> *OPERATION HELLRAISER*
> *A global cataclysm to deal some real motherfucking punishment!*
>
> *The world shall be swarmed by Lucifer's Worm, then burn and crumble from the wrath of the Seven Deadly Sinners!*
>
> *#1: Doctor Lucifer*
> *Fuck everyone who is full of pride, especially asshole doctors!*

#2: Investor Mammon
Fuck everyone who is full of greed, especially filthy billionaires!

#3: Chairman Leviathan
Fuck everyone who is full of envy, especially corporate cutthroats!

#4: Father Asmodeus
Fuck everyone who is full of lust, especially pedophile priests!

#5: Chef Beelzebub
Fuck everyone who is full of gluttony, especially fat-ass restauranteurs!

#6: Chief Satan
Fuck everyone who is full of wrath, especially racist police!

#7: Senator Belphegor
Fuck everyone who is full of sloth, especially lazy-ass politicians!

I shake my head. The Seven Deadly Sinners are out of their goddamn minds. Walter Laramie as Doctor Lucifer, Adam Tyler as presumably Investor Mammon, and five other yet-to-be-identified demonic hackers. Quickly, I pull out my cell phone and use its camera app to take a photo of this page. I do the same for the next few pages, which lay out the details of Operation Hellraiser in a flowchart. In essence, Doctor Lucifer sends copies of the email containing Lucifer's Worm to 66 random people, while each of the other six demons deliver the spam message to 100 recipients. These 666 total emails spark the exponential self-duplication that floods email servers while leaving insecure backdoors. The rest is history,

There is other stuff scribbled on the next several pages, something entirely different. It's all a messy mix of notes, numbers, and crude diagrams. One of the diagrams depicts a smartphone, and it's even labeled with a brand name: Microsoft. I have no idea what any of this is, until I find a packet of printouts slipped between two of the pages. They are portions of a user manual for a Medtronic pacemaker. I rapidly flip through those pages before stopping on one in particular. The page with technical specifications for the device has two sets of numbers circled with a pen.

Base rate and sensitivity.

I suppress the urge to hurl these notes onto the floor. Walter fucking did it, hacking Laverne McDonald's pacemaker. With my phone, I snap images of the circled specs and samples of the related notebook pages.

The remaining pages of the notebook are blank, so I put it back into the *Diablo* game box. Same for the game manual, which has nothing inserted or handwritten between its pages. I'm about to return the game CD case when I decide to be thorough. I open the CD case and lift the game disc from the black plastic tray. Nothing underneath. Then I pull apart the tray, separating it from the clear back portion of the case.

Whoa, there is something in between here, not just the square paper with the back cover. There is a small sticky note, with just two words written:

Lucifer_MD
DeeMin_666

I take a picture of this before putting everything back in the box and returning it to the same hiding place. At that moment, my hand feels something else behind the pile of sweaters. I pull it out right away. It's a Microsoft smartphone, just like what's drawn in Walter's notebook. Holy crap, he somehow jerry-rigged this thing to hack McDonald's pacemaker. Shuddering, I put it back and exit the closet.

I rush over to Walter's desktop computer, turn it on, and wait until the Windows 10 booting process finishes. Then I am at a login screen. Walter Laramie is already identified as the user, but I have to enter the password. Instinctively, I enter "Lucifer_MD," which does not work. Then I try "DeeMin_666."

Jackpot.

The Windows desktop background depicts a man in green armor fighting a horde of demonic monsters, along with the logo for a video game called *Doom Eternal*. Seconds later, icons fill nearly every available slot of the screen. I scan each one. The standard icons for "This PC" and "Recycle Bin" are in the upper left. Surrounding it are utility applications, for things like enhancing sound, playing videos, and optimizing the 3D graphics card. From there, the rest of the screen is a ton of icons for PC video games, like *Mass Effect 2, World of Warcraft, Call of Duty: Black Ops, Overwatch, Fallout 76, Borderlands 3, Grand Theft Auto V,* and *Halo 4*. Goddamn, this guy has no life.

But then I come across an icon labeled "The Gateway." Its graphic depicts red stairs leading up to an archway. It is so simplistic, too, with just a few shades of red and a blocky look to it. Unlike the surrounding video game icons that are detailed high-resolution miniature pics, the Gateway icon looks like it was drawn by a crappy artist. Naturally, I double-click it to run the application. A large window pops up, containing only three white rectangles in the center of a black background. I hover the mouse cursor over them. With the first two, the cursor changes from an arrow to an I-shaped text cursor, indicating that they are boxes where I could type in something. The cursor remains an arrow over the third rectangle, but when I click it, it turns a light gray, then instantly back to white. It's a button.

Even without labels, I have a hunch that these are boxes for a username and password and a login button beneath. I type in "Lucifer_MD" into the first box and "DeeMin_666" into the second box, then click the button. Nothing happens, other than the two text boxes clearing. Probably they are wrong. So I try the reverse, "DeeMin_666" as the username and "Lucifer_MD" as the password. I click the button.

The entire window goes black.

Seconds later, it displays a row of buttons along the top, along with two large boxes side by side and two single-line boxes above. The large box on the left shows a list of folders, and the narrow box above contains text for a file path, indicating these are the contents of Walter's computer being displayed. The two corresponding boxes on the right are empty. Then I look at the buttons at the top, which are labeled with commands such as "Edit," "Duplicate," and "Delete." There is also a strange button called "Preset Hacks."

I've seen enough to figure it out. The Gateway is a hacker's tool, to remotely connect to a computer, examine its contents, and sabotage them in whatever fashion. The Preset Hacks feature is used to store instructions that would be automatically followed at specified dates and times. Maybe that's what Walter did to erase every mention of an allergy from Doris Schafer's chart, and perhaps every instance of Clara Summers's blood type. How else could he be hacking without being physically at a computer?

The whole thing is just fucking sick. I'd beat the shit out of Walter if I could. Damn him to hell!

Going back to the top buttons, I notice another one labeled "Chat." When I click it, another window pops up on top of the Gateway window. It's some kind of chat room, with a text box, an "Enter" button, and a single long list of messages entered by the Seven Deadly Sinners, dating all the way back to last Saturday. Here, the seven hackers are distinguished not just by name but also by text color, involving different shades of red, orange, and yellow that give the whole thing a fiery look.

I read a sample of the earliest chat messages:

> *BELPHEGOR: u all ready?*
> *LEVIATHAN: Fuck yeah I'm ready*
> *SATAN: I don't get why we gotta wait until tomorrow*
> *LUCIFER: Sunday is a holy day, so fucking it up is perfect!*
> *BEELZEBUB: And a new seven-day week*
> *ASMODEUS: yep, it's hell week*
> *LEVIATHAN: give em hell. hehehe*
> *MAMMON: what time on sunday do we begin?*

> *LUCIFER: Send the emails out at noon*
> *SATAN: Why not midnight when Sunday starts?*
> *ASMODEUS: hey, even we gotta rest, you know*
> *LEVIATHAN: I could sleep in first. Lol*
> *LUCIFER: after the emails, wait three hours, then do your stuff*
> *BEELZEBUB: fuck, I gotta wait? Ah well*
> *MAMMON: dude, its only one more day*
> *BEELZEBUB: fine*
> *SATAN: this is gonna be fun!*

Next, I scroll down to some of the communications posted on Monday, when I first heard about Lucifer's Worm.

> *MAMMON: holy shit, the world is in a goddamn panic!*
> *BELPHEGOR: raising hell, motherfuckers!*
> *LEVIATHAN: look at the media talking about us*
> *ASMODEUS: they're talkin about the worm, dumbass*
> *LEVIATHAN: The world is still bowing down to us*
> *BEELZEBUB: bow down to us, mortals!*
> *SATAN: screw the minneapolis PD! Go to their site. Hehehe*
> *LEVIATHAN: damn, you did good, satan*
> *SATAN: thx L*
> *BELPHEGOR: take that, bitches!*
> *MAMMON: who r u talking to, Belph?*
> *BELPHEGOR: the whole world, fool*
> *BEELZEBUB: You're a maniac, you kno that?*
> *ASMODEUS: fuck yeah, we're crazy*
> *MAMMON: we r all maniacs!*

Skimming the following messages, the Sinners mostly chat about random stuff not related to hacking, like action movies and video games. So I jump to the end of the chat thread. Since yesterday, there have been only a handful of messages posted, at intervals longer than before.

Something tells me they are finished.

LEVIATHAN: shit, the feds got one of us
BEELZEBUB: hold on, it's a goddamn kid?
LEVIATHAN: he's young, but he can fucking hack
ASMODEUS: which is he? Satan?
SATAN: Adam tyler ain't Satan. I ain't that kid
BELPHEGOR: where is lucifer
BEELZEBUB: I don't know. he better tell us what to do
LEVIATHAN: is Adam lucifer or mammon?
BELPHEGOR: I don't know
SATAN: he must be one of those two
BEELZEBUB: yeah, we are the other five
ASMODEUS: maybe we should hide
LEVIATHAN: why?
SATAN: Adam is snitching. The fed knows there is a clan
BEELZEBUB: ah, fuck it. I'm getting off. Not sticking around
BELPHEGOR: later

What a bunch of losers. These seven had nothing better to do than stoke chaos and disorder. Of course, I only care about one of them, and he's missing in action. Lucifer said nothing in the chat today. Is Walter terrified of the walls closing in, too?

I close the chat window and return to the Gateway, looking again at the command buttons. There is one more curious button: Gallery. Clicking it leads to another new window popping up. Inside is a series of small thumbnail images, above a button labeled "Upload." Double-clicking on an image displays its full-size version. In this manner, I look at each of them closely. Many of the images are screenshots of internet and TV news headlines, all related to Lucifer's Worm and subsequent reports of hacking. It is clear that the gallery is for the Seven Deadly Sinners to celebrate the chaos they have stirred up. There seem to be around fifty of these kinds of images altogether.

I also notice that each of the Seven Deadly Sinners has an image representing their personas

Senator Belphegor: a hand-drawn image depicting men in suits sleeping in a congressional chamber, some of them having their heads ripped off by a giant winged red demon.

Father Asmodeus: a vulgar art piece, showing a priest getting sodomized by a giant demon, shown from their front sides.

Chairman Leviathan: two angry office workers being crushed in the fists of a demonic beast.

Chef Beelzebub: an obese demon in a chef's hat ramming food down the throats of equally fat humans.

Investor Mammon: rich old men holding bags of money, while a demon rips their hearts out of their chests.

Chief Satan: a group of pig-like monsters wearing police uniforms, with a text caption saying, "These Pig Cops are from the game *Duke Nukem 3D*, but they're so much like real-life cops."

Lastly, I open the gallery image for Doctor Lucifer.

Two bright orange flames, shaped like wings, burn on either side of a blood-streaked gold staff. A pair of dark red serpents coil around the staff multiple times. One of them has its head facing me directly, its jaw wide open to reveal massive bloody fangs. The other also faces me, at an oblique angle. Its mouth is only slightly open, but several drops of blood fall from its exposed teeth. The whole thing transfixes me, disgusts me, and especially pisses me off. The caduceus, the modern symbol of medicine, twisted by dark demonic forces.

Walter Laramie is one sick fuck. What the hell is wrong with him? What does he have against the medical profession, or me for that matter?

I close my eyes, thinking about it real hard. But it only gives me a headache, tightening my forehead. Then another pain explodes in my head, this time in the back. It's so intense that I hear it. Oh god, something hit me in the skull, really damn hard! Then a deep pain stings in my right shoulder, and the next thing I know, my whole body softens. I open my eyes, but everything is a blur. The blurriness fades as my head droops forward.

The world goes dark.

CHAPTER 27

The first thing I become aware of is my head.

Constant, relentless pain permeates it. The throbbing makes it even worse, knocking against the inside of my skull each second that passes. My brain is crushed and suffocated like a vise, and I can't do a goddamn thing about it.

Soon, I begin to feel my neck as well. It's bent forward at a sharp angle, way more than I normally like. My mouth hangs slightly open. At least I can breathe.

Basically, I'm not dead yet.

I slowly open my eyes. Gradually, I let my vision clear up until I can see that I am staring into my own lap. But I cannot move my arms. They're pulled behind me and locked into place. My legs are fixed the same way, spread apart but unable to come closer together no matter how hard I try.

Shit, I'm tied up in a chair. My limbs and torso are bound to it with long ribbons of duct tape.

I don't bother trying to look up. I am out of juice. Whatever strength I had before has pretty much left my body. Now I long to be unconscious again. Whatever horror is coming, I want to sleep through it. There is no escape, but at least make me numb to it all. No misery or pain for me while in captivity.

Please. Pretty please.

I stay like this for quite a while. For a few moments, I close my eyes. I savor the luxury of two minutes of sleep in the most uncomfortable body position imaginable. Eventually, my ears pick up a slight shuffling of the carpet. I open my eyelids a tiny bit.

Out of nowhere, a shoe appears in my field of vision, between my knees. Followed by a second shoe.

"Rise and shine, Dr. Lin."

A cold hand touches my forehead, then slowly lifts it. I now stare into the face of Walter Laramie, twisted by an ugly scowl. This face and his friendly one in the hospital are night and day. He slowly pulls his hand away and steps back. At this point, I can keep my head upright on my own, as long as I don't tilt it in any direction. For several seconds, Walter eyes me with furrowed brows.

"Are you just going to sit there and stay quiet?" he says. "Say something or else I'll make you."

"You're a motherfucking sonofabitch," I manage to utter hoarsely. "There. Are you happy now?"

He snorts and turns away. One of his hands comes into view, gripping a lead pipe and a syringe. So that's what he knocked me out with: a blow to the head and an injection into one shoulder. Damn.

"You know, I should've hit you twice, three times, even," Walter says.

"Guess you're not so tough after all."

He turns back to me while pointing the end of the pipe at my face. Then he transfers the syringe to his other hand, examining it closely.

"If only I'd stolen more of this," he says.

"What is it?"

"Just some sedative from a medication room. I know the code for the door, because I can snoop through nurses' emails."

"Just like you and my patients' records. I assume you have the Gateway installed on your hospital laptop."

"I do."

"You used it to delete medication orders and create your own, all in my name. Is that right?"

"Yep."

"You also changed the patient's name on an order for propranolol, so that it goes to one of mine instead."

"Absolutely."

"What about the blood type for Clara Summers?"

"That was me, too."

"The allergies of Doris Schafer?"

"Uh huh."

"With preset instructions, so that your hacking occurs hands-free?"

"Brilliant, don't you think?"

I have regained enough strength to turn my head to the side. Walter played me all along. What a sucker I am.

"How about the voice?" I ask.

"What voice?"

"The demonic voice over the phone. Is that you, too?"

Walter leans in close, his stinky breath hitting my face. He slowly smiles, revealing an ugly set of yellow teeth.

"*Fuck yeah, that was me,*" he says in that same voice.

"But wait a minute. How could I get a call from that voice even if I was in the same room with you?"

"You know about robocalls, don't you?"

I stay silent. Then I nod, as it falls into place.

"I prerecord a message, save it into an audio file, then have a robocall app automatically call you at preset times and play that file," Walter explains.

"Every call was automated?"

"Not all of them. The evening calls were me speaking to you live, in that other voice. You still never figured out it was me."

"But I figured out something else."

"What?"

"The pacemaker. You went right into Laverne McDonald's room to try hacking it, using that old Microsoft smartphone you modified somehow. Sadly for you, she lived to tell me all about it."

At that moment, Walter flinches slightly, then slowly moves back. For the first time, it looks like I've thrown him off.

"She gave me a pretty good description of you," I say boldly. "You probably thought you could kill her, didn't you?"

"Does it matter? I still got what I wanted: driving you nuts."

"Why me?"

"Because you're a doctor."

"Why do you hate doctors so much?"

"They're assholes, OK? Every single fucking one of them."

"You think I'm an asshole too?"

"You know how much it pisses me off to see people like you getting all the good stuff? All the success, respect, the high salary. Oh yeah, I know a lot about you. I've been watching your every move. Your routine, the hospital floors you usually go to, where you park, who your friends are. Even where you live and hang out, because I've been following you after work without you ever knowing."

"For how long?"

"Like a year or so."

"Really?"

"Uh huh."

"But I still don't get why you've been tormenting me specifically, not anyone else. Seriously, what have I ever done to you?"

Walter says nothing. His breathing becomes audible, air flowing heavily in and out of the narrow slit of his mouth, his chest rising and falling. Suddenly, I remember that face and heavy breathing before. It may have been a blur from earlier this week, but seeing it now, it has become crystal clear.

"Dr. Pierson," I say softly. "He's the one you really hate, isn't it?"

"Hold on a minute," Walter exclaims, flabbergasted. "What the hell are you talking about?"

"Don't lie to me. I remember that fight with him very well. Even the moment when you pulled him off me and practically threw him back really hard. Now I see it. It wasn't an accident. It wasn't you not knowing your own strength."

Walter freezes. Then I take a deep breath and look him in the eye.

"You *wanted* to hurt him, didn't you? You intentionally hurled him backward into those chairs because you've got some beef with him."

"So what? He's a fucking asshole, too, just like you."

"Then why not hack into his patients' charts? Why me instead of him?"

Again, Walter doesn't answer. But I no longer need that, because at that moment, it dawns on me.

"It's because you couldn't, right? He's a surgeon, and there's only so many medications he deals with, like blood thinners and opioid painkillers. Maybe you thought it was too risky to try to alter those medications under his nose. He could spot irregularities easily because there aren't that many for him to deal with. Plus, maybe the pharmacy's special safeguards against those drugs are too strong for you to get around and do some serious damage. So what do you do? You settle for a scapegoat. You find a different doctor to target, one who deals with a ton of medications per patient, not a few. Like someone practicing internal medicine. Someone like me, right?"

"Yeah, pretty much," Walter says grudgingly. "But don't think that means I don't hate you. You know how much it pisses me off to see you getting those Doctor of the Month honors again and again?"

"Why? You didn't get into medical school?"

"Don't fucking interrupt me!"

"Come on, Wally. I'm just asking a question."

Instead of a verbal answer, I get a physical one. Walter clenches a fist and launches it right into my gut, forcing out so much air from my lungs. Then he throws three more punches, straight into my face. I grunt loudly, gritting my teeth.

"Don't you *ever* call me that!" Walter screams. "It's bad enough that Patrick does it. Now you have to do it, too."

"I thought he was joking around."

"Not funny to me, asshole."

"OK, I'm sorry. All right? Just stop hitting me."

Walter backs away, but he keeps his stern face.

"Might as well," he says. "You're the one tied up, after all. But I can't still get over the fact that you broke into my house."

"You left the door open."

"It's still trespassing."

"What are you going to do? Call the cops?"

"Maybe I should."

"I don't think you will."

"And why not?"

"Because there's no point. I know everything, about how you created Lucifer's Worm and released it upon the world along with six hacker buddies. How you are the computer hacker known as Doctor Lucifer, trying to kill my patients with your hacking skills. The other six do whatever shit they want, and I bet that's all a smoke screen, so that nobody would notice what you're doing and I would not figure out it was you. Is that right?"

"Yeah, sure."

"Then you email me that poem concealing a riddle, to throw me off. I might get stuck trying to solve it, or get into trouble for accusing the wrong person. But no matter how many walls you put up, I climbed over all of them, until I spoke to the pacemaker patient who held the key to finding your sorry ass. So if you want the police to arrest me, I'll just tell them my trespassing led me to discover the root of Lucifer's Worm. The plot to unleash a cyber pandemic, starting right here in this house. Given how much damage you've caused compared to me, I'd say they'll be on my side, not yours."

Walter lets out a heavy sigh. Then he stomps one foot and turns away. He has no good comeback. Maybe he regrets not killing me the moment he spotted me at his desk. But would that do anything? Nah, he wouldn't escape the police so easily. My corpse would turn up, and they'd sniff him out.

Regaining his composure, Walter slowly approaches me.

"I will deal with you later," he says quietly. "Right now, I gotta take care of something else first."

"Like what?"

"I'm not telling you."

"Because I know too much already?"

"No. Because I want you to discover what it is. You will see for yourself what I have in store. Then you will be shitting your pants and begging for mercy."

Walter leans close to me again, causing me to flinch a little. I say nothing. I just keep my eyes trained on his, because I am not going to back down. Ever.

I hold this stare even as the phone on Walter's desk rings. I wait for the rings to stop. That is followed by an electronic voice telling the caller to leave a message after the tone. Then a beep. And then a live voicemail message.

From a very familiar voice.

"Walter, this is Patrick. Look, I'm not going to mince any words here. Rajesh and I were thinking about how you suddenly called in sick today. And I have to tell you. Your excuse about being ill with the flu is bullshit.

"This morning, Dr. Lin came into our office, wondering if the medical hacker is in fact someone in IT. Rajesh and I checked everyone else at the office today. We found nothing to suggest it's any one of them. So that leaves you, wherever the hell you are. Under the circumstances, we felt it was important to leave no stone unturned. So Rajesh logged into your work laptop with administrator rights. We looked to see if you're the hacker causing so much trouble for Dr. Lin this past week.

"Sure enough, you are. We found the Gateway program and figured out what it's supposed to do. There's also the preset hacking instructions you left behind, plus the robocalling application and the sound files with the monstrous voice. Now we know. You're the medical hacker, maybe one of those involved with Lucifer's Worm. Part of me wants to help you, if there are personal problems driving you to do this. But another part wants justice, because I believe in doing the right thing. Therefore, Rajesh and I notified the FBI.

"At this point, just give it up. The feds are probably on the way towards you as we speak. You can't run from this. The best thing you can do is just turn yourself in and not make it any worse for yourself. Think about what I'm saying."

The voicemail ends. A long silence follows as Walter looks down on the floor, undoubtedly weighing his options.

"Come on, Walter," I say calmly. "There's no point in hiding from this. Just do what Patrick says."

"No," Walter says, balling a fist. "I will not be silenced."

"Seriously, this is crazy."

"You stay right there."

Then Walter leaves the room.

Moments later, I hear loud shuffling and banging from the next room, which I recall is a stuffy storage room. What is he getting from there? Then I hear a continuous metallic squeaking before I see it. A wheeled cart with a flat-screen TV and some kind of electronic box slowly enters the room. Walter pushes it until it reaches my feet. He plugs the TV into an electrical outlet and turns it on.

Then I notice two more items on the cart: a roll of duct tape and a pair of wireless over-the-ear headphones.

"What are you doing?" I ask.

"Giving you a show," Walter says with no emotion. "The last one you'll ever get to see. You better fucking enjoy it."

I have no idea what he means. But something tells me it will be some kind of horror fest. I shudder.

Walter picks up the duct tape and headphones and moves behind me. I hear a loud unpeeling, then a tearing. A strip of tape comes down in front of me, then into my face, covering my mouth and sealing off all possible screams. Next, the headphones come down over my ears, blocking out all noise. Then another strip of duct tape, wrapping around my head multiple times to keep the headphones strapped to my ears. Walter comes back to my right side and gives me an evil smile. Then he walks to the door, flicks off the light switch, steps out of the room, and closes the door.

I am all alone again.

The room is almost pitch black. The only lights come from illuminated green dots in the mysterious electronic box. I hear nothing but muffled rubbing as I force my limbs against the bands of duct tape. Oh god, I'm so fucking screwed. What's going to happen next? The thought makes me shake all over, and the knowledge of being in captivity only makes it worse. I wait helplessly for several minutes. My heart pounds through my chest, ready to burst through my sternum and ribcage.

Then, an image comes on the TV.

It is showing some kind of wooden rod at an angle in a dimly lit room, probably the leg of a table. I hear a few clinking noises, as if various metal objects are being put onto some kind of surface. Suddenly, the image moves. The camera is quickly being rotated. Then it settles on a hideous sight.

Walter's entire face and neck are painted bloody red, along with his hands. Sharp pointed fangs, probably fakes, protrude from his mouth. He wears a red-stained long white coat, as well as a head strap with an attached head mirror, an obsolete physician artifact.

Doctor Lucifer in the flesh!

"*You like my new look, Dr. Lin?*" he says in that cold demonic voice. "*You should. You are about to get a taste of what's coming for you.*"

The unseen camera rotates again. Now I see a man in a chair, lower limbs and torso secured with duct tape in the same manner I am, and upper extremities taped to wooden armrests. He wears nothing but white boxer shorts. Duct tape over his mouth muffles his desperate moans. Then the camera zooms in so that only his face and upper chest are visible.

Dr. Samuel Pierson is crying helplessly.

CHAPTER 28

I shake violently in my chair.

Never before has so much fear flooded me, sending my heart into overdrive. A tsunami of grief follows, choking off my breathing. Is this really happening, the surgeon I've always considered the asshole with a scalpel now this close to who knows what? Now my eyes are soaked in tears. My head teeters close to fainting.

And then I freeze, remembering something Lucifer said yesterday, in the voicemail message.

"*If you fail, I will kill someone and leave the blood on your hands.*"

Now I get it. Lucifer is going to kill Samuel Pierson, and I would be the helpless one witnessing it. Goddamn, why does it have to be like this? I drop my head and let tears fall onto my lap. I let out a muffled scream.

"*You see that camera, Dr. Pierson?*" Lucifer says on the closed-circuit TV. "*You have an audience, an audience of one. Your special guest is Dr. Mark Lin. You know him, right? The internist whom you hate so much, and vice versa. Well, he's upstairs watching you. He is just dying to see you suffer.*"

Pierson's eyes widen. If only I could speak to him. I'd tell him I am so sorry and would do anything to get him out of this. But priority number one is breaking free. I jerk my body hard to the right in a swivel motion. The chair still faces forward. Fucking carpet!

On the TV, Lucifer's red hand holds up a pair of pliers.

"*Are you ready?*"

Then the pliers disappear. Seconds later, Pierson shuts his eyes and growls, uncontrollably. Even with duct tape, his wails threaten to shatter my eardrums. As suddenly as it started, his screaming ceases.

"*Maybe I should try it here.*"

This time, I look away. I focus on my chair, not Pierson's deafening yells. I force another right-turning jerk. Nothing. I do it again, this time with my toes pressing down on the carpet to lift the front chair legs slightly.

Whoa. I've just turned a few degrees to the right. Better than nothing.

I keep doing it, over and over, as quickly as my body can take it. I stop after ten tries, catching my breath through my nose. I have turned the chair about forty-five degrees already, and moved a bit away from the TV. Good.

By this moment, Pierson's voice has downgraded to a soft whimpering. Lucifer speaks again.

"*You must wonder how I got you here. I trust you got that email from your colleague, asking you to meet in the park to talk about your suspension. The one that, in reality, I wrote. And you believed every word of it.*"

Lucifer laughs, while I look around for something to cut through duct tape. There are no loose objects of any kind, let alone sharp ones. I turn my head towards the desk, next to the low-lying video game shelf. I hold my gaze.

The shelf's corners are sharp. The outermost one, about a couple of feet behind me, isn't right up against any bedroom wall, and there's enough space between that shelf corner and the computer desk.

I've found my ticket to freedom.

"*Once you stood at the trunk of my car, I snuck up from behind, injected some sedative into your thigh, popped open the trunk, and pushed you into it. Not a single person was nearby. Everyone was too far away to witness it.*"

I do more repeated jerks to rotate my chair. Toes down, turn. Toes down, turn. I master this in no time. Pierson's screaming starts up again, but never mind that. I am now facing ninety degrees from the TV and slightly closer to the shelf corner.

Time for a variation: swivels to the left.

Toes down, turn. Toes down, turn.

I am getting closer to facing the TV again, while being a few inches behind my starting point. Progress!

"*What's wrong? Candle wax too hot?*"

No time to sit. I go back to rightward jerks and turns. I've rotated another right angle, while moving another inch or two closer to the shelf. I breathe rapidly through my nose. Pierson does the same.

"*I bet you don't remember me at all. Take a look at my face. Do you not have any memory of what you did to my mother? Miami, 1988?*"

Even if this is intriguing, I keep it in the periphery. I jerk in left turns, moving slightly back. Then right turns, moving slightly back. Each cycle brings me closer to the single point that would tear my bonds.

"*Her name was Barbara Laramie. A really sweet lady, the nicest mother anyone could have. Unlike my father who would call me weak and stupid, hit me for doing anything wrong. You know his favorite punishment? Tying me up in a chair in the basement, and leaving me in the dark for hours.*"

My throat tightens. I breath hard to suppress the nausea, just as Pierson's continuous moan rattles the silence, double in intensity from last time.

I check my progress. Practically halfway there. Only about five more feet until I hit the shelf.

"*But she protected me. On any bad day, I always turned to Mom, never to Dad. She even got ready to divorce him and take me with her. Tragically, she came down with an inflamed gallbladder.*"

I am closer. Three feet left, maybe.

"*And you fucking botched the surgery! You accidentally made her bleed, but couldn't save her. You let the wrong person die, you bastard!*"

A sudden yelp from Pierson, but I don't care. I just focus. One more right-left swivel cycle should do it.

"*You fucking killed my mother!*"

I am facing the TV again, now a long distance away. Pierson's face is smaller, but not his latest muffled scream. My hands feel the pointed shelf corner behind me. I position my wrists against it, then quickly rub up and down. It starts poking deep into my skin. I ease the pressure before continuing.

"What did you do when you broke the bad news to me and my father in the waiting room? You hurt my feelings. I, a seven-year-old kid, looked up at you, grabbing your pant leg, demanding to know where Mom was. Instead of trying to soothe me, you kicked me aside. Then Dad slapped me and grabbed my wrist tight. After the talk was over, Dad yanked me out of the room, then back into the car where he slapped me again and again!"

Pierson cries through his duct tape. I scream through my own mouth-covering tape, but my sound cannot mask his one bit. I have to stomach it while slicing through the wrist-binding tape. It isn't one layer, but several I have to cut through. I can't tell if I've broken through at least the outermost one.

"Imagine living in torture, endless punishment and torment. A father who never loves you because you're not a man like him. Computers and video games are loser hobbies, he says, unlike sports and guns. You know what the happiest day in my life has been? The day my father died. Well, fuck him!"

More screaming from Pierson, more tape slicing from me. Wrists still bound together, but I keep going.

"Even with his death, you're still in the picture. I couldn't just let you get away with screwing up my life. That's why I looked you up. When I found your profile on the Ivory Memorial website, I knew my next move was to get a job in the IT department, then plan my revenge on you. Yet, you were just too damn hard to punish with my hacking skills. I settled for Dr. Lin because he's a much easier target. But that didn't stop me from watching you from afar, learning about all the shit you do. Talking down to patients. Calling a nurse a bitch. Throwing tools in the operating room. And don't forget your fight with Dr. Lin, and me throwing you back to make you fall. That's for all the pain you unleashed on me!"

At this point, the shelf corner easily pokes my skin. I guess I have one or two layers of tape left. I keep shutting out Pierson's voice of pain.

"*And now, I have the perfect way to finish you off.*"

The sharp point now hits my skin directly. I push my wrists downward to force the cutting further up the tape.

"*See that contraption right there? That shall be your punishment. A very fitting one, I must say.*"

I pull my wrists apart, hard. Then again, even harder. They separate a little. Another bilateral tug and my hands no longer touch. I wriggle them to force the strip of tape off one hand. Both hands free, I search for the start of the torso tape, then quickly unpeel it, round and round as fast as I can.

"*Say your prayers, Dr. Pierson.*"

Next step: the tape around my ankles.

"*It is time to end my misery.*"

Final step: the tape over my mouth, plus around my head and earphones. The last thing I hear is a deafening sound, like a harsh buzzing, before I rip off the earphones and hurl it aside.

I scream for help while sprinting out of the bedroom, then down the stairs. The noise is faint, coming from near the kitchen. I head that way, then pinpoint the buzzing to behind the basement door. I yank it open and rush down frantically.

And then, time slows down, as I take in everything I can...

A large table, with instruments of torture laid out...

A video camera, secured to one edge of the table...

Pierson duct-taped to a chair, facing the camera...

Two buckets on the floor, one under each of Pierson's hands that dangle past the armrests...

Lucifer standing with his back to me, holding the source of the dreaded buzzing...

A chainsaw, its teeth just inches above Pierson's wrists...

My own hands reaching forward, as my feet touch the bottom of the steps...

The chainsaw teeth lowering...

The gap between me and the demon closing fast...
My fingers grabbing the back of Lucifer's coat...
Me pulling back as hard as humanly possible...

Lucifer growls as he stumbles. I whirl around to heave him straight into the wall. The chainsaw blade strikes a metal cabinet, shooting bright sparks all around. The death machine drops to the floor, but Lucifer charges at me. He barrels his head into my stomach, pushing me back and then slamming me down onto hard concrete. Next thing I know, the devil is above my head, driving a punch down towards my face. I block it, as well as the next one with his other hand. Quickly, I roll to my side, dodging a third blow. I hit one leg of the table. I reach my hand up onto the table, feeling around for anything to use as a weapon. My fingers touch some kind of handle, and I grab it.

I hold a big knife, its tip stained with fresh wet blood.

"Hold it!" I command, pointing it at Lucifer.

For the first time, the demonic doctor shudders. I slowly get up. He throws up his hands in surrender. I also notice that I can actually hear my own breathing. The chainsaw has automatically shut off. Keeping the knife in my right hand, I glance at the table. There is the familiar pair of pliers, along with a lit red candle, a burning cigar, a hammer, a crowbar, a wooden awl, a long piece of rope, and another knife identical to the one I'm wielding. I pick up that knife with my left hand.

Holding two knives out at Lucifer, I turn to Pierson and examine him. Streaks of dried blood from both nipples, small round burn marks on his abdomen, bloody puncture wounds in his left calf, dried candle wax over his inner right thigh, and a bleeding incision along the inner aspect of his right forearm. With the knife in my left hand still pointed outward, I use the one in my right to slice through the duct tape around Pierson's limbs and torso, careful to cut only the portions stuck directly to the chair. I put the right blade down and use my free hand to pull off the torso tape, then the strips around his legs and his arms.

At that moment, the chainsaw whirs again. Lucifer is on his feet, charging in my direction!

I drop the knife in my left hand, then grab Pierson's arm and pull him back, off the chair. Then I pick up the chair by its armrests. I hold it in front of me, its legs extending toward Lucifer. I rush him head on.

All four points of the chair make contact with Lucifer's chest, halting his progress. I heave forward to force him back slightly. Lucifer thrusts the chainsaw at my stomach. It misses me by an inch.

During the struggle, I spot Pierson standing on the other side of the instrument table. He just looks at me.

"Get out and call the cops!" I yell.

"What about you?" he asks.

"Just go!"

Pierson stumbles a bit at the foot of the stairs, but otherwise moves up fine on his own. I turn back to Lucifer and scream.

"Drop the chainsaw, asshole!"

"*I'm gonna fucking kill you!*"

"Just give it up! There's no point in this!"

"*No!*"

Lucifer pushes against me. I still resist, but now my arms start burning. If I let go of the chair, I am finished. I need something else as a weapon. I look to my left. The instrument table is too far away now. But on my right side, there is an open metal cabinet within arm's reach. On a shelf about chest high is a can of WD-40 oil. I quickly stretch out one hand to grab it, then maneuver it to have its nozzle facing out. With my finger on the can's trigger, I spray its contents into Lucifer's eyes. His growl fills the void of the basement.

Now I have the upper hand. I quickly push his stumbling body all the way back to the wall. He slumps to the floor. Then I hear some harsh wet cracking, plus a deafening roar.

Lucifer's chainsaw, still in his grip, is slicing his own left leg!

I jump towards the stairs to avoid the blood splatter. I scramble up and out the door. I close it, then take a chair from the nearby dining table and wedge it at an angle under the doorknob. That should do it. I turn to the front door. It's already open. No doubt Pierson has escaped the house. I head that way, too, spotting a police car in the street through the doorway. Upon stepping out, two Anaheim cops on the sidewalk aim guns at me.

"Put your hands up!" one of them shouts.

"Wait, wait!" Pierson yells from across the street, standing near a third officer. "He's not the killer! He's the one who saved me!"

"The man you want is in the basement," I say. "I secured the basement door. Be careful. He tried to kill us with a chainsaw."

"All right," the first cop says in a no-nonsense tone. "Step away from the house, hands up. Join the victim over there."

Without pause, I move quickly, my hands raised to show compliance and earn their trust. Once I reach Pierson and the accompanying officer, I sit down on the curb. Pierson joins me. The officer, a young-looking blonde man, continues to keep a careful watch. From my vantage point, I can see there are actually four police cruisers parked at random angles in the street. Somehow, they know they have a bad situation to deal with.

I turn to Pierson.

"Are you OK?" I ask.

Pierson nods slowly. A tear washes down his right cheek.

"I wish I had arrived sooner," I say, slowly and solemnly. "My god, you were about to get killed."

"You still came in time," Pierson says, patting me on the shoulder. "Without you, I wouldn't be here."

"Sure, sure."

"Seriously, thank you. Thank you so much."

I nod, then bury my face in my arms. What a goddamn fucking nightmare this is. Too much death and destruction in a single week. I want this to end. Nothing else really matters. Not even the two faint gunshots coming from inside the house, or the subsequent police chatter. I suppose I am a hero in all of this, given how things would be even more awful had I not tried to hunt Lucifer down.

But this will still haunt me, for days to come.

"By the way," Pierson says. "How did you find me?"

I look up, then let out a quiet sigh before answering.

"It's a long story."

ONE WEEK LATER

CHAPTER 29

The world had thought the cyber pandemic of Lucifer's Worm was the weirdest thing since COVID-19. Boy, were they in for a surprise.

Over the past week, news and social media were flooded with chatter about that house of horror in Anaheim, the home of Walter Laramie, a.k.a. Doctor Lucifer, the computer hacker turned would-be murderer. It started with the local news, reporting that a neighbor had called 911 because he heard a man next door screaming for help. Good thing I didn't stay quiet after freeing myself from the duct tape. That would explain the quick arrival of the Anaheim police. Then the story continued with what the two foremost cops did next after entering the house. They moved aside the chair blocking the basement door. Moments later, Walter threw open the door and came barreling out, whirring chainsaw in both hands, one leg still pouring blood out of a gaping wound. Both cops, startled by the sudden charge, took no chances. Guns already drawn, they each fired a shot into Walter's chest, killing him instantly.

What made this coverage go national was the arrival of the FBI. They came about twenty minutes later, thanks to cooperation from the arrested teen hacker, Adam Tyler. I would assume that the FBI also acted on a tip from Patrick Flanigan. If I ever see him again, I'll buy him a drink or two.

It would be hours before the public learned about the Seven Deadly Sinners and the details of Operation Hellraiser. I, of course, played a part in that. During my interviews with both local and federal law enforcement, I did have to admit that I trespassed onto the property and into the house because of my suspicion that Walter was up to no good, based on all the events leading up to that day, which I had gone over in great detail. But ultimately, I earned their good graces, by giving them the goods, including the pictures I snapped in Walter's house and my account of what I saw on Walter's computer. Plus, I did save Samuel Pierson's life, which would not be possible if I hadn't gone as far as I did. The gruesome story from Pierson's perspective sealed the deal, too.

Naturally, Pierson and I stayed out of the spotlight. We requested anonymity, and both the police and the media respected our wishes. Everyone else could digest this twisted tale of child abuse, medical malpractice, cybercrime, hospital horrors, and revenge while still giving us space to breathe. At least, I hoped so. Even our respective chiefs at the hospital granted that luxury. Roger Garrison called me to confirm that the mandatory one month off still stood, in light of the terrifying events I survived. The Chief of Surgery passed along a similar message to Pierson.

The news, of course, didn't end there.

After Walter's job history surfaced, Ivory Memorial Hospital was also thrust into the spotlight. The lady from its public relations department maintained her poise during a press conference, in which she read an official statement expressing deep shock about the discovery of Walter's secret activities, along with a firm stance against individuals choosing to do harm and an ongoing commitment to patient safety.

That last item was in response to one thing happening in between, covered in a separate news item.

Ronald Schafer, the husband of Doris Schafer, had spoken out to reporters after the revealed connection between Walter Laramie and Ivory Memorial Hospital. He wondered if the antibiotic mishap sending his wife to the ICU with anaphylaxis had something to do with that computer hacker. Sure enough, he spoke with someone at the hospital and got confirmation. The best part was that he went on record to say that he no longer blamed the treating doctor for it, meaning I'm off his hook.

Sadly, Ronald also expected to withdraw life support for his wife, given extensive brain damage and no signs of recovery.

Beyond the news for public consumption, Dr. Garrison called me again to provide some behind-the-scenes tidbits. Based on the evidence that the IT department gathered about Walter's actions, Garrison had personally contacted Ronald Schafer to offer an apology and condolences about what happened. Ronald had not made plans to file a lawsuit initially and definitely will not now. In a similar way, Garrison had reached out to the families of Darnell Jackson about the mistake with propranolol and of Clara Summers about her blood typing scare. They were grateful for the concern and respect shown to them, plus relieved that the nightmare of Doctor Lucifer was finally over.

Not a word was spoken by anyone about Laverne McDonald and her pacemaker malfunction. But that's OK. She didn't need the attention anyway. Plus, she seemed to be doing fine when I last saw her. Best to leave her alone.

Amazingly, the news never covered the association between the hacker and the Flint family. In everyone else's eyes, supposedly, the parking garage assault on a doctor was a separate event entirely. If that's what they were thinking, good. I, who connected the dots and survived the worst of it, want this buried.

Speaking of secrets, there is one more I have to keep. Really, really deep inside, never to be heard by anyone.

On the night I ranted about Dr. Pierson to two strangers at a Newport Beach bar, about wanting doctors like him to be tortured, have their hands cut off, etcetera, I was letting out steam and a tidal wave of frustration. But I never wanted any of it to actually happen. Yet, the torture did, and the dismembering could have occurred if I had waited an extra second or two. Was it simply a freak coincidence? I'm not so sure. Walter had mentioned that he often followed me and that he knew my habits. He knew where I parked my car at work and where I lived. Is it possible that, last week on Wednesday night, he had followed me from the hospital all the way to Newport Beach, then sat nearby and overheard me?

I'm going to assume the answer is yes.

Now I wonder if my words had awakened a deep-seeded hatred within Walter. Did he suddenly decide at that moment that he would carry out a killing and not be satisfied with only malicious computer hacking? If so, he would need to get me out of the way. Hence, the complex riddle to throw me off. Maybe through his eavesdropping on me, he had learned who Jane's fiancé is, along with his occupation, then decided to lead me in that direction. Once I am farther away from Walter, he could figure out a way to kill the doctor he'd hated for so long, the one responsible for the death of his mother, who was the one and only person who gave him any kind of solace.

The more I think about it, the more plausible it seems. In the end, I have no way of knowing. But the mere possibility of it still makes me sick to my stomach.

Samuel Pierson almost died because of me.

All of a sudden, I have no desire to ever speak to him again, let alone see him. I have to take this secret to my grave, but until I really do leave this world, I will be carrying a massive weight in my heart. If I ever come face to face with him, I'll have a panic attack like no other. Hell, my life would probably end right there, with me collapsing, breaking my head, never waking up.

Shit, I can't take this anymore.

I pour out my grief in a torrent of tears, letting them soak the sleeves of my sweater. No one can hear or see me. I am lying on the living room couch, all by myself, too sad to do anything all morning. Just like this past week, really. I haven't left the house once since coming home last Friday.

I turn back to the TV, which is broadcasting a live report on Fox News. The network has just finished a segment about Doctor Lucifer. Now the current story is about something else entirely, though still a sad topic: the case of a missing child. I don't pay any attention. It's not going to help me feel any better. Should I just wait until this feeling passes? I suppose I could. After all, that's what I tried to do when two people I held dear to my heart died tragically. Then again, what did my father say after those painful, heart-wrenching losses? Move on and keep going?

Yeah, that's what he kept telling me, even many years later.

I now know what I must do.

I pick up the phone and call Samuel Pierson, who gave me his cell number before we parted last Friday.

"Hello?"

"Sam, it's Mark. I wanted to see how you're doing."

"Hey there. Thanks for calling. Didn't expect it."

I hear something for the very first time: Pierson laughing.

"You sound better," I say.

"Somewhat. Not too much, really."

"I know the feeling. I've been bummed out for days."

"I don't blame ya."

"Listen, I was doing some thinking for a while. Maybe it would be a good idea if we take the time to talk about things. In person. You up for it?"

"Seriously?"

"Absolutely."

I hear nothing. I'm guessing he's thinking it over. No matter what he decides, though, I feel a little better just from reaching out to him in the first place.

"Why not?" Pierson finally says. "I really need to get out some more. Plus, I'm getting hungry."

"You and me both. You want to have lunch?"

"Sure. You pick the place, and I'll be there."

* * *

Pierson and I share a booth at a Denny's restaurant in the city of Orange. After placing our orders, he and I chat about how we would be spending our time off. He talks about going to the beach and visiting his three kids, whom his ex-wife has custody over. He also opens up about his messy divorce and how it stemmed from him never being around because a surgeon's work is basically a lifestyle in and of itself. As for me, I'm finally using my time off the way I should, with a getaway trip. A real vacation.

Soon, our food arrives: a hamburger and fries for him, a turkey sandwich for me. Over the comfort of delicious food, our conversation gets into the heavy stuff.

"You still think about last week?" Pierson asks.

"How could I not? I was the hacker's target, remember?"

"Right, I know. Though you did say he might've wanted to go after me originally, but just settled for you because you were easier."

I nod. He had gotten the full picture of my side of the story just as much as I had gotten his. We talked about it outside Walter's house, while the police and FBI were still going about their business.

"What I can't believe is how, all these years, he wanted to get back at you so badly," I say, almost breathlessly. "It must be scary knowing that."

"It is. But the worst part is the beginning."

"What about it?"

"The day I was doing his mother's cholecystectomy, I was fresh out of residency. Got board-certified and everything. Yet I made a horrible mistake. I botched her surgery. Somehow, during that procedure, I nicked one of the hepatic arteries. Maybe it was the right hepatic. I don't know. But she was bleeding like crazy. I tried everything to stop it, but no, it all went downhill. She was dying before me. The objective went from removing a gallbladder to just making sure she lived. And... I failed at both."

Pierson closes his eyes and bends his head forward. He holds that position for a while. Then he continues.

"How was I supposed to break this to her husband and son? Could I just flat out admit I screwed up? No way. So I beat around the bush, saying she suffered complications during surgery. It didn't go well for the husband. He still accused me of being such an awful surgeon. I was so hurt by this that when his kid son demanded to know where mommy was, I just kicked him aside. Then I saw what I had done, but it was too late. Now, decades later... that same kid is grown up... and tried... to kill..."

I reach forward to pat him on one arm. His face is in his hands, which are muffling his cries. Our waitress passes by and stops to ask what is wrong. I tell her he is grieving. She follows my lead and places a hand on his shoulder. He picks up his napkin and wipes his eyes, as the waitress gives him a few extra clean napkins.

"Thank you," he says quietly.

The waitress slowly walks away, frowning. I have a feeling she'll be back to check on us again, which I don't mind one bit.

"I know how scared you must've been," I say soothingly. "I was too, having been forced to watch it."

"I thought I was going to die. I even believed I deserved it. I really did. I mean, look at how I treated everybody, you especially. I was a real jerk. No way I could deny that. So in those final moments, I just expected the worst. After all, I was divorced, my job was getting too stressful, everyone hated me. What did I have left?"

At that moment, Pierson grabs my left hand in both of his, holding it tight. He continues, both eyes teary. Plus, there is the faint hint of a smile.

"Yet, I was blessed with a miracle. I was saved, given a second chance. And of all the people who could've come into the basement to pull me out of that hellhole, it was you. Even after I physically attacked you the other day, you still came along. Seriously, I don't know how to thank you for all of this."

"The important thing is that you're alive," I say calmly.

"You didn't have to do this."

"Correction: I did have to. It's the right thing to do."

"Even with the mistakes I made?"

I nod. Speaking of mistakes, there is my own big one, the one that is going with me to my grave. I expect its weight to pull my heart down right in front of Pierson. But no, that doesn't happen. Instead, I have an epiphany.

"Even the worst mistakes can be corrected," I say. "Look, I've made mistakes, too. I've said mean things about you when you're not around. What happened last week definitely made me regret it. I want to move on from all of this as much as you do. It's going to take time, but I have a feeling we can heal. Time has a way of making the pain fade away.

Right?"

Pierson nods, while chewing his burger.

"It's just like what my father told me in times like this," I say, looking off into the distance. "Move on and keep going."

"That's smart. I'll remember that."

"And be good to yourself and others."

"Are those your father's words, too?"

"No. My mother's."

"You come from a wise family."

I smile as I drink a sip of water.

"Thanks, Sam."

On that note, the rest of the meal is pleasant. The food is delicious, and we talk about fun stuff, like restaurants and travel. Anything other than cheating death last week. We even avoid talking about work. That is, until he brings it up himself.

"There's something I have to tell you," he says calmly before taking a deep breath.

"What is it?"

"After all that has happened, it'll be really hard to go back to the hospital. I know you said time will heal, but that's not going to be easy. Not when the workplace is still a constant reminder."

I look at him, still holding my glass of water in midair. Suddenly, I know where this is headed.

"Are you saying...?"

"Yes, Mark. I will be quitting my job at Ivory Memorial. First thing after we leave, I'm calling the chief to issue my resignation."

"Sorry to hear that."

"Don't be."

"Are you sure about this?"

"Yeah. It isn't just best for me. It's really best for everyone. That includes you. From now on, you won't have to worry about me bothering you."

"Even if you've apologized to me?"

Pierson nods solemnly.

"Starting fresh is the only way to go," he says.

"So you'll look for another hospital to work at?"

"Yeah. Not right away, though. If you ask me, I think I might need two months off, not just one."

"You still have nightmares about last week?"

"Sometimes. I think I'll be fine as long as I get plenty of rest."

"Well, enjoy it."

"What about you? Are you still going to work at Ivory Memorial?"

I nod without hesitation.

"I guess I'm just used to the place," I say, laughing a little.

"Whatever works."

Soon, the meal is over and I pay the tab. We head out to our cars, which happen to be parked side by side. Before Pierson gets into his, I approach him.

"Hey, listen," I say. "I hope everything goes well. Honestly, I'm really glad we got to talk like this."

"Me too. And let me just say once more, thank you. I don't know where I'd be without you. And before I forget, I will seriously get my life together and stop acting like a bastard. Those days are going to be over."

"I'm sure your new hospital colleagues will appreciate it."

Pierson smiles and offers to shake my hand. I gladly take it. Then he pulls me to him and gives me a tight hug with his other arm. He holds me like that for a while. By the time he lets go, I am almost panting for air. He laughs.

"Good luck," I say.

"If you ever want to get together again, you have my number. Take care of yourself, OK? Don't do anything I used to do."

I nod with a smile. Then he gets into his car as I walk back around to my own car door. Before getting in, I see him reverse out of his parking spot. He waves to me, and I do the same. He turns and heads into the street. I watch him disappear into the distance.

Seconds later, I shed a tear.

A tear of joy.

CHAPTER 30

At last, my bags are packed. I am ready to go.

It is a beautiful Saturday morning when I pull out of my garage. The sun is shining bright and not a cloud litters the sky. I imagine my five-hour drive will be just as pleasant. Hopefully, my destination will be, too. Originally, I had thought about a scenic road trip along the entire length of California Highway 1, but I want to be more inland instead of being so close to the ocean. It doesn't take long for me to reach the I-15 and start heading north towards my chosen place of respite: Las Vegas.

While passing through SoCal cities like Rancho Cucamonga and Fontana, I look back on that week of horrors. I think about all the people who died, their lives cut short by anger and hate, either within themselves or in someone else. I remember those who cheated death, narrowly escaping its clutches. The memories may be more faded now, but they're still there. It's time I really put them to rest.

On the dashboard's Spotify app, I scroll through the playlist, looking for just one song in particular. I find it and hit the play button.

"Only Time" by Enya is the current track.

The rhythm here is soothing. The singer's ethereal voice, mesmerizing. The instrumentals, heartfelt. Altogether, it is magic, a wondrous piece of musical poetry. This is my go-to song for emotional healing, to move closer to inner peace. It is also a reminder about the passage of time. What the future holds is always a mystery. It may be dark or it may be bright. I can only wait and see. At least I can do it with a sense of hope.

For the next hour or so, I drive in total silence. It's the kind of commute that is boring most times but comforting when needed most. Passing through Barstow, I'm only thinking about Samuel Pierson. Specifically, how this twisted tale started and ended with him. How accidental death drew a path toward intentional death. How Lucifer brought him to hell while I pulled him out of it.

How humanity has come full circle.

Perhaps there is such a thing as treatment for disease of humanity. Every social ill has its polar opposite, its counterpart antidote, its cure if you will. Kindness for hate, education for ignorance, charity for helplessness, etcetera. Whatever problem comes up, I would throw in a solution. Whether it would work or not, I could only find out. It's not going to be easy. In fact, I expect it to be tough, always. But I will keep fighting, on the side of life. I suppose that makes me an angel.

Maybe I do have a place in the realm of healers after all.

The best part is that I've purged some demons. Doctor Lucifer is dead, of course. But so is Pierson's ego. The demon of pride no longer possesses him. He has gotten his wings back and he will surely soar. I could say the same about myself, but with a slight twist. The demon that I've expelled from within myself isn't arrogance, but self-pity. After what I've done, I have no need to play victim.

Because I am a hero, one that Hippocrates should approve of.

Is this truly the end of my darkest days? I wish, since I know I have more demons to conquer. Might I relapse back into misery, bitterness, and the like? Sure, anything's possible. But will I never stop trying to reach the light? Absolutely, because that's where I want to be. The journey will be a long one, almost eternal. But as long as I head in the right direction, I think I'll be fine.

It is only a matter of time.

Made in the USA
Columbia, SC
08 December 2024